THE PARALEGAL

i

DANIEL EASTERLING

The Paralegal

Daniel Easterling

The
Paralegal
A Novel

Daniel
Easterling

THE PARALEGAL

Other books by Daniel Easterling:

Paula Roberts Private Investigator – Johns Island
(sequel to The Paralegal)

Paula Roberts Private Investigator – Cayman Islands
(sequel to Paula Roberts PI – Johns Island)

ACKNOWLEDGMENTS

From this novel's inception, I gained inspiration from important friends who told me what I needed to hear: "You can do it, Dan," and, "Don't give up." Later, inspiration came from interacting with other authors, editors, and publishers at writers' conferences. During the final six months of editing and rewriting, I would be remiss not to mention the wonderful crews at Starbucks Coffee in Brenham, Texas, and on Harbison Boulevard in Columbia, SC. I spent more time at both of these establishments than I should have, but I was able to get a lot done and make friends of the baristas, who kept me pumped with toffee nut iced-coffee with breve'.

Finally, thank you, readers for your loyal support and for input you have given me. Please email comments to dsetoday@aol.com, or post them online where you purchased the book, or e-book. Feel free to "friend me" on Facebook at Dan Easterling to keep in the loop on the status of future novels and book signings. Two sequels to The Paralegal are planned for 2013, and 2014.

DEDICATION

I dedicate the completion of this novel to my late mother, Erma Moody Easterling who as a widow raised three boys, and a girl. She said, "God threw away the pattern after He made Daddy". She worked hard at a job where she could be home shortly after we arrived from school to cook a meal and be there for us. On Saturday mornings, she cleaned house, washed clothes, and made sure we were in church on Sundays. She was well read and always had a quip for us for nearly any occasion. I love you, Mom.

DANIEL EASTERLING

1

Paula Cooper rolled out of bed to grab a freshly brewed cup of amaretto coffee, her hair disheveled, her eyes struggling to open. She poured the delicious concoction into her favorite mug that she handpicked on a trip to the Charleston Market Place. Yawning, she stirred in cream and sugar until the mix was complete then she held her cup with both hands, her fingers clutched around the rim. This was her habit each morning as she made her way to the patio of her condominium, savoring each hot, invigorating sip. The bay view and caffeine infusion cleared her head to start her day, and she rarely talked to anyone, including her daughters, except to say, "time to get up, girls", until after her wake-up routine.

Her striking features shined like a morning star as she stood facing the warm sunlight, her soft ivory-colored terry cloth robe pulled tightly at the waist revealed her lovely, well-proportioned shape. Above average height with long, soft brown hair, Paula's deep green eyes sparkled, as the sun rose with radiant splendor over the water. The sunlight glanced off the water onto her face, lighting her up as if she was on stage. Orange and pink hues spread forth across the horizon, inviting the sun to burn brightly on the marshland beneath.

The Winyah Bay breeze gently blew through her uncombed hair as she watched a tugboat push a barge laden with barrels of chemical waste down the Sampit

River. The origination point was the Colonial Paper Mill that had done business in Georgetown for over sixty years. The barge slowly meandered its way around the final bend towards the open bay where a ship waited to load its cargo. The stench of the paper mill blanketed the entire town—pungent and odorous, and yet the population largely ignored it because of the economic benefit. Residents became offended when anyone criticized the dreadful smell.

Time quickly passed as she gazed out on the bay, daydreaming about better days. Paula desired a job where she could take pride in her work without the secrecy that shrouded much of what she did for her employer. Glancing at a small wooden cuckoo clock, she realized that she was running late as the bird popped out with its familiar sounds, indicating the time. Quickly placing her coffee cup in the sink, she darted off to the shower.

As the pulsating water beat down upon her body, she was in turmoil because she knew the plaintiff, the Environmental Protection Agency, had a just cause this time. The opposition had been right before, but that did not bother her until this case developed. This time, a lot more was at stake than just winning a case for the law firm where she worked. Protection of the waterways and marshlands of the home she loved was in jeopardy. She was sick of the shady politics and "money under the table" deals, which lined her boss's pockets. She wondered how much longer she could hide her resentment in helping him win these type cases.

The Denby Law Firm became an infamous site for more twenty years, ever since J. Thomas Denby first hung out his shingle in Georgetown. Denby ran a law practice that handled everything from corporate law to loan closings, wills, personal injury, and criminal cases, a one-stop shop for legal matters. He knew how to cut corners and skirt the law just enough to twist it in his favor and had a well-known reputation for taking cases which had a positive outcome, if you were his client. For this reason, his clients did not mind paying the exorbitant rates his firm charged. It was not so much the one hundred seventy-five dollars per hour Denby charged that made his rates high, but he padded the time just a little on nearly everyone's case. He kept the clock running, even at home, where he accomplished many of his phone chats to grease the wheels of "so-called justice." A few minutes were always rounded up to an hour.

For Paula, her discontent began after Denby pulled her into his web of deceit four years earlier, having her act more as a private eye than a paralegal. She began as a typical paralegal, researching cases for trial and looking up titles at the courthouse for loan closings. Soon afterwards, she was utilized on divorce cases to dig up smut on the opposition, for which she received bonuses for her investigative work. She needed the money and found the work exhilarating at first; one thing led to another until she was in over her head.

Paula tried to leave the firm once, but Denby threatened to ruin her reputation, labeling her as a troublemaker if she did not continue working for him. She inevitably backed down because she feared his reprisals and because she loved paralegal work. Denby had power, either to favor her at work or to assign her to a switchboard, fielding phone calls and typing voluminous briefs. She knew he could make getting work in the legal profession anywhere close to home very difficult. If she left her job, she determined that it would be on her own terms, with an offer from another firm in place.

Why Paula ever fell for Denby's proposals was something she could not understand. She had reconciled this lapse in judgment as an ill-advised decision influenced by the fact that she was bored with normal paralegal duties; besides, she needed the extra money for her daughters' college funds. Her salary of forty-five thousand per year, with bonuses and other benefits thrown in, made her the best-paid paralegal in the area. She was not hung up on money per se, but she was the sole supporter of her daughters since her ex-husband had moved out of state to avoid paying child support.

"Mom!" Rachel shouted from an adjacent room, "Chrissie and I are leaving now. It's almost time for the bus."

"Okay, honey, y'all be sweet. Remember, your grandparents are picking you up from school today, so don't take the bus home."

"Alright, Momma, we will," said Rachel.

Working full-time and raising two children as a single mom kept Paula very busy. Rachel and Christine, her two lovely daughters, were her pride and joy, and if not for her parents, who helped her with the children, her situation would have been much tougher. The girls were well adjusted and popular in school, excelling academically despite Paula's divorce to their father, who seldom contacted them. Since Denby paid her very well, Paula was relieved that neither she, nor her daughters, had contact with their dead-beat dad. The girls chose to look up to their maternal grandfather as a role model instead.

After completing her preparations for work, Paula hopped in her new black Ford Explorer, provided by the Denby Law Firm, and headed to work. Her drive took a route that traversed a mile-long bridge over the once pristine Winyah Bay basin. She drove across the bridge, occasionally glancing down at the bay and marshlands below.

She remembered fondly the occasions when her family went clam digging in this same waterway. Times were simpler then:

"Paula, don't get out too deep!" shouted her mom. "You're almost out where the fast current is, dear."

"Yes, ma'am, I'm coming back in closer to the bank." Paula hurriedly waded back to a safer location.

"We came here to dig clams, Paula, not to venture out in the river," chided Mrs. Cooper. "Don't you remember when Johnny Brooks was pulled out by the undertow and drowned very near where we are just two years ago?"

"I know, Mama, but there was a baby shark I was trying to catch with my net. You should have seen it swim. I think it was a sand shark!"

Paula was awestruck with wondrous excitement to see the beautiful aquatic life in the wild. She enjoyed tomboyish adventures as much as Huck Finn. Her parents had taught her not to fear trying new things, but had lived to regret it because she was too quick to venture out into potentially dangerous situations.

Mr. Cooper looked up in amazement at his twelve-year-old daughter's answer.

"The girl knows no fear," he chuckled under his breath.

Paula smiled, her heart warmed by the recollection.

Denby possessed the ultimate Machiavellian personality, requiring the new attorneys that he hired right out of law school to work for him for a minimum of two years. He figured that by then they would become indebted to him, and he craftily worked things to that end with all of his employees. There were a few other unhappy employees, like Paula, who resented Denby's ruthless methods; however, the money and opportunity kept them happy enough and their mouths shut, for the most part. With this slightly dysfunctional but talented team, Denby continued to turn out positive decisions for his clients and kept his practice on top as one of the most successful in the "low country," as the area near the coast of South Carolina is called.

New attorneys in the Denby Law Firm made a little more than half the money Paula did, as they eagerly jumped at the chance to learn under their renowned employer. The young attorneys were there to learn all they could about the legal profession before they branched out on their own. Some of them left the firm to start private practices; others took corporate jobs or filled positions in state government. Denby loved to assist his upward-bound associates in acquiring these positions so that later on, he could call in his cards when an opportunity arose.

He was not bad looking, tall with light brown hair and blue eyes, but he was beginning to bald and had a sizable beer gut. He tried plugs on the front of his scalp of hair, what was left of it, but they did not seem to take root fully. He wore his glasses on the end of his nose for reading and used this look as a way of intimidating people with condescending remarks, as he glared over the top of the rims.

Denby had scheduled a meeting with his trusted paralegal before regular work hours. At 8:00 AM, Paula pulled into the parking lot behind the restored 19th century brick building that housed the Denby law offices. Built in 1837, this grand building was originally used as the Town Hall. Its history was rich, which included occupation by Sherman's men during the Civil War. The two floors above ground provided their offices, and command post, the one below, a prison. The sturdy old brick building was one of few in their path that Sherman's men chose not to burn. Some said they allowed it to remain standing because of the lascivious times the officers had with the young women who visited them there. The basement was now the firm's legal library, while the two floors above ground were remodeled into stately offices decked with oriental rugs, traditional artwork, and fine furniture for the attorneys and support staff.

2

Denby arrived nearly every morning at 8:15 AM. Paula was ahead of him by fifteen minutes as she scurried inside to make coffee and set up for the meeting. She tossed her legal pad out on the long cherry-finished table in the back-conference room—the meeting room where Denby conducted most of his business with clients and subordinates. The front conference room was set aside for loan closings and depositions. Paula placed a cup of coffee, prepared the way he liked it, for her boss at the head of the rectangular table.

Denby pulled into the parking space reserved with his name and entered the back door to his office. Once inside, he stepped into the room where Paula waited, halfway down on one side of the table, in one of the eight matching black leather high-back chairs.

"Good morning, Paula," Denby said. He slid an envelope down the table in her direction, which she caught with one hand before it slid past her.

"Good morning, Tom. What's this?"

"It's an invitation to attend a Christmas drop-in that Judge Wilmont Parks is hosting. I wanted to go but decided it's best if you would be there in my place."

"Do you mean the one and only Judge Wilmont Parks, our federal judge for this district? That sounds interesting. What do you want me to do there?"

She opened the envelope, reading the embossed gold letters inviting J. Thomas Denby, Esquire, and Associates to the party. In the South, there is a drop-in to go to just about any time of year, with the bigger ones during the Christmas season. This one was more like a full-blown party.

"Paula, I've asked you to do many things for me in the past five years, but this one favor may mean a lot of money for both of us, and I do mean a lot. I want you to charm Judge Parks and somehow get him up to his bedroom in front of the large bay window facing the garden. Then, in your own sweet way, get him to hold you in his arms."

"What?" she gasped. "Have you lost your ever-loving mind?"

"No, now wait, Paula, hear me out. I know it sounds crazy and a bit dangerous, but I know what I am asking of you. We are going to paint the judge into a corner so that he will uphold a motion to throw out the Colonial case. You remember I told you how he is in the middle of a nasty divorce. His wife would jump at anything she could to take him to the cleaners, so I think he will want to prevent her from finding out what happens between you two."

"Are you serious, Tom? It's too early in the morning for a practical joke."

Denby ignored Paula's intonation and facial expression. "I understand he's an art lover; perhaps you can use this to get close to him? Didn't you study art in college?"

"You know I did, Tom. Don't play games with me."

"Dave McCaffery is going to the party and will work with you to get it on tape. He will be outside in the courtyard by the garden to record the encounter.

He's excellent at setting up electronics for this type of thing."

"Yeah, Tom, I know Dave. We worked together a couple of times before. You should know that, or have you forgotten?"

"Don't be irritated with me, Paula. You'll receive a sizable bonus for Christmas if you will do this. I promise that I will never ask this of you again."

The liar, she thought. Suddenly, Paula jumped up from her chair, smacking her legal pad on the table with a thud. "Damn it all, Tom! That's the same line you gave me the last time I did anything remotely close to this, and yet this scenario is far worse. I should walk out of here and never look back."

"Paula, I don't know what you're talking about. Refresh my memory, if you will?"

"Remember the older gentleman from Beaufort? You know...the real estate executive. He's the one I chatted with at Willie's Grill who got so drunk that he told me who he was sleeping with. I think his wife made out really well on that case, didn't she? You promised me that there would be no more roles like that to play!"

Denby did not miss a beat. He took a gulp of his coffee, placed it down on the table, and leaned back in his leather swivel chair. "But Paula, dear, I know of no other way to win this case. You have seen the evidence collected by the EPA; it's rather overwhelming, don't you agree? Colonial Paper Mill's alleged, prolonged dumping of toxic waste in the Sampit River and surrounding marshlands will most likely bring a fine that could cause the plant to go under. If Georgetown loses Colonial, it will have a huge, negative impact on the economy around here."

"Don't try to patronize me, Tom. I don't care if Colonial has to rob the bank to pay for its abuse of the marshlands. We both know that the fish and wildlife are dying by the thousands throughout the Winyah basin, and something needs to be done about it. I used to eat the shellfish from these waterways. Now, if anyone does, he gets sick. There are even signs posted not to eat anything caught in those waters because of the pollution."

"Okay, Paula, calm down. Please, sit down. Look, here is the bottom line. I'll pay you fifty grand if we win the case and twenty-five grand if you'll just get the tape made."

"Tom, is everything with you always about winning a case and making money? Are you even aware of the fact that I have a personal life or that the man I'm dating is special to me? We have plans this weekend," she said, taking her chair.

"Paula, you know I care about you. I know this isn't easy. That is why I asked you; because you are the only one qualified to do this job. Your boyfriend doesn't have to know about it."

"You mean, I'm the only one crazy enough to try, but that's not the point anyway, Tom. I wanted to be with him this weekend. Now, at the last minute, you spring this on me."

"I'm sorry for the late notice, Paula. It just came to me yesterday as I thought this case over. I know it's a risky proposition, but it's the only strategy I could concoct to win the win the blasted case. There's just no other way."

Denby did not care about Paula's personal life, though he put up a good front. The contract with Colonial Paper was so lucrative that he assigned his best three attorneys to the case with hourly rates. A twenty-five-thousand-dollar retainer, hourly rates, and a five hundred-thousand-dollar bonus, if Denby got the case thrown out of court, made this one of his best cases all year.

Paula shuddered to think what would happen to their relationship if her boyfriend, Jim Roberts, found out that she was involved with a shady dealing such as this. She wanted to make things work with him because he possessed the qualities that most women have only read or dreamed about in a man. She had been on a natural high ever since they had met on the beach at the Isle of Palms the summer past. Almost shouting now, she spoke with her jaw clinched, barely able to hold back the anger.

"Alright, Tom, this one last time, but I swear to you, if you ever need this kind of favor again, don't come to me! Are we clear on that?" Thoughts of Jim and of her daughters raced through her head. Her heart pounded at a faster than normal pace—blood vessels protruded in her neck.

"Yes, Paula, you've been perfectly clear," said Denby, his lips pursed with an insolent expression on his face.

Silence overcame the conference room as they both sat pondering their exchange. Paula fidgeted while she mulled over what she had just agreed to do. Denby assessed the situation, watching her body language with gratification that he had once again manipulated his trusty legal assistant into doing his dirty work.

There! I gave him my final warning. I do not care what is at stake in the future; I will not submit to his nonsense again. Besides, I'll move to Charleston to find a job in a firm there if I have to. I'll just lead the judge up to his bedroom and let Dave get a shot of our silhouette against the window. I cannot believe I am agreeing to this. I have sunken to a new low...far from the way I was brought up, she thought.

"Paula, you know you are the most valuable asset I have. You know what the odds are if we have to litigate this case against the Feds. Why don't they get back up north where they belong and leave the South for us to manage?"

Denby did not care that most of the "federal people" involved in this case were actually from the South. He equated Federal control with Northern aggression in the distant past. His prejudices came from the Civil War history he had learned as a child. In the fifties when he attended grade school, nearly every grammar school in the Southern states emphasized the heritage of the Old South under the glorious flag of the Confederacy. Schoolchildren were well versed on Sherman's troops and their needless burning, pillaging, and raping when they ransacked the South. This happened, they were taught, despite the fact that the war was over and the soldiers were going home.

New teachers from a younger generation, farther removed from these facts or biases, whichever the case may be, were teaching now. Still, old notions die hard, and Denby, like many Southern middle-aged men, carried a certain amount of prejudice against the North for imposing its will on their beloved South.

"What do you say, Paula? Let's get to work on this case? You can get back to me on Monday sometime before my meeting Tuesday with Colonial Paper."

"Okay, I'll have a report for you, and you can get the tape from Dave. You will keep all this in a safe, won't you? And I certainly don't want anyone beyond you, Dave, and me to know about this."

"Of course, I will, Paula. Only three people will ever know."

She glanced down at the invitation and then back at Denby. "This invitation has your name on it, Tom. What if they give me a problem at the door?"

"Don't worry about that. I'll notify them that I can't attend and will send you, as Renee Caldwell, in my place. The time, location, and a map are on the invitation."

"Oh, so I get a fake name for this assignment, nice," Paula said sarcastically.

"He doesn't need to know your real name. It could help you," Denby said.

"Thanks for that, I guess."

"When you get to Charleston, would you pick up one of those nice throws down at the Old City Market for Judge Parks? Also, grab a jar of homemade blackberry preserves, word is he loves that stuff."

Paula scribbled notes on a pad for reminders. "Is that all, Tom? I have to go soon if I am to get packed, and make it in time to get a room in Charleston tonight. I'll have to do some shopping, also. Expect to see the price of a nice dress and pair of shoes, as well as the usual, on the expense report when you sign my check."

"That's fine, Paula. Just do what you need to do. I won't complain as long as we get what we need on the judge. Judge Parks is a smart man, and I do not know how easy this will be. Good luck!"

"Just leave that to me. You said I was the only one qualified to do the job." Paula winked to portray a false sense of confidence and to hide her nervousness. She left quickly down the hall to her office. Reaching his door, Denby closed it behind him and was immediately on the phone.

"Good morning, Paula," said Frances. The perky legal secretary went to work for Denby straight out of technical college a couple of years prior. She was a bit naïve but very competent at her job. At twenty-five, the best qualities about Frances were her pleasant voice, fast typing skills, and proficiency at loan closings. During a loan closing, Denby had only to walk in, greet the clients, and sign the paperwork. Frances did the rest.

"Good morning, Frances," Paula replied. "You came in early today, didn't you?"

"Yeah, I did, just after you two arrived. We've got three closings today. After that, I need to research two titles for closings tomorrow."

"That will make the firm money. Way to go," said Paula.

Mortgage interest was at an all-time low, causing the public to buy houses at the fastest rate in thirty years. Paula had long since left the mundane, repetitive work for the more complicated skills where attorneys negotiated settlements and made deals— the kind of work that required skillful diplomacy, and quite often, secrecy.

"I do what I can, Paula. So, what's the hot new stuff going on around here?" Frances asked with a whimsical grin. She knew that whenever Denby and Paula met privately before work, some juicy circumstance was involved.

"Oh, just the usual, I go to a party, have drinks with some folks, pick up what I can about a case...nothing to it."

"Oh?" Frances replied. "You wouldn't be referring to the Colonial Paper Mill case, would you?"

Paula knew Frances liked to gossip. "No, nothing like that," she said, laughing the remark off. "Listen

Fran, I would like to chitchat more, but I don't have time."

"Okay, Paula, no problem. I know you are an important woman. I'm just making conversation."

"Talk to you later."

Paula went into her office and closed the door behind her. She dispelled the negativity of the meeting she just had with Denby, preferring to think of the good times she had with Jim. She felt at ease with him from the beginning. He had a sincere tone in his voice and an honest look on his face that was genuine. Paula shuddered at the prospects of him ever finding out about the blackmail plot. She visualized a dark cave in her mind where she could hide all this from him. Although they had an evening planned for dinner and a movie, she somehow felt that Jim would understand, despite his disappointment.

Now at her desk, Paula picked up her phone and pushed the speed dial button to Jim's store. She wanted to explain over lunch that she had to be out of town for the weekend, knowing that gently breaking the news to him in person was best. As the phone rang, she evaluated how much she could share about her assignment.

Jim trotted across the large floor space, darting in between antique furniture, grabbing the phone by the third ring. "Good morning, Unique Antiques, may I help you?"

"Jim, good morning, you surely may. How are you?"

"Hey, Paula, I'm kind of busy at the moment. What's up?"

"Nothing much, just wondered if you are available for lunch today? I need to talk to you as soon as possible."

"I might be able to do that, honey. By the way, are you ready for the evening tomorrow night with me as chef?"

Paula hesitated. "Yes, let's talk about it at lunch, okay?"

"Is anything wrong?" Jim had a sixth sense about him. He could always tell when Paula was upset. She loved the sensitive quality he possessed because she had never known it before in a man. Paula also knew that Jim was highly intelligent and would see through avoidance mechanisms; nevertheless, she tried.

"No, nothing's wrong. I'll explain at lunch, if you can get away?"

"Okay, how 'bout I meet you a little before noon at the Shrimp Shack?"

"Okay, sweetie, I'll see you there." She hung up the phone, biting her lip in turmoil.

Paula looked at the sticky notes on her desk, deciding if she needed to return any calls before the following Monday. Opting to let them wait because none of the requests was urgent, she locked her filing cabinet and desk, preparing to leave. Frances noticed Paula with her things in her arms as she passed by her desk.

"Leaving already, are we?"

"We aren't, I am. I've got some errands to run, and then I'm meeting Jim for lunch."

"That must be nice. Where's the party?"

"Out of town...I'll see you Monday, Fran, and listen, you know Mr. Denby's rules, right?"

"What's that, Paula?"

"What goes on here stays within these walls? If someone doesn't need to know something, then we don't tell them."

"Right, I know that, like no one here talks to anyone," Frances chuckled.

"No, I'm serious, Fran."

Paula abruptly walked out, leaving Frances wondering why she was so short with her. She was not in the mood for Fran's sarcastic humor or for sharing the details of her assignment. From the inquisitiveness that Frances showed, she knew she had inadvertently said too much already.

She decided to stop at a local dress shop run by a friend of hers to see if she had a party dress that would be appropriate for the Charleston gala, one that would accentuate her figure, yet classy. Luckily, she found a dress with matching shoes, which would save her time in Charleston as she prepared for her mission. Lunchtime with Jim would roll around before she knew it, and she was glad to have a little time for shopping therapy to relieve the stress and pull her thoughts together. Next, she ran by her condo and gathered the few things she needed for the weekend. Carrying all that she needed in both arms, Paula pulled the front door behind her and locked it. Concerned about how Jim would take the news of her leaving for Charleston, she drove back downtown to the Shrimp Shack for lunch.

3

Jim Roberts, a new resident of Georgetown, was breaking out on his own for the first time in business as a sole proprietor importing oriental rugs and antiques. He had made visits to the Charleston area and the South Carolina coast many times in the past to vacation with his family and to visit his great aunt. He discovered that an antique business, if run properly, would flourish in this region.

He received his goods on ships and barges via the Atlantic Ocean and the waterways that had helped industry in Georgetown from its founding. Before this undertaking, Jim had risen up the corporate ladder with a company that did business worldwide. His former home was New York, but he spent much of his time in Europe before moving to the South.

He returned to New York from one of his trips abroad to find his wife of fifteen years sleeping with another man. He was a loyal man but could not reconcile with her after that. He realized that getting a fresh start was better for the both of them than staying in a marriage with bitter feelings that could not be resolved. The divorce was more than Jim could handle if he was to remain in New York where he and his wife shared mutual friends. It was just too awkward. After much deliberation, Jim made his decision to resign his position as European manager with his company. He said his goodbyes to his sons and left for the coast of South Carolina to start his new life. He chose Georgetown as the spot for his business but made sure that he visited his sons as often as he could and brought them down to visit every summer.

Having always been an admirer and collector of fine antiques and rugs, purchasing many for his home, Jim was knowledgeable about the wares he now imported for retail distribution. He had always planned to venture out into this business after his sons finished college, but this plan moved itself up on the calendar due to the unfortunate series of unforeseen circumstances.

During one of his initial trips to the South Carolina coast after his divorce, Jim met a most unusual woman. He would never forget that scorching hot day in July when, on a trip to the Isle of Palms, he met her. He was still recovering from the awful ordeal with his ex-wife and just wanted to get away with his sons once more before they started school. A possible romantic encounter had not entered his mind; however, this hot summer day would prove otherwise.

Jim remembered walking gingerly onto the beach as the sand burned his feet, trying to locate his two teenage sons whom he had dropped off earlier. Hundreds of families lined the beach, frolicking about. Teenagers were throwing Frisbees and footballs both in and out of the water. Young adults were playing volleyball in the dry sand near the dunes and sea oats that swayed in the hot summer breeze. Men and women were jogging on the beach while small children played in the shallow salty water with parents nearby as the waves lapped rhythmically on the shore. There she was, sitting on a lounge chair positioned strategically toward the sun's rays, wearing big sunglasses, and reading an issue of

American Women. Her slim, tanned body, partially hidden by a sombrero-like straw hat, glistened with suntan lotion. Her long, shapely legs were exposed to full view, attracting the eyes of many men as they passed by, scanning the beach for eye candy.

While winding his way through a swarm of sunbathers, a colorful beach ball flying overhead flashed through the corner of his eye. Jim looked up and followed the spinning ball as it landed on the reading, long-legged woman's lap. It startled her so much that she fell over sideways in her chair onto the glistening white sand. The beach sand was exceptionally beautiful but not well enjoyed when mixed with suntan oil and plastered to the body. Despite being unceremoniously dumped onto the sand, she held tightly to her magazine, her body barely clinging to the chair. Covered with sand as she leaned on one elbow, Paula looked up to see a tall, handsome man standing over her. He was dressed in slightly baggy, colorful swimwear, just short enough to reveal the beginning of his well-defined thigh muscles, and a white casual shirt, unbuttoned. Jim held in his laugh but could not help grinning as he offered her a hand.

"Would you allow a stranger to help you up?" he asked, looking down on Paula with a smile.

"Oh, my goodness, I can't even move without falling more," said Paula. She cringed from embarrassment but was careful to provide a smile for this appealing stranger.

"I promise not to take advantage of the situation by dropping you for everyone to see."

Paula tried to hide her grin then glanced up at her rescuer. Their eyes met in the bright sunlight, and they laughed at the situation with a friendliness that relaxed them both. Jim extended his muscular arm with hand outstretched. To deny him now would be awkward, or so she thought.

"Well, I certainly hope not," she said. She reached out her arm to this mysterious knight on shining sand. "Do you just walk around the beach looking for such opportunities, sir?" asked Paula.

Jim gazed into Paula's eyes as she peered at him over the top of her sunglasses. "No not at all. There's no reason for you to think like that."

"Good, for a moment there I thought you were just another man with a fast line trying to pick up a girl on the beach, no pun intended."

An instantaneous romantic spark was lit as only it can be when certain chemistry exists between two people and Cupid finds his mark. Paula closed her magazine and stood to her feet. She gently brushed the sand from her arms, legs, and hands. She glanced at Jim taking in his masculine features with one quick scan. She admired his tan, as he stood tall, with a full head of thick black hair, parted on the left and worn touching his ears. A little gray mingled on his temples, providing a sexy salt and pepper look. His warm brown eyes and lean physique with hairy chest captivated Paula. The sit-ups and push-ups that Jim did regularly were paying off, and although he was quite proud of his body, he remained humble.

"Well, I guess I'd better be on my way," Jim said. "I have to locate my two teens. I dropped them off a few hours ago with explicit instructions not to stray."

"You have two teens? That's coincidental, so do I," she replied, not wanting him to leave so quickly. "My girls are on the beach out there somewhere throwing the Frisbee. They'd better not be far away," Paula said, as she looked around to spot them. "They love being active."

"That's a good thing. Mine do, too."

Jim was a bit surprised that this beautiful, young-looking lady could have teenagers. He was smitten by the way she carried herself, her shape, and her comely features.

"I told my boys to remain in this vicinity until I returned, but you know how kids can be. They're usually pretty good though."

Paula gave herself a final brush and straightened her swimsuit. "Yes, I certainly do. Would you like some help locating them? By the way, my name is Paula Cooper," she said, extending her hand to shake his.

"Nice to meet you, Paula, my name is Jim Roberts." Jim took her hand in his and held it briefly, but warmly, with his large, strong hand.

"Sure, if you would like to help, please do." Jim positioned his hands across his eyebrows to shield the sun as he scanned the beach for his boys.

"How old are your boys?" Paula asked. She followed suit, positioning her hands against her brow to scan the beach with this mystery man. Her heart quickened its pace. *What's happening to me?* she wondered.

"They're thirteen and fourteen, only eighteen months apart. There! Those are my boys by the lifeguard stand tossing a Frisbee with those two girls."

Paula saw the boys smiling and laughing, having fun with her daughters. "Funny, they weren't there just a minute ago. Those two girls with your sons are mine."

"Oh, they are? I see where they get their looks," Jim interjected, flashing his bright white teeth through his mustache.

"Well, thank you, Jim. And your boys have good taste," Paula added, returning a smile.

They both chuckled, enjoying the moment. This whole happenstance seemed to be providential bringing a bit of joy into their lives again. Jim turned to face Paula as he pondered this serendipitous event.

"Paula, I know we just met, but if you're single, would you like to have lunch sometime? I think we have some things in common."

"I'm divorced, Jim, and would be delighted to. How good is your memory?"

"Very good when I need it to be; try me," Jim responded eagerly.

"Okay, then, if you can remember my number, then I'll go out to lunch with you."

"You're on!" Jim said, with a sly grin.

Paula stepped over a plastic pail and shovel that a child had left by her chair, moving closer to Jim. He felt the blood warm in his body as her presence and perfume excited him, and was a little surprised that she had this effect on him. She softly spoke her phone number as Jim watched her lips, the movement almost mesmerizing him. He repeated it in his head several times.

"Got it, I'll remember that," he said. He committed the number to memory like a secret formula that could have saved the world from nuclear destruction. "It's a pleasure to have met you, Paula, but I need to get moving with these boys. They want to go watch an early movie after dinner, and we barely have time to make it."

"No problem, I do understand. Someone has to keep the clock. It's very nice to have met you also, Jim," she said sweetly.

Jim whistled loudly to get his sons' attention. "Excuse me, Paula; it's the way I call my sons when they're at a distance. I prefer it over yelling."

"Well, it sure beats my dad's hog call."

"What?" Jim said, surprised.

"Just kidding, Jim, don't worry; I grew up on the coast, not on a pig farm."

Jim laughed, a bit relieved, as well as, entertained by Paula's sense of humor.

The boys heard their father's distinctive whistle and ran swiftly to greet him. Paula's girls tagged along, gleefully skipping through the sand as they went. Jim left the beach with his sons, laughing and talking. Just before the boys got out of sight, they spun on a dime and turned to wave good-bye to Paula's daughters. The girls giggled and waved back. The next week, Jim phoned Paula, inviting her out to lunch. From then on, a movie or dinner at least twice a week became the norm, even though both of them had to juggle their schedules to see each other. On each occasion that they met, feelings grew stronger, but neither Paula nor Jim wanted to admit that they were falling in love. Both had been hurt before, and reluctance to commit remained a hurdle they had to overcome.

4

Many locals and tourists from near and far come for lunch at Cool Daddy's Shrimp Shack, situated on the boardwalk in Georgetown, overlooking the Sampit River about 1,000 yards below Colonial Paper Mill. Ron McKinnon, the proprietor, had sailed the seven seas and knew all there was to know about marine life and preparing seafood, so he said. His claim to fame was his Seafood Gumbo and Shrimp n' Grits, served with a delicate white cream sauce.

Although most of the world has not experienced grits, it is a Southern staple made of ground corn, a regular breakfast item on most menus in the South. The ground corn is boiled in water until it has the consistency of cream of wheat, but with a much different flavor. Just add salt, pepper, butter, and the flavor changes from bland to scrumptious.

This quaint little restaurant located beside the river allowed those who traveled by boat to dock while eating lunch or conducting business. On the walls inside the restaurant hung photos of anglers with their catches and paintings of boats going out to sea. A stuffed blue marlin and hammerhead shark were nestled on the walls between the many pictures. A fishing net draped behind several items on the wall added to the obvious décor. Paula and Jim preferred to dine on the patio at the dockside entrance when weather cooperated.

Paula arrived outside the restaurant just before noon. Her oversized tires on the SUV bumped the curb as she parked. Jim sat waiting on a dark green metal bench in a break between the buildings where there was a small public park. Walking to the car, he greeted her with a smile as he watched her step out of her vehicle.

"Hi, sweetie," Jim said with a boyish grin. "You look gorgeous, as always."

"Hi, Jim, thank you. You are sweet to say that." Paula smiled for the first time that day.

They exchanged a hug and a brief kiss without smearing her lipstick. They felt the closeness they had come to know over the past six months. Paula leaned against Jim's chest, wanting a deeper kiss than a small greeting.

"We are in public," Jim murmured, pressing his lips against her hair.

She leaned back and sighed, "I know."

They walked hand in hand to the boardwalk, built on the edge of the river. Turning left, they continued walking past several storefront businesses, which doubled as residences on the second and third floors. As the couple reached the back entrance of the restaurant, the sun had risen high overhead, a pleasant seventy-two degrees, even though it was early December.

"Should we get a table out on the patio?" Paula asked.

"Yeah, that sounds good to me, sweetie. Two for outside," Jim said to the host.

They sat down next to one another at a square metal table covered with a red-checkered tablecloth. The wooden chairs with straw-latched seats and backs were handmade by a local artisan. At Cool Daddy's menus were positioned on the tables between the metal napkin dispenser and the old-timey glass salt and peppershakers. A smaller slip of paper inserted in the menu indicated the lunch specials. Grabbing their menus, Paula and Jim decided what to eat as the server arrived to take their order.

"What can I get for you folks today?" she asked in her pleasant Southern twang, chewing her gum vigorously.

"I'll have a Shrimp Gumbo with a House Salad, please," said Paula.

"Give me the same as the lady and two iced teas," Jim said. He took in Paula's facial expression and knew that she forgot to order her beverage.

Cool Daddy's had the best iced-tea anywhere around. They served it with lemon and just a bit more sugar than most places and then poured it in a sixteen-ounce Mason jar filled with ice. Customers frequently ordered the iced tea by the gallon in plastic carryout jugs.

"What's going on, Paula? You sounded upset this morning on the phone."

"Well, I would like to laugh it off and tell you everything is fine, but I can't. I'm in a mess at work, and I don't know how to explain it all right now. I'm very sorry to tell you this, Jim, but I have to leave for the weekend to go to Charleston."

Jim's heart sank. "Why?"

Paula shrugged, disappointed with what she had chosen to do. "I've got to attend a party at Judge Wilmont Parks' home on Saturday night. I'll be representing the Denby Law Firm at the judge's annual Christmas party."

"Why can't Denby go?"

"That's the part I can't explain at the moment, Jim. Tom put me on the spot just this morning, giving me this assignment on the Colonial Paper Mill case. Please forgive me."

Jim did not answer but listened as Paula continued.

"I have to pick up a dress that I bought a little while ago. It has a minor alteration that the shop owner is doing for me, and then I am heading to Charleston to get a room for two nights. I have to get out early in the morning to have my hair and nails done, and find a couple of more things I need for the party."

Jim gazed into her eyes. "What about me going with you? That could solve our dilemma. We could spend the night in Charleston together tonight. I have a salesperson working on Saturday morning who could handle things at the shop until I got back."

Paula's heart fluttered at the thought of them being together but knew she could not include him this time. There was no way that she could juggle everything with Jim there. "Jim, darling, I would love that, but this is going to be more work than pleasure. I have to meet with Dave McCaffery early Saturday morning to work out some details, and the rest of the day Saturday I'll be getting ready. Trust me; it won't be a fun time for you to tag along with me doing all that."

Jim was curious about the "mess at work" that Paula alluded to earlier. The mention of McCaffery, who he knew was a private investigator, did not sound good, but he resisted the urge to pry. "No problem, Paula, if that's what your job requires, then go for it. Maybe we can get together on Sunday night when you return." Jim tried not to show his disappointment.

"Thank you, Jim, for understanding. I'll have to see how things go. We can discuss it over the phone while I'm away, if that's okay?"

"Sure, Paula, if that's what you want."

There was an awkward pause, as neither of them knew quite what to say.

"Well then, I guess you are on your way after we eat?"

"Yeah, I have to run by my parents' house and drop off some clothes for Rachel and Christine. After that, I'll be on my way."

Jim wanted to be supportive because he had a wife in the past that often criticized him at whatever he undertook. He had determined not to put anyone else through that.

"Will you call me when you get situated in your room tonight, Paula, so I'll know you are safe?"

"Of course, I will." She felt good that Jim was concerned about her well-being and safety. "I'll call you tonight and tomorrow night after the party." He was comforted that she seemed eager to call.

The food arrived, and the couple ate as they changed the subject to lighter topics, enjoying each other's company. After finishing lunch, they exited out the back entrance the same way they entered. Jim walked Paula back to her vehicle and gave her a soft, lingering kiss. They pulled back slowly from their embrace, allowing their hands to touch and then slide apart purposely while gazing deeply into each other's eyes for an enraptured moment.

Jim watched Paula drive away and then walked back to his shop where he had bills of lading that needed his attention. A new shipment of rugs and antiques had arrived from overseas which had to be inspected, sorted, and priced before placing them on the floor. He reflected on Paula's mood and the conversation at lunch. He thought at first that she was doing her usual social appearance for her boss, but knowing she was to meet with a private investigator caused him to wonder what role she was being asked to play.

He had heard about the Colonial Paper Mill case from a couple of its managers who were his customers and did not like the idea of her possibly snooping around a federal judge's home. Paula had spoken about the case in passing but revealed no details. She always revealed as little as possible to maintain confidentiality and to minimize complications if things went wrong. One never knew who might later be required to testify if law enforcement became involved.

There was a story around town about such a case that went wrong regarding a young attorney, Jed Simmons, who had worked for Denby a few years earlier. He supposedly opposed Denby at times, talking too much behind his back. Rumor was that Denby had him killed and fed to the alligators in a nearby swamp. No evidence, however, ever pointed to Denby as actually having done such a thing. People around town believed him to be a ruthless attorney, but did not believe he was vicious enough to kill. Deputies found the young associate's vehicle half-buried in marsh mud and the capsized boat not far away in the swamp. A boot and clothing fragments that belonged to poor Jed were all that ever surfaced. Others believed he simply fell out of the boat while fishing, but no one ever knew him to go alone.

5

Paula arrived at Magnolia Inn, a magnificent bed and breakfast located near downtown Charleston, late in the afternoon. She had stayed here before on overnight trips to the Holy City, as it is sometimes called because of the abundant churches. She loved the old home, which formerly belonged to Sir John Lafayette, a wealthy merchant during the decades preceding the Civil War. Parking on one of Charleston's numerous narrow brick streets built in the 19th century, she grabbed her suitcase and hanging bag then turned to admire the inn nestled among the many other fabulous mansions built at about the same time. She felt as if she had stepped back in time one hundred and fifty years or more as she climbed the steps to the elegant old mansion.

The home was 4700 square feet—the larger portion used for the guests. The proprietors, Sarah and Mickey Johnson, lived comfortably in another part of the home on the bottom floor. The Johnsons were longtime residents of South Carolina but not native Carolinians. They escaped the hustle and bustle of corporate life in Pittsburgh some twenty-five years prior. They remembered selling their home, cashing in their mutual funds and much of their savings, to purchase the Magnolia Inn for nine hundred thousand dollars.

Magnolia Inn had appreciated in value to over two and one-half million dollars now; however, the

Johnsons cherished it so much that there were no plans to sell. This was the life they chose to live, and enjoyed their guests sharing in Magnolia's splendor and warmth. They took great pride in showing off the beautiful home with its ten and twelve-foot ceilings. The stately halls and rooms were lined with off-white chair rail molding, the ceilings' edges surrounded with beautiful crown molding.

Tongue and groove heart of pine flooring provided the base beneath exquisite Oriental and European rugs. Magnolia Inn was furnished with the finest antiques of Early America and Europe. Each room, a masterpiece in its own right, captured the old South in its glory years. The National Registry for Historical Homes had the inn listed as one of the most interesting homes in the South that is more than one hundred years old. Its colonial elegance brought many guests back for a return stay.

A majestic crystal chandelier hanging in the foyer was one of Sarah's favorite furnishings in the home. It was originally crafted in Austria by artisans whose families no longer produce such pieces. Mickey loved the intricately designed framed mirror, which was hand-carved in early nineteenth century England and hung in the formal dining room.

"Hi, Paula," Sarah said, as she greeted her in the foyer. "I haven't seen you in nearly a year, I guess."

"Hi, Sarah, it's so good to see your smiling face. I think it was a little over a year ago at Thanksgiving that I was here."

The two old acquaintances exchanged a warm hug.

"You're just in time for dinner. We're having roast beef, green bean casserole, and potatoes all rotten, oops, potatoes au gratin, I mean," said Sarah, with a chuckle.

She loved playing with words to get a laugh out of her guests. Paula laughed politely, recognizing her antics. Sarah had a special affection for Paula ever since they first met three years earlier when attending an interior-decorating workshop together.

"Great, which room do I get this time?"

"You can have your favorite bedroom. You young folk don't mind the climb up to the top floor. Besides, it's all I have available."

"That's good. I need a little pampering after this week of work with Tom Denby."

"I remember you telling me about him. Is he still being an obstinate rascal?"

"Obstinate, overbearing, idiotic, snake-in-the-grass, and a few choicer words I prefer not to mention."

"Why don't you leave him and come to work in Charleston? You'd love it here, and we could get together more often."

"Aw, that's sweet, Sarah. I've often thought of making a move this way, but Mom and Dad help so much with my girls. I just might do it one day when they get older. Who knows? As for Tom Denby, I would rather not talk about him anymore. He makes my stomach queasy."

Even though she had come to Charleston, Paula was still in a dilemma about what she would do concerning Judge Parks. She was having second thoughts about carrying out her assignment, and her tension level was at an all-time high because of the ruthless, money-grubbing attorney for whom she had chosen to work. In a divorce case, an incriminating circumstance is almost as good as, being caught in the act of adultery. She hoped that if she pulled it off it would be enough.

"Did I hear you say something about dinner? I'm ready to eat some of Mickey's good cooking."

"I surely did. The food will be served shortly. Why don't you go spruce up and hurry back, so you can get it while it's fresh and hot?"

"I can smell the aroma from here," Paula responded as they walked to the staircase. "I'll just run up, put my things in my room, take a quick bath, and be back down right away."

"Okay, sweetie, dinner is served from 5:30 PM to 7:00 PM, buffet-style in the formal dining room, as usual."

"Sounds wonderful, I'll see you shortly."

Paula did not care much for the climb but loved the view from the third floor where she could look out on the Charleston harbor. From her window, she looked down to a lovely spot that was once a fort during the Civil War where brave young Citadel cadets stood their ground against the bombardments of the Federal Navy. White Pointe Gardens Park was bordered on two sides by historic homes and on the other two sides by rock wall on the harbor's edge, known as the Battery. On a quiet night, with windows raised, one could hear the sounds of the water lapping against the walls. A seven-acre tract of land with large, old oak trees and lush green grass provided grounds for Civil War era cannons and triangular piles of cannon balls fixed in their positions and spaced near the sidewalks that zigzagged through the park. Memorials to soldiers of various wars were positioned symmetrically throughout, frozen in time. A large statue of a famous Confederate officer, Sergeant William Jasper, stands near the front of the park. In the middle of the park stands an old gazebo where public speeches were delivered, politicians held rallies, or a couple got married.

One can also see Fort Sumter a few miles out in the harbor, where the first shots of the Civil War were fired. Fort Sumter's thousands of annual visitors take ferry rides from points in Charleston to reach the historic fort built on a sandbar just large enough to support it. Though once a functional, imposing fortress utilized by the Confederate troops to guard the entrance to Charleston harbor, it has now dilapidated. A movement to get a bill passed was before the South Carolina Legislature to restore it to its original specifications.

Charleston's rich history dates back to 1670 when the eight Lord's Proprietors, commissioned by King Charles of England, sent a single boatload of indentured servants to develop a location in Carolina as a business venture. King Charles granted this land to his faithful lords for their loyal service. At that time, Carolina stretched from the East Coast to the West Coast and comprised what are now North Carolina, South Carolina, and part of Georgia.

The Lord's Proprietors had handpicked their leader, William Sayle, from the colony of Barbados, to lead this new settlement. There he had already successfully developed a settlement exporting crops to Great Britain. Sayle had the foresight to settle first in Carolina at Albemarle Point, an inland peninsula safer from Indian attacks and planned later to move to a larger peninsula of approximately one hundred forty-seven square miles situated between the Ashley and the Cooper Rivers. Under his leadership, the American colonists grew in numbers to two thousand within ten years. In 1680, he moved the two thousand settlers, when they were better able to defend themselves, to where Charleston is located now. Importing and exporting would also be easier with the convergence of the rivers, the bay, and the Atlantic

Ocean. William Sayle later became South Carolina's first pre-Colonial governor.

Paula opened the door to her room. There it was, just the way she remembered. A beautiful Early American poster bed with an off-white cotton canopy stood centered in the room, the rich dark mahogany polished to a soft sheen. An exquisite hand-sewn linen bedspread with decorative frills covered the bed. After putting her things away, she turned the knob on the old radiator-type, steam-filled heater to break the chill. Hissing and popping, the old heater circulated its steam warming the room.

Paula turned the knobs on the old tub to draw her bath water as she slipped out of her clothes. She looked at the tub admiringly. *This antique must be a hundred years old with its claw feet and depth. A relaxing hot bath in this tub is worth a night's rate,* Paula thought. She turned the ceramic knobs to shut off the water and sank down into its soothing, hot depths. Breathing in the lilac aroma from dissolving bath oil beads, she soaked in the therapeutic water. She listened, deep in thought, as the bubbles burst so softly that only she could hear them.

Her mind drifted back to the time when she first kissed Jim. Each time they kissed was a new adventure of blissful excitement. She thought about the days before they met and realized how empty her life was, except for her lovely daughters and faithful parents. She thought of how the intimate relations with her former husband had become just an obligation, and she longed, once again, to give and receive real love, not just physical gratification.

No one Paula had ever known compared to Jim, who was manly, yet gentle. He knew how to treat a woman with respect and honor. He did the little things that matter to a woman. He opened doors, he pulled her chair out to seat her and most of all he listened. She respected him because he understood her desire to wait until she was ready before becoming intimate, and yet in her animalistic prowess, she wanted to have him from the start.

Soaking in the soothing water, a folded towel for a makeshift pillow behind her head, Paula closed her eyes intending to relax, but instead she dozed off for a few minutes. As she lay there, dead to the world, the telephone rang loudly, causing her to jerk wildly. She jumped up out of the tub, grabbed a towel, and wrapped it around herself, water dripping from her body.

"Hello?"

"Hi there, Paula, how are you?"

"Oh, Dave, it's you. I'm good, and you?" she responded, somewhat relieved.

It was the private investigator, Dave McCaffery, calling to set a time for them to plan their strategy. Paula thought it might have been Denby calling with some last-minute instructions, not that she wanted any.

"Very good, thanks for asking. You sound as if you were expecting someone else."

"Oh no, Dave, I had just dozed off for a minute, but I'm glad you called. What's up?"

"Not too much. I just called to find out when and where you would like to meet to talk about things."

"Yes, I was expecting your call. Why don't we meet at eight in the morning for breakfast here at Magnolia Inn? We can eat a bite and discuss things then."

"That works for me. I will be there at 0800 hours, ma'am," said the former Marine.

"See you in the morning, Dave."

"You got it, Paula. I'll talk to you then. Good-bye."

Dave was excited to work on a case again with Paula. Most of his investigations were stakeouts on divorcing couples or chasing witnesses for wreck cases. He had a secret crush on her, as did several men around their small town.

The bath water had begun to cool, so she left off bathing, and pulled the stopper. She toweled her body dry then tightened it around herself, tucking between her breasts. Pulling a towel from a rack she rubbed her hair vigorously for a few seconds then brushed it out allowing it to air dry. She threw on a comfortable pair of black jeans and a green cashmere sweater and tied her hair back in a ponytail. Trotting down the stairs to the dining room, her mouth watered as the flavorful aroma drifted upward from the dining room to her olfactory senses. She helped herself to the sideboard, a handmade English oak piece, covered with dishes of succulent Southern cuisine and took a seat by the other guests. Typical tourist banter filled the air.

She finished eating in silence, just listening to those who sat around laughing and talking, when Sarah came from the kitchen offering her a White Russian. She accepted as she rose from her chair to make the climb again. Paula enjoyed visiting with Sarah, but this was not the time. She had too much on her mind and wanted to try on the dress she had bought for the party. She also needed to plan her day and think about how to charm Judge Parks on Saturday evening.

In her room now, Paula turned around in front of a mirror, which hung on the back of her closet door, admiring the fit of her satin Ruched dress. The material of the poinsettia colored gown was amazingly comfortable. She slipped the three-inch heels on, as well, and thought the match was nearly perfect, then returned them both to the closet. She called Jim, but his answering machine picked up, so she left a brief message. Afterwards, she prepared for bed, as she tried to dismiss her worries.

"Darn, I miss Jim. Wonder where he is? He's gone out for dinner with some clients, I bet," she muttered.

Paula's head nodded as she read from the novel she brought for the trip. The drink was also having its sedentary effect. She wanted to be fresh for Dave's rundown on Judge Parks.

"Ten o'clock, I'm exhausted. Time for lights out," she mumbled.

Turning off the lamp, she sank down in the comfortable bed, as she wrestled with the events of the day. At ten-fifteen, tossing and turning, unable to get to sleep, Paula got up and took a Benadryl. She nestled in the covers again, letting out an exhausted sigh, frustrated that the White Russian alone did not put her to sleep. She flipped the pillow over to the cool side and laid her head down comfortably in the feather pillow, drifting this time into a deep sleep.

6

Dave McCaffery, a former Marine, served as a military policeman just before his discharge. He also spent two years in intelligence where he learned his skills in electronics. Not only did Dave know how to use video and wire tapping devices, but also if challenged physically, he could rumble with the best of them. He decided to get out of the military shortly after Benton came into office and implemented his "Don't Ask, Don't Tell Policy." Dave hated "faggots," as he called them, and made no bones about it. The thought of a gay man in the same shower with Dave was enough to set him off into a raging tirade. After being investigated for beating two gay lovers one night outside a bar, his Commanding Officer informed Dave that he would have to either take a job in the PX or take early retirement; he took the latter.

Now forty-four years old, but in excellent shape, Dave jogged two to three miles nearly every morning and lifted weights regularly. He was a chip off the block when it came to his father's looks and disposition and had the rugged jaw of a Marine-lifer. An NFL fullback had no better physique than he did. He still carried his Marine-issue, four-inch barrel Colt 38, hidden beneath his left arm by a leather holster that he wore strapped across his shoulder. Every year but one, during the five years that he was stationed on Paris Island, Dave won the marksmanship contest.

The year he lost was to his dad, Colonel McCaffery, who transferred to the training camp to be near his son.

Dave had a few quirks, such as the way he made his bed every morning in military fashion. He checked it by flipping a coin to see if it would bounce on the bed when it hit. If it did not bounce up just so, then he would tighten up the corners of the linens until it did. He was nearly impossible to live with because of his obsessive-compulsive disorder, which he developed as a child because of growing up with a father who ran the home like a military camp. The condition caused him to go into angry fits if things were not done a certain way. In Dave's marriage, his rigid control problems cropped up during the daily routine of family activity. He expected his meals at precise military times and wanted a hot meal at 1800 hours every night. His first wife could not keep up with the rigors of what Dave expected. His second wife had done the most to comply with him and to help him see how his childhood history and military training affected his personality. He even consented to counseling for a few weeks but would not continue because he did not like the counselor honing in on his faults.

Two divorces later, Dave had mellowed somewhat and was beginning to change gradually, but he just could not seem to completely break out of his rigidity. Although he was still a long way from being flexible enough for most women to tolerate him, that didn't stop him from dreaming that Paula could somehow be attracted to him. He considered her the Queen of the South, perfect in every way. Adept at hiding his emotions, he did not want Paula to notice his infatuation with her, but that was improbable.

Dave turned off Highway 17 onto Meeting Street in his red Dodge Ram pick-up early Saturday morning and drove through downtown Charleston. Just a couple of miles south down the street, several blocks from the Market District, and he would be there by the Battery at one of Charleston's fine bed and breakfast inns to meet with the savviest paralegal he had ever had the pleasure of meeting.

Down an old brick street, Dave's pick-up bounced and jostled past several gorgeous mansions to Magnolia Inn. A thick wooden sign hung from a white post in front by the sidewalk, which read: ~ Magnolia Inn ~ Welcome Guests ~, carved in script and surrounded by beautifully hand-painted magnolia blossoms. All of the homes in the historic district were painted only with colors approved by the City of Charleston in order to maintain the city's charm and historical features, signs included.

Dave pulled into the narrow street near Magnolia Bed and Breakfast Inn, parallel parked, then hopped out of his truck and bounded up the twelve marble steps to the front porch. As he stepped onto the long porch, he noticed a "joggling board" to his left. The joggling board made of cypress and painted black or dark green was commonly used by inhabitants of the 18th and 19th centuries. They often positioned the boards on the opposite side of the porch from the adults' sitting area. The board was ten feet long and sagged in the middle from its design and age. Cypress wood was chosen most often because of its flexibility, strength, and for its ability to repel insects. Propped up by two sturdy curved legs on either end, children enjoyed it as a fun-time bouncing board and rocking chair. It served mainly as décor now. *Cypress wood, well preserved, and rugged, like me in a lot of ways*, Dave mused.

Dave looked exceptionally dapper, decked out in his smartly pressed khaki pants and maroon knit shirt that he wore for the meeting with Paula. He usually wore jeans, a screen-printed T-shirt, and a leather-flying jacket with an old pair of deck shoes, but today he donned a pair of shiny brown loafers. He had kept the custom of spit shining his shoes after being discharged from the Marines. One of the quickest ways to get demerits in the military was to wear a pair of shoes that did not meet dress code, of which Dave was never guilty.

He rang the doorbell just to the right of the massive front door. Mickey Johnson, scurrying about in the kitchen preparing breakfast, buzzed him in. The security monitors that the Johnsons had installed in the kitchen allowed them to view the guests at the door before granting entry. A moving camera, inconspicuously mounted on an eave, scanned the front porch area. Mickey and Sarah hated to use these electronic devices, but after a robbery two years earlier, their insurance company insisted that an electronic security system would be safer and would keep their rates stable.

The Johnsons were still trying to settle a lawsuit with a guest who was assaulted when she walked in and found a burglar ransacking her room. The thief stole her purse, loaded with vacation money and credit cards, backhanding her to the floor as he ran out. The elderly woman had a history of heart problems, and the shock of this event caused her to go into full-blown cardiac arrest. Though the Emergency Medical Technician resuscitated her, the heart attack took its toll on this seventy-six year old tourist. Her brain ceased to function normally after that, though her heart did stabilize within reasonable limits.

One doctor diagnosed her with a mini-stroke; another one said that her brain was deprived of oxygen for too long, which put her in a comatose-like state. In either case, the poor woman was relegated to a sorry existence in a nursing home facility where she was being kept alive by breathing and feeding machines. The family did not have the heart to pull the plug because their dear mother had some brain activity, and they still hoped that she could miraculously recover. New America Insurance Company offered two hundred thousand dollars to the family, but they did not want to settle for that small an amount, knowing the medical bills and nursing home care would exceed that figure within three to four years.

Sarah tried not to think about the case. She was great at reassuring Mickey with her favorite saying, "Things will work out in time; they always do." If, on the other hand, things did not work out, which was Mickey's worry, the settlement might exceed the million-dollar liability policy causing them to sell Magnolia Inn to pay for the medical care of their former guest.

Dave walked into the foyer of the old mansion. He looked to his right where he saw Paula already seated in the breakfast room, having coffee and reading the daily news. "BENTON TO BE IMPEACHED," the paper read in bold block letters, as she scanned Section A.

"Good morning, Sunshine! It's a beautiful day out there," said Dave, as he strolled into the breakfast room.

Paula responded with a slight groan. "Sure, Dave, whatever you say. Grab a cup of coffee from the sideboard over there and pull up a chair."

Dave did as she suggested, pouring a cup of steaming coffee from a silver-plated pot, and pulled up a chair across from her. "Actually, Paula, I'm starving. The smell of that food has my stomach growling."

"Well then, Davie-boy, let's chow down."

Paula jumped up from the table, tossing her newspaper aside. Deciding to eat first before mapping out their game plan, the two Denby pawns would soon be at work on a case with one of the biggest fines the EPA has yet levied against a South Carolina industry. They both had healthy portions of cheese grits, eggs, bacon, and sausage links and then finished off their second cups of coffee with orange marmalade and strawberry preserves on homemade biscuits. The Johnsons had found a little old woman in the mountains of North Carolina, who made the preserves the old-fashioned way, and they used her exclusively to keep stocked with the luscious jams. The tourists, who shared the room with Paula and Dave, emptied out of the breakfast room, and the idle chat ceased. Paula and Dave looked at each other, recognizing that the time had come to attend to business.

"Okay, Dave, let's have it. I'm all ears."

Paula placed a small planner on the table to make notes, lest she let some of the discussion slip from her memory. She knew Dave would give her more information than she would need. She figured that she could review the notes in her room and then destroy them later. Dave withdrew two sheets of ruled paper from his back pocket and unfolded them, like a grade school boy reading a poem to his pig-tailed girlfriend. He read the following before he talked from his memory: "Motion detectors are set around the house. Lights come on if the perimeter of the home is penetrated but will be turned off during the hours of the party."

After he conveyed the layout of the home to Paula in detail, he told her the judge's habits, his mannerisms, his tastes in women, liquor, and his hobbies.

"So, how do you suggest I work my way into his heart?" Paula asked in a half-serious tone. She had her own plan for how and when but wanted to hear what Dave had to say, nonetheless.

"Well, ma'am, I guess you already know all about that. A woman with your looks and charm won't find that difficult, but whether you can get him upstairs is the important thing here. Denby tells me that we need to get a shot of the two of you embracing privately in his bedroom."

"Yes, that's right, Dave. I should be able to handle that."

"I did my research, Paula, and discovered that what Tom Denby said is very accurate. The judge has over a million dollars in Renaissance art hanging on his walls. He has beautiful artwork throughout the house, and from what I learned, some of the best pieces are in the master bedroom. He really is a pretty interesting character."

"Yes, I heard about his collection from Tom, as well. I was an art history minor in college, and I feel he will be amenable to show it off for me. I'll try and convince him to take me on a personal tour of the grand home and then let him lead me upstairs, after everyone leaves, of course, and then hopefully he will want to show me the fine art in the master bedroom."

"I can see him doing that for you," said Dave, grinning. "I hear he is quite proud of it, not to mention the fact that he does notice attractive women."

"Tell me what normal man doesn't, Dave."

Dave looked at Paula sheepishly as if she had corrected his stupid comment stating the obvious. From their discussion, the plan was taking shape in Paula's mind.

"What time do you think you can pull this off, Paula?"

"Well, the party starts at 7:00 PM and goes until 10:00 PM; I'll have to find a way to stay after the others leave. That way the judge won't be distracted by having to socialize with everyone. I should be able to get him to relax some by then, assuming, of course, that I get to talk with him at the party. I'll just ask for a tour of the art collection after he warms up to me. Surely he will prefer waiting till the party's over since people would gossip if we went strolling throughout his entire home during the party."

"Excellent, Paula, I'll have everything set up by 9:00 PM under the cover of darkness and will position the camera in the shrubs on the side of the house by the garden. I'll train the camera on his large bay window. He keeps those drapes pulled open most of the time."

"Got it, Dave. Did you make sure that you tested that camera after dark to insure the infrared is working correctly? Remember, the last time we did one of these night gigs, it malfunctioned?"

"Yes, I do. That was an older model. I purchased a new one for this project, and I have already tested it...works like a charm. I promised you that I would never let that happen again, and I won't."

Denby paid Paula for her efforts on that job, but he did not pay Dave because the video was so dark that the parties involved were unrecognizable.

"Very well, then, it's all set. One more thing, Dave, do you have the small recorder that Denby wanted me to use?"

"Yeah, I've got it right here. Here it is," he said, pulling it from his pants' pocket. Dave nodded to Paula, looking downward, and then slipped the mini-recorder to her under the table, out of view of anyone who might be passing by. Paula took it, as smoothly as a baton in a relay race then slipped it in her purse. She shuddered as she thought about the complexity of this case and at what she was preparing to do.

"Good luck, Paula. You deserve better than this from Denby, but somebody has to do it, I guess."

"Yeah, I do need some good fortune. Thanks."

"I'll talk to you on Sunday to let you know how things came out with the video."

"No, it can wait till Monday, Dave. Just call me at work, please. I have to get back early Sunday to be with my girls, and I want to forget about this last hurrah that I'm about to perform until after I see them."

"I understand. Okay then, you may not see me tonight, but I will see you. Take care, Paula."

"You too, Dave, stay safe."

McCaffery briskly arose from the table and left abruptly, the heavy front door thudding behind him.

Last hurrah, what did she mean by that? Dave wondered, as he skipped down the front steps of the inn and returned to his truck.

Now that the accomplices had parted company, they were on their way to complete the last-minute details before the party. Dave ran by the store to get videotape for his camera and then settled down in an average motel. Paula returned to her room and dressed casually for errands and a trip to the salon.

7

Situated in a ritzy area of Charleston, the Salon de Paris employed European women, for the most part. A woman could get a manicure, pedicure, and her hair styled under the same roof. Facials with a neck and shoulder massage were available, as well as other esthetic enhancements, i.e. waxing and hair removal. Unlike the Asian nail salons and chain hair shops that have mushroomed across the country, this one had authentic Old-World flavor.

For Paula, trips to the salon in the Market Place district were a rare treat. The last time she came here was the weekend that she met Jim. The circumstances could not be more different this time. Unfortunately, Paula only had time for her nails and hair today.

"Good morning! You've not been vaiting long, I hope?" asked the Swedish nail artist, in her Scandinavian accent.

"Oh, no," Paula replied, "I just walked in. Thank you for asking."

"That's good. Then you have good timing, madam. Ve are very busy today, but I just had a cancellation. How can I help you?"

"That's great. I can't believe I don't have to wait," Paula replied. "In that case, I want as much as you can do to these nails in thirty minutes, please.

Afterwards, I'll just get a quick wash, trim, and hairstyle from the ladies across the hall."

"You came to da right lady. My reputation is for fast, but excellent service. Come back to my station and have a seat, madam. Here, give me your hands," said the nail technician, reaching out to her client.

She stretched out her hands to be examined. "Please, call me, Paula."

"Vunderful, Paula, I'm Erika. I suggest ve shape and paint your nails, and then I have a few lotions you can choose from, or would you prefer I put some nails on for you."

"I'll keep mine, Erika. The first thing you said sounds good to me."

"What color would you like your nails?

"Something in a deep red that would blend with a poinsettia party dress."

"Here, choose from these shades," Erika said, as she held up a tab of color samples from which Paula could select.

"That one will work for me," said Paula, as she pointed to the deep red.

By coincidence or fate, another nail artist from Germany next to Erika's cube was busy working on the nails of the estranged wife of Judge Parks, Eleanor Parks. As Erika began clipping Paula's cuticles, she could overhear the voice of a woman apparently in a great deal of turmoil and stress.

"Yeah, and to think I was dumb enough to leave our beautiful home for a modest townhouse by the water. We were going to counseling, attempting to reconcile, but I don't really think that my husband cared anymore about working things out. He skipped two counseling sessions before informing me that he didn't want to continue. He didn't even invite me to his Christmas party tonight, and half those people attending are my friends, too."

"Oh vell, not to worry, Mrs. Parks," said Greta, as she buffed her client's nails and smacked her chewing gum, "From vhat you have told me, his day is coming, is it not?"

"Oh, yes, my dear, what goes around comes around, and his turn is not far off. Just one slip up, and I'll live in that family home of his for the rest of my life. I'll get alimony and might even decide to get me a younger man," retorted Mrs. Parks, with a maniacal chuckle.

Eleanor knew that she had brought the divorce upon herself with excessive drinking and inappropriate behavior but did not realize the severity of the situation for a long time because she lived in denial. She wanted children to gain status with many of her friends who were constantly talking about theirs. She felt like a fish out of water among them and gradually fell out of most social activities they were involved in together.

Although she had the material things they possessed, she did not have the contentment of a happy marriage with children. The Parks never had children because Eleanor had ovarian cancer not long after their marriage. The doctors were able to successfully treat the cancer with chemotherapy, but the chance for pregnancy was fifty-fifty until she reached thirty-five. After that, the chances had diminished appreciably, and although Eleanor sought the best medical care available, she was unable to conceive.

With a heavy workload and reaching his middle age years, the judge would not consent to adoption, though Eleanor had tried to persuade him on numerous occasions. Quite often, they ended their discussions in shouting matches over this issue and her drinking. For Eleanor, at forty-nine, the relentless nagging about adoption had given way to depression, drinking, and arguments, while Judge Parks immersed himself more and more in work and workouts at the local gym.

Before their final attempts at marital counseling failed, Judge Parks sought help for Eleanor by convincing her to try a rehabilitation facility, but the treatment she received was too short to have a permanent effect. Their next option was residential treatment at the Betty Ford Clinic, but Mrs. Parks refused to go. When she refused to receive further treatment, the judge asked for a separation, citing her alcohol addiction and verbal abuse.

When Court was in session last, Mrs. Parks exploded into the courtroom in a drunken fury, shouting obscenities at the judge. She cited him for all the wrongs he had ever done and accused him of adultery. That proverbial straw broke the camel's back. The judge was so embarrassed that he had her removed from the courtroom and committed to Mercy General Hospital for a psychological evaluation and brief stay.

Eleanor awakened with the worst hangover she ever had, and though she begged his forgiveness, he had heard her empty apologies all too many times before. He filed for divorce, citing irreconcilable differences. In South Carolina, a divorce takes a minimum of one year, unless one party can prove that the other is having an affair or has been physically abusive. Eleanor had thrown away an upper-class lifestyle, and was unlikely to recapture it, unless, the divorce court ruled in her favor.

"The only thing I can say for sure, Greta, is that somewhere, someday, I'll get him for this humiliation he has put me through."

"I understand," said Greta in her German accent. "Yah, he vill get vat is comin' to him."

Greta could see through Eleanor Parks' charade straight through to her problems. Eleanor had come to the salon reeking of vodka, and to Greta, she was just another spoiled, wealthy American woman who could not find happiness from within. Whether it was a new Miata or a piece of jewelry, Eleanor continually acquired new things in an effort to satiate her thirst for happiness, but to no avail. Greta knew her role, however, and it was to provide a look of glamour for her clients while listening to their personal problems and gossip. At thirty bucks for a full manicure, plus a decorative jar to catch unreported tips, she did not find difficulty in being adept at listening. This was the best money she had made since she was a flight attendant with the Lufthansa Airlines when she lived in Germany.

Greta finished drying and touching up her client's nails. "How do your nails look, Mrs. Parks? Will this vurk for you?"

"They look fine, Greta. Thank you."

"Guten abend, Mrs. Parks, I hope you have a vunderful veekend!"

"Thanks, Greta. I'll try, but I don't have much to look forward to."

Paula, sitting adjacent to Eleanor Parks' station, overheard the venom that Mrs. Parks had spewed out towards her husband and, to an extent, felt sorry for her. To desire to have a child and yet never be able was something that she could not fathom. Paula thought about her two daughters and about how blessed she was to have them. Eleanor's threat sounded serious, but Paula did not know how to read her. She continued to prepare her mind to carry out the plan developed by Denby, not wanting to bog down with Eleanor's problems. Her stomach knotted up as she pondered the possible scenarios that could result, if she was pulled into the middle of the Parks' divorce case.

What if Mrs. Parks has a private investigator staked out at the judge's house tonight? My God, this could be very embarrassing to my family, if I'm caught alone with the judge, she thought. Paula's nails shone, freshly painted with a brilliant deep red. She slipped her hands from underneath the tiny fan to admire the work and new look. After settling with Erika, Paula walked through an archway to the adjoining room to begin the next stage of her beautification, and took a seat in the hairstylist's chair.

"What shall I do for you today, ma'am?" the stylist asked.

"Yes, I need a shampoo, cut the dead ends, and style it sorta like you see it now, please."

"Yes, ma'am, sit here. We'll trim it first and then shampoo before the blow dry and styling."

Paula sat in the bulky, black vinyl chair with padded stainless-steel arms. Deep in thought, she barely noticed what was happening to her hair. Fear gripped her as second thoughts rolled through her mind like a freight train barreling down the tracks at break-neck speed.

Is it too late to call this plot off? I could call Tom when I get back to the room. I can't go through with this for any amount of money, she thought.

The stylist finished her hair with a brush, the touch of her hands, and a shot of hair spray. "Have a look in the mirror, ma'am, and tell me what you think."

"I like it a lot. Thank you so much. I think this will do just fine."

Paula turned to get her purse, and although she was coddled and pampered at the salon, her experience was not extremely enjoyable. Images of Eleanor Parks and of possible scenarios that could evolve flashed in her mind like lightning bolts striking in a furious summer thunderstorm.

She returned to Magnolia Inn a little after lunch but was not hungry. If caught on a private investigator's tape, she would lose the respect of her teenage daughters and the love of a special new boyfriend. She hurried up the three flights of stairs to her room and fell face first on her bed like a falling tree.

With her head buried in a pillow, she rehearsed what she would tell Denby to back out of this hellish plan. *I'll have to just level with him*, she thought. She knew that confronting Denby, a master manipulator, very determined and ready to do whatever was necessary to win this case, would not be easy. She knew very well how angry he became when things did not go his way.

She struggled to sit up on the bed as she lifted the handset on the phone on her bedside table. Dialing Denby's number, Paula breathed in deeply and then exhaled slowly a couple of times, like in a Lamaze class, to gain her composure.

"Hello, Tom Denby, here. Can I help you?"

"Well, yeah, I hope you can, Tom, because I don't think I can carry out this scheme of yours."

"Would you like to tell me why not, Paula?" Denby asked coldly.

"Because it's too dangerous, Tom, not to mention, there's this little matter of illegality. I was at the salon this morning and Mrs. Parks was there vowing to get back at the judge. I think she's having him tailed. I don't want to be caught up in the middle of their divorce case."

"There you go worrying again. You ought to get that crap out of your head and focus on making the bonus money. Besides, there's no one else who is capable of pulling this off, but you, Paula."

"I don't care that much about the money, Tom. We both know I could use it for my kids' education, but don't throw money in my face again. The risk is just not worth it."

Denby responded in a softer tone, realizing he had to give this conversation more thought and effort. Paula had experienced too many of his tricks to swallow his hook readily. "Paula, I know you can do it. I have all the faith in the world in you, so please don't let me down. It will all be over in a matter of six hours."

"No, it won't. You know it will go on until the case is wrapped up, and maybe even after that. Thanks for understanding. I'll talk to you on Monday."

Denby cringed as she slammed the phone down in anger.

Highly distressed, she picked up the phone again to call Jim, tears trickling from her cheeks. On the third ring, Jim grabbed the phone as he excused himself from a customer.

"Hello, Jim Roberts speaking, can I help you?"

"Jim, darling, I'm so glad it's you."

"Yeah, Paula, I got your message last night. Sorry, I missed your call when I was out with clients. What's the matter? You sounded upset."

"Yeah, I figured you were entertaining clients. I needed some rest anyway. I've had so much on my mind, and I'm really stressing here. I feel like I'm about to lose it."

"I see, well, whatever it is you're doing up there doesn't sound too good to me if you are feeling like that."

"It's not, Jim, but this is the last time I'll go to one of these parties for Tom. I am in the middle of a situation on a must-win case."

"But you don't have to be, Paula. That's his problem."

"Well, it's my problem too as long as I work for him. May I confide in you, Jim? Bear in mind that if I do, you won't be able to share this conversation with anyone?"

"Of course, you can, sweetie." *What had she gotten into with the sleazy snake Denby?* Jim wondered. She paused to gather her thoughts. "Go ahead, Paula, tell me what's eating at you?"

"Well, I don't want to tell anyone, but I have nowhere else to turn. I know of no one, but you, that I trust so completely and who might understand."

She cried softly, and for a moment, could not speak for choking up inside. She knew that if she was to share all the details of her plight, she might lose Jim's respect and love, so she closed up. "I can't talk about it, Jim. I'm sorry. I shouldn't have brought it up."

"It's going to be okay, Paula. Just be strong. The sun will shine in the morning, and this dark cloud, whatever it is, will pass. Hang in there, and just do what you think is best."

Paula appreciated Jim's encouraging words, but the clichés rang hollow somehow. She was in too deep and could not muster the courage to turn around.

That is what upset her the most. If only she had the courage to tell him, then things might be different, but she could not take that chance.

"I will, Jim, thanks. I'm sorry, if I'm not responding as I should. I'm just so overwhelmed. I feel as if I'm a character in a book with a bad part to play who can't help but act it out."

"Are you sure you don't want to talk about what's bothering you?" Jim asked, thinking that confessing her troubles might do her good.

"Yes, I'm sure. Thanks for being there for me though. That means the world to me."

"Well, I'll tell ya what, Paula. Just say the word and I'll leave for Charleston after work."

"No, thank you, Jim. Not this time. Listen, I don't want to hang up now, but I have to get moving," Paula said, biting her lip.

"Good-bye, Paula. I'll be thinking of you."

"Same here, thank you."

Paula opened her purse to read one of two letters from Jim that she carried with her. He wrote it to her the day after the first time they kissed. The romantic interlude occurred at a dinner party on a boat that regularly toured the Charleston harbor. She gently unfolded the creased paper. She needed to refresh her memory of the beautiful words that Jim had written. Paula briefly forgot her troubles as she read:

Dear Paula,

I know that this is a little too soon to say I love you, but how else can I describe this overwhelming sense of warmth and joy that I feel inside? I felt it from our first date. I think it was even there since the time I saw you fall out of the beach chair at the Isle of Palms. What began as a rosebud of warmth is bursting forth to open into a full bloom in all its glory for the entire world to see. Our love is growing so sweetly, like a fragrance unmatched by the sweetest of magnolia blossoms.

I realize we both need time to see where this relationship is going, but I am willing to work at it as carefully as an artist paints a portrait. I have wanted so much to be in love with a woman like you, but my lot has been to be "unlucky in love," until now. From the things you shared with me about your first marriage, I would say that you have been, too. Nevertheless, there is something good about failing, only later to succeed, about losing, then later to find victory. The victory is always savored and cherished more.

So, my dearest Paula, I want you to know that I cherished our time together last night. I was lost in the warmth of your caress as waves gently rocked us in the boat. My head is still spinning, my heart beating like a bass drum, as I contemplate your beauty and the wondrous time we shared. The closeness we felt as we slow danced in the cabin to Johnny Mathis's "Chances Are" was incredible. When we kissed the way we did, I thought our hearts would explode into the night, like fireworks on the fourth of July.

My heart and mind are centered on you. I have to force myself to focus on work to take my thoughts off you. I see constant reminders of you all day and smile inwardly until we can meet again. My life is now incomplete without you, and yet I know that if I was to lose you, then my life is better for having known you.

I am with you in all that you do, and I pray that this wonderful beginning will have a beautiful future that is special for us both.

Love always,

Jim

She loved the encouragement that reading his letter gave her and sensed his sincerity as he expressed his feelings to her. Paula knew this proclamation of love would be tested this weekend. *If he sticks with me through this mess and still loves me, perhaps he is the love of my life,* she thought. Paula felt the same way towards Jim, but trusting anyone completely again was hard after all the hell she had been through in her first marriage. She had no indication that her first husband would become dependent on drugs, though they did experiment a little together in college.

She had since figured that not dealing with another man in her home was much easier. She ran things the way she wanted without interference or having to compromise; yet, in her heart, she still clung to her values that marriage was the proper context to have a lasting intimate relationship. At least, those were her morals, and she was comfortable with them. Regardless of what others did, she could not stray too far from her upbringing where two people in love married and lived together as a family. To marry this man would be the ultimate expression of her love, and if the relationship was to be, it was worth waiting.

Suddenly, Paula shook her head clearing the cobwebs from her fantasy, as she awakened, as if from a dream. Aware of the time drifting by, almost panicking, she thought about what she had left to do before she made her way across town to the party. She contemplated two or three scenarios that could unfold, depending on which variables she would encounter. She closed her eyes in anguish, wishing her predicament would go away. Gaining determination, she refused to yield to her inner voice, which tried to warn her to pull out. Instead, she focused on pushing through and getting it behind her.

8

Tom Denby channel-surfed with the remote while watching college football and checking bets he had placed on a couple of parlay cards. A bookie ran by the back entrance of his office during football season, and collected cards from the attorneys and staff who wanted to play. He jotted notes on which teams were winning and by what score, but his mind went back to the conversation with Paula. He was concerned about her tone, revealing her bitter attitude. She had always pulled through in the past, but in this case, attempting to sway a federal judge from due process made him very nervous. Denby knew this type of thing does occur, but he had never had the gall to try it before with a federal judge, regardless of his underhanded dealings in other cases.

Denby phoned the CEO of Colonial Paper, Paul Walker, to bring him up to speed on the case. He wanted to rehash his plan concerning the judge and hoped Walker would offer some words of encouragement.

"This is Paul Walker. Can I help you?"

"Yeah, Paul, it's Tom. I just wanted you to know that I may have some difficulty pulling this off. My gal on the inside is pretty nervous and a bit shaky."

"Tom, like I told you before, I don't care how you get it done, just get it done." responded Walker, irritated that Denby was calling him on a Saturday.

"Well, it's complicated when you set out to do something like this. To be honest, I really think the bonus is too low for what you are asking me to do."

"Oh, come on, Tom, are you telling me that you want to renegotiate now on what we already agreed?"

"I'm just saying that the offer is low. Can you do any better?"

"So, you are saying that. You take the cake, man. I thought the offer was more than fair."

"Not when you consider that it involves tampering with a federal judge, Paul."

"Alright, Tom, I'll personally guarantee that your bonus for getting the case thrown out will be doubled."

Denby was so surprised and taken off guard at the generous offer that he failed to respond immediately with enthusiasm, which disappointed Walker. Instead, he offered a neutral response to nail down the offer.

"Could you fax me a letter to that effect, Paul?"

"Why do you need a fax? My word has always been good with you."

"Well, yeah, but this is a much larger transaction. You can't blame me for that."

"I'll do it first thing Monday morning. In addition, Tom, I do expect some sort of kickback since I'm upping the ante. This has got to be one of your biggest cases in a while, buddy."

"I've always taken care of you on referrals that you have sent me, Paul. You know that. Tell me the amount you're looking for, and I'll tell you what I can do."

"I don't know, Tom, you make an offer."

"How about twenty-five g's?"

"How 'bout fifty?" Walker responded.

"Alright, Paul, for you I'll do that."

"Yeah, I guess you will, you ole codger," replied Walker. "Look at the size of your bonus, but then you do have to pay taxes on it, don't you?"

"Yes, I do, you weasel, and I do have lawyers and staff to pay. I'll talk to you later."

"Alright, Tom, just get it done, for Pete's sake. You are supposed to be the master at this sort of thing."

Walker hung up without another word, leaving Denby with mixed emotions. The potential bonus had jumped exponentially, but still, he felt the pressure without the affirmation that he sought from his friend. Denby put down the receiver and paused for a moment with his arm extended to the phone. Walker and Denby had been childhood playmates growing up in Georgetown County together, but neither trusted the other implicitly. It was certainly not the kind of trust, which did not require a written document with this amount of money involved. With the stakes now higher, Denby became even more obsessed with the case.

Should I let my concerns go and just trust Paula to come though, or should I take matters to another level? Denby wondered. The tone in Paula's voice caused him concern about how she would perform. Not once had she let him down. Why should he not trust her now? On the other hand, what if she bailed and did not through with their plan? How else could he get the judge to throw the case out? How much time would they buy, if a new judge was appointed, and the current judge be taken off the case?

Denby thought about the people in New York who were willing to help him once before. Walking to the phone, he had a sick feeling inside as he dialed the number that was hidden on a business card in his drawer for five years. He heard the phone ring twice.

"No, I can't. I'm not going to do this," Denby muttered, as he hung up the handset. He was willing to do about anything to win the case, but he did not want to call on underworld figures, even if they would help. He had kept their contact information just in case, but the very presence of the business card made him uneasy when he considered it. He was questioned about the disappearance of Jed Simmons, but he claimed that he had no knowledge of the incident.

Denby knew from his study of the law and experience in his career that "the hand of one is the hand of all" when it came to authorizing a murder or committing a crime. He might as well pull the trigger if he was to pay someone to be murdered. He thought back on his childhood days, going to school with his friends, attending church, learning the golden rule. He wondered if he would ever be able to find his way back to a life with honesty and integrity. He had slowly seared his conscience for the love of money since the earlier years of his practice. A cesspool of trickery and deceit had become his way of handling tough situations.

9

The party was almost ready to start. One of the better private Christmas celebrations in Charleston, with great live music and libations, it had a guest list that read like a Who's Who List of the community. People were arriving at Judge Parks' residence car by car, a valet service tightly squeezing them on a side area of the lawn roped off as a temporary parking lot. A few guests rode in taxis for the ride home without having to be concerned about a designated driver, or fear being caught under the influence behind the wheel.

Inside, the band tuned their instruments, and hors d'oeuvres were in their final stages of preparation. Bartenders, servers, and kitchen workers all scurried about striving for perfection to please their kind, but very particular employer, as they placed various items at designated positions throughout the judge's spacious residence.

Double-checking the start time, Paula glanced at the invitation that indicated the party commenced at 7:30 PM. Since arriving at a party the very instant it began was not fashionable, she thought being a little late would be better. Besides, that way she would not be as noticeable among the socialites who wanted to comment on what everyone was wearing upon entry, and of course, figure out who each person was. Paula slipped into her poinsettia party dress, put on her matching high heels, and stood in front of the mirror. She added her string of cultured pearls with matching earrings and put on her red lipstick. She looked at herself in the mirror approvingly as she pressed her lips softly together and then touched up her application with a tissue, removing the excess. Last, she touched her finger to the opened top of a small expensive perfume bottle, applying it to the pulse points on her neck and wrists.

Her trip to the salon, getting all gussied up, gave her the appearance of a model more than a paralegal. She fastened the matching pearl bracelet and backed up a few steps. Turning sideways to gain a complete view of her profile, she took a deep breath, checking her look from the side. Forcing a smile, she tongued her teeth for any lipstick residue. Next, she fluffed her hair, and completed the final touches with a misting of hair spray,

"That's it, time to get going before I change my mind," Paula mumbled.

A knock on Paula's door startled her causing an uncontrollable flinch. "Paula, honey, your taxi is waiting," said Sarah Johnson through the door. "I just saw them arrive out front."

Paula had chosen not to drive to the party but to travel in a cab since she intended to be one of the last guests to leave Judge Parks' residence and she did not want to be seen in a particular car where a description and tag could be traced.

"Thanks, Sarah, I'll be down shortly."

The time had come for Paula to dive into action. She drew upon the drama courses she took at camp in the Catskill Mountains as a young high school junior, and then later on in college. Those were the days when she dreamed of being an actress, going to New

York to try making it on Broadway, or to Hollywood to pick up a part as an extra in a movie or soap opera, hoping to one day make it big. Those days of innocence for Paula had come and gone. She was about to play a part in a real-life play. The only problem with this play was that the lives were real and the scenes portrayed were unchangeable. Where this drama would end, she could not be sure.

She opened her purse, peeked inside, checking to see if the mini-recorder was enclosed, and then left the room, trotting down the wooden stairway, her high heels clicking as she made her way down the long staircase and out of the inn to the curbside where the taxi waited.

"Have fun, and knock 'em dead!" Sarah called out to Paula, as she opened the front door, hinge creaking.

Paula winced as she heard what Sarah said, forcing a smile as she looked back in Sarah's direction. Inwardly, she was shaken to her core. "Okay, I sure will, Sarah. You and Mickey have a good evening."

Sarah closed the door with a thud. Paula loved Sarah and Mickey and felt guilty for staying at Magnolia Inn while engaging in deceitful activity. The taxi driver stood by the curb, waiting. By the time she reached the sidewalk, he leaned over to open the back door for her. There is nothing like the view of a gorgeous woman to get a man moving, and this cabbie had noticed that Paula was an extraordinary woman the moment she began her descent from the porch. He had seen many women in this tourist and college town, but none more gorgeous and stunning than she was.

Paula entered the taxi, taking a seat as the driver closed the door carefully, so as not to close it on her knee-length dress. The driver might as well have been a private chauffeur especially assigned to Paula with the treatment he gave her. His endocrine glands came alive with her presence and the scent of her perfume, which permeated his cab.

"Where we going to, ma'am?"

"Sir, could you drive down around the Market Place District for about a half hour before taking me to the residence of Judge Wilmont Parks? It's called Wellington Place, at 22 East Bay Drive. Do you know it?"

"That's not a problem, ma'am. I know exactly where that is. It's down near the Battery, isn't it?"

"That's correct. You know your city well."

"Well, the city is not that big, ma'am. I was born and raised here...been driving a cab for ten years, too, so there's not many places I don't know," the cabbie said.

The driver made a right turn at the next stop sign and headed for the Market Place, a famous tourist attraction situated in the center of town. Here, one could find all the crafts, artwork, and souvenirs to take home for remembrance of a Charleston visit. There were handmade sweetgrass baskets, woven by African-American families who passed down the craft from generation to generation. Many of these families conversed among themselves in the Gullah language spoken only in the coastal region of South Carolina. The local traders of many other authentic Low Country items, as well as imported trinkets, rented tables in the three-block long Old City Market where they sold their wares. There were T-shirts, sweatshirts, and other collectibles to commemorate Charleston's history in the Revolutionary and Civil Wars.

The cabbie turned down Market Street and rode by the shops and restaurants that lined the narrow brick streets. Paula looked out the window to see the tourists and locals walking the sidewalks. It was nearly eight o'clock in the evening, and the shops were open late crowded with people taking advantage of Christmas sales. Paula lowered her window to hear the sounds of live bands playing on the patios of the restaurants. She thought about how wonderful moving to Charleston and having access to this atmosphere any time she wanted would be, rather than making the hour's drive down the coast each time she traveled from Georgetown.

"Ma'am, I don't mean to disturb you, but from what you said, isn't it about that time to head out to Wellington Place?"

She glanced at her watch. "Yeah, so it is. Thanks for noticing. Let's motor to Judge Parks' residence."

The driver made a right turn out of the Market District and on to King Street where many fine retail and restaurants are located. They passed Hyman's Restaurant where Jim and Paula had eaten seafood the last time they came to town. She reminisced briefly but then snapped her mind back like a rubber band to her business tonight.

"I can get through this," Paula whispered as she attempted to reassure herself.

"Pardon me, ma'am?"

"Oh, nothing, I was just thinking out loud."

The driver continued north on King Street and then turned left on a side street to Rutledge, where he drove south in order to avoid the heavy traffic downtown and to add mileage to the odometer. Paula peered out of the window at the storefronts they passed. After a few minutes' ride, the cabbie made a left on Calhoun.

"We're almost there, ma'am."

"That's great. I'm ready to stretch my legs and see this beautiful home."

"I wish I could, ma'am, but I gotta keep working."

Paula reached in her purse, pulling out a small compact to touch up before her entrance. With a tissue, she cleaned a small smear of lipstick from the corner of her mouth. She plucked the mascara tube from her purse and gingerly gave her lashes a brush. The driver made his final turn onto East Bay Street en route to Judge Parks' residence.

"I'm looking forward to this party. Judge Parks has a fine art collection which is written up in magazines, the kind of stuff you find in museums."

"Is that right? Well, I hope you have a good time," said the driver, as he pulled into the drive where a man from the valet service waited to open the backdoor of the cab.

"Thanks, you take care, and don't work too hard," she said, greasing his palm with fare and a tip.

The judge had acquired his home from his mother's estate when she passed away. It was an easy transition because he had only one sibling, a sister, who wanted to live in the Midwest with her husband and two children. The sister, younger than Judge Parks, received much of the mutual funds, the family silver, and her mom's jewelry. The judge got the gorgeous three-story mansion.

Judge Parks was from an old Charleston family whose roots went back to England. His lineage was traced to the scholars who served the eight Lords of Great Britain commissioned by King Charles to develop Charles Towne. Evidently, one of the Parks' ancestry came to Charleston as a historian to record the progress of the settlement, and out of his loins, several generations later was born Wilmont Charles Parks. The honorable Judge Parks had the mettle and fortitude of a Victorian Queen and was often cited by law review magazines for his wise jurisprudence. He considered only the law and the evidence when making his rulings, interpreting the law as a Constitutionalist.

Like other federal judgeships, his appointment was for life, which made discharging his duties without showing partiality to anyone easier. Many a lawyer had tried to buy the judge's favor with rewards of varying descriptions. He had been invited on hunting trips to exclusive lodges and to golf trips to various beach resorts, but he always paid his way if he accepted an invitation. He did his best to carry on the tradition of his English ancestors who helped influence how the laws were written in the United States.

If a lawyer came into Judge Parks' courtroom unprepared, without proper attire, or without an acceptable demeanor, he had best be ready for a confrontation with sarcastic retorts from the *bench*. Outright rebuke was the norm, if an attorney tried to upstage traditional practice in any way. Once, in Judge Parks' courtroom, a lawyer was extolling the virtues of a defendant who had allegedly committed rape. The attorney was busy listing all the good deeds that the accused had supposedly done, painting his client in the most favorable light. When Judge Parks had heard enough of the crap, he surprised the young attorney with a funny, yet harsh rebuke. "Tell me something, counselor. Have you seen a halo floating over the defendant's head?" Everyone in the courtroom laughed aloud at the embarrassed attorney, who turned three shades of red, each one darker than the one before.

Judge Parks' father and mother were always busy with their business of importing but hired a nanny who practically raised him. She was an English woman of proper standing who lived with the family and schooled him at home. Not until high school, did young Wilmont Parks receive formal education outside his home. He attended high school at Porter Gaud, a prep school nearby, and completed his undergraduate degree at the College of Charleston before going to Harvard Law School. With a ratio of three to one at the College of Charleston, he could choose from many young women. He chose Eleanor, a bright-eyed college co-ed, who majored in finding a good man to marry. She was easy to get along with, at the time, and allowed him to concentrate on his studies. Reasonably attractive, as well, Eleanor seemed to be the perfect fit for him.

The judge resumed a dating relationship with her when he returned to Charleston to practice law. She was one of the few young ladies he knew and got along with from his undergraduate years who had not yet married. He did not want to work at the dating scene because of the demands on his time as a young lawyer. Dating Eleanor seemed to fall into place as she worked hard at landing the young attorney with a bright future. Not very many Harvard trained attorneys were based in Charleston, and she figured he was bound to rise to the top of his profession.

The judge, now fifty-two, had restrained himself from extramarital affairs since their separation, although there were several women who would have succumbed to his charm and handsome looks. Will, as his friends called him, kept in shape by playing racquetball and lifting weights. He ran rings around most men his age and rarely missed a day at the gym. Keeping physically active was his way of avoiding his home life as long as he could before he had to return to an unhappy wife, who was usually drunk out of her mind by the time he arrived back home.

After twenty-four years of marriage, living much of that time with a woman who was miserable, the judge had remained faithful, although she accused him of having an affair with his Clerk of Court. He desired greatly to be in love and to be married to someone who did not have as many personal problems as his present wife. His goal was to remain celibate for a year in order to get a quiet divorce from Eleanor, but lately, his libido had been rising to a state of constant readiness.

Judge Parks thought that if he encountered the right situation, he might not remain chaste. He remembered the many divorce cases he handled as a young attorney, advising his clients to keep busy and occupy their time until the divorce was final. He always stressed that the divorcing parties were to stay free of intimate relations with anyone until the divorce was final. Keeping his own advice was harder than he ever imagined.

If I can find an attractive, single woman tonight to be with, I just might consider it, Judge Parks thought. He continued to stroll through his home greeting the many guests attending from local law firms. Most were considerably younger than he was, but this fact did not deter the judge from dreaming. After all, he was successful, fit, and nice-looking. He scanned the gathering crowd for lovely, single women from time to time, as he made idle chat with his guests.

Groups of persons mingled throughout the fine home while the catering personnel walked back and forth with trays of heavy hors d'oeuvres. Bottles of champagne and various wines circulated, courtesy of

Judge Parks, and the wait staff who offered the bubbly to all with an empty glass. A long table of food situated in the ballroom beckoned appealingly, causing guests to salivate and graze its contents. At the side of the food table, was a portable bar with two jolly bartenders pouring whatever mixed drink anyone desired, or twisting the top off a favorite beer.

10

Paula arrived exactly as she planned, thirty minutes after the party began. Strings of white lights bordered the driveway that led up to the Southern mansion. Multi-colored lights were strewn around the garland on the porch railing. Inside, the home was decorated with Christmas ornaments from one end to the other setting the tone for a festive evening.

The judge hired a party service that provided the band, and who coordinated everything. The service also provided a master of ceremonies to announce when the dancing began and to direct the flow of the other activities. There were awards for the best slow dance, the best fast dance, and the best "Shag", the South Carolina State Dance. In addition, for laughs, about a dozen men who participated paraded around with their pant legs rolled up above their knees in a "bare legs contest". The volunteering female judges inspected their hairy legs for the best-looking pair then voted based on how loud the crowd cheered for each one, which always brought loads of fun and laughter.

The party was now in full swing with a house full of people mingling and enjoying the festivities. The crowd was so thick that people were turning sideways, as they passed by each other. Some of the ladies were tapping the toes of their shiny, colorful heels to the live music. The band set up in the corner of the ballroom for maximum exposure to the crowd. It was early, but lively beach music, with an occasional Christmas song tossed in, put the guests in a festive mood.

Paula, waiting nervously on the porch, rang the doorbell. The inlaid brick porch was half the length of the house, with large, dark green wooden rockers spaced uniformly from one end to the other, a common theme in the Southern decor. Eight tall, intricately designed Corinthian columns supported the outside front entrance to the grand home. Their stately appearance yielded an elegance that captured times past.

"Good evening, ma'am," said the butler. "May I have your name, please?"

"I'm Renee Caldwell from the Denby Law Firm. I think that "J. Thomas Denby" is the way the name is listed on your roster. He couldn't come tonight and sent me in his place." She smiled as the butler dutifully marked number one forty-one off his clipboard with a sense of pride.

"Yes, ma'am, I see you are listed here by Mr. Denby's name. May I take your wrap?"

"Yes, sir, thank you." She stepped into the foyer, turning her back to the butler, who assisted with removing her lightweight, three-quarter length camel-colored coat to hang in the large closet. "Also, here are a couple of Christmas gifts that my boss sent for the judge, sir."

"That's fine, ma'am. I'll take those to the kitchen. Your coat will be safe here with me. It won't go nowhere 'cuz I'm good at remembering everyone's coat with their face," said the butler.

His grin, a Louis Armstrong smile, showed off his pearly whites with genuine friendliness. Domestic workers made a good living by being extraordinary at their simple jobs when done with a flare like this African-American gentleman did. Paula slipped him a tip to ensure he took extra care of the silk-lined cashmere coat.

She walked past the foyer into the hallway that led to the ballroom. Amused as she heard the band playing their popular tunes, she sashayed to the banquet table for hors d'oeuvres. She carefully placed a few delicacies on her plate then glanced up, looking around for Judge Parks. Dave had given her a photo of the judge earlier that morning, which she had studied carefully before she left for the party. She hoped that he would not be hard to recognize, knowing that pictures can be tricky.

He's not in this room, she thought, as she walked to the end of the table abounding with every type of finger food and sweets available. Licking her fingers stained with sauce from chicken wings, Paula approached the portable bar for a beverage.

"Yes, ma'am, what can I get for you tonight?" asked the bartender.

"I'm not sure. What's your specialty?"

"I do it all. How about a rum and coke, or a Cape Cod?"

"Actually, I'll have a diet coke with a twist of lime," she said, as she winked at the bartender.

"I'll see what I can do, we don't get too many requests for the hard stuff," he said playfully.

The bartender was all too glad to dig around under the set-up table and locate a bottle diet coke. Diet coke was a drink that was seldom ordered, but one that had a little redemptive value with a slice of lime. The way she carried herself energized the bartender, who was eager to give her whatever she wanted.

"Here ya go, ma'am, one diet coke with a twist of lime."

Paula took a sip of her soft drink, scanning the room again for the judge, all the while taking in the party and crowd.

"How's your beverage, ma'am?" the bartender asked.

"It tastes great. Thank you," Paula replied.

Paula reached in her purse and fished out a couple of bucks to drop in the bartender's tip jar. He used a thick glass fish bowl strategically placed on the top of the bar to collect the gratuities. Finding an inconspicuous place to stand for a few minutes while listening to the band and observing the crowd, Paula saw several people she thought looked familiar from when court was in session.

The dimly lit ballroom was humming with excitement as the guests took to the floor to the sounds of "Jingle Bell Rock." For their next number, the versatile band performed a slow song, originally sung by the Drifters. Dance partners stayed on the dance floor, changing from a slow dance to the Shag without a hitch. Paula wished Jim were here, holding her in his arms and sliding across the floor to the rhythm of the soulful sounds. She finished her beverage and found a place to deposit the small plate and glass. The Swedish meatballs and other hors d'oeuvres she consumed were just enough without getting bloated and sleepy.

A short walk to an adjacent room brought Paula into the large formal living room. A baby grand piano prominently displayed in one corner and fine antique furniture aptly placed on an exquisite Persian rug blended perfectly with the decorum of the room. Leather and fabric chairs filled the remainder of the room, with oil paintings perfectly positioned on smartly wallpapered walls. A room full of people stood discussing cases, talking shop, and swapping jokes about Veronica Kowalski and Bill Benton.

Although President Benton was the first president in over a hundred years to be impeached, he was still hanging on to his office by his uncanny ability to slip out of a noose, much to the chagrin of Republicans. Teflon Bill had truly earned the nickname of his detractors, "Slick Willie." Hilary loved the White House prestige so much that she demanded he not resign. Some believed she aspired to become President of the United States. He was willing to do anything to appease her since the discovery of his affair with the young intern that rocked the core of the nation. Up to this point, he had never paid much out of his pocket for legal fees in the face of alleged affairs. That all changed with this affair and with the Claudia Jones case that surfaced, as well. With the news of Veronica giving the President oral sex and Claudia Jones and others going after him, William Davidson Benton set all-time records by a sitting president for legal bills.

Since the President was a master at deception, he wanted to blame the whole debacle on Hilary's lack of consistent affection. She often claimed she was too tired when he wanted intimate relations, reliable sources said, so he stayed up all hours working, while finding other ways to gratify his lusts. Benton figured that Veronica provided some of the things he missed in his relations with his wife, but she was the worst mistake of his life, and he knew it. He would probably have chosen to resign without his wife's support, but he reasoned that he could keep his job and position as President of the United States as long as Hilary stuck by him. *The nation is forgiving, no matter what, if I play my cards right*, he thought.

Paula smiled, even laughed, at some of the ridiculous jokes she overheard, as the group bantered and cackled. Not seeing Judge Parks yet, she slowly eased her way out and into the next room, the study, which was a rather large room lined with built-in mahogany bookshelves filled with law books and classic novels. On one wall, there were many other books, such as histories of Early America, the Civil War, and South Carolina. There were also leather-bound antique books from England and France in one section.

A crowd of twenty-five to thirty people milled about making conversation barely heard above the music. A close circle of a dozen people gathered around a prominent-looking man with gray temples. It was the judge surrounded by colleagues and their wives. There was no mistaking his identity, as Paula observed him discreetly. The crowd laughed as he told stories of comical events that happened when court was in session. There was group of ladies who stood nearby, probably workers at the Federal Courthouse and nearby law firms. Within four blocks of the court, there were the city and county courthouses and thirteen law practices with numerous attorneys and staff.

Many of them looked at him in ways suggesting that they would say, or do, nearly anything to gain his favor. Parks could see through these charades but enjoyed them just the same. He maintained a certain amount of grace and humility that befitted his office and was true to the code of conduct for a judge on the federal bench. Though many had tried, the judge had never allowed anyone to penetrate his armor. He had made his reputation as a brilliant Federal prosecutor before his appointment to the bench.

Eleanor Parks had so repulsed her husband that he did not want to perform his marital duties for some time prior to their separation. It had been six months since Judge Parks had a restraining order issued to prevent his wife from coming on his premises, and even longer, since he had sex. The lonely road of celibacy had now lasted longer than nine months, but still he knew waiting was best until his divorce was final. Not seeing anyone at the party who attracted him, he figured he would just fantasize and keep his lusts safely tucked away in his head.

"Yes, that was a complex case to prosecute the drug cartel king pin, Hernandez," said Parks to his circle of guests. "With all the publicity surrounding the case, the many interruptions, and so on, gleaning enough evidence to put him behind bars was difficult. The Nicaraguans wanted to extradite him to face trial there, and the prosecutors had to prove that at least one large shipment of cocaine was directly tied to him here in the States. I remember the break came when the District Attorney received a phone call from an informant in Miami who had worked with the shipment. He had an audiotape, on which Hernandez was recorded orchestrating a deal with the Mafia. That was what we needed to put that lowlife dealer in the penitentiary."

"I remember that," responded one of the judge's assistants. "We were all about to snap from sleep deprivation and stress when the break came. Remember, Judge?"

"How well I do. I don't care for bodyguards all around, but we had them everywhere we turned. I understand that I made some folks pretty mad just doing my job."

At the time of the case, there were threats on the judge's life nearly every day. A team from the Secret

Service was dispatched to protect him. For the next six months, there was at least one bodyguard assigned to watch him twenty-four hours a day until things calmed down.

Parks was a distinguished-looking gentleman with gray temples and a thick head of medium brown hair. He stood six-foot two, average build, with piercing blue eyes that seemed to take in the whole room when he looked out into the crowd around him. Indeed, he possessed the ability to take in many events, facts, and the personal demeanors of those in the room in a moment, while listening to a conversation in his circle.

Paula glanced in his direction, studying the judge. *Not bad looking, this won't be as difficult as I feared. Perhaps he will even be pleasant*, she thought, as she quickly looked back in another direction, not wanting to attract attention. The judge looked up, seeing a strikingly beautiful female guest standing out from her group, as a lone diamond among rhinestones. He noticed she had been looking in his direction, which piqued his interest.

He looked again in her direction and saw no wedding band on her finger. *Could it be that my dream has come true before I expected?* he wondered. His heart picked up a few beats, manly hormones stirring within. *I had better make my rounds and mix with the guests,* the judge thought. He politely excused himself from his colleagues and acquaintances and approached to a group next to Paula. He figured that he would slip in to talk to her in a moment. She noticed the judge on the move and waited to see what he would do.

"Good evening, ladies," said Judge Parks to the group. "I hope you are having a good time at my little party."

The group of ladies nodded in unison, laughing and smiling to ingratiate their host. "Yes, sir, we are. Thank you for inviting us," said one of the women.

"Great, then please enjoy the rest of your evening. I'll see you ladies around."

He smoothly dismissed himself and turned to approach Paula, who had slipped away from the group of women and stood alone a few feet away, appearing as if she was watching the band.

"Hi, are you enjoying the party tonight? I'm Wilmont Parks, and you are?"

"I'm Renee Caldwell, Judge Parks. It's a pleasure to meet you."

"Oh, so you know who I am."

"Most people do who are in the legal field. You're well-known."

"The pleasure is mine. Is there a fortunate man who escorted you to the party?"

"Not tonight, Judge Parks. I came alone."

"Well, I'm honored you came, Renee. Are you an attorney here in the Charleston area?"

"Oh no, Judge Parks, I was sent to represent J. Thomas Denby Law Firm from Georgetown. Mr. Denby sent you a couple of things, which I left with your butler."

"Yes, I believe I saw them on the kitchen table. Please tell Mr. Denby thanks for me. He doesn't miss a trick, that boss of yours, does he?"

"You have no idea, Judge," Paula retorted.

"Are you enjoying the party thus far, Miss Caldwell?"

"I sure am. The music and food are great, and the way you have your home decorated is fantastic. Did you do that yourself?"

"No, but I can say that I directed most of it," the judge said, as he laughed.

"I see. You have a good eye."

"Thank you. I try."

"Judge, I also noticed you have many beautiful works of art throughout your home. When Mr. Denby said that he needed someone else to come, I really didn't want to miss the party because of an opportunity to see your fine home and art collection. To be honest, I read an article about your home in the Southern Gazette Magazine," she said.

"Oh, so you saw that little-known article, did you? I don't think the magazine sales were up that month," said Judge Parks.

"That's not what I heard about the sales. I think you're being modest."

"I was fortunate to have inherited much of the artwork and my home from my parents. Some of the paintings I picked up myself on trips to Europe. So, you have a keen interest in art?"

"Yes, sir, I sure do. I studied art in college with an emphasis on the Old Dutch and Italian Masters."

"That's very interesting, Renee, but please don't call me sir. Court is out of session and the term makes me feel old."

"Sorry, that's just the way I was raised."

"I understand perfectly. It's not a big deal. Listen, if you would care to accompany me back to the ballroom, I'll tell you a little about the paintings as we go."

"That would be wonderful, Judge Parks."

"And please, call me, Will."

"Okay, Will, I can do that," she said, smiling.

They meandered through a couple of rooms, taking in the art. Her grace and charm mesmerized the judge. In his own right, Judge Parks looked rather dapper in his suit and tie, shiny shoes, and starched blue button-down shirt, a monogram, WPC, prominently displayed on his coat pocket.

Tom Denby and Dave McCaffery had done their homework correctly, discovering the judge was lonely and desired female companionship. Paula walked alongside him listening as he elaborated on two paintings in the hallway. They wound their way through the crowd and out the doorway to the ballroom. Judge Parks had as much chance as the proverbial "snowball in hell" not to melt to the bewitching charms of this Southern belle. Though she was beautiful from a distance, up close, her looks and perfume were captivating. The judge was slowly becoming paralyzed, like a fly bitten by a poisonous spider waiting in its web to devour its prey. He had not been attracted to anyone like this since his college days.

Paula did not want to overestimate her effect on the judge, so she continued to pour on the charm, but she did so in a subtle way so as not to appear disingenuous. Surprisingly, Paula enjoyed his company, although she did have ulterior motives. Her interest in his art collection went as far as needed because her ultimate goal was to get into his heart and win his trust.

They walked together into the ballroom, brushing arms unintentionally, which set the judge off with sparks of curious delight. The band was performing a favorite beach music tune in the South titled "Under the Boardwalk." The crowd danced, enjoying the looseness in their limbs from the effects of the adult beverages, as they sang along to this former sixties' hit.

"Would you like to dance, Renee?" asked Judge Parks as he turned, looking her in the eyes.

She had the softest green eyes that he had ever seen in his entire life. They sparkled like emeralds, yet with a softer sheen, jade-like and rare.

"Yeah, Will, let's go for it!" responded Paula.

No one seemed to notice, or care, as the judge took Paula's hand and began to dance, shuffling back and forth across the floor with her. A few of his close friends looked on with excitement and were glad for him, knowing the hell that his wife had put him through. The band performed a slow song next, and Judge Parks and Paula slipped into each other's arms as easily as the band making the transition from one song to the other. They danced until the song ended.

Knowing that he should mix more with his guests before he continued showing Paula the rest of the artwork, the judge decided that *discretion is the best part of valor*. Two songs were enough for now.

"Thank you for dancing with me and for your interest in my art collection," said Judge Parks. "Would you be willing to resume our tour later tonight? Showing you the rest of the paintings would be my privilege. You do seem to enjoy them."

"I would be honored, Your Honor, no pun intended."

"Great, I'll find you when the guests leave, if you will wait around for me."

"That's no problem, Will. I'll be out of the way somewhere, like a wallflower," she said, smiling.

"See you later then, Renee."

Her response amused the judge. He returned the smile, thinking how lucky he had become this night to meet the lovely Renee Caldwell. Judge Parks circulated among the various groups of people, greeting and thanking them for coming. The guests complimented him on what a fine party he was hosting, the kind that normally would have an admissions price. Parks did not mind throwing the extravagant party because he had a great year with his investments and because he enjoyed seeing his friends in a different, more relaxed setting.

Paula strolled to another room, making small talk with a person or two, but mostly, kept to herself. After an hour or so, she checked her watch, ten o'clock. Trepidation crept back in as she realized the enormity of the evil in which she was involved. The fact that she had pushed her conscience aside simply to try to please her boss and to meet a financial need came crashing down on her.

She remembered growing up in church and being taught right from wrong by all her teachers. Thoughts of her daughters and her parents, who had faith in her as a decent moral person caused her to shudder. She gulped down the remainder of her diet coke, pulled the lime perched on the rim of the glass, bit into the semi-sour fruit, and tossed the triangular rind in the bottom of her empty glass before placing it on a convenient oval tray nearby.

11

The front entrance to Wellington Place was a good fifty yards away from where Dave McCaffery set up. He was busy adjusting the focus on his infrared camera in the garden area to the east of the judge's bedroom window. He had sufficient cover in the highly wooded area on that side of the property with large pine trees, thick camellia and azalea bushes, and flowerbeds with tall gladiolas. A prominent statue stood in the middle of the garden pouring a continuous stream of water from its mouth to a surrounding shallow pool of water. Stocked with Japanese coy, the bottom was sprinkled with coins from wishers who tossed them in for luck. With a state-of-the-art infrared camera with high definition and zoom lens, the judge was easy prey from his bedroom window, should Paula succeed in getting him in front of the bay window, as planned.

The band began breaking down their set. The guests were filing out leisurely, wishing each other a Merry Christmas. The ones who indulged heavily were wobbling as they left and were under the watchful eye of the butler. He politely convinced most of them to take one of the taxis he had arranged per Judge Parks' instructions to get any intoxicated guests home safely. The only people Dave had to worry about spotting him were guests leaving the party and the valet staff who were parking the arriving cars. Dressed in camouflage, Dave completed his setup and crouched in the bushes waiting.

Just inside the front door of the estate, Judge Parks looked over his shoulder hoping to find his lovely guest. Paula waited, standoffishly, inside the entrance to the study. She was thumbing through a rare book while watching people leave as they filtered out the front door. A portion of her profile was barely visible. The judge left off with his guests for a moment to walk back and speak with her.

"Are you ready to see the rest of the paintings, Renee?"

"Whenever you are, Will," said Paula, closing the book and holding it with two hands, one finger inside to keep her place. "Don't you have more guests to talk to now?"

"Well, yes, I do, but I'm almost ready...listen, I'm quite sure you're aware that I'm separated, and my divorce is not final yet. Would you mind waiting in the kitchen for a little while until the last few guests leave? I'll have time to say my good-byes to them, and we won't start any unnecessary rumors this way. As you can imagine, some of these women are no doubt friends with my soon-to-be ex-wife."

"Certainly, Will," she replied. "Oh, I understand completely. Besides, I didn't get enough to eat when I passed the food table." Paula smiled politely. "You just go ahead and do what you have to do. I'll have a cup of decaf and a bite of dessert while I get acquainted with your kitchen help."

"Thank you, Renee. I won't keep you waiting any longer than I absolutely have to. I shouldn't be more than ten or fifteen minutes."

"Not a problem, Will. I'll be waiting," she said sweetly.

This was just as Paula had planned, and he had no idea that she was playing him into her trap. He thought that she was a truly unique and lovely woman, a lover of art, someone with whom he could enjoy spending some time. She was all of that, but oh, how first impressions can lie. Still, he liked his chances with the vivacious paralegal. Paula, on the other hand, now realizing this elaborate plan was working, got a grip on herself, and continued the act in which Denby had cast her. She was taken aback that the plan was evolving so precisely.

Paula allowed her feelings to empathize with the judge and his marital problems. She knew from information given by Denby and McCaffery that he was an honorable man, and she had experienced firsthand what a gentile spirit he possessed. He was much more interesting and thoughtful than she expected.

Judge Parks turned and went back to the living room and adjoining rooms, exchanging small talk and saying his farewells to the remaining guests. Paula returned the book to the shelf and left for the kitchen, in need of a restroom. She felt her cold, clammy hands, and her stomach was queasy and knotted. Her neck had developed knots in the muscular area around her vertebrae.

"Ladies, Judge Parks said that I could get a cup of decaf here. Is that right?" Paula asked, as she entered the kitchen.

"Yes, ma'am, we'll brew some fresh for you," said one of the workers.

"Thank you, ladies. Could you also direct me to the closest restroom, please?"

An African-American woman, dressed in a loose, mid-calf length frock with a white cotton apron draped from her neck and tied behind, pointed out the back entrance of the kitchen to the breakfast room. "Right that way, ma'am, there's a restroom over there."

"Thank you, I'll be back in a jiffy for the coffee."

Once inside the restroom, Paula brushed her hair, touched up her lipstick, and checked the functionality of the micro-cassette recorder. It worked perfectly. *Too bad for Judge Parks*, she thought. *He seems like a decent man.* She exited the bathroom, returning to the kitchen where a cup of freshly brewed decaf coffee was waiting for her. Picking up the cup of hot, refreshing decaf, she took a sip as she watched the three women.

They worked in unison, each helping the other clean plates, rinse dishes, and load the dishwasher, like an assembly line in Detroit. The women got the job done with ease while they laughed and chatted with each other. They all knew each other from growing up in the same dilapidated community, in sections of Charleston readily visible to passersby, yet, not far from the business districts and wealthy neighborhoods.

"Yummy, this is good! Thank you for this wonderful cup of coffee, ladies. What kind is it?"

"It's a Christmas blend that Judge Parks picked up, ma'am, but we haves tah grind da beans over here in dis coffee grinder. I don't know why he don't just buy da stuff already ground up, but dat's the way he do it."

"Ah, I knew there was something I liked about him. I grind my coffee beans, too."

Paula smiled and took a seat at the breakfast room table, forgetting about the dessert that she had fancied earlier. Her stomach tightened again as she considered the next phase of the deception. Soon the judge would be back, and she had to pour on the charm once again to complete the mission. *That good-for-nothing Denby will have his man, and he can go straight to hell,* she thought, *but what if the plan backfires somehow?*

Surely, the plan could not go wrong because Judge Parks has too much to lose. If his wife got a big settlement, his career on the Federal bench would be tarnished, if not over, and aspirations for future higher office dashed. He could not afford for anything to go wrong. One day he wanted to serve on the Supreme Court, or perhaps be Attorney General, if Americans would vote a Republican back in the White House.

"Good night, and Merry Christmas to you," Judge Parks said to the last guests. He stepped out on the porch and waved to them as they walked to their cars.

Anxious to return to his lovely guest, he quickly closed the front door and walked back through the foyer and down the hallway to the kitchen. His pulse quickened as he thought of this elegant woman waiting for him. His eyes captured her in the adjoining room, coffee in hand. Her perfectly shaped red lips pursed, slowly touching the edge of the cup, aroused primal urges.

"There you are. I trust I haven't kept you waiting too long."

"No, you're fine, Will. I needed a break from the chatter and crowd. I really prefer one-on-one conversation to talking in groups. Are you ready to finish my guided tour?"

"I certainly am. It's fantastic to have your company, Renee."

"Aw, thank you, Will. I'm glad to be here, too."

Taking advantage of someone was not her cup of tea in the first place, but this handsome man seemed to genuinely like her more than a little, thus her guilt deepened. He led her around the remaining portions of the home downstairs that she had not seen earlier and then climbed up the grand staircase with hand-carved mahogany banisters. The staircase steps, covered by oriental runners, led to the second floor of four bedrooms. They turned down the hallway, entering a guest bedroom that the judge had converted into an upstairs study, which he used more often than the formal study on the main floor.

"This painting, Renee, is by one of the Old Dutch Masters. Isn't it amazing how well preserved the rich color and detail is? So lifelike, it is incredible. It was painted in 1537."

"Yes, it is. These artists had very intricate methods for mixing paints from naturally occurring elements, I understand. The clarity they produce, after all these years, is beyond any medium used today. It's a shame that the process can't be duplicated anymore."

"Exactly, so you know about it already. I have to set specific temperatures and the proper humidity throughout the house at all times, or Lloyds of London won't insure the paintings. Having a backup generator, should the power be lost, is also mandatory."

"I bet you do. I believe this artist studied in Italy and brought some of his methods to Holland before painting most of his works that remain today. Are there any more?" inquired Paula.

"Oh, yes, there're about six more, two in each of the bedrooms. If you feel comfortable with me taking you there, we can go see them."

"I'm fine with that, Will. We're just looking at art."

Paula continued to maneuver the judge, although he believed she was the one who was being manipulated. It was close to 11:00 PM, and Dave McCaffery was ready and waiting for the pseudo-lovebirds to strike a pose in the bay window. They passed through two other guest bedrooms, viewing paintings by Italian artists, and then they walked down the hall to the master bedroom. Judge Parks' most prized painting was in the master suite, one by Bernini, and a student of Michelangelo. He stepped aside, motioning her to enter first.

He was thinking that just maybe she was giving him a signal. He reasoned that she might want to be with him since she was willing to view the paintings in the bedrooms. As they were walking, the aroma of her perfume saturated the night air with an intoxicating fragrance. The view of her back with the low-cut, strapless dress, together with her fragrance, captivated him like a prisoner in shackles. *If she gives me a few more smiles and keeps looking at me the way she has been, I'll attempt to kiss her,* the judge thought. *She must really like me. Why else would she be alone with me tonight at my home?*

Thirty more minutes, she thought, *and I can get out of here.* Anticipating what was about to transpire, Paula started coughing. "Is there a bathroom where I can find a tissue, Will?"

"Sure, be my guest, it's over there," said the judge, who motioned politely to the master bath.

She went in and pulled some tissue from a box to feign its use. Quickly, she opened her purse to press the RECORD button but hesitated. She could not do it. Closing her purse quietly, she came out of the bathroom to hear the description of one of his most prized paintings in the collection.

"This painting, by Bernini, is my favorite," said Judge Parks. "He's responsible for the many sculptures in the courtyard of St. Peter's Basilica and for completing the construction of St. Peter's after Michelangelo's death. And, although he was better known for his sculptures, he painted a few masterpieces of his own."

"I remember learning about him in school. This painting is amazing! Just look at the detail in their facial expressions."

Paula maneuvered the judge quickly past the bay window for them to have a different view of the painting. She knew Dave could not record them moving that fast. "This angle gives a different perspective, Will. Take a look from here."

"Yes, it does. I never get tired of viewing these paintings and I see something new each time. No wonder they're called masterpieces," the judge said.

Paula was truly enthused by the painting, but at the same time, she had decided to keep the judge away from McCaffery's camera lens. Judge Parks had seen the painting from every angle, but to please his beautiful guest, he gladly walked wherever she wanted. She tugged gently on his coat sleeve to get him a little closer.

"Stand here, Will."

He stood next to her, brushing against her side, and took her hand in his. Paula accepted his hand, clutching it softly. Flesh now touching flesh; the warmth of both of their hands was taking their clandestine meeting to a deeper level.

"Will, I appreciate your taking the time to show me the paintings that you love. I've had a wonderful evening," said Paula softly.

She turned to face him, thinking how she could graciously exit now that she had decided to turn back from the insidious Denby plan. Before she could make another move, the judge reached out, taking her other hand in his. As they smiled Judge Parks moved in closer and gave her a hug. He leaned back a little from embracing. He moved in again, and she allowed a short kiss. They hugged, holding each other in their arms for a few moments, her head resting on his strong shoulder.

"What are we doing, Will? You're married," she whispered gently.

"I'm legally separated, Renee, with no intention to reconcile. There's a big difference."

"Of course, you're right. This just feels a little awkward. We should be careful...you know, take things slow. You don't want people delving into your business with a divorce pending, do you?"

Paula, out of view of the camera now, pulled back to look into Judge Parks' eyes. She saw his eyes yearning for her. The judge gazed into her eyes hoping she felt the way he did and moved in for another kiss. She allowed a longer one this time, not knowing why, maybe because she did not know what to do, or maybe because she felt sorry for him.

Dave's camera was running the moment he caught a glimpse of them, but he wondered what went wrong because Paula and Will had moved quickly through his focal point. Without getting the incriminating evidence recorded on his camera, he became agitated. "What the hell is she doing?" he muttered.

Suddenly, Dave McCaffery felt a cruel, cold steel wire quickly tighten around his neck with tremendous force. The attacker worked so efficiently that he did not have time to react. Dave attempted to reach the man behind him, but his larynx crushed like a paper cup by the strong twist from the assassin's muscular arms. Dave gurgled and sputtered, losing consciousness in a matter of seconds, his arms falling limply by his side. The assassin dragged Dave's limp body off into the bushes and took the camera down from the tripod, replacing it with a high-powered rifle with blazing speed.

Special Forces around the world had produced many deadly mercenaries. The man in black clothing was one of the better ones. He adjusted the rifle's scope for a good view while peering in to spot two people in the bedroom. He could barely see them on the side of the bay window. Waiting impatiently, he paused with his finger on the trigger until the embrace had ceased.

"Will, I can't do this, I'm sorry. I need to leave now," Paula said apologetically.

"Are you sure, Renee? I don't mean any harm."

"Yes, I'm sure. It's not you. You've been very nice."

"Okay, then, let's go back downstairs, and I'll show you out."

Paula lost her hold on the judge when she interrupted the enticing moment, and before she could react, Judge Parks crossed back in full view of the bay window. The deadly assassin aimed with the crosshairs of the infrared scope on Judge Parks' head and fired three quick pops from the muzzled rifle. The bullets crashed through the window, shattering the glass into thousands of shards. Paula lunged toward the judge to push him out of the line of fire, but she was too late.

The first bullet missed them both, lodging in the far wall. The second one found its target, piercing the back of Wilmont Parks' neck and exiting without hitting his spine, but it grazed Paula's head enough to burn her scalp, leaving a surface wound. The third bullet hit Judge Parks squarely in the middle of his right lung. He fell headlong onto Paula with a tremendous geyser of blood spattering her face, arms, and dress. She tried holding him up to catch his fall, but the weight of his limp body proved too much for her. Stepping back in horror, she let Judge Parks' body crash to the floor, like a tree felled by a lumberjack. She did not know what had happened for a moment, but when she felt the warm blood on her body, she screamed at the top of her lungs.

"Oh, my God, he's been shot! He's been shot!"

Suddenly, and without any apparent reason, a calm sensation overcame her. She ran to the phone and called 911, her heart throbbing erratically in her chest. Frantically, she explained to the dispatcher.

"I don't know for sure what happened...just get someone here as quick as you can. Judge Wilmont Parks has been shot! His wounds are serious. Please, hurry!"

"What is your location, ma'am?" asked the dispatcher. "I need to verify that the information on my system is correct."

"I'm at Wellington Place at the Battery on 22 East Bay Drive, the residence of Judge Wilmont Parks."

"Yes, ma'am, we'll have an ambulance there in a matter of minutes. Can you tell me where the judge was shot?" the dispatcher continued.

Paula dropped the phone to the floor, barely able to keep her composure. The sight of the bleeding judge lying on the floor caused her knees to grow weak, as she drifted into shock from the awful incident. The operator attempted to keep her talking to no avail. She glanced at Judge Parks' bloody body again and then at her dress.

How can I explain being with the judge in this situation? Who will believe that I pulled him away from the bay window when we embraced? Who could have done this? she thought. Her head became light, and her knees buckled, her body crumpling to the floor.

The women in the kitchen and the butler were the first to hear the commotion. Paula's screams sent shivers down their spines. One of the women, fearing something happened to Judge Parks, sent the butler scurrying up the stairs to investigate the loud noises. He saw the judge and Paula lying on the floor and grabbed the portable phone, which was lying next to the bodies. He put the blood-spattered phone to his ear.

"Hello, is anyone there?"

"Yes, it's the 911 dispatcher, please state your name."

"I'm James Singletary, Judge Parks' butler. There's been a shooting, and the judge and one of his guests are down."

Paula had passed out, draped across Judge Parks' body, a picture of death. The butler thought that both of them might be dead because of all the blood that covered their motionless bodies.

"Yes, sir, the incident has been reported. Emergency workers and police have been dispatched and should be there shortly. Please be available when they arrive to direct them to the injured parties."

"I will," said James. His hands clutched the phone like a vice grip as he ran down the stairs to let the EMS workers in the home to treat his beloved boss and the mysterious woman who lay across his body.

Sirens blared as they arrived at the front entrance of Wellington Place. The EMS and police department were less than two miles away, so the response was quick. A team of four EMTs in two ambulances arrived and ran inside the house as the domestic workers pointed towards the grand banister, shouting, "Upstairs! Upstairs!"

The EMTs bounded up the stairs to the master bedroom skipping steps as they ran. One EMT checked Judge Parks, discovering a weak and erratic pulse. After the quick triage, they determined that Judge Parks was the one in greatest danger of bleeding out. Efficiently, another EMT assessed his wounds and wrapped his neck with sterile gauze, applying pressure to stem the tide of blood. The first EMT removed the judge's jacket and cut away the shirt and tee shirt from his body with a large pair of scissors that he drew from a holster on his belt. He wrapped gauze around the judge's thoracic region, covering the wound on his chest. Quickly, an oxygen mask was applied and an IV was inserted into his left arm, as they loaded Judge Parks onto the spinal board to stabilize him.

Simultaneously, an EMT checked Paula for a pulse and discovered that it was strong. He rolled her over on her back and applied an oxygen mask. Paula awakened, frantically trying to roll, but the strong arms of the medical worker kept her flat on her back.

She felt the sting from the bullet, which grazed the side of her head.

"Just lay still, ma'am. You're going to be alright."

Already, the knowledge that this case would require extensive investigation was apparent. Judge Parks was a high profile, well-known, powerful man who presided over important federal cases. CNN and Fox got wind of the incident and had affiliated news teams dispatched to the scene almost as quickly as the police arrived. The news crews were not allowed inside the home; however, and they had to get their footage and report from outside.

The medical team continued moving with precision and sped down the staircase to the waiting ambulances. The news crews flashed their night cameras for still shots of the bodies of Paula Cooper and Judge Wilmont Parks, which were being loaded into the emergency vehicles. The journalists shouted questions to the medical personnel as the victims were wheeled into position and locked down.

"Who was shot?" shouted one reporter.

"We have reason to believe that one victim is Judge Parks. Is this so?" shouted another.

"Who is the lady?" yet another questioned.

The EMTs ignored the reporters, doing their jobs with efficiency and proper ethics, consistent with HIPAA guidelines. The only response from the medical unit was the screech of tires burning rubber and high-pitched sirens. The blinding lights of the emergency vehicles flashed in the reporters' faces as they drove out of the gate and sped away to the Mercy General ER, escorted by three of the many law enforcement units, which had arrived at the behest of the 911 call.

The crime scene was quickly cordoned with yellow tape to prevent contamination of evidence, and the Charleston police quarantined the estate. The lead detective on duty led the effort upstairs in the Parks home to glean any possible evidence. Everyone, including all staff who remained cleaning up, and all who worked at Wellington Place in any capacity had to stay for questioning. All remained, except the valet staff, whose duties had been completed. They left before the incident occurred in their own vehicles, except one, who left when a car arrived for him.

12

The private hospital room where Paula was recuperating from shock was brightly illuminated with morning light piercing through the opening in the soft blue cotton curtains. Long, slender rectangles of light, then shade, alternated like a tapestry across the room from the sun's rays insisting their way in. She opened her eyes and struggled to rollover from her back, but the sedative had produced severe grogginess, weighing her down like a huge anchor holding a ship in bay. Her initial efforts to sit up were slug-like and futile. Her throat was dry as she pressed mentally, like a pregnant woman giving birth, to awaken. She squinted, and her vision adjusted from a blurry condition to a painful focus on reality. *Is this just a bad dream?* she wondered. Unfortunately, it was not.

Her fortune, though bleak, turned out much better than Judge Parks, who did not survive. The wound in his neck, where he bled out from a severed jugular vein, proved fatal. A police officer stood guard outside Paula's door. Two men investigating the shooting of Judge Parks were waiting in the hall, pacing like lions in a cage, back and forth, panting restlessly.

A female seemed to appear out of nowhere wearing faded scrubs with the name of the hospital stamped above her shirt pocket. "My name is Gina, your nurse, how are you feeling this morning, ma'am? Is there anything I can get for you?"

"I'm okay. Yes, Gina, just some cold water, my throat is parched. What did they give me, for Pete's sake?"

"It was a sedative to help you rest. You went through a lot last night, so I hear."

Paula coughed as she slowly raised her head looking for the mechanism to raise her adjustable bed. Finding it, she pressed the green button to bring the bed to an upright position, thinking how much these devices have improved since she last raised herself in bed eleven years earlier when giving birth to her youngest daughter. The nurse poured a cup of cold water in a plastic cup, which Paula drank down without pausing.

"Thanks, Gina. That hit the spot. May I have another one, please?"

"Absolutely...here you go. By the way, do you feel well enough to answer some questions, Miss Cooper?"

Without thinking whether she was ready or not, Paula attempted to compose herself. "Yes, I suppose so. What do you want to know?"

"Well, it's not me, ma'am. The men in the hallway have been waiting for you to wake up, and my orders are to allow them in when you are ready." Without saying another word, the nurse quickly strolled to the door and poked her head out. "Okay, gentlemen, she's awake and will talk to you now."

Paula did not have time to object. She quickly ran her fingers through her hair, fluffing it a little to appear more presentable. Two men, one in a gray, and the other in a dark blue suit, both with white shirts and neckties, entered the sterile hospital room.

"Hello, Miss Cooper, I'm John Dibbs, Special Agent with the FBI," said the man in the gray suit.

"This is my associate, Agent Albert Mendez. We would like to ask you some questions about your presence and activities at Judge Parks' party last night. We regret that you went through such a terrible ordeal. This shouldn't take long."

Paula did not want to appear as if she was hiding anything. Her head was still spinning from the previous night's events, yet she had confidence that she would know when to stop or request an attorney, if she felt the need to do so. Scantily clad in a pale green hospital gown, she pulled the covers close to her chest for warmth and security.

"Yes, gentlemen, how may I help you?"

"As you know, Miss Cooper, Judge Wilmont Parks was shot last night under very unusual circumstances. Can you tell us anything about who might be involved with this murder?" asked Agent Dibbs.

"He died? I didn't know he passed away. All I remember is the crash of the bullets through the window and blood from Judge Parks splattering me. I called 911, and after that, I passed out."

"His wounds were serious, and he bled out before paramedics could get a blood transfusion started," stated Agent Mendez. "So, Miss Cooper, you mean to say you were found in the room of a married man, who had just been shot to death, and you can't tell us anything?"

"No, sir, I don't have a clue who on earth would have done such a horrible thing. I can't believe this happened."

"What were you doing with Judge Parks in his bedroom at the time he was shot?" asked Dibbs.

The line of questioning aggravated Paula, as she sensed the tactical pressure that the agents employed to get her to talk. "I was taking a tour of the home to see his renowned art collection. He invited me to see it after I met him at the party. I was attending on behalf of the law firm where I work. I don't know why anyone would have wanted to kill him."

"Yes, ma'am, I see. Are you aware that a private investigator was found murdered outside in the bushes? What can you tell us about that?" asked Agent Mendez.

The agents were good at using a "tag-team approach" in questioning witnesses and suspects. They had worked together for five years and had perfected this method of interrogation.

"No, I was not. What is his name?" Paula asked. She feared the worst but wanted to make sure. The situation seemed so surreal.

"David McCaffery, ma'am; did you know him?"

"Oh my God!" Paula shrieked, as she burst into tears. As quickly as the tearful floodgate started, she shut off the flow, demanding of herself to be strong. "Yes, I know him."

"Was any of this pre-planned between you and Mr. McCaffery?" inquired Dibbs.

"Was any of what pre-planned?" she responded, as she sniffled. Paula reached for the box of tissues to catch her tears, and wipe her cheeks. She straightened herself and clinched her jaw in resolve, determined not to break down emotionally again.

"Were you and Dave McCaffery planning to record Judge Parks and yourself tonight when you the two of you were in his bedroom?" asked Agent Mendez.

"I'd rather not answer that question," Paula said.

"Just tell us what you know, Miss Cooper, and things will be much easier in the long run," said Agent Dibbs, waiting intently for Paula's answer.

"Dave and I had talked earlier that day. All I can tell you for sure is that I know nothing about why Judge Parks and Dave McCaffery were murdered."

"Then why were you in his bedroom with him standing in front of a window where he was an easy target? Exactly what is your relationship to the murdered David McCaughey? We've determined from his driver's license that he is from Georgetown, same as you," stated Agent Dibbs.

Gaining her composure, Paula spoke firmly to Agent Dibbs. "If I had anything to do with Judge Parks being shot, Agent Dibbs, do you think for a minute that I would have been standing near him at the time? Why would I have risked my very life, if I knew what was going to happen? Do you see this bandage on the side of my head? It's a wound from the shots that were fired. I assure you that I do not have a death wish."

Paula's intonation did not deter the agents.

"Yes, ma'am, we're sure you don't, but we have to ask these questions. We do intend to find out who killed your acquaintance, Mr. McCaffery, and who killed Judge Parks," responded Mendez.

Paula knew better than to go any further without the presence of an attorney. She had already said too much in an effort to be cooperative.

"I understand, gentlemen. Well, I'm sure you understand that I'll have to ask an attorney to be present before I can answer any more of your questions. Besides, I let you two men in here without even having a chance to wash my face or put clothes on. So, if you will excuse me, please?" Paula said curtly.

"Very well, Miss Cooper," said Dibbs, "if you want to play hardball, fine, but let me inform you that, as of this moment, you are under arrest for conspiracy to commit blackmail of Judge Wilmont Parks. You will be detained at the Charleston County Jail when your physician releases you from care. In the meantime, there will be a federal marshal positioned in the hall by your room to check on you from time to time. You are not to leave this room without his presence. Are we clear on that?"

"You're placing me under arrest?" Paula asked, her voice rising and her expression in disbelief.

"Yes, we are. You have given us no choice. You're the only living person at this point that we know of, who has firsthand knowledge of the crime. We have reason to believe there is a conspiracy and that you are likely involved."

Paula knew that everything happening to her was part of the investigative process, but it still rattled her. She had never been confined in a jail but had seen things happen to people who were incarcerated, especially women. Other people were in jail for long periods before they were released without a cause for their stay.

Dibbs wanted to detain her for questioning and to frighten her into telling everything she knew. He personally did not suspect her of murdering Judge Parks, although he did not know for sure at the time. The connection with the private investigator who was killed, and why McCaffery was outside the Parks' residence with a camera, led him to believe there was some sort of conspiracy operating. At the least, he felt sure that Paula was withholding information when she chose to hire an attorney to represent her.

"Let us know as soon as you acquire an attorney, Miss Cooper," said Agent Mendez. "We'll resume our conversations with the two of you then."

Agent Dibbs stepped forward, handing his card to Paula. "If anything at all comes to your mind that may help us in the investigation, please call as soon as possible. We'll see you later, Miss Cooper."

"I'll have my attorney contact you, Agent Dibbs. Thank you."

The agents exited the hospital room with a sense of finality that frightened Paula. She glanced at her clock on the bedside table. It was only 9:00AM, and she wondered if Jim knew anything about her whereabouts or the incident that had occurred the previous night. Thoughts of her daughters and her parents raced through her head.

"Gina, has anyone else come to the hospital or called for me?"

"No, ma'am, not that I am aware of, only the FBI agents and Charleston police have been here so far."

The nightmare of the windows shattering, Judge Parks being hit with bullets, and the horrendous sounds of him gurgling, as his blood spattered her face, neck, and chest kept replaying in her head. A few minutes passed, and then three gentle raps on the door followed. Gina walked over to answer the door. She opened it just enough to see a visitor standing in the hall. The FBI agents had barely missed him coming up the elevator, as they went down the other side.

"I'm here to visit Paula Cooper," the man said. "Is she awake?"

"Who are you, sir? We have orders for family visitation only."

"I'm Jim Roberts, her boyfriend."

"Just a moment, sir, I'll check with Miss Cooper. She really needs her rest."

"Are you up for another visitor, Miss Cooper?"

"Who is it?" asked Paula.

"He said his name is Jim Roberts. He says he's a friend of yours."

Paula's heart both rose and sank in quick succession, much like a ride on a Myrtle Beach roller coaster. She knew she could lose Jim's love because of her headstrong and stupid actions, but at that instant, there was no one else that she wanted to see more than him. She could use a steady, nonjudgmental friend, if that was possible.

"Please ask him to wait just a few minutes, Gina. I need to freshen up a little."

Paula hurriedly jumped out of bed and scooted to the bathroom to wash her face. Afterwards, she ran a brush through her hair, feeling pain on one side of her head. She pushed her hair back to see the red streak where she suffered the burn on her scalp from the grazing bullet. She brushed her hair lightly so that the burn was mostly covered. Last, she dabbed a little make up on the bags under her eyes then applied lip-gloss. Her toilette took all of three minutes and she was out, back in bed, ready for her visitor.

"Okay, Gina, you can let him in."

Jim wore jeans and a pale blue polo shirt, Paula's favorite clothing on him. Without hesitation, he hurried to Paula's side, giving her a much-needed hug, and then sat in a chair that he pulled close to her bed.

"Hi, honey, I hear you had a rough night."

"Yes, Jim, I certainly did. I really screwed up this time."

"Well, it's still nice to see you under any circumstances. I called Magnolia Inn earlier this morning, and the Johnsons said you didn't come home last night, so I was concerned and made some calls until I found you. I would have waited at home until I heard from you, but the hospital would not give out any information as to how you were."

"No, I'm glad you are here. Jim, I wanted you to be the first to know what happened last night. I wouldn't blame you if you walk away from me today and never look back."

Paula's humble sincerity touched Jim, yet he was curious as to exactly what did happen. He responded before she could finish, trying to provide a little levity for an otherwise very somber situation.

"I couldn't do that. I searched too long to find someone who can put up with my driving," Jim said, chuckling. "I'm just glad you're alright."

Paula was overwhelmed with his kindness and reached out hugging him tightly. Inwardly, she was ashamed and did not know where to begin.

"Thank you for being you. I know I've gotten myself into a mess here, but if I get out of it, you'll never see my face again in a predicament like this," she said.

Jim gently kissed Paula's forehead as they slowly withdrew from the comforting embrace. He sat down on the edge of the bed, and cradled her hand between his palms. She was so relieved to see his smile, which did more to help her recover than any medication could.

"What happened, Paula? All I have heard are rumors."

"The situation's too complicated to explain, Jim. And, to be honest, I'm ashamed of myself."

"Have you been questioned? Who is that man in the hallway?"

"Yes, I have. The FBI just left, and the man in the hall is a federal marshal."

"Paula, I don't know what's going on here, but you need to get legal representation as soon as possible."

"You're right. I'm not thinking clearly yet. It's all happening so fast. If I had taken your advice earlier, then I wouldn't be in the fix I'm in now. I just didn't see how I could back out. So, I just plowed ahead with an assignment like I usually do, and being too stubborn has really cost me this time."

"It's alright, just stay calm, and tell the truth to the authorities. Your attorney will help you with that." Jim wanted to know more about what happened, but she was not ready to tell him everything yet.

"Who do you know who can help me, Jim? I'm embarrassed to ask anyone from Georgetown."

"My cousin, Luke Bradley, might be able to represent you. Remember me telling you about my great aunt in Charleston? Luke is her son and a partner in a small firm specializing in criminal law. I'll give him a call to set up an appointment, if you want me to. Perhaps you two can meet when they release you from the hospital."

"Sure, I'll meet with him, but I don't think the arrangement will be that easy. I've been placed under arrest. As soon as the doctor releases me, I'll most likely be at the county jail, awaiting arraignment. The circumstances are not looking good."

"Good grief, Paula, what did you do?"

"I can't tell you everything now, Jim, but I didn't go through with the plan. Please give me some time."

"Paula, there's no time to hide things now. You may as well get everything out in the open."

"You don't realize what I have to tell them."

Jim was alarmed by the tone in her voice. "What, Paula?"

"I have to tell them all I know about how Tom Denby sent me up here to secretly entrap the judge in a blackmail scheme. I knew about it and conspired

114

with Dave to shoot pictures of the judge and me embracing in his bedroom window."

"Oh my God! I can't believe what I'm hearing."

"There's more, Jim. The next thing they will do is arrest Denby. I don't know what will be worse…to tell them nothing or to tell them everything."

Jim was shaken to his core to hear what Paula had told him. He felt as if a ton of boulders were placed on his shoulders. He tried to hide the disappointment he felt by attempting to keep a poker face.

"That's why you need a trustworthy attorney who can take an objective look at this. You can't see the forest for the trees from where you sit. You need to hear sound counsel, and Luke's your man for that."

"You're right, Jim. I'm just afraid of what Denby might do when he's confronted with an arrest. And, I'm worried about Rachel and Christine and how much I will have to share with them, and my parents, for that matter."

"Denby won't do anything to harm you or your kids, Paula. He's crazy but not that crazy."

"I hope not. Will you call Luke for me and ask him to call me as soon as he can at the hospital? After I discuss my situation with him, perhaps he can come to the jail. I should be released from the hospital later today. I'll probably be sporting an orange jumpsuit soon, courtesy of Charleston County Sheriff's Department."

"It could be worse," Jim said. "From the looks of that redness on the side of your head, you're lucky to have any choices right now."

Paula reached up and felt the side of her head where she was grazed, tender to the touch. "Jim, I know I'm very fortunate not only to have lived through this, but to have you here means everything to me. I'm fortunate to have my two girls, as well. Please don't let anything happen to them."

"You can rest assured that I'll go by and visit them long enough to make sure they're fine as soon as I get back to Georgetown today."

"Please don't tell Mom and Dad any details. I'll call them later today, but I can't bring myself to talk to them just now. I don't want the girls to know anything about this, Jim."

"I understand, Paula. I'm leaving now to get things set up with Luke. I'll give him a call and be in touch with you on Monday."

"Here, take this," she said, passing Agent Dibbs' card to Jim. "Luke will need the names and numbers of the FBI agents."

"I'm so sorry," she said. He turned to leave. "Thanks, Jim. I appreciate what you are doing."

Jim did not answer as he left. He was upset and needed to leave quickly so that Paula would not know. He did not want to further complicate things for her by expressing anything negative, and he had to get back to his business preparations for the coming week, after calling his cousin to arrange the telephone call. He stopped in the hallway by a pay phone station. Fortunately, he reached Luke on his first call and arranged for him to call Paula. He explained the situation a little, as best he could. Luke had seen the news on television and read a sketchy article in the paper because not much had been revealed, yet.

Jim jumped in his vehicle and drove the hour's trip back to Georgetown. Although he had hidden it from Paula, he was worn out from lack of sleep and pacing the floor the night before, worrying about her whereabouts after not talking to her on the phone as planned after the party. Still, he had some thoughts pent up inside that had to spill out. Love for this woman who had captured his soul the previous summer washed over him, but now they were complicated by her lack of good judgment.

He wasn't the best with romantic words in person, but with a pen in his hand, the innermost depths from his soul flowed out like water from a deep artesian well. Though he knew Paula had done wrong, he saw how remorseful she was and felt compassion for her. He pulled in his driveway, went inside his modest condo, and walked to the kitchen to retrieve a beer. Popping the top, he walked over to an antique secretary he used to pay bills and folded it down. He took a seat and picked up a fountain pen and two sheets of stationery to express his thoughts as he wrote:

Dearest Paula,

I do not know why or how you became involved in this predicament, but I want you to be assured that I'll be with you until you get through this. I have never felt so deeply for anyone, and I trust that you will put this all behind you in time. Hindsight is 20/20, so they say, and we all learn from our mistakes.

If I had known that you were in the hospital, I would have been there sooner. I want us to retreat from this chaos and be together where we belong, in peace. Every minute that we are apart, my thoughts are filled with you. My life is without purpose, if you are not in it.

This time apart, though, is good for me to evaluate how much you mean to me and how close I came to losing you. Forgive me for letting you down in your time of need by only advising you to "do what you think is best." If you ever ask my opinion again, I will tell it to you straightforward.

I long for the day we can be alone, to hold you in my arms, to feel your caress and your body next to mine. The warmth of having you with me, the smell of your hair, and the touch of your lips against mine, are the simple pleasures in life I treasure. When I am with you, there are no problems so big that our love cannot overcome them.

With love,

Jim

He placed the letter in an envelope and addressed it to Paula in care of his cousin, Luke, to be mailed in the morning, but when morning arrived, he could not mail it. Doubts had crept in overnight. He enjoyed being in love again and felt fully alive for the first time since the demise of his marriage, yet to deny that this event had not rocked his world would be a lie. He needed to wait to mail his letter until he felt that he was fully sincere, when the doubts had subsided. The incident that occurred shook Jim to the core, like an earthquake, which sent a tsunami rolling over his soul. He had to recover mentally and emotionally and there was no use pretending.

Paula, on the other hand, needed the solid encouragement from Jim, as much as a desert flower needs rain. She knew he was in a place where he would gradually drift away, never to return to what they enjoyed, or he would come back by her side to stand with her. Paula knew that Jim helped her out of a reaction to be kind, but whether it would last was her concern. The remorse she felt was overwhelming. A ton of bricks and debris was upon her chest, and she had to find a way into the sunlight again.

13

At the Charleston County Jail, reality set in hard as Paula paced back and forth in her cell, feeling the shame for what she had done. She waited in her cold, drab cell for Luke Bradley. The cell, a nine by eight-foot rectangle, had one bed—a thick slab of steel attached to a sidewall by two metal brackets and hung by two thick, cold, steel chains. A three-inch thick foam mattress encased in gray vinyl covered the bed. A green army blanket was provided for warmth. It gave little comfort, but was better than the men's unit, which had thinner mattresses and not enough blankets to go around.

Luke drove to the entrance to the Charleston County Jail. The weather had turned cooler but was still mild for December. He maneuvered his red BMW 325 convertible into a parallel parking space with ease. Like most successful attorneys, Luke worked all sorts of hours and had a penchant for detail. He wore wire-rimmed glasses with a neat, short haircut. To be considered top-notch in the legal profession, one not only had to be good at practicing law, but also had to don the proper attire. Since it was the weekend, he gave himself a break from the unspoken dress code expected of attorneys in the South, a starched shirt, dry-cleaned suit, and silk tie with shined shoes. Today, Luke sported a brown polo shirt, faded Levis, and leather deck shoes that he loved to wear without socks. If the weather held up, Luke hoped to take his schooner out for an evening run in the Charleston harbor.

He entered the complex and nodded to the deputy operating the metal detector as he placed his change, watch, keys, and cell phone in a red plastic bowl, which the deputy dropped on the conveyor belt, sending the contents through the scanner. Luke walked through the metal detector quickly and then turned to get his belongings from the bowl. A few deputies who were changing shifts greeted him.

"Good evening, Luke," the deputies said, passing by him. Luke thought they were being too chummy, but they knew some of the attorneys by first name, and he knew them.

"I bet he's coming to see the lady in D-5," said one deputy. "She's the only one in here who could afford Luke." Laughter followed this deputy's comment.

"I hear you're charging one-hundred fifty an hour nowadays, Luke?" asked another deputy smugly, picking at the attorney.

"That's two hundred for you, Curt, if you ever need my services," the attorney fired back.

The other deputies howled with laughter. The deputies were a little jealous of the young, affluent attorney, but they liked him just the same because he knew how to connect with them. He could take their heckling and give it back just as good. Luke grinned.

He walked to the next door where the dispatch deputy was stationed who controlled the automatic switch to open the door that led to lockup. Luke looked in the direction of the dispatch deputy, who was taking a phone call. The deputy turned sideways, barely glancing at Luke, and pointed down for him to sign in on the clipboard on the counter that tracked all visitors to the unit. Luke disliked the procedure, since they knew him, and tried to get by without it. He was successful sometimes but not with this deputy, who played everything by the book. He moved over to the counter and signed the log. The buzzer sounded, unlocking the door just as he put down his pen. Luke pulled the heavy metal door open and passed down the hallway, which led to the wings of cells. He stopped at the next counter where the deputies who ran lockup were gathered.

"Could you men tell me where I might find Miss Paula Cooper?"

The three deputies barely looked up from their table where they were playing five-card draw. One deputy spoke, glancing up at Luke, "Yes, sir, you mean the beauty queen? She's down in D-5 where we don't have anybody else locked up."

"And which one of you deputies is assigned to that wing?"

"I am," said the deputy, who gave him Paula's whereabouts.

"Then why the heck are you over here playing cards?" retorted the young attorney. "I realize I am not Sheriff Jacobs, but he's a personal friend of mine, Deputy, and I really think you ought to be on your wing keeping watch."

"We're just playing a few hands of cards, man!" said the deputy. He knew that he should have been at his station. "I'll let you in to see her. Do you have some ID?" The deputy was somewhat irritated that he had to leave his poker game.

Luke pulled out his ID, showing it to the young deputy as the two men passed through the door that led to D-Wing. It was the smallest of the triple-winged jail facility, usually left empty unless a female prisoner or an affluent person was incarcerated.

From a recent lawsuit and history of questionable treatment of prisoners, the county jail was under a court order to provide women "separate and secure facilities when incarcerated." After two rapes and other harassment accusations, the courts had ordered this remedy to preclude recurrence. The case was settled with a sizable amount of money paid to the victims in a class action lawsuit. Luke had represented one of the women in the case three years earlier. From that experience, he knew much more than the average attorney about what went on in the confines of some county jails. He did not want to take a chance with his client and wanted her out as soon as possible.

"Deputy, I want an extra thirty minutes with my client. If I stay a little beyond the time limit, I don't want to be bothered. Otherwise, I know your boss's home phone number, and I am sure he would want to know about the card games and you leaving your post. Are we good with that?"

"Sure, mister, whatever you say. You don't have to be so hard about it. Sheriff Bates has a temper. I would be written up for sure, maybe lose my job. You just stay as long as you need to, okay?"

The deputy approached the cell where Paula sat with her head in her hands, looking downward. The orange jumpsuit, intended for uniformity, looked like something an auto mechanic would wear. With the turn of a large metal skeleton key and the loud creaking sound of an old metal hinge, the deputy opened the heavy metal cell door for Luke to enter.

"Hi, Miss Cooper, I'm Luke Bradley, Jim's cousin. You are expecting me, right?"

"Yes, I am, and I'm glad to meet you, Mr. Bradley," Paula said. She extended her hand to him. "Call me Paula."

"Will do, Paula, and call me Luke, most everyone does. The first thing I want you to know is that you don't have to talk to the FBI anytime soon, okay. So, rest at ease about that," Luke said, in a gentle Southern twang.

Paula was immediately relieved as she let out an audible sigh. "Whew, that's good news. I know they were just doing their jobs, but those guys were getting on my last nerve."

"The second thing, Paula, is that you are getting out of jail today. This is not the safest place to be, though they have increased the level of safety here, but with your looks, who knows?"

"But I thought the FBI wanted me in jail here until arraignment?"

"They may want you here, but they can't keep you here, not until they have evidence for filing formal charges. I took care of that as soon as you explained on the phone what was going on. They like to get suspects in jail as soon as they can to scare them into divulging more information. I called the Assistant Solicitor, who's on call this weekend, and he agreed with me to let you go on a personal recognizance bond."

"That's awesome, Luke. Thanks for that."

"You're welcome, ma'am. Agent Dibbs can take a hike for now. I'll be in touch with his office on Monday, or vice versa, I'm quite sure. We need a safe place for you to stay for a few days until I have more time to assess the situation thoroughly."

Luke gave her a change of clothes from a paper bag that Jim had sent with him. The party dress, undergarments, and shoes soaked in blood were seized as evidence of the crime scene. She never wanted to see those clothes again anyway. Paula could not believe her ears. She was accustomed to more red tape from attorneys who played games with their clients to exact higher fees.

"You might as well be an angel sent from heaven, Luke!"

"Well, thanks, Paula, but back to reality. Do you know any place where you would be safe for a few days?"

She thought for a moment, and then she remembered the beach cottage on the Isle of Palms where she had taken her girls on vacation for a week the previous summer. "I think I might. The owners of Magnolia Inn where I am staying have a beach cottage on the Isle of Palms. The Johnsons use it to get away when they need a break. I hear they rent it out some to people they know. We can run by Magnolia, and I'll ask them."

"Good," responded Luke, "let's get out of here."

Paula was a smarter client than Luke was accustomed to having. He motioned the deputy to come to the cell and showed him the emergency papers signed by a federal judge, ordering that Paula be released.

"Good day, Deputy, I hope your poker hand gets better."

"Have a good day, Mr. Bradley," said the deputy, who was extremely relieved to be rid of this troublesome pair.

Paula changed from the orange jumpsuit into her clothes, and then they hopped in Luke's BMW and set out for the bed and breakfast. Paula and Luke arrived at Magnolia Inn late in the afternoon. She opened the entrance door and started across the foyer to climb the stairs to retrieve her things from her room. Luke accompanied her inside.

"I'll need to run upstairs for a minute. Could you wait in the parlor for me, please?"

"I can do that. I'll be sitting right here," said Luke, as he turned and took a seat in a tufted Queen Anne chair.

Sarah Johnson heard Paula's familiar voice in the foyer and ambled over to welcome her back.

"Paula!" exclaimed Sarah. "I'm so glad you are okay."

"Hey, Sarah, thanks, I'm fine…sorry I didn't call you. I knew you would be worried, but I've had so many things on my mind. I need to speak with you; it's urgent."

Upon hearing the explanation that Paula offered, she agreed to let her stay at the beach house on the Isle of Palms.

"Excuse me please, Sarah, let me say good-bye to Luke."

"Sure, honey, take your time."

Paula returned to the parlor and motioned for Luke. They stepped through the foyer and onto the porch for privacy.

"Sarah Johnson is letting me take the cottage for a while, Luke. I'm sure she has to clear it with Mickey, but she runs the show around here for big decisions, so consider it a done deal."

"That sounds good. I like the way you get things done."

"Likewise, Luke. So, what is the game plan now?"

"You call me once you get settled at the cottage, and we can go from there. Just lay low and keep your eyes open. In the meantime, I need to make some calls and do more research. Can you call my office and leave the address of the cottage when you go back inside?"

"I will," she said, as she gave him a hug of appreciation. "Thank you so much for getting the FBI off my back and for bringing me here."

"No problem, Paula. Please let Jim know that we met and what's going on."

"I'll do that for sure."

Luke turned and trotted down the stairs to his car. "Good-bye, Luke," she said, waving as he rounded the back of his car to hop in.

Luke opened his car door, plopped down in his bucket seat, then tossed his hand up in the air, as he got in and zoomed off to the landing where he kept his sailboat. Paula went back inside to discover Sarah, once again, not far away by the staircase, where she had to run the gauntlet to get by her gracious, but nosey host.

"Paula, you can get through this. Just do as Mr. Bradley says. He's a fine young attorney from all I've heard about him."

"Oh, I intend to, Sarah."

"Why don't you come grab a bite to eat before we put up the food? You'll feel better, sweetie."

"Sarah, give me thirty minutes and I'll be down. I want to shower and freshen up before I do anything else. I feel as if I haven't showered in a week after being in that dreadful place."

"That's fine, Paula. I'll see you in a few. Dinner is open for another hour."

Paula, somewhat relieved, thanked Sarah who had to return to help her husband in the kitchen. She did as Sarah advised, and then quickly returned to her room. She relived the past few days in her mind as if she was fast-forwarding a movie. The whole ordeal was too much to take in. She grabbed the novel she had been reading on the trip to distract her mind and find solace, settling in to read for an hour, or more. Her mother had trained her as a little girl to read for enjoyment, education, and peaceful solitude. The training was invaluable now.

Getting sleepy, she pulled off her clothes, draping them around the chair, and grabbed a nightie from her small travel case. Slipping into the negligee, she brushed her teeth and gargled. After applying some lotion to her body and face, she curled up once again, reading until she drifted to sleep with the book falling across her body.

Early the next morning the yellow sun peeked out on the Charleston harbor. Paula rolled over in her bed with a groan, stretching, her mind alerting her to the unfamiliar surroundings. She thought about where she needed to be. Once out of the shower, she drank her flavored coffee in the same manner she did from the patio of her condo, fingers clutched around the rim of her cup, only this time faster. Although the coffee maker in her room was only half-sized, it still provided the quick jolt of energy she needed to keep pushing forward.

Bed and Breakfast Inns were famous in the South for the personal touches that make one feel at home. Soon after these quaint inns made a comeback because of the increased travel of Americans, hotels began imitating this kind of service with much success. With competition being so keen in the motel business, any amenity provided for the extra touch helped attract customers for repeat business.

Paula sat in a French provincial chair in her white terrycloth bathrobe, her legs and feet folded Indian-style beneath her. She stared out toward the harbor, seeing a few sailboats glide past. On her second cup of java now, the caffeine kicked in, having its wonderful effect. Paula's mental wheels turned like the RPMs in Luke's BMW when he revved the engine changing gears.

I'll tell Luke everything I know. After all, that's the purpose of having an attorney. I'll have to trust this young man. He seems nice enough and very intelligent. After all, he is Jim's cousin, and the bottom line is that I really don't have any choice. She sighed. She had to rely on him to defend her but shuddered to think about the repercussions with Denby. He knew that Paula was arrested but continued to lay low as he evaluated what strategy he would employ when the FBI came knocking on his door. Denby had already received word that Luke Bradley was representing Paula. He always did have a knack for finding things out faster than most people could.

The urgency to make the drive out to the Isle of Palms pressed upon her. She hopped up off the chair, dressed, and threw her things together in a jiffy. As she reached to open the bedroom door, the phone rang. Dropping her luggage to the floor, she grabbed the phone on the bedside table to hear a familiar voice.

"Hello, Paula...too much excitement for one weekend?" inquired Denby.

Paula wondered when he would catch up to her. She had hoped it would not be this soon. "Tom, what kind of a crack is that, with Dave and Judge Parks being murdered last night? You're more of a jerk than even I imagined!"

"Calm down, Paula. I don't mean any disrespect to Dave, or Judge Parks. I know you're going through a very tough ordeal, and I wanted to offer my assistance to you."

"I bet you do...you snake in the grass!" Paula barked.

She was more intent now than ever on exposing the infamous J. Thomas Denby for what he was, a self-centered liar who had been left to his own devices much too long for the well-being of the community. Not willing to tip her hand, Paula softened her initial reaction with a conciliatory, dishonest response.

"Tom, I haven't said anything to anyone about why I was at the party, and we would be well-advised not to talk on the phone. Too many people know where I am staying, and I don't trust anyone right now."

Denby thought for a moment. He realized that the FBI could not move that fast to tap her phones, since a court order would be required. "Paula, do you realize that you will be in danger of prison time since I'll deny knowing anything about you being there?" Denby left her hanging with that cruel statement and hung up the receiver.

"The nerve of that man, to threaten me," Paula muttered.

After going through a near-death, experience and it somehow freed her from fear. Denby made a serious mistake in underestimating her intestinal fortitude. Though she had submitted to his secret schemes in the past, he would never intimidate her again. She wanted to do as her new attorney had advised, get to the safe location and stall, so that the authorities would have time to do their work.

Paula's drive would take her north out of the city on Highway 17 across the wide expanse of the Ravenel Bridge over the Cooper and Wando Rivers to Highway 517 across the connector bridge to the Isle of Palms, about fifteen minutes away. She got on the road and immediately flipped open her cell, dialing

Luke Bradley to give him an update on Denby's call. She told him how she tried to position Judge Parks out of Dave McCaffery's camera view, despite her reason for going to the party.

"We'll cover everything when we meet later, Paula."

"Okay, Luke, I'm just upset that the sleazebag would try and threaten me. I'll talk to you later. Thanks."

Keeping quiet was not an option now. The only way out of this mess was to tell everything, and she knew it. Daydreaming as she drove by the picturesque scenery, which led to the Isle of Palms, she remembered days of innocence when the only thing she worried about was passing Algebra, making an SAT score worthy of college admission, and hanging out with her high school friends on the weekends. A vision of her ex-husband passed in front of her mind. *How did I go so wrong in selecting him to marry? At least I have two beautiful daughters and for that I can't be sorry,* she thought, justifying her otherwise poor decision.

14

The weather forecast for the next two days included cloudy skies with rain and temperatures climbing to the mid-sixties. The warm weather had pushed its way up from the Gulf of Mexico with days of sunshine and some with rain. It was the time of year that cold Canadian air and warm weather fronts struggled with each other for control, and sometimes they compromised.

Paula made the trek over the drawbridge that rose high up over the city. From here, she had a panoramic view of the boats below and the general layout of North Charleston. She looked down on another mill that did its share of polluting in a different waterway. In the distance, she could see Fort Sumter and Sullivan's Island. She remembered history lessons in middle school in which she learned that many Southerners lost their lives defending the only way of life they had ever known.

The bridge sloped back down, depositing Paula onto a flat stretch of highway until she reached another bridge with a gentle slope, a newer bridge that shuttled her to the Isle of Palms. She crossed it, glancing over the side railing to the water below. She could see the boats in the channel moving about and seagulls dipping and flying upwards, gracefully dancing on the wind. She watched, as they seemed to take turns dive-bombing the surface fish. A pod of dolphins played in the water, bobbing up and down on the surface near one of the boats.

On the island at last, Paula thought. *I wonder if the Johnsons have any groceries in the house, or if I'll have to go out to buy some.* Paula made the final turn down Ocean Boulevard and drove four miles of winding road, which led her near the coast of the island to the Johnson's beach cottage, known as "Pelicans' Nook." Nearly all of the houses on the island had either a special name or the owner's name prominently displayed on a wooden sign hanging above the front door. Some had a signpost by the driveway. The plaques gave each house a bit of charm befitting the beautiful island; moreover, this was just the tradition here. Oak trees thick with Spanish moss graced the roadside like giants standing watch in the front and back yards of many of the homes on the Isle of Palms. Palm trees were prominently spaced on properties everywhere.

Many styles of homes were scattered on the island, some with no front porch, other homes with huge screened-in porches, and still others with open porches that wrapped around for outdoor seating. Usually a few rockers, a chair or two, and maybe a hammock were placed on the porches for regular use. Pelicans' Nook was situated on the oceanfront and had a back porch with a deck that overlooked the water.

A few hundred yards from Pelicans' Nook, the small business district had several restaurants, a few bars, and shops for practical and souvenir items. The Isle of Palms Police Department made most of its money from parking tickets, especially in the summer season when families and tourists flocked to the small downtown area to access the public beaches. There were several entrances to the beach through the shops, as well as between the buildings, which were not attached to one another. In the summer, tens of thousands of people came to visit this tiny town to enjoy the fun. The ocean at the Isle of Palms did not produce large waves because it was located on the inner side of the peninsula. The waves were large enough for local surfers, but small enough that families with children could swim and use their body boards and floats without excessive danger.

The sandy shore of the island stretched about one hundred yards from the sand dunes, where the sea oats grew, to the ocean water at low tide. The distance reduced to ten or fifteen yards at high tide. An abundance of seashells washed up on the shiny bright sand. An occasional horseshoe crab, jellyfish, or a sand dollar left by the tides to dry out and die, only to be sucked up again by the ocean for recycling in the rhythm of life.

Out in the ocean three hundred yards, shrimp boats passing by dropped their nets to make their catches of the tasty Carolina crustaceans. The water here was a deep green, rich with plant and animal life. It was not quite the way it was hundreds of years before when the Indians inhabited the coasts, but it was not far from its previously unspoiled condition. The strategic location of the island helped it to remain pristine because it was up the coast from the polluting factories of North Charleston.

Here, on the island, where Paula started falling for Jim is the reason this summer spot would always be special to her. It seemed fateful irony that her favorite summer place for relaxation had become a haven of safety in the winter from imminent danger. Her vehicle rolled into the shell-filled, unpaved driveway to the cottage. Pelicans' Nook stood with grace, warmly inviting her to come inside and share the setting.

It's a shame that no one lives here all year round, Paula thought. The cottage was simply too quaint and cozy to be used on an occasional basis. The Johnsons did plan to retire there after they reached an age when their aches and pains hindered them from their rigorous chores and schedules at Magnolia Inn, but they still had a few more years before that time approached. Paula quickly unloaded her vehicle, placing her things in the house. She walked through each of the rooms for peace of mind and adjusted the blinds and curtains to suit. It was daytime so she latched the front screen door leaving the main door open for the time being.

Her sleep the night before had been rather fitful as she tossed and turned, thinking about how she would unveil Denby's shady business dealings, in particular, the blackmail plot. She had promised to meet Luke Bradley at noon for a working lunch, and began to organize her thoughts as to the information she would give to him.

Luke looked forward to the conversation involving a confidential disclosure and account of exactly what transpired to put Paula Cooper in Judge Parks' bedroom when he was murdered. Agent Dibbs had contacted him, bringing him up to speed on what they knew thus far, but he did not know what Paula would share. He only knew that he would defend his client, as his duties required, and collect his well-deserved fees. He knew Paula was not wealthy, but his cousin had pretty much guaranteed his rate if she could not pay him. He was good at what he did and happy to be in the criminal defense field. Most of the time, he found his work exhilarating and intriguing.

His time on this case was already four hours, with a retainer he would negotiate with Paula.

Paula poured a glass of wine and took a quick sip. 10:00 AM was too early to begin drinking, but she needed something to calm her nerves a little. She sipped the red wine; deep in thought about how Denby's legal empire would likely crumble when she revealed all of his shenanigans. She hated the thought of dealing with his nasty tactics and threats, and what he might say to the people of her hometown. Paula knew there was no getting around his bullying, so she fortified her mind to make a stand and tell her story.

She rehearsed several events that led up to the ultimate price Denby had asked her to pay. From experience, she knew recording a timeline was the best way not to leave out anything. She gathered a legal pad and pen that she always kept in a side slot of her carryall. Taking a shawl for cover from the cool breeze on the deck, she sat down in a folding chair to record the events to the best of her memory. Feeling the ocean breeze blowing on her face, she looked out at the water, the shore, and then back at her legal pad. Focusing on what she wrote, time flew by as the ink flowed on her paper. She could barely keep up with her mental processes churning like a fast freight train.

Now 11:00 AM, Luke would be arriving in one short hour to garner as much information as she could give him. Taking a deep breath and exhaling with a sigh, Paula could not write fast enough to tell everything she had pent up inside. She realized and admitted that she was at fault for agreeing to go to the party but recited the facts more like a chronology of events than an accusatory statement. This way, Luke Bradley could draw his own conclusion as to how he would plan his strategy to exculpate Paula from the awful situation in which she was currently involved. The chilly wind caused Paula to shiver, but she refused to quit writing until she had the full account on paper detailing what she knew about the already infamous case, Colonial Paper Mill versus the United States Environmental Protection Agency.

Luke was to arrive at noon to meet Paula at Mango Moe's for lunch. After she finished writing her account, she walked out across the short front lawn and took the sidewalk by the two-lane road that led to the Isle of Palms business district and ran the length of the downtown area. She walked to the restaurant and waited on a public bench by the sidewalk, arriving a few minutes ahead of Luke. He pulled up in his shiny, red BMW into a parallel parking space and got out with a briefcase in hand.

"Hi, Luke, we don't get many fancy lawyers up here on the island," Paula said, as he approached the bench where she sat. She stood to greet him, extending her hand. Luke shook her hand warmly.

"Yeah, I know, right. How about that?"

"So, how was your drive up?"

"It was uneventful and nice, thanks. I actually love this drive to the Isle of Palms, passing over Shem Creek with the view of the marsh. Nature doesn't get much prettier than that."

"Exactly, Luke, I love it, too."

"Shall we go in to get a bite?"

"Sure, I have an outline of the events and information that should tell you all you need to know. Afterwards, we can go back to the cottage to fill in the details if that works for you."

"That sounds good to me," Luke said.

They shuffled up the sandy steps to enter Mango Moe's Restaurant where a host escorted them to their table on the rooftop deck with an ocean view. In the distance, a pier extended out into the ocean about seventy-five yards. People gathered on the pier to see the various seafaring vessels and seascape. Tourists and a few locals fished from the pier, hoping for an occasional flounder or sheepshead. Paula and Luke took their seats at their table overlooking the water.

"Here, I wrote down everything you would want to know about Tom Denby and some things you don't, but nevertheless, it's the truth. All the events regarding the Christmas party at Judge Parks' home are listed chronologically. I have learned the hard way on this "last hurrah" of mine how important truth and justice are," said Paula, with a humble smile.

"I believe that, Paula. Tell ya what, let's order first, and we'll get down to business in a few minutes, if that works for you. I skipped breakfast this morning, and I operate much better with food in my stomach. What do you recommend in the way of a good sandwich here?"

"I don't know the whole menu, but I know they have the best grouper sandwich anywhere around. I suggest you give it a try."

"Grouper sandwich, aye? That sounds good to me. You can't get that everywhere."

"Trust me, it's wonderful! And they serve it with great-tasting coleslaw and fries, or onion rings."

"I'll tell you what, Paula...since you've decided to trust me with your life, I guess I can trust you with a lunch recommendation," Luke laughed.

The waitress arrived to take their order.

"Can I get you folks started with a beverage, or would you like to order now?" she asked.

"I think we're ready to order. Go ahead, Paula."

" I will have the shrimp burger," said Paula.

"I'll have the grouper sandwich and fries, against my better judgment," he said to the waitress with a grin. He looked quickly at Paula and winked to assure her he was kidding.

"Two sweet iced teas?" asked the server.

"That will be fine for me, and you, Paula?" asked Luke.

"Yes, the same for me, Miss, with plenty of ice."

"So, what do you have for me? I see a familiar-looking legal pad sticking out of the top of your bag."

Paula handed the pad to Luke. The restaurant was not crowded to capacity as it usually was every day during the summer. There were some tables unoccupied on the rooftop where they sat so that Luke and his client had sufficient privacy. A local guitarist sat on a wooden bar stool with the minimal equipment for his acoustic-electric sound and sang James Taylor tunes to entertain the lunch guests.

"If you have any questions as you read it, just fire away."

Luke did not look up from the legal pad as he carefully read the chronology of events. Written in a short time span, it covered all the important information. Luke paused a minute as he reached the part about the decision to attend Judge Parks' party.

"Now, tell me why you went ahead with the plan when you knew it would be dangerous and was potentially blackmail?"

"It's like I wrote, Luke, I wasn't thinking very clearly, and Denby took me by surprise. I thought that would be the last time I ever did this sort of thing. Yes, I attempted to do a terrible thing, and I wanted to back out, but Denby was persistent. When he offered me huge bonus money, I thought about my daughters' education and caved in. I know I made a stupid mistake, but the plan was all Denby's directive, and now he has the nerve to threaten me."

"Paula, I believe you. Denby won't learn a thing until he's caught. He has no shame and reminds me of another man in a position of power. He will most likely follow the same pattern as our current president; deny, and deny, until he is painted into a corner. Here's what I want you to do. Next time you talk to him on the phone, if there is a next time, record him, if you can. The tape won't be admissible in court, but the FBI agents might like to hear him in action. We can show this pattern of behavior you allege. We might get other witnesses at the firm to come forward, but they are likely to remain loyal to him, even if they are deposed. Since Dave McCaffery is dead, we will need a little more than the chronology you have set forth here to bargain with the FBI."

"I will do whatever it takes, Luke. I know I was wrong to go to the party, but as I wrote, I did pull out of the plot when I maneuvered the judge out of the line of sight of Dave's camera. I'm hoping the FBI has Dave's camera and can see that much."

"If the assassin didn't take it, they probably do. Listen, do you have any idea who had the judge killed? He was a decent man, regardless of his reputation for being tough on the bench. I have heard that he had a hard time with his wife, trying to keep her under control during years of nasty, alcoholic-related episodes."

"Yes, I also learned that about him. All I can say is that I'm pretty sure he had several people who wanted him dead, from all that I have been able to learn about him."

"From what Agent Dibbs told me this morning regarding the style of this assassination, a professional was involved. McCaffery, your private eye friend, had his throat crushed by a flexible steel wire, the kind used by a trained killer."

"I agree that this guy must be a hired killer. Several people hated the judge and had the resources to have him killed. Look at his unstable wife, whom I overheard saying that the judge would get what was coming to him. There's also the incarcerated drug lord, Hernandez. I read where he swore in Judge Parks' courtroom after he was sentenced that he would kill him one day. And lastly, there's Denby, but why would he commit murder, if he was going to blackmail him?"

The food arrived, and they ate their succulent dishes as they mulled over several scenarios, contemplating who might be the culprit in this double murder. From their lofty vantage point, seagulls swooped down to snatch pieces of bread and French fries, dropped intentionally by children sitting with their family, then flew quickly back to safety to their air currents high above. Bright blue skies with a few cumulus clouds took hold, as the sun looked down from its lofty position in the picturesque seascape.

"Shall we go to your place to finish up our business?" asked Luke, as he pushed his chair back from the table.

"Sure, I'm stuffed and need to get back to make a call, or two, anyway. I haven't talked to my daughters since this whole ordeal began."

Paula rode with Luke back to the cottage. The little kitchen table with a blue-checked, linen tablecloth became Luke's office in the field. Luke presented the contract for Paula to sign. She read it carefully then cleared her throat when she read that a ten thousand-dollar retainer would be required. Luke noticed where she was reading and interjected that his time spent thus far would be deducted from the retainer.

"If you exceed the retainer, which, to be honest, you likely will, I'll have my secretary contact you so that you will know where you stand."

Paula gulped. She knew that criminal defense would be expensive but had never been on the wrong end of it before.

"Paula, I think I can get the cooperation of the FBI, if you turn state's evidence against Denby. Your conspiracy charges could be dropped, or lessened, but obtaining that optimal scenario will take some doing. Some of this depends on what Mr. Denby does, as you can imagine."

"I am aware of that, but do you have any idea what my defense may end up costing, Luke?" asked Paula. "I may have to move some money around before this is over," she said, biting her lip.

"To be honest, Paula, I don't know. It may only cost you the amount of the retainer, which is the minimum I accept in a case like this. On the other hand, it may climb up to twenty-thousand, or more, depending upon what happens."

"I can get the additional money if necessary. Just notify me, like you said. I trust that you will do your best for me. I'll leave it at that," she said.

Paula laughed to keep from crying as she realized that clearance from these charges might cost her life's savings. She lamented her huge lapse in judgment. "The expense will be worthwhile to me if we can put Denby out of practice and help find who killed Judge Parks and Dave McCaffery."

Luke gathered the papers and a check for ten thousand dollars from Paula and turned to go out the opened front door of the cottage. He pushed the screen door half-way open then looked back at her.

"Paula, call only whomever you absolutely need to. Realize, too, that if Jim comes up here, he may be in danger. Whoever murdered Dave McCaffery and Judge Parks is a ruthless, cold-blooded animal. You need stay here a few days until I can determine that you are safe, and then I'll likely move you somewhere else."

Paula nodded her head in agreement.

"I have a man working for me who will keep an eye on the cottage while you are here. In fact, so that you will not to be alarmed, he is in a dark green LTD down the street. He followed me up today and will be driving around periodically. He'll look for anything unusual in the neighborhood."

"Thank you, Luke," Paula said.

"If anything happens where you feel you are in danger, call 911. My detective has a police scanner in his vehicle, and will be listening. If anything occurs, I assure you that he will be quicker to your defense than the police will. I will talk to you when I know something more, but I need to get back to Charleston now."

"Thanks again for your help. I do appreciate it, especially that you have a man to keep watch for me."

"Don't mention it. See ya soon."

The screen door slammed, bouncing a few times before resting against the frame. Paula closed the front door, locking it, and retreated to the deck again. This time she gravitated to the handmade Pawley's Island hammock as her resting spot. She was emotionally drained from the meeting. Partially sedated from the glass of wine, she lay back in the hammock. She thought of Jim, her kids, and her parents.

A flock of brown pelicans flew overhead in a group of seven, one leading at the point. *Seven, my lucky number*, she thought. *Maybe it's a good omen.* Paula watched the pelicans flap their wings in unison from three to five strokes and then glide for quite a distance before repeating the same motion. If only she knew the secret of the pelican who sojourned in life with such grace. The loss of sleep the night before and stress had rendered her zombie-like. Her eyes fluttered then closed, as she fell asleep in the hammock for a couple of hours until mid-afternoon.

"My goodness, what time is it?" Paula muttered to herself, as she awakened. She had promised her kids, and Jim that she would call.

She rolled her body halfway from the hammock in a quick burst of energy, only to find that a sudden exit was not an efficient method to extricate her from the sagging rope mesh. She fell back into the hammock, swaying for a moment, holding onto the sides for dear life, which barely prevented being dumped onto the deck. Determining that this next attempt would be more deliberate and thoughtful, she stretched with a yawn and rolled slowly, her feet touching the wooden planks. She held the sides of the rope swing tightly as she stood to re-enter the house and make her calls. Dialing Jim's work number, she waited as the line rang several times. This was his busiest time of day, just after people got off from work and before he closed his doors.

"Hello, this is Jim Roberts, may I help you?"

"You already have, Jim, darling. I want to thank you for the way you took care of me through Luke and for your visit to me at the hospital."

"Paula, where are you now?"

"I'm at the Johnsons' cottage on the Isle of Palms. Luke wanted me to stay here for a while until things calm down."

"I can be up there by nine tonight if you want me to? Just say the word."

"That will be great, Jim, but Luke said to tell you that being with me right now could be rather dangerous."

"Let me worry about that, Paula. I appreciate you telling me, but wild horses couldn't drag me away from being near you."

"You say the sappiest things, Jim, but I like it. I'll run out and pick up a few things for dinner...not sure what. Does something like baked fish and a steamed vegetable medley sound good to you?"

Jim was elated that Paula sounded better, almost back to herself. *She always did have a remarkable way of recovering from crises*, he thought. "That sounds absolutely wonderful, honey, I just want to see you. It doesn't matter if we eat peanut butter and jelly sandwiches."

"Aw, that's sweet. I'll have the meal all ready when you get here. Say...can you do me a big favor, please?"

"Sure, honey, what is it?"

"Will you have time to go by Mom's to pick up some clothes for me? I didn't plan for more than a weekend's stay. I'll call her so she can get them ready."

"Sure, I can go by your parents' home. Tell them I'll be there around seven."

"I will. Thanks, Jim, I appreciate it. On another quick note, I believe Luke has made the right moves with all that he's done thus far."

"Well, he's my cousin, after all, and a very smart man."

"I've got confidence in him. I like his style and demeanor."

"That's good, dear. I was hoping you would. I'll pick up a chilled bottle of Chardonnay and see you around eight or a few minutes after, okay?"

"Works for me...please be careful on the way."

"Good-bye, Paula. I'll see you soon."

"Bye-bye, I'll see you soon, Sweetheart."

The two lovebirds hung up their phones, hearts beating faster than before, hearts that would only be satisfied in each other's arms. Paula made the call to her parents to arrange for clothes and spoke with her daughters.

Jim arrived at Pelicans' Nook as filets of orange roughy, his favorite fish, and a steamed vegetable medley were cooking and within five minutes of completion. The aroma of the cuisine and scented candles Paula lit filled the cottage drifting out onto the small front porch creating a delightful ambience. A sea breeze blew in from the half-opened deck doors with the fresh smell of the salty air. Jim exited his car with a quickened pace, much as he did on a Saturday in his store hurrying across the floor to wait on a customer. He raised his hand to knock on the screen door, but to his surprise, Paula opened the inner door and stood there smiling.

"Come in, honey. You're a sight for sore eyes," she said.

They embraced with a kiss then walked to the kitchen. Paula took the bottle of chilled Chardonnay to the kitchen, as Jim followed. He opened the bottle pouring a glass for each of them, as Paula served the plates of succulent baked fish and steamed vegetables. They sat down to enjoy their dinner at the same small table where she had earlier signed the contract with Luke. She quickly dismissed her legal problems from her mind and engrossed herself with Jim. The lovebirds gazed into each other's eyes, making small talk about missing each other, their kids, and his work.

"That was great, honey. Everything was perfect. When do you meet with Luke again?"

"Let's not talk about the case now, Jim. I'm so tired of thinking about it."

"I understand, honey. Would you like to go for a walk?"

"Yes, let's do that. I'll get my jacket."

The couple put on windbreakers to prevent a chill from the cool evening breeze coming in off the water, but not walking on the beach while a beautiful Carolina full moon beamed down like a soft spotlight seemed like a crime. The waves beckoned all who caught a glimpse to come and walk by their sandy shores and enjoy their soulful rhythm as they tirelessly played their peaceful refrain.

The abundant constellations and the Milky Way lit the sky, blanketing the bedazzling backdrop, and adding to the gorgeous setting. Paula and Jim walked across the wet sand by the rolling waves, which crashed on the shore. They arrived at the point where a jetty was built to soften the currents in the channel that cut through the south end of the island. They paused and embraced, enjoying the touch of each other's body. The breeze danced through their hair, shifting directions periodically.

"It's strange, Jim, but as alone as I know we are out here, I feel as if someone is watching us."

"I guess that's possible, but I don't think we are being followed."

"Well, there is the man who Luke has stationed keeping watch, but I feel as if evil is lurking somewhere. I don't mean to spoil the mood, honey."

"No, I totally understand, sweetie. Let's head back."

They started walking back to the cottage when they saw, off in the distance, a man with a large dog coming towards them. The ocean breeze was so strong that they could not hear anything beyond ten yards. The only audible sounds, besides their voices, were the sounds of the relentless waves pounding the shore, rolling up and then back to their appointed boundaries, and the sounds of the wind whipping through their loose clothing. Only twenty-five yards from them now, suddenly, the man and dog shifted sharply at an angle towards the couple.

"Stay calm, Paula," Jim said. She had never heard his voice so serious.

Paula's body tensed, her hand squeezing Jim's large hand. Ten yards apart now, and the man and dog cut in front of them. Jim readied himself, remembering the defensive skills he had learned in the service. Paula braced herself.

"Good evening, you two. Fine night for a walk," said the man. The dog bounded towards the water to wet his pads and lower body.

"It surely is," replied Jim, with a chuckle of relief. "Is that a Black Labrador?"

"Oh yeah, he's all boy, too," said the stranger. "Sorry to cut in front of you like that. He's as strong as an ox, and I can't keep him out of the water." The man jogged away with the muscular dog pulling him, as if he was on a sled. "Take care."

"See ya," Jim responded.

Paula and Jim were amused as they returned to the cottage; very relaxed from what they thought might be a confrontation. Once inside, Paula put in a slow jazz CD and they danced in each other's arms. The hugs and kisses they shared soothed away the toughest times ever in Paula's life. That evening, the slow dances led them across the threshold to the bedroom and they spent the night together for the first time.

The next morning Paula awakened, stretching with her eyes closed, then realizing the bed was empty on one side. She swung her arm behind letting it fall where the covers were rolled back on the bed to verify Jim had gone, even though she knew he had. The only sign of him having been there was an envelope with the letter he had written a few days before, but not mailed.

Paula went to the kitchen and brewed a short pot of coffee. With a cup in hand, she returned to her bed and read the letter she carefully pulled from the envelope. *I've never read anything so assuring and beautiful in all my life,* she thought, then smelled the page hoping for a scent of Jim's cologne. It was there, and she smiled.

15

Special Agent John Dibbs, accompanied by Agent Mendez, entered the law office of J. Thomas Denby with an arrest warrant. Another FBI vehicle with two agents waited outside as backup. Since Paula had agreed to cooperate fully with the federal and other enforcement authorities, Luke Bradley had been able to arrange a deal resulting in her complete amnesty. Additionally, the Feds could not prove she did not reconsider the plan anyway, as she stated. For her, cooperating was not difficult because she wanted to cleanse her conscience.

"Good afternoon, gentlemen. May I help you?" asked Frances.

"Ma'am, I'm Agent John Dibbs with the Federal Bureau of Investigation. This is Agent Mendez. If Mr. Denby is in his office, we would like to speak to him. This is an urgent matter that cannot wait."

"Yes, sir," said the receptionist, "I'll ring his office now. Mr. Denby, some men with the FBI are here to speak with you."

"Tell them I'll be out in just a moment, Frances."

Tom Denby knew that this scenario could unfold eventually. He only wished that Paula had complied with him once more, but she would not. He walked out to the spacious waiting area where the agents were standing.

"Good morning, gentlemen, would you care for some coffee?"

"No, thank you. Are you James Thomas Denby?" asked Agent Dibbs.

"I am. How can I help you?"

"Mr. Denby, I'm Agent John Dibbs, and this is Agent Mendez, my partner. You are under arrest for conspiracy to blackmail a federal judge. Anything you say can, and may be used against you in a court of law."

"You have no proof of this allegation," Denby said.

"On the contrary, Mr. Denby, we believe we have plenty of proof," said Agent Dibbs. He put Denby in handcuffs and turned him around, facing his partner, who held up a document for him to read.

"This is a subpoena duces tecum to seize your computers, files, and records pertaining to the Colonial Paper Mill case. Also, Paula Cooper has signed this release for us to obtain her files and all correspondence you have had with her during the time she has been employed here," said Mendez.

Denby scanned the subpoena and release, and finding everything in order, he realized there was nothing else he could say that mattered. With his jaw clinched, he looked over his shoulder at Agent Dibbs. "You can do this if you choose, Agent Dibbs, but you are making a grave mistake."

Another federal judge, Robert Tolson, was presiding over the district now. Substituting for the late Wilmont Parks, he signed the warrant and would hear the cases that were interrupted by the tragedy. Tolson served his country as a prosecutor for fifteen years before running a private practice in Charleston.

He was well respected among his peers, before being appointed to the bench.

"Let's go, Mr. Denby; my men are waiting," said Dibbs, not impressed by the infamous attorney.

The FBI had their man and did not intend to let him go.

One day later

Paula awakened with the sunlight shining in her window. An orange-yellow hue cast its shadows across her bedroom. She heard the sounds of seagulls crying out their familiar refrain as they swooped down, scanning the beach for their version of breakfast. Paula got out of bed and was moving at a leisurely pace. She had not slept that well in quite a while and saw no reason to be on a schedule at the cottage while she was in limbo. A grin came to her face as she stretched with a yawn.

I'm in love with this man, she thought. *It's the real thing; he's a man who respects me and has been nonjudgmental throughout this whole fiasco.* Paula and Jim had found the kind of love that is very hard to find. In a fast-paced society where most of the emphasis is on money and not on the qualities of life that make living worthwhile, they had discovered this love growing between them.

The phone rang loudly, rattling Paula out of her daydream. "Hello?" she said, haltingly.

"Paula, it's Luke, you can make arrangements to leave Pelicans' Nook and return home to Georgetown. Denby is in custody now and won't be getting out anytime soon. You are not a suspect in the murder case, and they are dropping the conspiracy to commit blackmail charges because of your cooperation. The investigation is well under way, and all leads are being pursued. My man who's been watching says there has been no unusual activity around the Isle of Palms, specifically where you are currently lodged."

Paula breathed a sigh of relief, but for the past twenty-four hours really had not given the case too much thought. She was wrapped up in the glow of being with Jim the previous night. "Thank you, Luke, that's great news. How did they decide to cut me a deal so quickly?"

"I think they have a lead as to who the killer is. They would not divulge specific information, except that for some reason, they are ruling you out on any plot to kill McCaffery, or assassinate Judge Parks. Just be ready to share everything you know without hesitation when we go before them, okay?"

"I hear what you are saying. I can do that without a problem. So, I am free to go?"

"Yes, Paula, you are for now. I'll be in touch with you. Be careful on your drive back to Georgetown."

"I will, Luke. Talk to you soon."

The FBI agents took Denby to their offices at the Federal Building for questioning. He had decided to negotiate for leniency since they would likely seek the maximum sentenced allowed. Agent Mendez removed the cuffs and seated Denby at a table in a bleak, sterile-looking room with a picture of the current president and director of the FBI on the wall. All else was very plain. A small one-way mirror was inset inconspicuously overlooking the table for observation. One man sat behind it with earphones and a laptop.

"Can we strike a deal, Agent Dibbs?" inquired Denby.

"We can ask for a deal from the Attorney General's office, but I'm not sure what can be done now. You had your chance when Paula Cooper was arrested, but instead of coming forth, you asked her to comply with your efforts to conceal information. All of that is on record now."

"That's her word against mine, but suppose I used my office personnel to aid in the murder investigation?" asked Denby.

"What do you know that can help us in the case?" Dibbs inquired.

"I might have some information to help, if I was assured leniency."

"I'll have to ask the Attorney General what she thinks about that and get back to you, Mr. Denby. We might be able to do something, but if you know anything or can help us in any way, I wouldn't sit and wait for an answer from the AG, if I were you. We have a good rapport, and she depends on me for input concerning how well you cooperate."

"Well, there are two possibilities, as I see it," said Denby. "There is the Nicaraguan drug lord, whom Judge Parks had locked up for life, and there is his separated wife. Get me word of a deal from the Attorney General, and I'll get my staff to get information on both of them."

"I'll see what I can do. Let me go back to my office and make a call now. Maybe I can locate her, and we can resolve this," said Dibbs.

Agent Dibbs placed the call stating Denby's willingness to help, and was instructed to tell the counselor that whatever he did to help would weigh in his favor, but he would not be totally exonerated from prosecution. Dibbs came back to the interrogation room to inform the detained attorney of the situation.

"Her assistant was in, Mr. Denby, and said that you will be treated fairly and with leniency if you divulge everything you know with regards to this case."

"Get your pen and paper out and turn on your tape recorders, gentlemen," said Denby. "Let's get to it. I may as well get this over with."

Dibbs snapped his fingers to get the entire team's attention. "Okay, guys, we're doing a statement. Get everything ready now!"

The men and one woman scurried quickly to make sure that the taping equipment was functional. The court reporter flipped the switch to a Dictaphone and put a cup over her mouth to record what was said. A man, who sat next to her, prepared to take notes.

"Okay, we're ready, Mr. Denby. Go ahead with your statement."

"When I did my research on Judge Parks, I discovered through my private investigator, Dave McCaffery, that the judge had two primary enemies who were motivated to kill him. One is the Nicaraguan drug lord, Manuel Hernandez, who has an amazing capability to get things done, even though he is in a federal penitentiary. The other person I would suspect is Eleanor Parks, who is very bitter about her separation and pending divorce from the judge. I understand that Paula Cooper, a paralegal under my employ, overheard the judge's wife at a hair salon in Charleston on the day of the party, stating that the judge would get his, in the end. I also had Dave McCaffery pay a nail artist to tell him everything she knew from conversing with Eleanor Parks. This was communicated to me the afternoon before he was killed. She's a bitter woman and very disturbed."

"Yes, I understand she is, Mr. Denby, but this style of killing hardly fits the mold of a bitter woman," said Dibbs.

"That's true," Denby replied, "unless she hired a hit man and wanted it to appear as though someone else may have done it."

"I'll concede that you do have a point there, Mr. Denby, but that idea doesn't sit well with me for some reason. Please, go ahead."

"The thing that intrigues me about Eleanor Parks is that she insisted that Judge Parks take out a two-million-dollar life insurance policy, with her as the beneficiary, just six months prior to his death. That was the only way she would leave the house. He already had a five hundred-thousand-dollar policy made out to her."

"That is interesting, Mr. Denby, please continue."

The FBI had two other suspects in mind, as well, two of whom Denby was unaware. One was the CEO of Colonial Paper, and the other sat in the room testifying to the FBI. Dibbs did not want to tip his hand that Denby was also a suspect in the murder case. He only wanted him to believe that the FBI had him nailed for conspiracy to commit blackmail. He figured that if Denby were guilty, somehow, he would slip up. At least this was Dibbs' theory.

"Hernandez, on the other hand, had vowed to kill Parks when he was sentenced to his prison term in the judge's courtroom. There was an article in the Charleston paper detailing the outburst several years back. Hernandez reportedly said, "I will have your heart cut out and fed to my falcons. It won't matter if I spend the rest of my life in your filthy prisons," said Denby.

"What other enlightening things can you tell us?" asked Dibbs.

Denby understood that he had to come up with more information to satisfy Dibbs. He thought of the floppy discs containing all the notes of the filings and meetings pertaining to the EPA versus Colonial Paper Mill case.

"Load those discs you confiscated from my office, and you will find more on the case. I only wanted to trap Judge Parks in a compromising situation in order to convince him to throw the case out of court on a technicality. That way, my clients wouldn't have to bear the expense of defending themselves in a nuisance lawsuit."

"I read about the case in the papers, Mr. Denby. Do you call dumping chemical toxins that kill fish and birds of all descriptions a nuisance case? Seems to me that we need to preserve our wetlands, or don't we? The marshes and the waterways provide food and are important in the ecological chain, aren't they?"

"My, my, I'm impressed with your interest and knowledge of the wetlands, Agent Dibbs," said Denby sarcastically. "I would not have thought that you cared."

"What if I told you that Green Peace plans to picket your law firm and Colonial Paper soon, with a huge editorial being released simultaneously in the local newspapers, Mr. Denby?"

"That doesn't surprise me. There's always some bleeding heart liberal ready to cause trouble in the name of nature."

At the Denby Law Firm, a very able associate vying for partner, Daniel Boswell, had taken the lead in the case, but he was not of the same mold as his boss. The phone rang from Colonial Paper. Frances answered efficiently.

"May I speak to Daniel Boswell?"

"Yes, sir, may I ask who is calling?"

"This is Paul Walker, CEO of Colonial Paper."

The receptionist, eager to transfer the call, perked up as she recognized the voice with the name he gave. "Yes sir, just a moment while I transfer the call."

"Mr. Boswell, Paul Walker of Colonial Paper, is on line two for you."

"Thanks, Frances," said Boswell, "I'll take the call."

Grimacing, Boswell answered, "Daniel Boswell speaking, how can I help you, Mr. Walker?"

"Mr. Boswell, this is Paul Walker, CEO of Colonial Paper; I hope you're doing well. I've got a few questions and concerns for you. Is what I hear about Tom true?"

"What's that, Mr. Walker?"

"Well, I have heard from a reliable source that he is in the custody of the FBI regarding circumstances surrounding the death of Judge Parks. Is that correct?"

"I believe what you said about Mr. Denby may be correct, Mr. Walker, but there is no reason to suspect him of doing anything wrong. He has more sense than that. I personally think that the FBI is just trying to get what they can out of him."

"Mr. Boswell, as you know, we employed the Denby Law Firm to handle our case with the EPA. In fact, you have been one of the main attorneys on the case, is that right?"

"Yes, sir, that's correct," said Boswell.

"Well, I'm sorry to inform you of this, but I am not pleased at all with the recent developments, and Colonial Paper cannot afford to be associated with a law firm whose owner may be committing federal crimes in his efforts to defend us. True enough, we wanted Judge Parks to throw out the case, but we didn't want him to be shot. And as for this local private investigator that was killed also, well, it's just way more than we bargained for."

"I understand how you feel, Mr. Walker, but these are routine procedures with the FBI to detain anyone they can to acquire information. Surely you are not implying that Tom had anything to do with the murder, are you?"

"I'm not implicating him, Mr. Boswell, but frankly, we don't know what to think. We are just no longer happy with the representation we have been receiving, considering all that has transpired over the past few days. I understand that Tom was attempting some sort of blackmail scheme to get the judge to toss out the case. Were you aware of that?"

"The FBI cited conspiracy charges involving blackmail, but I know nothing about any such scheme."

"Well, in any case, Mr. Boswell, please understand your firm's services are terminated, and you may bill us for what is owed to date."

In Denby's absence, Boswell led meetings with the other staff assigned to the case. The only persons privy to the blackmail scheme connected to the Denby Law Firm were Tom Denby, Paula Cooper, and the belated Dave McCaffery. Boswell was shocked but did not doubt that his boss to have tried such a stunt.

"Very well," said Boswell, "I'll inform Mr. Denby as soon as he calls. He will not be happy that we have lost your trust, and I'm sure he'll want to talk to you about retaining you as a client, if possible. I think this will all blow over soon enough."

"There is nothing to discuss, but give him my message. He knows how to reach me," said Walker, as he hung up the phone.

Both Dibbs and Denby were developing cottonmouth and sweaty palms from the interview process.

"Agent Dibbs, I need a break, and I would like to use the men's room and to call my office briefly. Would that be okay?"

"I guess we can accommodate you, Mr. Denby. I could use a break myself. Escort him down the hall to the restroom and then to the phone, Agent Mendez."

"Yes, sir, my pleasure," responded Mendez.

Denby finished using the restroom and was shown to the phone. Dialing his office, Frances answered the phone, and hearing Denby's voice, nearly dropped the receiver. "Mr. Denby, the CEO of Colonial Paper just called."

"I figured he would, Frances. Get Boswell on the line for me."

"Yes, sir, Mr. Denby, hold one moment, please."

"Boswell, here, can I help you?"

"Daniel, it's me, Tom. What's going on since I've been detained?"

"Not much, except that everybody here is worried about their jobs, and Paul Walker called to fire us from the Colonial case."

"Are you kidding me? He did what? That sorry, no-good, son-of-a-gun, and after all I have done for him. He knew what I had in mind and is running now. I guess that is to be expected, but he won't get away with it. You watch, I'll have his butt nailed to the wall for this," said Denby.

"Yeah, I hear you, Tom, but you need to hear this from me. I didn't know about any scheme to blackmail a federal judge and certainly would not have approved of it. I have done some pretty underhanded things to expedite cases since I came to work here, but I never knowingly committed a felony in an effort to win cases."

"I knew you never would, Danny boy; that's why I didn't involve you."

"Hear me out, Tom. You are a manipulative, selfish man who is always slithering like a snake for your next big payday. You deserve what you have coming to you. I quit! Good-bye."

Before Denby had a chance to respond, he slammed the receiver down, immediately cleaned out his office, and left the law firm. Later, Boswell was questioned by the FBI and was cleared of involvement in the conspiracy case.

16

Feeling good from Luke Bradley's telephone conversation, Paula was on her drive back to Georgetown. She was crossing the "connector," as the locals call it, from the Isle of Palms to the mainland when she noticed an old, faded blue van very close on her tail. Without warning, the van sped up and rammed her with a jolt so hard that she nearly lost control of the wheel. She looked in her mirror to get a look at the culprits' faces. Again, there was a thud in the rear of Paula's Explorer; this time they hit even harder as she slammed into the guardrail and back across the centerline. Her SUV bounced up and down from the shock of the impact on the narrow two-lane bridge. Sparks and sounds from metal clashing and tires squealing added to the fray.

She pulled her vehicle steady again in the center of her lane—both hands gripping the steering wheel tightly. The two men in the front seat of the van wore ski masks so that Paula could not get a good look at their faces. She floored the accelerator, pulling away for a moment, but the van kept closing in on her. The traffic in front prohibited her from losing her attackers. Suddenly, Paula spotted an opening to pass and did so quickly, swerving out into the passing lane and then back in before a long line of vehicles met her, passing head-on from the opposite direction. The frustrated drivers in the van could not pass.

"These bastards are trying to kill me!" Paula screamed.

She banged one hand down on the steering wheel and continued speeding and passing vehicles until she reached Highway 17 North, where she set out for Georgetown. She managed to extract her cell phone from her purse. Flipping it open, she dialed *47, the number for the South Carolina Highway Patrol.

"Highway Patrol Dispatch, how can I help you?" inquired the dispatcher.

"This is Paula Cooper of Georgetown, SC. I'm heading north on Highway 17 about two miles off the Isle of Palms, and a blue van is tailing me. It's already hit me in the rear twice, causing damage and nearly making me wreck," Paula exclaimed.

"Try to keep your wheel steady, Miss Cooper, and don't stop, whatever you do," advised the dispatcher. "What are you driving?"

"I'm in a black, late model Ford Explorer."

"I'll send help now. Can you remain on the line while I contact the highway patrol, ma'am?"

"No, I can't. Please, hurry, I've got to keep two hands on the wheel and drive," Paula said, and snapped her cell phone shut.

Three patrol cars were dispatched, and the chase was on to apprehend the persons in the blue van. Blue lights flashed, and sirens screamed as the Highway Patrol approached the van, closing in on it like a blue tick hound on a swamp coon. The driver of the van, knowing the Highway Patrol was in pursuit, turned off the highway onto a dirt road that led through the marshlands, hoping to lose them. Speeding and driving recklessly, the van careened side to side. The driver almost lost control, but he managed to hold on, as the road sloped to a clearing at a dead end by a boat dock. The men, with their masks off now, were shouting obscenities in Spanish, each one blaming the other for their plight.

Two patrol cars turned in, one after the other, with a third one close behind blocking the entrance to the dirt road from the highway. The lead patrol car was twenty-five yards behind the van when it slid to a sideways stop, nearly turning over, the doors flew open. The men grabbed their guns and ammunition clips and ran behind the van for cover. They began firing rapidly as the first patrol car approached.

The crooks unleashed a barrage of bullets that shattered the highway patrolman's windshield. The patrol car flipped and rolled until it landed upside down, then suddenly caught fire from the bottom near the leaking fuel lines. After a few minutes of burning, the flames ignited the gas tank, which exploded and sent the car ten feet straight up in the air before it plummeted back to the ground. The patrolman struggled to get out but didn't have time to save himself from the hellacious inferno.

"One down, two to go," shouted one man to the other. The two patrolmen in the next car, seeing their partner's car crash, came in with their pistols blazing. Both men returned fire, still hiding behind the van. One patrolman ran to a nearby tree to get a better angle on the men. The patrolmen trapped the suspects in crossfire, killing one man, and taking the other one into custody.

The loss of life by the South Carolina Highway Patrol, not unusual because the major route for drug trafficking passes from Miami to New York through the Palmetto state. The violence was typically reserved for Interstate 95, the main artery, but this time the deaths found their way to the coast. Both suspects were of Hispanic origin, the patrolmen noted.

Aware of the pursuit by the Highway Patrol, Paula was relieved that she was able to lose the van, although she did wonder who was trying to kill her. She arrived in Georgetown and went straight to her parents' home to see her daughters. She had a change of plans and needed her parents to continue keeping the girls.

Rachel and Christine saw their mom's vehicle pulling into their grandparents' driveway and darted outside. "Mom, Mom, you're here," the girls said, excited to see her.

"Yes, I am girls. Let's go inside and talk to Papa and Nana."

"Aw, we want to go home now."

Mr. and Mrs. Cooper watched from the bay window in the kitchen as the girls hugged their mom then walked with her up the sidewalk, bordered with yellow daffodils, to the front door. The Coopers left the kitchen and greeted their daughter in the foyer.

"Are you staying for dinner, Paula? I've got enough food cooking for all of us," said Mrs. Cooper.

"I don't think I should," Mom, but I'll take a rain check, if that's okay.

"Honey, why don't you stay long enough to eat and visit with us a little while?" Mr. Cooper said.

"Dad, I told you what happened, and it's going to be a while until things return to normal. My attorney wants me to move around."

"That's not a problem. We can deal with that. I want you to stay here tonight," said her dad. Mrs. Cooper stood by, silently trembling from what she just heard her daughter explain.

"Okay, Daddy, I will, as long as you and Mom promise to give me a little space. I may have to leave on a moment's notice, and I can't talk about what is going on much at the moment, not until this ordeal is closer to being over, anyway."

"What's going on, Mama?" Rachel asked.

"It's nothing, Rach... just grown-up talk."

"I'm grown up," Rachel said defiantly."

"You are getting there, for sure. Let's go in the den with Papa and Nana," Paula said.

Paula hugged and kissed her girls, spending time with them catching up on what was happening in their lives for the past several days.

"What time will dinner be, Mom?" Paula asked Mrs. Cooper.

"Not long, honey, maybe forty-five minutes, to an hour, tops."

"Okay, I'm going to run downtown to see Jim and be back very soon," said Paula.

Taking leave of her daughters, Paula trotted out the front entrance and drove a few miles to Unique Antiques. She parked near Jim's store and walked down the sidewalk to find him in his office reviewing paperwork. She hugged him tight as he stood up to greet her on her unexpected visit.

"They're after me, now," she said, her body trembling as she closed her eyes, trying to forget the black ski masks in her rear-view mirror. She had done such a good job hiding her fear in front of her parents and daughters that the pent-up emotion welled up and overflowed on Jim.

"Slow down, Paula, who is after you?"

"I don't know, but I was nearly run off the bridge as I was leaving the Isle of Palms on the way home. A van hit me in the rear twice, and I was lucky to evade it. I had to call the Highway Patrol for help. I hope that they apprehended the thugs."

Jim drew back a little so that he could see her face. "Take a deep breath and try to calm down, honey. Why don't you plan to stay with me for a few days? I have a gun and know how to use it if anyone suspicious comes snooping around."

"That sounds too dangerous, Jim. Besides, I told Mom and Dad that I would stay with them. The girls need me, too...you understand."

She was not in any shape to be amorous, and he quickly understood that. "Yes, I do. I was worried about you. I'm glad to see that you are safe and at home again."

"Well, I'm here, but I'm not sure how safe. I'm going to get Luke to send his man back. I don't know where the heck he was today, but I could have used his help."

"Who do you think might be doing this?"

"I don't know who would want me dead, other than Denby, and surely he can't orchestrate an attack from inside jail. Could he?"

"Don't underestimate the weasel. You've seen him in action for five years. Who all is he connected with anyway?" Jim asked.

"Oh, God, he has connections with all sorts of people, some of whom I know nothing about. I've never seen a man like him who has a person and plan for every situation. With all of this going on, I still can't believe he could cause such a calamity. I know he's highly irritated because I have turned state's evidence, but he's in custody and fighting a battle of his own now. I'm sure that his phone calls are limited and screened, don't you think?"

"I would think so. What about this drug lord guy you mentioned to me?"

"I know, but why would he want me dead? I've never even heard of him, except on television when he was jailed more than a year ago."

"Maybe he hired the assassin and thinks you know something more about the death of Judge Parks. If he is involved, that is."

"I guess that's possible. Listen, I need to get moving. I'll call you soon, okay? I needed to see your face and hear your voice to calm me down."

"Alright, be careful, Sweetheart. We'll talk later."

"Promise me you'll be careful, as well, Jim. These people are serious and seem to be on the move to intimidate or seriously hurt people involved with the case."

Jim held her in a tight embrace before letting her go on her way. The trial of their lives would either pull them together or tear them apart. Jim continued to be supportive, but Paula felt bad for putting him through all this. She allowed him to be with her as long as he wanted to because there was no other place she felt so safe and secure. They dreamed about being married, but their dreams seemed so distant now. Where else was she to go, if not to the man who had captured her soul?

17

The phone rang at 7:00 AM.

"Hello?" said Mr. Cooper.

"Hello, sir, this is Sergeant Hunter from the South Carolina Highway Patrol, may I speak to Miss Paula Cooper?"

"Yes, sir, just a moment while I get her to the phone," he said, surprised at the call. "Paula, it's for you. Sergeant Hunter with the Highway Patrol," Mr. Cooper shouted through the door of her bedroom, while muting the phone with his hand.

Paula picked up the phone on the bedside table. "Yes, sir, this is Paula Cooper, how can I help you?"

"Ma'am, I'm Sergeant Hunter with the South Carolina Highway Patrol. We need you to come to Charleston as soon as you can, concerning a van which reportedly rammed your vehicle. I believe you made an emergency call to us for help, is that correct?"

"Yes, sir, I did. I was afraid for my life, so I sped up and continued my drive to Georgetown, where I live. I was fortunate to get away from whoever was attacking me."

"I understand, and we don't blame you at all for that, but we need you to come file a report in person. Were you aware that we responded to your call, and that we apprehended one suspect? The other man was killed in the shootout. One of my men died, also."

Paula tossed the covers aside and slid into her bathrobe and slippers. She paced the floor while concentrating on the conversation. She hated being awakened from a dead sleep with serious business.

"I'm very sorry for the loss of your patrolman, sir," said Paula, as she put her hand to her mouth. "I was aware the Highway Patrol responded, but I didn't know what happened after I saw the patrol cars and the van disappear from my rearview mirror."

"Thank you, Miss Cooper. We do have the man in custody who was tailing you. We would also like to see if you could give us a positive ID. Maybe you will recognize him. We suspect from talking with the FBI that this man may be working for the same people who killed Judge Parks. It's just a theory, but it needs to be checked out. How soon can you be here?"

"It's 7:10 AM now, and you are in Charleston? Hmm, I can be there around 9:00 AM at the earliest, Sergeant Hunter. Could you give me directions?"

"Yes, ma'am, we will be at the Charleston County Jail. Do you know where that is, Miss Cooper?"

"Oh, yes, unfortunately I do." *How ironic*, she thought, *I can't get away from that place, it seems.* "I'll call my attorney and see if he's available to join me. That would be alright, wouldn't it?"

"Yes, ma'am, you certainly have that right; however, we are not questioning you. We are just asking you to help us identify this man, if possible, and file a report."

"Will the FBI be there by any chance?"

"I believe they are sending an Agent Dibbs, ma'am."

Paula walked to the bathroom with the portable phone, and opened a drawer where her mother stored the towels. She reached inside the shower and turned the knobs to heat up the water.

"In that case, I'll call you back to confirm the time of my arrival, Sergeant Hunter. I need to call my attorney. I would like to have someone present with me, if all you guys are going to be there. I'm sure you understand."

"That will be fine, Miss Cooper. I'll look for your call."

The hunt for the murderer of Judge Parks and Dave McCaffery had developed quickly. Every branch of law enforcement was working together, following all leads. Special Agent John Dibbs' office was appointed as lead man in the investigation. Signs were quickly posted, and there were public service announcements on television for a reward of one-hundred thousand dollars for information leading to the arrest and conviction of Judge Parks' murderer.

Paula explained to her father what had just transpired, then jumped in the shower. Her head was spinning as the water beat down on her body. *Who is trying to kill me, and who the heck is this guy they have arrested?* she wondered. The hot shower at her parents' home felt great compared to the tepid water of the county jail facilities. The creature comforts of freedom, compared to what a jail provided, were as different as summer from winter. She remembered the cold, stained tile flooring and ancient showerhead that barely trickled water. In the jail facility, she had to turn carefully to wet her body enough to feel as if she had showered. It was something she never wanted to repeat.

As Paula shampooed her hair, she racked her brain, thinking about the party and everyone she had noticed. She remembered seeing a man in the valet crew who had dark features, possibly one of the suspects the FBI was trying to find. She heard him speak to others with a broken accent when he took the keys from a guest to park his car. *Oh, my God,* she thought, *what's going on? I have been the target of someone who wanted both the judge and me dead.*

Paula stepped out of the shower. Water trickled down her body as she dabbed her face with a hand towel and then toweled off. She ran the blow dryer through her hair and found a change of clothes. Quickly, she put them on, applied her makeup, and brushed her hair.

Time to go, let me call Luke, she thought. She rang the attorney's office and found him in early, preparing for a hearing.

"Hello, Luke Bradley, can I help you?"

"What? No receptionist, Luke?"

"She's out picking up the mail...who's calling, please?"

"It's Paula, how soon you forget," she laughed.

"Oh, sorry, I didn't recognize your voice, Paula. I'm still waking up with a latte from Starbucks. It hasn't kicked in yet, I guess."

"No problem, I'm just kidding you. Listen, Luke, I need a big favor. If possible, could you meet me at the county jail around 9:30 AM?"

"I thought we were done with that place. What's going on?" Luke sat back in his chair and sipped his coffee, sliding a legal pad closer in case he needed to make notes.

"I'll tell you more when I get there, but to make the explanation short, an attempt was made on my life yesterday while driving home. This guy rammed the back of my vehicle, and the police have one of the suspects in custody. The FBI will be there when they question me about this man. Get the picture?"

"Clear as Kodak on fine paper, Paula. I have a hearing at 1:30 PM that I'm preparing for, but I can squeeze that in. I'll see you there. Take care."

"Good-bye, and thanks, Luke. See you soon."

The drive to Charleston was uneventful for Paula. She called the sergeant, adjusted her arrival time to allow for Luke, and arrived at the Charleston County Jail a little after nine. A deputy, watching at the entrance, opened the front door. Luke was already there in the lobby, chatting with Agents Dibbs and Mendez. She entered the building, catching the men's heads swivel around to look up and down her tailored frame. She was tired of the excessive attention and despised their obvious crudeness. *At least Luke is more of a gentleman, than these two,* Paula thought, smoothing her reaction so that it wouldn't show.

"Good morning, Paula."

"Hi, Luke, how are you this morning?"

"I'm well, thanks. Excuse me just a moment, will ya?"

"Sure, do what you need to do; I'm good."

"Deputy, can we have a conference room for ten minutes please?" Luke asked. "We have a lineup to go to at 9:30."

"Yes, sir, Mr. Bradley, right over there," the deputy said, as he pointed to the left side of the lobby. "Use that one. It's not exactly a conference room, but it oughta be big enough for the two of you."

"Thanks, Deputy. We appreciate the accommodation," said Luke. He tugged at Paula's sleeve ushering her into the small room before anyone could approach her.

"Paula, just stay calm and relaxed in there with those men. I know you don't know exactly what to expect, and lineup identification can be a little intimidating. If you recognize the man, just say so. The prisoners won't be able to see or hear you. If law enforcement asks you anything that I disapprove of, I'll be with you in there and let you know."

172

Paula nodded, gripping her purse strap.

"Yeah, sure, I can do that," she said.

"Okay, let's get out there and do what we need to do. Take a deep breath and focus on the task at hand," Luke said.

Paula inhaled slowly, her chest rising, and smiled, thinking about how fortunate she was to have Luke representing her. The various representatives of the Highway Patrol, the FBI, and the Sheriff's office were all assembled, some seated, others standing in a room on the second floor behind a one-way glass, which overlooked the ground floor where the prisoners would be brought in for the lineup. As Luke and Paula entered, they all stood and greeted the now famous duo, at least in their circles.

"If you will sit here, ma'am," said Sheriff Bates. "Luke, you can sit there, next to your client."

They were seated at a small table directly against the one-way glass with optimum viewing of the area where the line-up would occur.

"Thank you, Sheriff Bates; it's a pleasure to see you again."

"Alright, bring in the prisoners," said Sheriff Bates through a microphone.

Three men walked in, bound with handcuffs and leg chains, clad in their gaudy orange jump suits with white letters on the back, indicating Charleston County Jail.

"Keep walking to the blue tape on the floor, men. Okay, stop right there and turn to face the glass wall," commanded the deputy escorting the prisoners.

The men stopped on the blue tape in the shape of an x, which indicated where they were to stand. They turned in unison as the deputy barked, one man expressionless, and two men with smirks on their faces trying to show their insolence for law enforcement.

"Paula? Do you recognize any of the men assembled here?" asked Sheriff Bates.

John Dibbs leaned forward with interest to view the lineup and Paula's reaction as she studied each one carefully.

"There," she said gesturing, "the one in the middle looks like a man who parked cars at the judge's party, but I don't know if he was in that van."

"Are you sure about that, Paula?" asked Luke.

"I'm pretty sure," she said. "I remember seeing that scowl on his face."

"Then this may be one of the men who tried to kill you yesterday on the bridge," said Dibbs.

Paula's heartbeat quickened as she heard this. "The man who may have killed Dave and Judge Parks now wants me dead, but why? No matter what he or his superiors had against the judge, why would he try to kill me? If Hernandez had ordered Judge Parks killed, chances are high that he didn't even know who I was."

"Don't count on it, Paula. Think about these men very carefully. Look closely at them. Your life may depend on recognizing the culprit," said Dibbs. "Is this the man who you saw working at Judge Wilmont Parks' house last Saturday night?"

Sheriff Bates gave a hand signal for the prisoners to turn sideways to the left. Paula looked carefully at a scar—long and jagged. She remembered seeing it across the man's cheek at the party. "Now turn to your right and hold," said the Sheriff.

"That's him. It has to be him...the one with the wavy dark hair and angry-looking eyes. I know it's him by the big scar on his face," she said.

"Are you sure?" asked Agent Dibbs.

Her heart pounded in her chest so strongly that she thought it would explode. Luke tapped his foot and then cleared his throat, trying to get her attention. Paula appeared to be daydreaming. She stared deeply, as if in a trance, at the man, without making a sound. After a moment, she blurted out again loudly, "That's him! I know it. That's him...the one in the middle."

"Alright, men," said the Sheriff, "take the prisoners back to their cells."

Luke clutched Paula's perspiring hand to comfort her. She needed a moment to compose herself before signing a statement acknowledging the identity of the suspect. "Paula, we will have to take our chances with the Feds now. How they want to pursue this is really up to Agent John Dibbs. Are you up to answering any more questions?" Luke asked. "I'm sure that Agent Dibbs is going to have a few for you."

"I can handle that, Luke. I think I'd rather get it done now. I'm relieved that the perpetrators are apprehended."

"Agent Dibbs, Sheriff Bates, and you other gentlemen," Luke said, as he turned to face them, "if you have any questions for my client, she would be happy to answer them now. Also, if you have any papers for Miss Cooper to sign, she is available to do that, as well."

"Yes, Mr. Bradley, we'll be right with you," said Dibbs.

Sheriff Bates nodded his head to the Highway Patrol official, accepting other paperwork from him. "Luke, give us one minute," said Sheriff Bates. The law enforcement officials had a brief conference before walking to the other end of the room where Paula and Luke waited at their table.

"Mr. Bradley and Miss Cooper, this is Sergeant Bill Neeley of the South Carolina Highway Patrol. He has some paperwork for you to sign regarding the blue van and persons you saw rear-ending you yesterday," said Sheriff Bates.

Paula and Luke looked over the papers. Luke muttered some of the verbiage aloud, as he speed-read the document then indicated to Paula where to sign on the appropriate line.

"Thank you, ma'am, and good luck to you," said Sergeant Neeley, as he turned to leave the office. "I hope things settle down for you soon, ma'am." He tipped his hat in typical Southern fashion.

"Thank you, Sergeant, I certainly hope so," said Paula graciously.

"This is Special Agent Dibbs of the FBI," said the Sheriff. "I believe you two have met him already?"

"Yes, we have," said Luke. Paula and Luke braced themselves, not knowing what strategy he would pursue or what questions he might have for them.

"Miss Cooper, as you are aware, this is a high-profile case, with every major paper and news station watching very closely. You also know that someone wants you dead. We do not suspect you to be a part of these murders; however, please be aware that you will be called on to testify in court regarding the identification of this man you saw today in the lineup."

Paula nodded to Agent Dibbs. Luke responded for her. "Yes, Agent Dibbs, we are aware of that."

"Further, Miss Cooper, if there is anything you can tell us to assist in the investigation we would appreciate your input. As you may know, your former boss is in our custody, facing charges of conspiracy to commit blackmail. You stated in a sworn statement that you were a part of his plan in going to Judge Parks' home last Saturday night, but that you did your best to pull out of the plot. Was Mr. Denby involved in any way with this murder?" asked Agent Dibbs.

Paula looked at her attorney for guidance. He leaned over whispering in her ear that she was free to speak if she wanted to.

"Agent Dibbs, we've been over this before. All I can tell you is that Mr. Denby is a tricky and ruthless man. He had a lot to gain by having the judge throw the EPA case out of court, but I can't see why he would have wanted to kill him. He sent me there to do a job. Denby wanted Judge Parks and I on camera in an embrace. I don't know what else he had in his twisted mind."

"Very well, Miss Cooper," said Dibbs. "We'll be in touch with you if we need further assistance. These are papers ordering you not to leave the state. You are a prime witness in this case, and we may have someone following you for your protection."

"My client amicably agrees to those stipulations and arrangements, Agent Dibbs."

Luke could tell her nerves were frayed and that she needed the security of knowing help was nearby, if necessary, so another protector on her trail couldn't hurt since his man had gone missing in action during the last incident. Luke did tell the man he thought the critical danger was past for now, so he blamed himself, as well. The private investigator, usually very conscientious, typically would have followed Paula off the island to her home. Still, Luke was puzzled at the detective's lack of skill at a crucial time.

"Agent Dibbs, you don't really think I'm involved any more than I have already told you, do you? I have told you everything I can remember," Paula added.

"No, ma'am, we don't suspect you at this time, other than what we have already discussed. That is all I can say at this point."

"Thank you, Agent Dibbs."

"You are free to do as you please, Miss Cooper. We are not going to restrict your movement as long as you stay within the state of South Carolina," said Agent Dibbs. "We may need you again on short notice. Thank you for coming down this morning. Have a safe trip back home."

"Yes, I will, Agent Dibbs."

She opened her purse, pulling out a compact mirror to check if her makeup and mascara were still in place. Still pondering the situation, she knew that the suspect was there at the party as a member of the valet staff, but she thought she had seen him somewhere else before. She hoped that in time her memory would come back.

"Paula, that's all for today. We're done here, and you did great. Let's get out of here," said Luke, as he gathered the paperwork given to them by the law enforcement

"That sounds good to me, Luke. I don't like the smell of these places."

Luke and Paula left the viewing room and exited the complex. He escorted Paula in the parking lot to her SUV positioned not far from his vehicle.

"I'm glad you made a positive I.D. Maybe it's something they can work with."

"I sure hope so. I do not like being in the middle of all this. I feel like I have a target on my back."

"Yeah, that's gotta be tough. I am sorry, Paula, but once again, I have to get rolling. Call me if you need me. Otherwise, I'll be in touch with you when we need to get together again."

"I appreciate you coming on such short notice, Luke."

"No problem, I'm glad I was available. You didn't need to be here alone. I'll mail you copies of these papers for your files. See you later, and watch your backside, okay?"

"Yeah, I will. It's about time I do. For years I have left that to you men," she said purposefully, to lighten the somber mood a little.

Luke chuckled and wagged his head. Paula smiled that she was able to make him laugh.

"Luke, I'll call you if anything else comes up. And thanks again."

"It's my pleasure, Paula. Where are you heading now?"

"I think I'm going to go to the Market Place, since I'm already in Charleston, to browse a few shops and maybe check out a favorite bookstore of mine. I need to try to relax and to take this stuff off my mind for a while."

"Sounds like a good plan. You know how to reach me. I'll see you later."

"Yeah, I do. I have your cell number now. You're in trouble." Paula said, half-joking. "You take care, as well."

18

Federal Penitentiary: Miami, Florida

"Hernandez," shouted the guard, "you have other visitors."

Manuel Hernandez looked up at the guard from his station where he sat across from a female visitor.

"Okay, señor, I'll finish up with my friend, and be ready in a couple of minutes."

The guard acknowledged his reply and made the visitors comfortable showing them to a seated waiting area. Hernandez was fortunate to be in a federal prison where naps after meals were optional. Recreation was encouraged with table tennis, shuffleboard, weight lifting, various board games, television, and movies in the evening. Phone privileges were liberal with time served for good behavior and exemplary work. Hernandez was only allowed certain visitors, so he had no idea who was coming to see him unannounced.

He had a local man he contacted from prison who ran his drug-smuggling operations. The money trail ran through banks in the Cayman Islands. The only thing that he lacked was his freedom. Through Maria Garcia, his so-called wife, he delivered messages too sensitive and detailed to handle by phone. Recently, Maria had become pregnant on one conjugal visit when Hernandez was in a state prison before his transfer to the federal prison, which hindered her business dealings. She was responsible for conducting many of the final negotiations on large shipments of cocaine and marijuana; including how and where the shipments would arrive. Many times, things would go wrong, and she intervened to get them back on track. Her word was the same as that of Hernandez, and no one challenged it.

Maria and Manuel never cared much for convention or the laws of man. They wanted to be powerful and rich, no matter whom they hurt, or what they did to accomplish their goals. They trusted each other with their lives, but now that Maria was five months pregnant with their first child, she had new concerns. Manuel was upset that she was pregnant at this particular time of the year because the cocaine harvests and shipments were in peak season. Negotiations on sealing deals were backed up until Maria could make her rounds, and morning sickness prevented her from operating at full speed.

"Manuel, I have to find someone else to train for this work. You know that I am carrying our baby now."

"I know," said Manuel, "why don't you have an abortion? You know we are not married and the church will frown upon your pregnancy anyway."

Maria's facial expression turned from concern to displeasure as she waved one arm in front of her. Her blood pressure elevated, and a vein in her forehead protruded.

"Manuel, look at you talking about what the church will think. With all that we do, how can you say that? What does the Catholic Church say about abortion, huh? Do you think that I am going to abort my first baby? I am going to have this baby. I was raised Catholic, too."

Surprised at her vehement reaction, Manuel knew better than to push the issue. Maria did not put her foot down often, but when she did, he knew how to read her. "You're right, Maria. I'm not thinking straight. It just came as a surprise, and I'm concerned about our future with me in this joint. I guess we can have our baby."

"I'm glad to hear you say that, Manuel," she said, as she put her hand on her tummy rubbing it a little as if to soothe the hurt feelings of their unborn. "Something else is bothering you though. What is it?"

"You read me like a book, Maria. I'm concerned about who we can trust to be our negotiator. Who do we know that can handle this kind of responsibility? Name one person for me so that we can train him pronto."

Maria was hoping that Manuel knew of someone, but he was not sure of anyone else to trust to make the deals, collect the money, and handle the deposits. He could not make decisions like this from jail and had to rely on Maria, since she knew better than he did whom to trust. He had been out of the field too long.

"I can suggest someone to you, but you are so jealous that you might not want him."

"Who are you thinking of?"

Maria thought of a former lover that she had off and on before she met Manuel. "What about Antonio Norrez? We have known him for years, and he has always been a good employee of the family. He has worked with the middle transactions to the street dealers for five years now and has never brought any money back short."

"I should have had that traitor killed when I found out he was messing around with you two years ago. If I ever catch the two of you alone together again, I will have both of you shot. Do I make myself clear, Maria?"

Maria hated it when Manuel went into his jealous rants. Antonio was the only lover she had that Manuel knew about, and it was before she officially became his girlfriend, but that did not matter to him. His outrageous temper tantrums had killed men in the past. Still, Maria knew that Antonio could be trusted and she felt that he was the correct choice for the job.

"Very clear, Manuel, what was between Antonio and me is long past. You are too possessive. I have to have room to do my job. He knows what you are capable of doing, and he won't fail us. Just pay him well for the risks he takes and be fair with him, as you would do for a brother, and he will serve the family well. I'm sure of it."

"I guess he's the only one who can step in and do what you have been doing, but if he screws up or double-crosses me,I'll have him shot and left for the dogs to lick his blood."

Maria was used to Manuel's tirades and learned to change the subject to get him on to something else. "By the way, Manuel, did you hear about Judge Parks being shot last Saturday night? Didn't you want him dead? Whoever shot him granted your wish."

"Yeah, I heard about it, but I didn't have anything to do with that."

She knew that if he did, he would avoid saying anything about it, but out of curiosity, Maria wanted to see his eyes. She could read him as well as anyone but was not sure what she saw this time. Some things Manuel did not share with her because he did not want her involved, especially with things like assassinations of judges or political figures.

"Hello, down there, Miss Garcia, visiting hours are over now," belted out the prison guard. "It's time to clear the visiting room of all guests. Prisoners are to remain until all guests have exited and then file out single file for a body search before returning to your cell," said the sturdy guard.

"Yes, sir," Maria replied. "Manuel, I'll set things up, don't you worry."

"Okay, baby, I love you."

She stood to her feet and exited like a toy soldier. On a previous visit, she ignored the guard for a few minutes, and their visitation was suspended for a month.

"Hernandez, stand by until the others leave. You will meet with your visitors in the conference room."

"Me? Are you sure, guard? What did I do to deserve this privilege?"

"Just shut up and wait, Hernandez. If you smart off to me one more time, you'll lose your television time for the rest of the week, you got that?"

"Yes señor, I got that."

Hernandez waited quietly as the other prisoners exited the visiting area. The guard led the way out of the visitation area to a conference room used by law enforcement and attorneys to meet with the prisoners. The visitors for Hernandez were two men. One was Agent John Dibbs and the second, Agent Albert Mendez. With less experience than Dibbs, Mendez still proved to be very valuable because he was bilingual. Another guard opened the door to the conference room and entered with the agents.

"Hello, Mr. Hernandez, I'm Albert Mendez with the FBI, and this is my partner, John Dibbs," said Mendez, in Spanish.

"Hola, Señores Mendez y Dibbs. How can I be of service to you?"

Hernandez was being polite against his nature because he was scheduled to come up for a parole hearing in a couple of months. Additionally, his subconscious enjoyed a Hispanic person greeting him in his native tongue, even if he was law enforcement.

"We have some questions to ask you regarding the murders of Judge Wilmont Parks and Dave McCaffery. Can you tell us anything that may be of help?" asked Agent Mendez.

Dibbs and Mendez did not have anything concrete on Hernandez, but were fishing, hoping to flush out a lead that might lead them in the right direction. Pablo Esteban, the apprehended suspect and culprit, who attacked Paula, was not talking from his prison cell at the county jail.

"Señor Mendez, I have every reason to behave here. Did you know that my sentence carries a parole for good behavior? I'm sorry to disappoint you men, but I had nothing to do with the murders, and I don't know anything about them. You are wasting your time here," said Hernandez.

"We have reason to believe you had a motive to have Judge Parks killed. Why should we believe you, Mr. Hernandez? He was the judge who sentenced you to the maximum time allowed by law. Didn't you swear that you would kill him as you were being escorted from the courtroom?" said Dibbs.

"People say things in anger they do not mean, gentlemen. It's as I said, Señores Dibbs and Mendez, I am up for parole on good behavior. Why would I want to jeopardize that? Did you see that beautiful woman who was leaving as you were coming in? She's my woman and pregnant with my child. I want to be with her and raise a family."

"You may be telling the truth, but if you are lying, it will come out when we get to the bottom of this. You are mistaken if you think we can't get Pablo Esteban to talk. He's facing murder one and behind bars as we speak," said Mendez.

"Who is he? I don't know a Pablo Esteban." Hernandez spread his hands flat on the table and leaned forward. "Look, I know that you men are anxious to solve this case, but again, I didn't have anything to do with it. Let me ask you men this...if I am able to find out who your man is, can you swing a deal for me at my parole hearing?"

Agent Dibbs was not convinced that Hernandez was free of guilt but agreed with him anyway to gain assistance. A break in the case seemed far away at this point, except for the arrest of Esteban, and the police could not hang their hats on his testimony because he was not talking. The press hounded relentlessly with articles titled, "No Suspect Arrested in Murder of Judge Parks." Dibbs wanted to solve the case on its merits and because he was up for promotion. He wanted one day to become a Deputy Director with the FBI, and he knew that solving this case would be a big step forward in his career.

Dibbs, after holding his peace, spoke out, "If you are able to point me to the killer, Manuel, I will give a statement as to your cooperation in helping us. That is the best that I can do. The rest is up to the parole board."

"Very well, Señor Dibbs, I'll do what I can."

After Agents Dibbs and Mendez left, Hernandez was escorted back to his cell. He thought about what he could come up with to improve his chances at parole.

Dibbs started the car and pulled out of the parking lot, heading back to Miami International. Pulling out on the freeway, the agents rehashed the interview.

"Okay, Mendez, what do you think?"

"I don't like the drug pusher. I'm not sure what he knows, but I know I don't like him."

"I didn't ask you if you liked him. I asked what you thought," Dibbs snapped, as he glanced at his partner.

"I've got a hunch that he's not involved with the murder of Judge Parks. I think he's trying to help us, if we'll help him. I bet he's afraid that one of his punks is messing with his pregnant girlfriend, and he wants to get out of prison as soon as he can to take care of her," said Mendez.

"You do have a point there. He's like a caged animal in there. I need to think about all the players in the case some more."

"John, what have you been able to find out from Denby? I think he knows something, and his firm is already falling apart."

"That may be true, Mendez; keep talking."

"Well, Denby had the most to gain, and he does know an awful lot about Judge Parks. He put a very thorough team together to study the judge. There was the private investigator, McCaffery, Paula Cooper, and the other young attorney we discovered who was assigned to study cases that Judge Parks ruled on for the past five years. Also, as I read the files confiscated from Denby Law Firm, I ran across something interesting."

"What was that, Albert?"

Mendez flipped through his briefcase and pulled out his notepad. "Denby made a reference to the CEO of Colonial Paper offering a huge incentive bonus, if the firm was able to get the environmental case thrown out of court. You knew that the EPA was fining them five million for pollution of the wetlands, right?"

"Of course, if the Feds win that case, then many parties who are affected by the same pollution are sure to jump on board with their own lawsuits. That's why I'm thinking that the CEO of Colonial might know something," said Dibbs.

"There's a very strong possibility that he does. Agent Blanding, who we sent snooping around Georgetown, says the CEO is up for evaluation by the Board of Directors and seeking a five-year contract extension. I'm sure that Mr. Walker is hoping to get more money. He runs a very lucrative and profitable company, and his future with Colonial Paper is hinging on this case. I would venture to guess that he was not depending on Denby alone to get the job done."

"That's exactly right, Mendez. We'll follow that lead and see where it takes us. In the meantime, Denby requested to see me about some new information that he wants to share. Why don't you set up an appointment with the CEO of Colonial Paper, Paul Walker? I'll follow up with Denby to get what I can out of him, and we'll commiserate tomorrow."

"You know, John, as we go deeper in this case, it's plain to see that there were several people who wanted Judge Parks dead. The man didn't have a chance. His death was imminent. When we get back, I'll get right on it," said Mendez, making a note on his calendar."

"Whoever killed Judge Parks bought some time before the case is heard. How much? Well, we'll just have to wait and see. We will know more after we interview Paul Walker. Have a background check run on him as soon as we get back to the office, as well," Dibbs replied.

"Ten-four, good buddy. We'll talk later after more has developed. Oh, one more thing... let's not leave out Eleanor Parks, who stood to benefit from Judge Parks' death, also," Mendez interjected.

"Oh, yeah, no way; she's down for a good scrutiny, too," said Dibbs.

The agents got out of the car at the parking lot of Miami International Airport and headed up the elevator to the main concourse.

"You called the local office to pick up the car, didn't you?" Dibbs asked.

"Yep, I left a message with the secretary. We're good to go. Loaning us the LTD was good of them."

"What time is our flight? Do you know off the top of your head, Mendez?"

"Sure do, Flight 714 should leave at 3:15 PM, according to this ticket," Mendez said, as he pushed it back in his shirt pocket.

"Cool, we won't have to wait long then," Dibbs said.

The agents rode the crowded airport train to their gate and exited as the automatic doors opened.

"Let's grab a seat over there and peruse a magazine or paper while we wait," said Dibbs.

"That works for me. I wouldn't mind getting off my feet for a while. I put on the wrong shoes this morning, and my feet are killing me."

"What did I tell you about wearing those pointy alligator shoes, Mendez?" Dibbs asked, laughing at his partner.

"Shut up, John. These shoes never did break in as they should have, but they are too pointed. They are going back to the far side of my closet as soon as I can get them off my feet."

Mendez joined his partner in a cushioned seat beside him. He grabbed an abandoned magazine to flip through, while Dibbs rifled through USA Today.

"Flight number 714 is now loading at Gate 44. All women with children, and pregnant women, and persons with disabilities are asked to board now," the announcer boomed through the intercom.

The agents peered over the tops of their periodicals sporadically until the next announcement came allowing all remaining persons to board.

19

Denby, now released and on bail, was back working at his practice in Georgetown. Since his arrest, he had lost three attorneys, his most valued paralegal, and one secretary to the blackmail fiasco. He was in a foul mood and racking his brain, trying to figure out how he could create enough usable information to obtain a favorable plea bargain on the conspiracy charge. The District Attorney's office had only agreed to allow him freedom for the time being, with charges pending. If he did not provide pertinent information, and fully disclose every source he had, which might lead the authorities to the culprit, then he most likely would receive a stiff sentence in federal prison.

Hunched forward with his chin resting on his left hand, Denby sat at his desk, his right hand tapped his desk repetitively in rhythmic fashion from little finger to index. *What more do I know that would be of interest to the FBI?* he thought. His motivation to help was high since he had never spent a day in his life behind bars, before he was arrested. The only thing that occurred to him was his telephone conversation with Paul Walker. He remembered how Walker bumped the already generous bonus of one-half million to one million dollars, providing that Denby got the case thrown out of court. He also remembered how upset his childhood friend became when he shared his doubts about the plot possibly not working because of problems with his heretofore-trusted paralegal.

Denby went to the filing cabinet and rummaged through the Colonial folder, looking for the faxed confirmation. *It should be here*, he thought. He worried for a second that he had misplaced it, but he knew that he would not have discarded such an important document. Suddenly, a memory flashed through his brain like Haley's comet lighting up the sky. He bounded up from his desk and went to his secret safe, hidden behind a large framed picture of an old English foxhunt. Hurriedly, he turned the dial on the combination lock. No one, not even Paula, who had access to the most sensitive files and records at the firm, knew about his hidden strongbox in the wall. Hidden in the metal box were documents and secret agreements, which could get an attorney reprimanded or disbarred by the South Carolina Bar Association.

He extracted a locked metal box the length of a legal pad, but considerably thicker, which he took to his desk and opened with a small key. Denby set the folder and all of the box's contents before him. Among the other items were a few thousand in cash, a small black address book, and a loaded nine-millimeter automatic that he kept on hand in case of an emergency. An irate person on the other end of a divorce case had threatened him a couple of times in his career. Once, a man came into his office waving a loaded pistol looking for him, but Denby was privy to the situation and left after calling 911 for the police to apprehend the idiot. He opened the folder marked with the letter C and located the fax.

Should I turn this note in to the FBI? he thought. *If I do, they will think I was withholding information. If I don't, I may not provide them with anything substantial enough to exculpate myself from a long prison term.*

Never before had Denby ever contemplated suicide, but the thought did rush through his mind, like an NFL linebacker bearing down on a doomed quarterback. The pistol lay there on his desk and seemed to say, "I'm your easy way out of this embarrassment. Pick me." Not being the kind of man to do such a thing, he resisted the fleeting thought.

"Oh, well, that bastard Walker will have to do some explaining," Denby muttered. "I'm not taking the rap all by myself."

He left the folder on his desk and returned the rest of the contents to the metal box. Placing the box back inside the wall safe, he spun the dial, locking it. *Serves him right for dropping me like a hot potato as soon as I was arrested,* he mused. He hoped that this would be his ace in the hole to deliver him from a long sentence, which he most certainly faced unless a deal was struck. On the other hand, would Denby find that his efforts to help the FBI were insufficient? He had always been an expert at making things seem more significant than they were, so he liked his chances nonetheless. The possibility that Paul Walker was behind an elaborate scheme to murder Judge Parks did seem highly unlikely to him. He dismissed the thought that this homegrown product of Georgetown, SC, the CEO of Colonial Paper, would have dared to do such a thing.

Leaning back in his armchair he thought again about who might be involved with the murder. Earlier that morning, he had read an article in the paper on Judge Parks' life. It was a complete biography of his childhood forward to college years. It continued with interesting facts on his career mixed with blurbs about his unhappy marriage to his estranged wife.

Being separated from her husband and having hard feelings over the proposed settlement seemed to give her motive, he thought. Two large insurance policies, one less than six months old of two million dollars, seemed rather fishy. Denby also suspected Hernandez, remembering the drug lord's revengeful outburst in the courtroom when Judge Parks read his sentence.

Determined to do all he could to obtain leniency, the attorney called Agent Dibbs and agreed to fax the secret document he had received from Paul Walker. He dialed the fax number on his outdated machine, pressed the green SEND button, waiting for the irritating fax signal to screech. "Transmission Complete" flashed on the LED, and a printout verifying the fax slid out from the bottom portion of the machine, automatically chopping off with a guillotine-like motion. He thought about decapitation and realized that what he had done was similarly self-destructive. Reversing what had been set in motion was now impossible, and the worst of outcomes was falling down on him.

20

The executive board of Heartland Insurance Company convened at nine in the morning to discuss their quarterly business reports. The usual items were covered: premium increase proposals, claims payments, and actuarial reports. Special investigation reports were authorized for claims to be paid on policies that were under two years old due to the contestability clause, which was included in all policies. This clause allowed insurance companies to challenge the validity of a claim and deny payment where cause was found. Numerous cases were discovered where foul play had occurred with owners and beneficiaries of policies that were within these time limits, saving insurance companies millions of dollars. The Chief Executive Officer of Heartland, Bob Tisdale, called the meeting to order with three sharp raps of a wooden gavel.

"Members of the Board, we call this meeting to order to bring you up to date on last quarter's earnings and to forecast the next quarter's growth. Mr. Beckley, would you give us your report, please?" asked Tisdale.

Mr. Beckley, the Chief Financial Officer, recited the numbers from the last quarter's earnings forecasting strong growth for the next quarter.

"Thank you, Mr. Beckley. In addition, we're investigating one large policy, less than a year old, whose payout, if legitimate, is two million dollars. The suspicious circumstances of this policy, which was taken out just six months before the death of the insured, alerted our claims department to take a close look before paying the beneficiary. The decision to hire a private investigator has been implemented."

The meeting adjourned; some members of the executive board returned to their jobs within Heartland and others headed home, this being their only function for Heartland. Insurance companies had ninety days either to pay the claim or to offer some reason for the delay.

After the small crowd dispersed, Mr. Tisdale returned to his office and dialed the phone number of a private investigator, Nancy Bailey, who lived in the Charleston area. "Miss Bailey, this is Bob Tisdale, CEO of the Heartland Insurance Company. You have worked for us on another case, I believe?"

"Yes, Mr. Tisdale, I have. Thank you for calling. How can I help you?"

"We need you to investigate a potential two-million dollar claim on a beneficiary. We need to know all we can on this person. She's a local resident in your area and has a life insurance policy which is only six months old."

"I sure can, sir. What's her name and information?"

"Her name is Eleanor Parks, the widow of the late Judge Wilmont Parks, who was killed a couple of weeks ago. Her address has not been updated in our database since her separation from Judge Parks. You can find it though, right?"

"Yes, I've seen the incident in the news, Mr. Tisdale, and actually followed the case out of my own curiosity. Terrible thing that happened to Judge Parks...he was an honorable man, from all accounts I have heard. As far as finding her address and the information, that's what you pay me for, sir. It won't be a problem."

"Very good, then, Miss Bailey, I'm sure that you are aware that he was murdered. Our position is that we need to rule out Mrs. Parks before we can pay the claim."

"Yes, sir, I'm aware of the insurance laws. I will check everything possible on her. How often do you want reports?"

"Let's say twice per week, on Monday and Thursday by noon. If you run across anything of super importance, contact us immediately."

"That works for me, Mr. Tisdale."

"Will the fees and arrangements be as before, Miss Bailey?"

"About my fees...I did go up a little since a year and a half ago when I worked that last case for your company. I get four-fifty per day now, plus expenses, instead of four-hundred."

"That's fine; just submit your invoice and expense report to our payroll department weekly like you did before. We will mail you a check each week, as soon as the reports are submitted, and our CFO authorizes it. Is that fair enough?"

"It sure is. I'll be in touch, as we agreed."

Bailey hung up her phone and immediately began a stakeout of Eleanor Parks. She tailed her to the Salon de Paris, which was doing its usual brisk business on an early Saturday morning. Now, two weeks after the death of Judge Parks, Eleanor dropped in at her usual 10:00 AM appointment time. She had a complete hair and nail appointment scheduled today. Afterwards, she was heading to King Street to purchase new clothes, swimwear, a straw hat, and sandals for her cruise.

Eleanor would soon embark on a cruise with a beau she had been discreetly seeing just before her separation from Judge Parks. She knew gossip would fly if she appeared to be partying so soon after her family tragedy, but Chuck Eastwood, a jazz musician by trade, had swept her off her feet. He convinced her that she needed to get away from the rumor mill and stress, if only for a short while.

Chuck built Eleanor up in many places within her mind and heart that were torn down by her failed marriage to Judge Parks. She had fallen head over heels in love with him, and they planned secretly to marry on the cruise in the Caribbean. It was the best choice for them because the quick marriage, so soon after the judge's death would certainly be viewed as improper by their friends and the public at large. They planned to have a public wedding in Charleston later, one that her friends could approve of.

"Guten morgen, Mrs. Parks," said Greta, the nail technician, as she seated Eleanor at her station. "How are you? And how is that hunk of man you were with last Saturday ven you came in?"

Nancy Bailey arrived just a little after Eleanor and was seated in a nearby station to get her nails done. As she chitchatted briefly with the technician, she eavesdropped on Eleanor and Greta.

"Yeah, he's a musician, nice-looking, and very good to me. We're going on a cruise tomorrow for a few days. You need to tuck that under your little hat, Greta, okay? I know I shouldn't be talking about a relationship so soon, but I can't help myself. I haven't felt this way in years."

"No problem, anything you say to me is kept behind these four walls. Are cruise lines running any specials?"

"No special, just two lovebirds looking for a place to get away for a while," she said, giggling.

"This sounds serious. How long are you two going to be gone?"

"Five days and four nights…I'm so excited."

"I bet you are, Mrs. Parks."

"You have no idea, Greta. I'm not going to worry about a thing. I plan to do whatever my heart desires since I don't have to answer to anyone about how I spend the money for once in my life."

"Oh, that must be nice," said Greta. "I have to watch how I spend mine."

Nancy Bailey turned her head at a better angle to capture what Eleanor said, over the buzz of electric fingernail files and fans. The new earpiece that Miss Bailey wore in her ear made her hearing four times better, like that of a canine, the salesperson had told her.

"Yes, Greta, between you and me, Judge Parks left me well-off with life insurance benefits, and all but one company has paid off."

"Oh really, vell, that's always nice in the middle of a tragic situation, not to have to worry about financial matters."

"Yes, there were three policies in all, and the one that hasn't paid yet is a big one that I took out just before we separated. I don't know what made me do that. I'm expecting the benefits on that one any day now, but as you have probably heard, they are still looking for my deceased husband's killers."

"Did you say killers plural? I read in the paper that law enforcement was looking for one man."

"Yes, from what I have been able to gather, the authorities think there may have been some sort of conspiracy with a hired gun. They don't release that stuff immediately."

"I'm so sorry that this tragedy happened. I know it must be tough on you."

"Thank you, Greta. I'll bounce back in time."

"I'm sure you vill, Eleanor. There, your nails are all set. You have a vunderful time on your trip, and try not to worry."

"Thanks, I appreciate that. My nails look great," said Eleanor, as she looked at them approvingly.

Eleanor tipped Greta with a twenty and moved on to the hair salon within the spa. Eleanor rarely tipped more than five dollars, but like many people who come into an unexpected sum of money, she felt the urge to be more extravagant and share in her good fortune. As she walked down the short hall, she remembered driving by her former home the night of the judge's party to view all the cars. She remembered tipping the taxicab driver a twenty the night of her husband's death. *Odd*, she thought. She reflected on what had been hers at one time when married to the prominent Judge Wilmont Parks.

Reaching the styling salon, she sat down in the waiting area, waiting her turn in the hairstylist's chair. She grabbed a large colorful book of hairdos and thumbed through the pages. Nadine finished up with her current customer, swept the floor, and turned to greet Eleanor.

"Come on over, Mrs. Parks. Have a seat, and tell me what we're doing today," she said.

Eleanor handed the stylist the large book, pointing to a modern style that belied her age. "I've been dying to have my hair done like this for some time. Let's see what you can do to make me look like this one, Nadine," said Eleanor, with her index finger on the picture.

"Very good choice…you do realize that it would look better on you, if you allow me to color your hair like the woman in the book, don't you?"

"Of course, Nadine, but I'm not in a flamboyant mood and don't have time for that today. Just style it like her this time, okay?"

"No problem, just trying to help."

"I know you are, honey. I'll go for the color next time I come in."

"Okay, let's go back to the shampoo sink and do the wash and then we'll come back here and get your style going."

She took her seat by the sink for the shampoo and rinse. The hair stylist worked her magic then draped a towel on Eleanor's head while she walked her client back to her chair.

"By the way, Nadine, I know you are probably aware of my deceased husband's tragic death about two weeks ago. While I know this might seem too soon, I met someone unexpectedly, a Godsend, and we are going on a cruise tomorrow. He's a hunk, and he's the sweetest man I've ever met."

Eleanor had downed a double Bloody Mary that morning before she left her townhouse and was running her mouth like a fast-talking used car salesman. Smacking her gum, she could not shut up about her money, her boyfriend, her shopping, or her trip.

"Yes, I'm aware of your misfortune. I'm glad you found someone to help you through your grief and loneliness." Nadine was a consummate professional at saying what each client wanted to hear to raise customer satisfaction in hopes of maximizing her chances for good tips.

Eleanor felt a little guilty because she did not feel as much grief after Judge Parks' death as she thought she should. She mainly felt relief that she would get what was coming to her after all. She had dreamed of a high station in life when she married the young attorney straight out of Harvard Law School. She wanted to mourn deeper, but when she thought about the way their relationship had deteriorated, she could not feel much one way or the other.

Although, her husband had done practically all that was humanly possible to help, Eleanor did not have the capacity to readily accept blame for her own problems. The judge stopped showing much compassion for her illness of alcoholism after many years had passed when she showed no signs of wanting to change. He was more business-like with her after years of suffering with her embarrassing problem, which she chose to make painfully public at times.

Miss Bailey moved on to the hair section to get a shampoo and trim, as she hung on every word that fell from the loose-tongued widow's mouth. *This will make a good report for Heartland Insurance,* she thought.

❀

Chuck Eastwood was five-feet eleven and had medium brown hair, which he wore combed back with a slight part on one side, giving his face a clean-shaven, boyish look. His five-piece jazz band was the newest hot sensation in the yuppie pubs of Charleston. He had been in town about a year now and had found a niche among the upper crust, the educated, and college students. His band was becoming known for his own brand of New Orleans-style jazz. Charlestonians were smitten with the sound of his band, and delighted that they did not have to travel all the way to New Orleans to experience it.

Eleanor was drinking with a girlfriend the night she met Chuck seven months earlier. He was breaking down the set with his drummer, who stayed late to put the equipment away. Amps, speakers, keyboards, and drums had to be broken down and packed into a small cargo trailer. The following morning the floor space would be used for the buffet breakfast served to the hotel guests.

Eleanor and her friend Jackie had stayed until closing that night. They were up front, clinging to each beat and swaying with the rhythm like a couple of groupies, until the music ended. They sat at their table, making idle chitchat, never minding the fact that they were too inebriated to drive. Chuck was not in the habit of picking up women from his work place, but these two seemed to need help. He had heard several stories of drunken people leaving his gigs, and being arrested for DUI or getting into a bad wreck as they tried to make it home. Noticing the women were the only ones left and inebriated, Chuck decided to be a Good Samaritan.

"Ladies, can I help you in any way? It's almost 2:00 AM, and they are about to lock up. If you two need a ride, I can call a cab for you or take you home, myself, but I hope you're not planning on driving tonight."

"That is awfully sweet of you, sir," said Eleanor with a slur.

"No problem, ladies. Please don't be offended, but I'd do it for anyone in the shape you two are in."

"We're not offended. Let me speak to my friend a minute."

"Jackie, he's right. I can't drive home like this. Can we go to your place? I'll call Will from there and tell him I'm spending the night. I don't feel like hearing a lecture about my drinking, which I'm sure to get if I go home tonight. I need to sleep this bender off before I face him."

"Sure, Eleanor, let's go, but who's going to drive? We're both in no shape to get behind the wheel," said Jackie.

"That's what I'm saying," said Chuck, "Where do you live, ladies? I'm almost finished here and can drop you two off on the way to my place."

"I live near Montagu on Gadsden," said Jackie. "We're going to my place for the night. Would it be too much out of your way?"

"No problem. That's right on my way, in fact. I live about three blocks from there."

"We would appreciate the ride very much. I can come back tomorrow in the daylight and get my car," said Eleanor.

Chuck got a good look at Eleanor as she stood and was attracted to her, even in her woozy state; moreover, she looked like someone with class. *Maybe these ladies will stay out with me to eat some breakfast,* he thought. The three of them climbed in Chuck's van and rode down four blocks and up two, to Jackie's apartment. The two women invited Chuck up for a nightcap, not that they needed one.

After becoming acquainted, Chuck was leaving to get breakfast when he asked Eleanor to keep him company. They shared breakfast, and one thing led to another. She had sobered somewhat, but was enamored with her new musician heartthrob. Chuck took her back to his place and the two were kissing and in the sack in a New York minute. Eleanor was not normally that easy, but she was drinking and had a thing for musicians. She was caught up in the thrill, and in finding someone who made her feel special again without judging her behavior. From that night on, she did not sleep with the judge. Sneaking around town, she continued to sleep with Chuck. Judge Parks was suspicious and got the goods on her from a private detective through a tip from a friend, who had seen them out a few times. He planned to save this information in case he needed it when the negotiations for divorce became critical. He really did not care that Eleanor had slept around on him at this point. He knew the marriage, for all intents and purposes was over, as did Eleanor.

After a couple of weeks of seeing Chuck, she moved out of her home with Judge Parks and into her townhouse by the waterfront. She had fallen in love with Chuck, and he enjoyed having someone to care for him who could be there when closing time came. He was sick of the groupie chicks that would hang out, hoping for a chance with a musician.

Chuck strolled in the Salon de Paris and walked past the busy receptionist locating Eleanor not far from the front. "Well, honey, are you about finished? You said we have shopping to do, and you wanted to get to Hyman's for lunch."

"Chuck, darling, I'm almost done. Would you be kind enough to wait for me in the lobby? Give me ten minutes, and I'll be there."

"Okay, Darling, will do," said Chuck, as he turned on a dime, heading back to the lobby.

Chuck had not been on a cruise for pleasure before, but he knew what to expect because he had a few gigs on cruise ships. Eleanor had taken many cruises, but none like the one she would embark on this time.

Nancy Bailey assessed the couple with a careful eye without them noticing her. Chuck walked past the private investigator to the lobby and winked at her. *The rascal, here he is about to go on a cruise with one woman, and he's winking at me,* she thought. *He's probably an opportunistic dirty dog of a man, taking advantage of his "sugar mama."*

Chuck had been trying to raise funds for a CD that he recorded to market on the Super Stations, but had not found anyone willing to back him. However, his financial problems were solved when Eleanor fell for him and offered assistance. He would soon launch a marketing campaign to sell his CD nationwide with her help. During the cruise, although for pleasure, Chuck arranged to meet with two television executives via videoconference on the last leg of the trip. He needed fifty-grand in start-up money, twenty-five thousand for each television station that would give him short, twenty-second ads for the period of a month. By then, the CD should begin to pay for itself for additional ads, according to the television experts. Chuck thought it was worth a shot. If he could catch a break, he might come into his own with a recording contract, and then be set.

Eleanor chose to back Chuck and not take a percentage of the profit, if he was to make any. This was her wedding gift to him. She figured she had two million dollars coming to her soon, and that she could afford what amounted to the least of her policy benefits, fifty thousand.

Ten minutes elapsed, and Eleanor met Chuck in the lobby. They scampered off to Hyman's Restaurant, voted one of the best restaurants for local seafood many years running, and enjoyed the local fare. After lunch and shopping, they went to Eleanor's townhouse to finish packing and then to the airport for their flight to Miami, where they caught the Caribbean Queen for a five-day cruise.

Nancy Bailey arrived just in time for the cruise ship to leave and blended with the crowd. She wore over-sized dark shades and a straw hat, staying under the radar of the lovebirds. So far, things were looking interesting, but she had nothing that she could really hang her hat on at this point. *A cruise in the Caribbean to tail two possible accomplices in an insurance fraud case...tough job, but someone has to do it*, thought Nancy. More than a thousand bucks per week, and expenses would work out nicely. This would likely continue for a week or two until she prepared a final report for Heartland Insurance. Upon her final report, Tisdale would take the information to the Executive Board on a special sessions meeting, and an official company position would be adopted as to whether the claim would be denied or paid.

21

Calm in the middle of a storm came for Paula and Jim. It was almost February now, and Paula began to send out resumes to Charleston law firms, but no one would hire her until she was officially cleared of all charges. She had to disclose the fact that she was a material witness in Judge Parks' murder case. She did not have to disclose the details of why, but rumors flew, which was not good for her reputation, as she tried to hire on with a quality law firm.

Paula was spending much needed time with Rachel and Christine, who were pummeled with nasty comments and questions at school by some of their peers. Their friends had heard enough of the news about the murder from their parents and media to give them ammunition to harass the girls. Their mother hated this the most, and knew she was to blame. She disclosed as much as she could of what happened, and the reasons why to them to their satisfaction.

Jim's business was going quite well. He invested a large percentage of the profit to build up his inventory. Filling special orders from his clients had become a large portion of his business. He hired a full-time employee to assist him with managing all aspects of the store. Now that Jim had a new employee, Paula's desire to get away for a day or two heightened. They decided to make a trip to the Isle of Palms for a weekend get-away to recharge their batteries. What better place to do it than at the ocean with a friend whom you love. Paula's last trip to the island was to Pelicans' Nook, and though she was with Jim for one night, that trip was not planned totally for pleasure, as this one was.

Jim drove out to Paula's condo around dusk, and picked her up, heading south on Highway 17. They stopped for a simple, early dinner of homemade hamburgers and fries at a popular mom and pop joint along the route. They enjoyed their roadside restaurant fare, and then continued their trip, arriving as the sun set at the Isle of Palms. Driving down the boulevard through the downtown business district they came to a sports bar and grill with a dance floor called the Swinging Hammock. The building that housed the popular spot was erected on stilts, as all of them were on the water. It had a front entrance facing the business district and a back entrance from the beach side. There were two flights of stairs with a landing in the middle, which led up to the main floor. During the daytime, there were volleyball games on at the beach side, in a sandy pit-like area, just below the deck that surrounded the back half of the building.

The main attraction of the evening was the Latino band called Los Hermanos Bravados, or, for short, Los Bravados. They were from Miami but played Charleston and up the East Coast quite often as the newest rage in dance music spread. The Latino-flavored rhythms, such as the salsa and the merengue, were not new but were the current fad in this part of the country.

The band was set to start at 9:00 PM, and the bar began to fill. The arriving crowd, anxious to get a good seat, already occupied most of the tables. The couple climbed a flight of stairs at the front entrance. The outer door was propped open, and a host greeted them from a small table, collecting the admission fee as they stepped inside the foyer. A large man, about the size of a WWF wrestling star, stamped each person with a little red hammock symbol before they entered the next door. One could move in and out of the establishment, if the stamped mark appeared under a black light. Jim spotted a location for them to sit just to the left of where the band had set up.

"There's a table, Paula, let's get it before someone else does."

"Do you think you can handle the music this close to the band? That's why it's available," Paula said.

"I can if you can," retorted Jim, with a smile. "Besides, we don't have too many choices left. The only seats left are at the bar, and it's going to be too crowded there when it fills up in here."

The couple plopped down quickly before anyone else claimed the last bastion of privacy. The music would get too loud later, but that did not matter to them. The most important thing was that Paula and Jim were together and away from their problems for the weekend. A cocktail waitress arrived almost as soon as they sat down.

"What kind of drinks can I start y'all with?" she asked.

"I'll have a sea breeze," said Paula.

"And I'll have a screwdriver," said Jim.

"Yes, sir," the waitress responded. "Shall I start a tab for you?"

"Yes, please," he said, as he offered her his credit card.

The young waitress scampered away to fill the orders, and returned as briskly as she left with drinks decorated with tiny, colorful paper umbrellas. They sipped their drinks while they caught up on each other's week. The band tuned its instruments in preparation for its second appearance at the Swinging Hammock. Los Bravados had played in and around Charleston several times, and Paula and Jim had attended one of their previous appearances. The rhythmic Cuban American sounds of Miami would soon begin to fill the air, with many people taking to the dance floor to salsa.

The couple knew the dance somewhat, but had never seen it performed live until the first time they heard the band. Paula bought one of their CDs and practiced the repetitive steps until she could hold her own on the dance floor. The salsa is a dance, aptly described by one writer as a combination of the shag and the cha-cha. The spinning and twirling movements make it fun for the energetic dancers who love to dance with the rhythmic beat of the music.

"Look, Jim, there's Ernesto, the one who plays the marimba. He's the guy who gave me the two for one deal on their CDs."

Paula looked at Ernesto whose eyes met hers as he waved to them. The couple waved and smiled back enthusiastically, glad to see him again. Ernesto continued his sound system check and tuning an instrument or two. Other members of the band appeared and started their fine-tuning, as well.

"Is he the leader of the band, or is it the guy in the middle testing the microphones?" asked Jim.

"It's the two of them," said Paula. "They are two of four brothers out of the seven band members. I believe these two, Ernesto and Roberto, are the oldest," he said. "He told me they came from Cuba when they were very young and grew up in the Little Havana section of Miami where they learned to play musical instruments in school. He said they learned guitar from their dad, who also used to play in a band."

"Hey, that's pretty interesting, hon. Listen, they are about to start."

"Good evening, ladies and gentlemen, we are Los Hermanos Bravados, all the way from Miami, Florida. We want to welcome you to the Swinging Hammock tonight where we are going to rock the house!" The crowd applauded and cheered. "We have come to share our musical heritage with those who don't know who we are. Those who do know us, we have come to party and have some fun!" said Ernesto.

The band started to play, and the crowd applauded again. The music picked up intensity and volume. "Most of all, we have come to play the music of the salsa and other Latin dances you will learn to love as much as we do," said Roberto, shouting to the adoring crowd, as he let go a rift on the marimba. "Now, get up on your feet and show us what you can do!" The crowd roared.

The trumpet player, the drummer, the percussionist, the bassist, and the guitarists all followed suit. Paula and Jim were tapping their toes as they watched some of the crowd move out on the dance floor. They noticed that, like the previous time when they heard Los Bravados at another appearance in Charleston, there was a large contingent of the Hispanic population present to enjoy their native music.

The couple quickly finished their first drink and ordered another round. Paula was glad their quick stop for dinner along the way helped her avoid a premature head rush from the alcohol. Los Bravados played on as the people danced with great enthusiasm, leaving no question why the new dances were all the rage. The music and dancing was upbeat with unmistakable magnetic Latin flavor.

"The cardio workout that people get by dancing the salsa for an hour is equivalent to a good gym workout, don't you think, Jim?"

"Yeah, I'm sure it is, Paula. God knows I need a good workout after shuffling papers all day at the store. Today was month-end inventory, and sales were slow. Are you ready to loosen up with a dance?" he asked, grinning.

"Sure, let's go for it," Paula said, as she stood sliding her chair back with her legs.

"Cool, I've been waiting to see these new moves you told me you've practiced."

She grabbed her drink and siphoned the remainder of her sea breeze from the tiny red and white striped straw. Jim followed her lead as he pushed his chair away from the table and headed to the small dance floor. They slipped into an open spot in the crowd as the band transitioned into the next tune. Paula and Jim sashayed back and forth across the dance floor, holding each other's hands. A pass and a twirl, and the couple moved with ease across the old wooden floor, which had been prepared for the dance with a thin layer of sawdust to ease the gliding movements of the dancers. Jim, with his cool, deep-set brown eyes, and Paula's eyes of a rare green gem, sparkled at each other. They spoke a language to each other that neither partner could utter. They were in love in spite of the turmoil that surrounded their lives.

The percussionist cracked out a few syncopated beats on the bongos, followed by the trumpet, and then the marimba joined in; a measure or two, and the bass and drums joined in. Now the guitar player jumped in, and the band was in full swing, rocking one of their new hits.

The two lovebirds danced until they were both almost out of breath. Just as they were about to take their seats, Ernesto thanked the crowd for being there, stating there would be a fifteen-minute intermission. The break went longer because the band members were perspiring heavily from their performance in the close quarters of the sports bar jammed with people. They needed enough time to down a drink, smoke a cigarette, and recover. Paula and Jim sat at their table, faces glowing from the joy of the dance, waiting for one more set from the band.

The whole crowd was having a good time, with everyone in party mode, when suddenly there was a loud crash that rang out from the back of the club by the pool tables. A Caucasian man had shoved a man against a wall, shouting, "It's my shot, you filthy wetback!" The Hispanic man was not from Mexico and was extremely offended. He reached into the back of his pants and pulled out a switchblade large enough to clean a deer.

"You want some of me?" shouted the angry Latino. "I came here to have fun, but you white folk think you are better than we are. You take another step towards me, señor, and I'll teach you a lesson about your bad manners."

The Caucasian man was shocked that his opponent wielded a weapon so quickly. The Hispanic man was smaller, but more agile. He tossed the knife from one hand to the other, as if he was juggling. He crouched like a leopard with hungry eyes ready to pounce.

The other man raised both hands in the air apologetically. "Hey, man, it's only a game of pool. I didn't mean any harm." Then, he suddenly lunged for a beer bottle, breaking it on the side of the pool table, creating a weapon of his own. "Put the knife down, you wetback!" he shouted. "Or, we will see who can cut the other one up for fish bait."

"Not till you apologize for shoving me against the wall. You know it was my shot, and you were just trying to pick a fight. Now apologize!"

The muscular bouncer hustled from the front door to where the trouble was with a pool stick turned upside down in his hands. He slugged the Hispanic man on the side of the head and dragged him out the door, relieving him of his knife. Luckily, the Hispanic man had a friend who tended to him until he woke up after a few minutes with a headache and a knot on his head.

The bouncer from the back of the room was just as efficient, and with a stick in his hands, shouted to the other man. "Drop the beer bottle and get the hell out of here, Joe!" Joe was a local who could not stand the sight of other races in his frequently visited places. He looked upon African-Americans as freed slaves and other races as inferior foreigners invading his homeland. A high school dropout who did construction work for a living, Joe never could rise above the prejudices he held from his redneck upbringing.

The crowd settled down after the ruckus temporarily interrupted their jovial mood. The band came back to play their final set. Paula and Jim were seated on the far side of the room away from the fight that had broken out. Luckily, they were not affected by it as much as the people near the pool tables. The dancing resumed, and business as usual continued in the bar after a quick clean up of the area where the bottle was broken.

The Latino and his friend, still hanging around outside, saw Joe leave the bar and head toward his car. They slipped into an alley and watched him approaching. Joe passed by one business and then another. He was glad that he knew the bouncer, who could have bopped him on the head, as well. He was woozy from the half-dozen beers he drank in the space of an hour. Staggering down the sidewalk, he came to a break in the storefronts where there was an alley.

Without warning, Joe was collared by the two men. They spun him around and shoved him face first against a wall of an adjacent building. He never had a chance as he was beaten and dropped in the sand, nearly unconscious. They dragged him off in the alley to finish their job. The shorter man of the two pulled a blade of his own to finish what his friend started to do in the bar. Joe lay in the sand, bleeding from his nose as he gasped for air. He tried to crawl back to the sidewalk to call for help, but the other man kicked him in the ribs, and poor Joe fell prostrate in the sand.

"Hey! Stop that, now. Leave him alone!" shouted a bystander from the sidewalk.

The unknown man accompanied by a few friends, startled Joe's attackers enough for them to flee. The two attackers ran down the beach about fifty yards and came out between two storefronts on the boulevard where they had parked. Quickly, they drove off, laughing about what happened. The man, who saw the beating transpiring and took the initiative to shout, unknowingly saved a life. He saw the man kick Joe, but not the knife. The three men who saved Joe helped him to his feet and escorted him to his track.

Inside the Swinging Hammock, the music continued to play. Everyone was oblivious to what had happened just outside the doors. Fun inside and pain outside, an ironic juxtaposition, yet it was a microcosm of the world at large.

"Jim, it's getting late. Let's dance to a song or two then leave. What do you say?"

"Sounds good to me, Paula, the music is beginning to get to my ears near this speaker anyway."

The couple danced to a fast song, and then the band played a slow number as they mixed the tempo in the second set. The romantic tune set the tone for the rest of the evening. Jim drew close to Paula, slipping his arm behind her, his hand placed on the small of her back. They took each other's hands as their bodies closed together for an embrace. She clung to Jim, holding him closely as she followed his shuffling feet in the slow dance they both enjoyed. The music was sweet and flowed through their bodies. They danced as one, bodies melting together.

"Let's go, honey," Paula said. "I want to take a moonlit walk down on the beach."

"Do you think I'm going to argue with that?" Jim asked, as he leaned over, whispering in her ear.

He kissed her on the cheek and held her tightly as they finished the last few steps in the dance. They returned to their table, picking up their things, and went out the back door by the pool tables where things had returned to normal. People on the deck were laughing, smoking, and drinking as they enjoyed the ocean breeze. A couple was in the corner of the deck kissing. They walked past the crowd on the deck and down the flight of stairs where a wooden walkway built over the sand continued toward the beach. As the couple reached the last portion of the boardwalk, it rose up a little with a short, bridge-like structure at the end of it. Paula took Jim's hand as they walked down the stairs covered with fine, white slippery sand to the entrance of the beachfront. He loved to feel her hand in his. It made him feel that he had arrived and that the world was his oyster.

They walked north on the beach down close to the water and headed towards a point on the island. The full moon lit up the night as it pulsated its warm light down on the couple from a sky filled with stars. The Milky Way, showing its splendor, swathed the middle third of the firmament above. The swell of the dark ocean rolled its waves gently up onto the shore. As the soft, warm wind blew the couple walked hand in hand, not saying anything for a while. They enjoyed the closeness they felt to each other and to nature. Although their feelings were seldom communicated in words of, "I love you," they both held them in their hearts for each other, like a closely guarded treasure.

The sound of the music from Los Bravados slowly faded away as they walked closer to the water's edge. The only sound they could hear now was the ocean rolling up on the beach and its waves crashing then sliding back into the dark abyss from which they came. They looked up to the houses to get their bearings and turned to embrace each other. The couple kissed lovingly under the moonlight, which blessed their love with a kiss of its own. They turned to walk on up the beach, and Paula opened up. With arms around each other's waists, they strolled and talked, contented to be together.

"Jim, do you ever wonder why life turns out like it does?"

"What do you mean, Paula?"

"Well, so many things that have happened to me seem to teach me a better way, if I listen to and learn from what is being said. You know... when life's circumstances show us new ways to handle things. We have choices everyday for how we choose to live, but it's up to us to choose what's best. Our decisions often control our destiny. Then there are times when we are caught in a swiftly moving current downstream when there is nothing we can do about it. We're only making decisions in response to what has happened to us."

"Wow, wax philosophical on me, one time," Jim said. "Seriously, though, I know what you mean. Take us, for example. We have made choices that have affected us in positive ways, and other decisions were the result of things that just happened to us externally."

"You mean the world to me, Jim. I am sorry for the problems that have complicated our lives. I know I made some wrong decisions, which set all these problems in motion. Forgive me?"

"Of course, I forgive you, Paula. I said I would be with you until this thing is behind us. You remember what I have written to you...I meant every word. I had plenty of time to think, and I couldn't see my life going on without you in it. If I can be with you in the close romantic times and enjoy you so much, why should I not be able to stand with you in the rough times when you need me the most? I mean, if two people love each other, then they grow in that love, desiring to help one another, no matter what."

"That's very sweet, Jim. You're almost making me cry. But how can you say that, after all I've put you through?"

"It's because I have this wonderful, overwhelming feeling when I am with you. It's like the ocean with its ebbs and flows, but it's always powerful and constant. That's what I feel for you, and if those feelings mean going through some tough times, well, tough times are only temporary. I wanted to take the chance that this feeling would grow and last, and it has, despite the setbacks."

Paula took in what Jim said. The words seemed to burn within her branding her heart to be only his. She squeezed his hand, and cleared her throat.

"Jim, I knew from the first time I saw you here on the beach last summer that you were special. I am so fortunate to have met you, and I know it. Otherwise, I would be going through all this by myself. Life is so strange and downright scary at times, but it's so much easier to handle knowing that you are here with me. I appreciate your loyalty, sincerely. I only hope to repay you in some way for the confidence and trust you have placed in me, though I don't deserve it."

"Don't worry, Paula. Just consider it a gift of love and know this: I am a man who wants love as much as I want to give it, and I'm willing to risk everything to gain it. When I found you, I knew I had found one in a million."

"Oh, stop, you are making cry now. You have already repaid me many times over."

The waves crashed and the tide rolled up, past where their feet sloshed through the shallow standing water, depositing seaweed, shells, and remnants of crustaceans on the beach. They jumped up as the chilly water unexpectedly wet them to their knees and splashed their bodies.

"Jim, your pants are wet now. Good thing I wore this dress, ha-ha."

"They will dry out; I'm not worried," said Jim.

Adjusting their walking path to a higher position, they continued walking with their shoes in hand, after laughing at what just happened to them.

"As I was saying, you didn't have to be honest with me, but you took the chance that I would run or stay. I stayed because you are a straightforward, lovely individual who respected me enough to tell the truth. You are not only a lovely person outside, Paula, and though you made a big mistake, the important thing is that you turned it around. I want to be with you when this is all over."

The couple could see the lights from the back of Pelicans' Nook, which they had rented for the weekend, inviting them to make their way off the beach. They held each other's hands as they trudged their way through the soft sand past the dunes with sea oats swaying in the breeze. Stopping at the end of the short sidewalk, they washed the sand off their feet from a faucet placed there for that purpose. Laughing and feeling like no problems were too big, they entered the quaint house, making their way to the bedroom. They took their windbreakers off and held each other.

"Paula..."

"What, dear?"

"The car is at the Swinging Hammock," said Jim. They both laughed.

"I knew that. We can get it tomorrow; it's not far. Let's get under the covers. It's cold out here," she said. She pulled away from an embrace and began to disrobe.

Jim took a step back delighted with the way she opened up to him like a morning glory. "I'll be back in a flash," he said, as he checked the lock on both doors. Gleefully, like a little boy, Jim returned to where

Paula waited under the covers. The couple embraced and kissed, temporarily relieved of all their worries and concerns. Sweet sounds of romance with a soft background of crashing waves from the beach whispered their splendid rendezvous that starlit night.

"I love you, Jim."

"I love you, too, Paula."

They fell asleep in each other's arms until the light of day.

22

Georgetown, South Carolina: Colonial Paper Mill

Agents Dibbs and Mendez arrived promptly at 9:55 AM to visit the CEO, Paul Walker.

"Yes, may I help you, gentlemen?" asked the executive secretary.

"Yes, we are here for an appointment with Mr. Paul Walker. I am Agent John Dibbs, and this is my partner, Agent Albert Mendez.

"Please have a seat. Mr. Walker is expecting you. I will notify him that you are here."

The secretary opened her boss's door. "Mr. Walker, the men from the FBI are here."

"Very well, send them in."

Paul Walker had taken no chances and had the company attorney present in his office. The attorney and Mr. Walker had reviewed the case and correspondence with the Denby Law Firm in preparation for the meeting.

"Good morning, gentlemen; you're right on time. I admire your punctuality. This is our company attorney, Bill Black. I trust you don't mind him sitting in. Company policy requires him to be present any time its managers are questioned by law enforcement about company business. My secretary will also sit in to take minutes of our meeting, if that is okay with you, gentlemen?"

"That is fine, Mr. Walker. Then you won't mind us recording the conversation, will you?"

"No, sir," responded Bill Black, "not at all. We'll just need a copy of the tape before you leave."

"That's not a problem, as long as you have a duplicator," said Agent Dibbs.

"We do, Agent Dibbs."

Miss Gentry, Walker's secretary, turned on the tape player then flipped open her legal pad, taking minutes as Mr. Black spoke.

"From what Mr. Walker explained to me, after he set this appointment, is that the FBI is investigating our contract with the J. Thomas Denby Law Firm and our correspondence with them with regards to the EPA versus Colonial Paper Mill case. Is that correct, gentlemen?"

"That's correct, Mr. Black. We are here to ask specific questions about the contract, the correspondence, and the phone calls that Mr. Walker had on behalf of Colonial Paper with J. Thomas Denby of the law firm by the same name. And you understand that anything said here may be used in a court of law as evidence, as determined by the FBI and the District Attorney's office, correct, Mr. Black and Mr. Walker?"

"Yes, my client, and I understand that, Agent Dibbs. Let's proceed."

"I'll let Agent Mendez go first," said Dibbs.

"Mr. Walker, you entered into a contract with the J. Thomas Denby Law Firm to defend Colonial Paper against charges by the EPA that your company is polluting the Sampit River, as well as the Winyah Bay and surrounding marshlands, is that correct?"

"Yes, sir, that is correct."

"Would you explain the terms of the contract to us, Mr. Walker?"

"They consisted of the usual things in a business contract involving corporate law, Agent Mendez. Our attorney has a copy of the contract for you."

Mr. Black handed a copy of the contract to Agent Mendez, who passed it to Agent Dibbs. Dibbs scanned it briefly, while listening, and then stowed it away in his briefcase for FBI attorneys to study.

"Mr. Walker, how long have you known J. Thomas Denby?" asked Mendez.

"Since we were about seven years old, so about forty years I'd say. I moved here with my parents and attended grade school all the way through high school with Tom...I mean Mr. Denby."

"Mr. Walker, would you say you have a close relationship with Mr. Denby?"

"We have a cordial business relationship, as any longtime friends would, but we are not as close as we were in high school."

"Would you say that the two of you do each other favors when you can, Mr. Walker?"

"I object to that question, Agent Mendez," Mr. Black blurted out. "What "favors" they may, or may not, do for each other is irrelevant!"

"I'll rephrase the question, Mr. Black. Have you, in the past, done things for each other which would be considered favors?" continued Agent Mendez.

"I object, again. It's irrelevant to the contract Colonial Paper had with the Denby Law Firm."

"It's not irrelevant when we have evidence of an offer of an extraordinary bonus to Thomas Denby by Mr. Walker, if he could get the case thrown out of court. Such an offer does not appear in this contract as part of the agreement for fees and services. Are you aware of this offer, Mr. Black?" interjected Agent Dibbs.

"No, I am not," said Bill Black. He looked at Paul Walker for an acknowledgment of the offer. "What do you know about this, Paul?"

"I made a comment to Tom that if we were able to avoid long, expensive litigation, there could be a bonus that the company would consider."

Agent Dibbs pulled out the copy of the note that Walker had faxed to Denby and passed it to the attorney. "Look at this, Mr. Black. Your client may want to refresh his memory."

The attorney perused the document. It read as follows: "The sum of one million dollars will be paid to J. Thomas Denby Law Firm, if said firm is able to have the pending case of EPA versus the Colonial Paper Mill thrown out of court", and signed by Paul Walker.

Mr. Black passed the fax to the CEO. "What about this fax, Paul?"

"Oh, that," said Walker. "I forgot about that fax. Tom wanted a hard copy of what I was saying about settling early. I knew that I had to take the offer to the board for a vote before we could do it, Bill."

"But you put us in the position of being liable for payment of this offer without consulting the board, Paul. Any time you go outside what is written in a contract that I have drawn up, you should consult me first for legal advice."

Walker knew he had screwed up, not realizing that Denby would have ever allowed the FBI to get the fax. In past dealings, he and Tom were able to pull off a few shady deals without any consequence. At this point though, he was not surprised at anything since everyone was trying to save his own hide from prison time.

"You're right, Bill, my mistake. I'll discuss it with you later."

"The document specifically states that a one-million-dollar bonus would be paid to J. Thomas Denby Law Firm if this case is thrown out of court, Mr. Walker. How do you explain that?" asked Agent Dibbs.

Both Mr. Walker and Mr. Black were silent for a moment, and then Walker spoke up. "I was motivated to get the case settled the best way I could, Agent Dibbs, but you wouldn't know anything about that in your line of work, would you? We are staring a five-million-dollar fine in the face. The offer made good business sense to me. Do you have any idea what a fine like that would do to our insurance premiums?"

"I can imagine, Mr. Walker," responded Dibbs.

"I made an executive decision that I regret and put it in writing because Denby, an old friend, insisted that I do so. He claimed he had to put more attorneys and personnel on the case. He told me that he thought he might be able to get it thrown out on a technicality."

"Did he mention anything about sending his paralegal, Paula Cooper, to entrap the judge in a compromising situation, Mr. Walker, and thereby be able to blackmail Judge Parks into dropping the case?"

"Well, he did say..."

"That's enough, Paul. We need just a few moments to consult, gentlemen," said Mr. Black.

"Sure, take your time," responded Dibbs.

Mr. Black ushered the CEO just outside his main office by a coat closet adjacent to the bathroom. "Don't answer any more questions about the case unless they place you under arrest, Paul, and even then, you make sure I am with you. This conversation may be leading them to arrest you for conspiracy to commit blackmail, or worse."

"How the heck can they do that?" asked Walker. "He has no proof."

"If you had prior knowledge of the conspiracy to commit blackmail and did not report it to the authorities, then you may be charged, as well. There is no purpose or advantage in us continuing with this fishing expedition."

"I understand, Bill. I just didn't want them to think that I'm unwilling to cooperate."

"Right, but they're asking questions that could land you in jail and embarrass the heck out of the company. You know how we work hard to keep a good public image in the community, and we certainly don't want our CEO arrested."

"You're right once again, Bill. Thanks."

The men reentered Walker's office where the two FBI agents were waiting.

"Agents Dibbs and Mendez, our attorney knows far more about the law than I do and has advised me not to answer any more questions about the case at this time."

"I see, Mr. Walker," said Dibbs. He nodded and looked at Mendez.

Agent Mendez reached into his inside coat pocket for the subpoena. "We sort of anticipated this might happen, gentlemen. Mr. Walker, this is a subpoena duces tecum regarding the case of United States EPA versus Denby Law Firm. It orders you to surrender all documents related to the case. Later, you also will be required to give a sworn deposition, in which your attorney may be present. Our legal staff will be contacting you as to the precise time and location of the deposition."

"Is that all, gentlemen?" asked Mr. Black.

"Yes, for now, Mr. Black," responded Agent Dibbs. "Thank you for your time, gentlemen, we will be in touch soon. Have a good day."

Agents Dibbs and Mendez shook the corporate executives' hands as they exited the stately office then found their way back to the foyer.

"I would like to be a fly on the wall in there to hear what that attorney has to say to Mr. Walker, now," said Mendez to Dibbs.

"Me too, buddy, me too," said Dibbs, chuckling. "Did you see the expressions on their faces when we served the subpoena?"

"They looked like they had seen a ghost," retorted Mendez. "Obviously there were things Walker knew that the attorney didn't. Black was smart to stop him where he did."

"Exactly, there's a connection with Walker and Denby that runs deep, and I can't put my finger on exactly what it is just yet. If we keep the pressure up, perhaps something will come out of it. Good job in there, Albert."

"Good job with your questions, also, John. You had them sweating, and I dare say that Walker is going to get a good butt chewing by the board once he explains what happened. His deceit could spell the end of his job. Walker overstepped his authority in making an offer like that to Denby."

"No doubt he did," said Dibbs.

The agents left the mill and headed back to their Charleston office.

Inside his office, Paul Walker and Bill Black were still in conference.

"Now, why in the world did you tell Denby we would pay a bonus like that without prior approval of the Board of Trustees, Paul?"

Walker began to squirm as he formulated his response. A nervous tick he had as a child caused his face to twitch. "Because I figured the money was a detail that we could work out if Denby was able to shorten the time frame considerably. You know how long the case could drag out. Estimates I received indicate that the cost of litigating the case to its conclusion could be enormous, Bill."

"I'm aware of that, Paul. That was my staff who prepared that report for you, and we have a fund for that. Some of those funds can be written off, but we don't have a slush fund for payments to get things done by unethical or illegal means. Besides, your "detail that could be worked out" is a million dollars! Tell me, Paul, what do you know about the blackmail conspiracy? It will stay in this room."

"It was just a passing comment that Denby made on the phone to the effect that he was going to send his paralegal to help persuade the judge to throw out the case. There is no written proof that I know anything about that, to my knowledge. I told Denby I didn't want to know, didn't care how he got the job done. I just wanted the case dismissed and the problem to go away. When he said how difficult that might be, I upped the ante to a bonus of a million. The board has already approved a half-million; I figured that they'd agree."

The corporate attorney observed Walker's body language, and felt that the CEO may not be totally honest with him. "Well, you should have waited until you took it to the board."

"I know I should have waited to get the board's approval, but time was running out, and I made a decision on the fly. I thought that Denby may be trying to back out, and his firm is the one that gets things done around here. You know that. I felt the pressure of trying to get this case behind us without paying five million in fines to the EPA and did what I thought was expedient."

"You do realize how this bonus offer you made compromises us? It puts us in bed with the conspiracy to commit blackmail with that fax the FBI has. Denby told you in detail on how he would try to get the job done, and now there's a murdered federal judge."

"Yes, I do, Bill, and that's one reason I fired the Denby Law Firm."

"Denby must be pretty hot, and he's trying now to divert attention away from himself by sending the FBI over here. I heard that he struck a deal for leniency to help them find the killer," said the corporate attorney.

"That wouldn't surprise me at all. His whole career will go down the tubes if he gets a long prison term. If he helps out a lot, he just might be able to get a light sentence, unless he was involved in the murder somehow," said Walker.

Still not sure what to make of the talkative CEO, Attorney Black indulged Walker to ramble on then decided to confront him to get a reaction. "I guess you are right. Do you think your old friend would have also conspired to kill a federal judge? He did have a lot to gain if he got the case thrown out, but then, so did you, Paul, no offense. Aren't you up for a bonus, if you meet your performance criteria?"

"You know I am, Bill. I resent that remark, damn it!" Walker pounded his clenched fist on the corner of his desk. "I had nothing to do with either the blackmail or the murder. It was all Tom Denby's idea.

I was only sticking my neck out for Colonial to get the job done."

"I know you were, Paul, but the appearance of things is not good. Let's just circle our wagons before the deposition so that we won't have any surprises," said Black.

"Can you hire a criminal attorney, the best in Charleston, to work with us on the deposition? He should be able to find out what the FBI is trying to uncover and keep them off our backs," said Walker.

"I was thinking the same thing. You will need good representation," said Black.

"Good, Bill, can you take care of that for me? I've got other business to handle at this time."

"Alright, Paul, I'll start work on it and get back to you tomorrow morning. Remember, no comments to the media or anyone about this."

"No, of course not, but I don't think that we have anything to be too concerned about. I'll talk to you tomorrow," said Walker. "Thanks for your help."

Bill Black gathered his file and left his office. Paul Walker was troubled that he may have said too much to Dibbs and Mendez. *What was Denby saying about him?* Walker wondered. *Moreover, why would they come knocking on my door for answers about the murder case when there were other suspects who were much more likely to commit a crime like that?*

Walker had read the newspaper articles on everyone, from Hernandez, to Denby, and to the widow of the late Judge Parks. He did not see why the FBI would even come knocking, except to uncover more of the truth on his longtime friend, J. Thomas Denby. After all, Paul Walker was well-known in the community as a benevolent man, who helped with many charities and civil functions. He ran a great company, which provided hundreds of jobs for the citizens of Georgetown.

23

The Caribbean Queen was lively with its normal array of entertainment. It was February, but felt like spring in south Florida. The ship was loaded with vacationers, honeymooners, and party animals of all description that wanted to cruise the Caribbean on its inaugural voyage since a revamping after a fire, which had gutted a good portion of the cabins and entertainment area. The renovations were complete, and the smell of new paint, wallpaper, and other components was in the air.

Chuck and Eleanor were dancing in the ballroom of the majestic ship to the sounds of a live band performing a variety of dance music from the last three decades. Tomorrow was their wedding day, at noon. They were to be married in the cruise ship's chapel when they docked for the day at St. Croix.

"Chuck, I can't wait until tomorrow," Eleanor said.

"Me either, honey. We will be secretly official."

"That's not funny," she said playfully.

"Well, it's true. We will be married but cannot tell anyone until later when we have a public marriage. Isn't that what you said?"

"You know the reason why, Chuck. Stop teasing me. I'm very sensitive about the circumstances until more time has passed."

"I know you are, dear, and rightly so. I didn't mean any harm."

The band began another tune with an upbeat tempo.

"Let's sit this one out; I'm getting tired."

"No problem, Eleanor. I echo that sentiment."

He led her off the dance floor, back to their round dinner table covered with a white tablecloth, and decked with an ornate silver candelabrum. The honeymooning couple had long since finished an excellent meal and was among many others on the cruise ship there to dance and have a good time for the evening. The waiters had snuffed out the candles for safety and turned the ballroom chandeliers on low.

Chuck seated Eleanor and turned to face her as they sat next to each other at the table for four. "Honey, I'm going to light the candles on this fancy candle holder and tell you what each of them represents."

"Aw, Chuck, now you are being sweet."

Chuck flipped open his shiny stainless metal lighter and spoke as he lit each candle in order, "This one represents you, and this one represents me, and the tall one in the middle is for a higher love that will see us through to cement our future together."

"That's the sweetest thing I've ever heard you say."

Nancy Bailey walked down the hallway of the living quarters with a listening device hidden in her closed hand. She arrived at cabin number 42 on the lower deck, assigned to the couple, and paid for by Eleanor Parks. She insisted on paying, and Chuck acquiesced. He was a very good musician, but not great with finances. He spent his money too fast and never could get a handle on saving.

Miss Bailey picked the lock using a small tool she pulled from her purse, which was converted to house various items for her trade. In a flash, she slipped inside the cabin almost as fast as one would have opened it with a key. Once inside, she spotted the best place to hide the bug, underneath a decorative table lamp resembling a seafaring vessel from the eighteen-hundreds. She tilted the lamp on its side, holding it with one hand as she added a putty-like substance to secure the bug on the spindly frame beneath the lampshade. Carefully, she placed the lamp back in its exact location then stealthily moved to the exit, pressing her ear against the door. She listened for sounds coming from the hallway. A noise from a couple got louder as it approached then subsided as they passed cabin 42.

She heard a door close down the hall. Nancy opened the door and exited, locking the door behind her. She walked at a normal pace down the hall and back up to the deck. She had followed Eleanor and Chuck to the ballroom earlier and took a chance that they would be dancing a while. Her calculations were correct, as usual, and her subterfuge went off without a hitch. The private detective placed a tiny earphone, which looked like a hearing aid, in one ear, connected electronically to the device under the lampshade.

She had not been able to pick up much more than a few words from Eleanor about how she would spend the two million dollars when she received it. Heartland Insurance Company delayed the payment with a notice they sent to the South Carolina Department of Insurance and to Mrs. Parks. The letter indicated that while the investigation was still ongoing, they were obligated to wait until Mrs. Parks was cleared of all wrongdoing with respect to the death of her late husband. Mrs. Parks received her letter the day she left for her cruise.

Miss Bailey returned to her cabin about the time Eleanor and Chuck finished dancing and retired to their cabin. She hoped for a break in the case, but all she heard were two drunken people making love, then fall asleep. She turned down the volume on the surveillance device and went to sleep hoping that tomorrow would be a better day in the world of private investigating. The next morning, Bailey tailed the couple to breakfast and hung out not far from them. While the soon-to-be-married couple lounged on the deck after breakfast, Eleanor let a statement slip.

"If I had known that an investigation would be launched, I would have chosen a different method for Judge Parks to die, if it was up to me."

"Eleanor, I can't believe you said that. Someone could get the wrong idea."

"I know, Chuck. That was crude and never should have been said."

"Let's stay focused on our wedding today. It should be a day of happiness."

"You're right. I think the Bloody Mary I drank at breakfast to calm my nerves was doing the talking. I forgot to bring my nerve pills on the trip."

Whether Eleanor's statement proved to be anything, or not, remained to be seen. It did give Bailey some hope that perhaps she could report something more damning, if she just kept at her job. *One thing for sure,* she thought, *it was a puzzling statement for a recent widow to make,* but then again, that was Eleanor Parks at times. Alcohol nearly always caused her to say whatever was on her mind without regard for others around her. She figured people on the trip did not know her, so why did it matter?

The time drew near for the wedding as the ship docked in St. Croix. Chuck enjoyed reading the paper and doing his crossword puzzle. Eleanor gulped the last of her second Bloody Mary down and kissed Chuck on the forehead before excusing herself. She ran by the beauty salon on the third deck to get her hair styled. Afterwards, she went back to the cabin to put on a spring party dress that she had bought for the occasion. Since this was a secret wedding, they prearranged a small private affair with the chaplain of the cruise ship. Of course, nothing on a full-service cruise ship could ever be mundane, so the chaplain had convinced them to accept the smallest package offered. The cruise line provided members of the crew to serve as bridesmaid and best man, and a choice selection of libations.

Chuck figured it would take him about thirty minutes to shower and jump into his suit. He was very relaxed about the whole ceremony anyway. Marrying Eleanor would provide stability in his life and catapult him into a better position to mass-produce his CDs. He would be able to play with his band without the pressure of making ends meet for the first time in his life. He did not care for Eleanor the same way she did for him, but he figured he could if given time. Eleanor sure beat the heck out of the groupies Chuck had met over the years, who just wanted a good time with a musician, and then were gone about their merry way.

Eleanor was mature, settled, and she had bucks—two million of them, coming in soon. The struggling musician would struggle no more. He played for the love of music, but marrying Eleanor would give him an instant boost to a new level in society. It would surely open some doors for gigs at private parties and nicer clubs. With his new credibility, Chuck hoped that a financier might finance him to record future albums without Eleanor having to risk any of her funds. He really did not want to take advantage of their relationship to the extent that she would resent him. He wanted her to be happy with him, with the both of them profiting in a mutual relationship.

Eleanor's dream was to marry a younger, good-looking man who did not judge her. She paraded him around as her prized possession. She showed her love for Chuck by how she freely spent money on him. Eleanor also provided a quasi-motherly security for Chuck, always building him up and loving him unconditionally, reciprocating for the way he treated her. He knew that she had had a tough time with Judge Parks because she tried to measure up to his intellect, which she never really could.

The depression and alcoholism that resulted from him not letting her adopt a child, and from their lack of communication, had subsided now with Eleanor's discovery of Chuck. She acquired a new sense of pride in herself and slowed down quite a lot on her alcohol consumption. On average, she only drank two drinks per day now, and not every day—a substantial drop from the previous ten years.

Eleanor turned the key to the door of the cabin suite. "Are you ready yet, honey?" she asked. "It's almost time to head to the chapel."

She was a woman of forty-six with an extra few pounds, but she looked great with the proper makeup, hairdo, and spiffy clothes. Chuck's love for her was originally born out of a concern for her safety, and a lusty mutual attraction in the wee hours of the morning. He learned that she was an interesting person with a big heart, regardless of her alcohol problem. He could see the real Eleanor emerging and liked what he saw. He had been through enough in life to know they were compatible, and if they treated each other right, then their love would grow. The ideas of love at first sight were not foreign to him, but he had a much more realistic viewpoint of love.

"Yes, dear, I am almost ready. I have to put in my contacts so I can see to put a wedding band on your finger. Would you grab my coat from off the door handle?"

He finished putting the second contact in his eye. Eleanor lifted the black suit coat off the door handle, a typical place for a man to hang an article of clothing, and helped him into it.

"My, my, what a handsome stud you are. I'm the luckiest lady on the boat today."

"Thanks, Darling, on the contrary, I feel that I am the luckiest man here. You came into my life in such a peculiar way and surprised me with your love and attention. I can't believe we've only been together for seven months, and our wedding day is already here."

Eleanor reached up and smoothed Chuck's collar, her hands lingering on his chest. "Isn't that peculiar, Chuck? I hate to say this, but the most tragic thing that could have happened has helped bring about the climax to our relationship. That's the supreme irony of it all."

Chuck took her hand in his and softly spoke to her, her eyes welling with tears. "Don't you know I have thought about that? On one hand, I am glad that I have you, but on the other hand, I wish our relationship didn't blossom as a result of the murder of Judge Parks."

"It didn't stem from his murder, Chuck. My marriage was in demise well before the tragedy. All we can do now is move forward. It wasn't meant to last. I do feel badly about his death—especially the way he died."

Eleanor sniffled then composed herself, as if nothing had happened. She did not want to spoil what was about to occur. Taking a tissue from a box, she dabbed the corners of her eyes, and touched the end of her nose.

"You're absolutely correct, Eleanor. I understand. Are you okay?" Chuck asked, as he squeezed her hand for assurance.

"I surely am, Baby. Let's go. This day will change our lives forever."

Miss Bailey continued her electronic eavesdropping, but she almost did not want the couple to be guilty of anything after hearing their mushy exchange. She reflected on their conversation, trying to decide what she would report to Heartland. Though the information seemed incriminating, it stopped just short. She decided to reserve judgment and keep observing, but she knew that statements she recorded would be of interest to the Heartland executives and was glad that she was able to catch their morning conversation.

The couple walked arm in arm down the hall to an elevator, which led to the deck where the majority of party rooms were located. There were hundreds of people lying out in the sun, rubbing each other with lotion and swimming in the large pool. An older crowd played shuffleboard nearby. Chuck and Eleanor stood out with their semiformal clothing as they passed by the scantily clad vacationers.

The disc jockey caught a glimpse of the couple and spun an old favorite, Chapel of Love, as they headed toward the marriage chapel. The on-looking crowd joined in and sang the tune loudly as Chuck and Eleanor picked up their pace to avoid extra attention. Eleanor was a little worried about some of the guests on the ship possibly knowing her. Chuck grabbed the entrance door to the foyer of the chapel and swung it open for her. The crowd clapped, sharing in the happiness that the couple felt. Inside the chapel, although they had just a few crewmembers present, Chuck and Eleanor turned facing each other and grinned with excitement.

Chuck leaned over to kiss her. Eleanor leaned back, placing a finger on his lips to block him. "Not yet, honey, you know kissing the bride before we take our vows is bad luck."

"You really don't believe that, do you, Eleanor?" He chuckled, embarrassed by his blunder. He thought briefly about losing his freedom as a single man but it really did not concern him that much. He had been single too long and was turning forty-two on his next birthday. He was slowly falling in love with this incredible woman, who had changed like a butterfly after going through its metamorphosis.

Everyone took their positions, with the chaplain at the front of the little chapel and the bride and groom, the best man, and bridesmaid at the back. On cue, as the chaplain nodded his head, a crewmember pressed the button to play the familiar refrain, "Here Comes the Bride." The bride and groom walked slowly down the aisle, both a little nervous, but not as much as if they would have been married in Charleston in front of hundreds of people. The music subsided. Eleanor looked marvelous in her beautiful dress. She had even dropped a few pounds for the cruise, and she looked as if she had lost five years since meeting her soon-to-be husband. Naturally, he was quite pleased with the transformation.

"Dearly beloved, we are gathered today to celebrate the love between these two people. The institution of marriage has been around as long as the beginning of the human race," said the chaplain. He continued with more of the usual repertoire that preachers use at weddings. The bridesmaid and best man stood statuesque as the marital rites were completed. "Chuck Eastwood, do you promise to love, honor, and cherish this woman for as long as you both shall live?"

"I do," said Chuck, while gazing at Eleanor with a smile. It touched his heart to see tears form, and then run slowly down her cheeks.

Turning to face Eleanor, the chaplain continued his refrain. "Eleanor Parks, do you promise to love, honor, and cherish this man for as long as you both shall live?"

"I do," Eleanor responded, with a lump in her throat, barely holding back a floodgate of emotion.

"Then, by the power vested in me, I now pronounce you man and wife. You may kiss the bride."

Chuck leaned over and planted a big kiss on his new bride. She was more than willing this time, and they lingered a little longer than normal. On a cruise ship wedding, much of the traditional protocol was set aside. The small gathering of people clapped and cheered as the couple walked down the aisle to an adjoining room. The crew and other well-wishers who joined the wedding party rained down grains of rice on the newly married couple.

Their wedding package included a modest reception where anyone who wanted to wish the bride and groom well could stop by to congratulate them. A few acquaintances they had met on the cruise and the participating crewmembers enjoyed their wedding cake and champagne. Afterwards, the couple took some pictures before they headed off to their room like a couple of teenagers.

They planned for a night of dancing, which did not begin until 8 PM, so they had plenty of time to kill. They made love and slept off their buzz until dinnertime when they awakened, showered, and dressed for the evening. They participated in the usual things couples do on a cruise. They ate a fine seven-course meal and enjoyed the entertainment. Chuck liked the ring of the name, *Mrs. Eleanor Eastwood*, as did his new wife.

Nancy Bailey was not far away when the newly married couple ate dinner and arrived at the bar for a nightcap. Although she was unhappy with the amount of information she had gleaned, she did enjoy the festive atmosphere. A couple of men tried to hit on her because of her looks, but she set them straight immediately. The Eastwoods retired to their cabin, and after giving everything thoughtful consideration, Miss Bailey returned to her cabin to complete her notes.

The next day Miss Bailey prepared her initial report to fax to Heartland Insurance. She opened her laptop beneath the shade of an umbrella on the deck where a gentle breeze blew intermittently. She reread the words of the letter that she prepared for the executives of Heartland:

Dear Mr. Tisdale,

I am sending a tape overnight of a conversation between the parties under investigation regarding the Judge Parks incident. Whether they incriminate themselves, or not, is tough to decide at this juncture. My personal assessment is that Eleanor Parks Eastwood and her new husband, Chuck Eastwood, seem to be clear of any wrongdoing in the matter. Eastwood is Eleanor's new last name since the couple secretly married on the cruise ship yesterday.

If you have any questions about any of the information I have gathered, feel free to reach me on my cell, or we can address them when I call you for the conference call at our next appointed time.

Sincerely yours,

Nancy Bailey, Private Investigator

Miss Bailey finished her task and returned to her cabin to put her laptop away. She knew from experience that whenever she could save insurance companies big payouts, she was treated royally with not only her own fees, but also with bonuses, which were unwritten in her contracts. She was hopeful, but really had nothing to hang her hat on, now.

Time has a way of healing all wounds, as well as revealing all truth, and this would be no different. If the Eastwoods were involved, their conspiracy would come to light eventually, no matter how discreet they were; something would be said or leaked to indicate their guilt. Bailey knew her profession well and taught firsthand by her uncle, who had brought her into the business fresh out of college. The intrigue and challenge of being a private investigator had always driven her to be good at what she did. Even if she did not find that Chuck and Eleanor were guilty of insurance fraud and possibly murder, she would know that she had done her best.

24

At the FBI crime lab in the District of Columbia, the ballistics report came back from in-house experts, as well as from two outside consultants. The shots fired at Judge Wilmont Parks were from a high-powered .30-30 Winchester rifle. The bullets were slender hollow points, designed to tear up the inside of their target. If the judge had lived, he would have had a long recovery, and permanent debilitation because of the way this type of projectile spreads when it enters an object. The assassin knew exactly what kind of weapon and ammunition to use for deadliness and accuracy. He was not a run-of-the-mill gun for hire, but someone who had handled weapons many times before and who was skilled at killing with high-powered rifles, the type of assassin most likely trained in Special Forces as a sniper, or else an avid hunter with an expert eye.

Agents Dibbs and Mendez were at the lab to pick up copies of the findings, instead of waiting for a fax. The main purpose for being in Washington, though, was so that Dibbs could talk to his old friend, Glen McAlistair, who had completed FBI academy with him. They went back further than that, attending George Washington University together while majoring in criminal justice. Dibbs remembered the time that the FBI sent recruiters to their campus for a job fair, trying to land a few of the brightest students as prospective agents. John Dibbs and Glen

McAlistair fit the FBI criteria and were recruited successfully. They signed up as soon as they received their diplomas and never looked back. Mac, as Dibbs called him, had transferred out of the field five years earlier, was proud of the fact that he had been promoted twice, and became assistant director of the crime lab. Dibbs loved fieldwork, while McAlistair loved discovering and interpreting empirical evidence through lab studies that could pinpoint a suspect.

"We haven't yet found the location where the bullets were purchased, John, but we do know that these loads are not standard-issue. They were most, likely bought through a mail-order magazine, or on the black market. I'm having the casings analyzed to determine their metallic content, which should help us narrow down the country, and possibly the factory, in which they were manufactured. We won't be certain of their origin for another couple of days," McAlistair stated.

"Sound good, Mac. You are on top of things as usual. Good work," Dibbs said, nodding his head.

"Thanks, John. I'll be in touch with the results as soon as they come in. How are you coming with your investigation? Have you found out who the perpetrators might be yet?"

"Well, it's coming along, but so far, we don't have anyone in custody and charged with murder. All we have are suspects who might have had a motive, and there seems to be several of them," Dibbs said, with a look of bewilderment. "I just wish whoever did this, or had it done, would screw up somewhere so we could nail him. I haven't seen anything like this in a while."

"What else ya got, John?"

"Here's the list of possible suspects who had both motive and opportunity. There is Thomas Denby, an attorney, and then the CEO of Colonial Paper, who hired Denby to defend his company in a case that the belated Judge Parks was presiding over. There's also Eleanor Parks and her boyfriend, who had more than two-million dollars to gain in insurance benefits."

"That's complex, John," said McAlistair, as he furrowed his brow and started to give input.

"Wait, Mac, there's more. There's Pablo Esteban, whom we have in custody, and Roberto Solis, his partner, who died in the shoot-out they had with the South Carolina Highway Patrol after ramming Paula Cooper's SUV with their van. She is the paralegal who Denby sent to the judge's party in a blackmail scheme. We think that these people are lower-level soldiers in the scheme. Finally, there is Manuel Hernandez, the drug kingpin, who, when Judge Parks sentenced him, swore in his courtroom that he would kill him one day. Though he's in the federal penitentiary, we have reason to believe he's still active in crime."

"Sounds like maybe you need to put the pressure on the man in custody and figure out a way to make him crack. Got anymore on him?"

"He's a Puerto Rican man, who's been in the country for a number of years. He married a Cuban American woman in Miami, and has been working in Charleston. We think Esteban knows more, but he's not talking."

"I see," said McAlistair. "Sounds like you've got your work cut out for you."

"What doesn't make sense to me is why those who wanted the judge dead also want Miss Cooper dead. What did she have to do with the judge, other than the fact that she was involved in the blackmail plot? She heard the sound of the gun go off and witnessed the hideous murder of Judge Parks. She was in shock for several hours afterwards. Paula

Cooper has no more idea of who might have killed Judge Parks than a man on the moon."

"John, whoever killed, or had the judge killed, may not know that. Sounds like the person who authorized the blackmail plot would want her dead, if that same person had the judge killed. Then again, what about the drug lord Hernandez and his henchmen? Those guys are accustomed to assassinations."

"That's true, but I have a hunch that whoever murdered Parks knew about Hernandez's threats against the judge, and he decided to make the crime appear as if he was the perpetrator. I can't be sure, and I don't have any hard evidence. I just have a feeling," said Dibbs, as he tossed his arms in the air and let them flop to his sides in exasperation.

"Hang in there and keep the pressure up. Something will break eventually. Do you remember the last case you had that came to the lab? You had hunches about that one too, but the empirical evidence led you to the murderer."

"True enough, Mac. The local police in Charleston are saying that the way the private investigator was murdered indicates a trained killer at work. The murderer used a steel wire instead of a knife to help keep his DNA off the victim. The precision with which he did his job, and left the crime scene without a trace is incredible; no clues where he came from or how he left. The only thing we know is that there was at least one unidentified Hispanic man in the valet staff who was parking cars. When we ran an ID on him, it came back as Jose Fernandez, the Spanish equivalent of John Smith. Do you have any idea how many Jose Fernandez there are in the world? It was a bogus name, social security card, and driver's license—the whole works. He had everything fixed as airtight as a CIA agent would. I haven't seen anything this good since the disappearance of Jimmy Hoffa."

"That is all the more reason why you need to get that Esteban dude to squeal. Just keep following every lead you have and I'll contact you if I come up with anything new. You can do it, man. Oh yeah, and get some sleep. You look like crap," said his old college friend with a chuckle.

"Thanks a lot, you old fart," Dibbs fired back. "If you weren't such a wimp, you would be out here with me on the case instead of hiding behind these walls in your lab coat." Dibbs laughed and shook hands with McAlistair. "Well, we better take this report and get back to Charleston; there aren't too many flights out of DC that way."

Although Mendez was with Dibbs, he was along as his sidekick, and he knew his role. Dibbs was lead investigator on cases they worked together. Mendez led his own cases at times, but when with Dibbs, he deferred to him to learn all the tricks of the trade. Dibbs appreciated that about Mendez, as well as the fact that he contributed immensely in his own quiet way, when appropriate.

"One more thing," said Dibbs.

"Yeah, what's that, John?" McAlistair looked up from his report.

"If my buddy here ever needs any help, see that you do what you can to treat him like you would me, okay?"

"Sure thing, John, I can do that, but does he really understand what that means?" asked McAlistair, laughing. "Good riddance, now get out of here and bring in the murderer."

"Ten-four, we're out, until next time," said Dibbs.

Once inside their black Crown Vic on the drive to Dulles International, the two agents opened up about their impressions of the investigation.

"Well, what do you think at this point, Mendez? You have access to as much information about the case as I do," Dibbs said.

"John, I want to depose five people before I can give you anything much. I think that one of these five will slip up somewhere. I am confident that if we hold our course and be patient, the killer will surface. I'm thinking that the double murder was not premeditated but was the result of the private investigator being in the wrong place at the wrong time," Mendez replied.

"I agree with that totally. Sad to say, but our bosses are not concerned about the death of McCaffery. The Charleston Police and Charleston Sheriff's Office were given that jurisdiction. We have to exhaust all our efforts in finding the murderer of Judge Parks," said Dibbs.

"That's true, but as I'm sure you are aware, we can't ignore the facts surrounding the murder of McCaffery because the same man may have killed Judge Parks."

"Yep, but keep in mind that the murderer was after the judge and that McCaffery was merely in the way. So, we know that the one who authorized the assassination only had the judge in mind," Dibbs said.

"Not necessarily, John. What if the one who authorized it, knew of the plot to blackmail Judge Parks? He would have known that McCaffery was privy to that and wanted him out of the way, also."

"Good point, Albert. I thought of that, but I sort of let the idea go to the back burner because I'm thinking of ruling out Denby, even though I know I shouldn't at this point. We cannot underestimate the author of such brutality, especially when this person planned everything with such depth and detail. Take a look at the way two murders occurred and another one attempted on the life of Paula Cooper. I am not so much referring to the technique as I am to the timing and the ones who were attacked. Does that not tell us anything, or could this just be the way a murderer works to eliminate any chance for those who might be able to testify?"

"Like I said, John, the case is still too complex for me to narrow down until I can get those persons deposed. I think that something will come out then. All I can say is that the evidence poses quite a mystery at this point, and unless something breaks soon, the trail may cool off. The killer could have time to cover his tracks."

25

The agents arrived at Dulles International, found their way to the gate, and checked in just in time to claim their seats before the final warning was given. They chose two seats on one side of the plane where they had privacy to chat. Dibbs tossed his bag in an overhead compartment, and Mendez followed suit. Upon take off, they resumed the conversation where they left off.

"Then let's stay at this around the clock, twenty-four seven, until we crack the case. Do you think your wife will allow that? If she will, I'll get clearance for more overtime," Dibbs said.

"I'm willing," said Mendez. "She knows overtime comes with the territory of being married to an FBI agent. We got married when we graduated from college, and she's been supportive of my career. The deal was that I would work while she raised the kids, and that's what we've always done. If my career requires more time than we like, then we put up with it, as long as I enjoy my work, and I do. Besides, you know if we can solve this case, we will likely be in for promotions. I need that to happen so I'm not stuck on my current pay grade. We've got three kids, and she's a stay-at-home mom."

"That is true dedication, Mendez. You'll make a fine FBI Director one day."

"Oh, I'm dedicated alright. I have no comment on your second wise crack. By the way, are you going to call me "Mendez", "good buddy", or "Albert"? You're confusing me, dude."

"I've always called you whatever, good buddy," said Dibbs, chuckling.

Mendez had great qualities about him and being a minority helped his chances. The fact that he was a veteran would also help him advance within the FBI, if he played his cards correctly. Dibbs had never seen him shrink back from anything.

"Oh, shut your mouth, John! You know what I'm saying. I would be satisfied with your pay grade. You're the one who has his sights set on becoming the big cheese in the ivory tower, not me."

"Yeah, right, whatever you say."

"Seriously, John, let's get the depositions and see what shakes out."

"I'm with you on that one hundred percent," said Dibbs.

The plane carrying the two agents touched down on the runway in Charleston. They heard the tires on the MD-80 screech as it hit the runway, and then felt the bump as the aircraft slowed to its taxing speed as it rolled toward the terminal to dock.

"All passengers are to remain in their seats with their seatbelts fastened until the plane has taxied to a complete stop and the red-light changes to green. The weather is fair with a temperature of sixty-five degrees. Thank you for flying Celtic Airlines," said the pilot.

The flight attendants scampered around, making final preparations as the plane continued to taxi towards the concourse.

"Why don't we divide and conquer to get the depositions arranged? That way, we can get them done quicker and you won't have too much on your plate, Mendez."

"Good idea, John. Why don't you get the three English speakers, and I'll get the two Hispanics since I'm the bilingual one here," Mendez said.

"Alright, that's sounds like a great plan. I'll arrange the depositions for Paul Walker, Thomas Denby, and Eleanor Parks. You make the arrangements for Manuel Hernandez and Pablo Esteban."

"We need to get court orders issued fast to get them to the depositions, and we need to move quickly before the trail cools off, or someone else is killed," Mendez said.

"You got that right. We have to get the court orders signed and delivered, to give parties sufficient notice to appear. First thing tomorrow, please make sure that the Federal Judicial Center can accommodate us with a conference room for the depositions. I am going to interview Paula Cooper one more time by phone to find out a couple of answers I need regarding Thomas Denby and Paul Walker. Apparently, she also knows Walker rather well, so she might know why he was squirming so much when we interviewed him at work," Dibbs said.

The green light came on, and the passengers were up, quickly moving about, gathering luggage from overhead compartments, trying to be the first down the aisle to exit the plane. A young businessman pushing his way down the aisle bumped a woman out of the way and then shoved Dibbs. He may as well have pushed *Dirty Harry*.

"What's your rush, sonny? You just pushed this lady who was ahead of you out of your way, and now you are leaning on me?"

"Get out of the way, old man!" cracked the businessman. "I don't have time for you Southerners parading about to right every wrong. That woman stood up in my way on purpose. She could see I was in a hurry."

The insolent young man was so self-absorbed that he did not realize how much he had overstepped his bounds. Dibbs stood upright in the aisle, loosening his shoulders. His height filled the space, the cabin seeming to shrink around him. Without another word, he pulled the man up by his necktie until they were standing inches apart.

"I don't have time for punks like you who think they have the world by the tail. Look down, son. Do you see the holster and gun under my left arm?"

"Yes, sir, I see it," the man said, his pitch higher than before.

"It's a government-issued weapon, son, and you know what? I don't need it to teach you some manners."

Mendez jumped up and laid his hand on Dibbs' back. "Easy, John, easy, he's not worth the trouble."

John jerked his shoulder, shaking off Albert's hand. "Yeah, I know he's not, Mendez. I can handle this. I'm just trying to teach this young man a lesson."

"Sonny boy, now turn around and apologize to the lady and go back to your seat until the rest of the passengers get off the plane. Understand?" said Dibbs.

"Yes, sir, I do."

He held the frightened young man on his tiptoes, glaring at him with a scowl that would have scared the paint off a new car. As Dibbs released him, the young man did exactly as he was told, straightening his tie as he went back to his seat. Passengers close by the incident applauded Dibbs for what he did. The scene occurred so fast that the flight attendants were unaware of what had happened because the crowd was in the aisle.

The young man could have filed a complaint, but he knew he was in the wrong. Ashamed, he ducked his head and exited the plane at the tail end of the line without saying a word to anyone. Embarrassed and shaken that Dibbs had pulled him up off the ground with one hand, correcting him publicly, he wanted to disappear into a crowd as quickly as he could. He had learned a lesson that would save many others the aggravation of engaging a prideful jerk in the future.

The agents walked through the airport making small talk. When they reached the front of the airport, they took an escalator downstairs where they picked up their luggage and a rental car.

"See you later this week," said Mendez. He shook John's hand and laughed at his partner.

"Yeah, will do," said Dibbs. "I'll be around."

The next two days were spent churning out subpoenas to the suspects in the murders of Judge Wilmont Parks and Dave McCaffery: a drug lord in federal prison, Paula Cooper's attacker incarcerated in the county jail, the CEO of Colonial Paper Mill, a crooked attorney, and the widow of Judge Parks.

Empirical evidence pointed to a military-trained assassin hired by someone with a motive to kill Judge Parks. Whoever hired the killer had left very few clues, except that he may have also tried to kill Paula Cooper, which made the investigation very tough. There was nothing left for the agents to do but depose the five suspects and see what developed. So far, none of the five had cracked, if any of them were involved with the murders.

J. Thomas Denby had returned to Georgetown on a temporary release and was trying to resurrect his struggling law practice since several attorneys and staff had quit. Clients were falling off like quail targeted by a group of expert hunters with double-barreled shotguns. Tom had not done anything else to help the FBI after giving them the fax from Paul Walker. It was his last best chance to get leniency.

Walker had contacted several of his prominent friends in the area, suggesting they drop Denby, and everyone followed his recommendation. Payback for Denby was hell. Walker even recruited some of Denby's clerical help, asking them to leave the law firm and come to work at the paper mill in jobs with equal pay but much better benefits. The retirement plan and insurance plan at Colonial Paper was something everyone in the community envied.

Denby deflected much of the attention from himself and his conspiracy charges to a back compartment in his mind. He realized that his case, a federal offense, would be adjudicated in the same court as the Parks and McCaffery murders, but it would take a backseat to those cases. If only he could provide enough information to satisfy the District Attorney's office, he would be happy.

Denby had gambled one too many times on the unpredictability of the human spirit in complicated schemes of deceit. Paula Cooper could not tolerate his lies anymore and was willing to risk everything to break free. Redemption from this colossal disaster was the glimmer of hope to which she clung. Denby was so cocky that he did not see it coming until it was too late.

26

Pablo Esteban was offered consideration on his charges ranging from attempted vehicular manslaughter to murder of a Highway Patrolman, although he claimed not to be a shooter. Mysteriously, when he surrendered, a gun was not found on him. There was a search underway, but the abundant water near the shootout probably hid the missing weapon. Esteban refused to sing the song the authorities wanted to hear because he knew that the person who hired him would kill him, if he were to point the finger.

The day for the depositions at the Federal Judicial Center adjacent to the "Four Corners of Law," drew near. This famous corner in Charleston, at the intersection of Meeting and Broad Street, is where St. Michael's Episcopal Church was constructed between 1752 and 1761, located on the southeast corner. In its churchyard are the graves of Charles Cotesworth Pinckney and John Rutledge, signers of the United States Constitution. On the northeast corner of the Four Corners is Charleston City Hall, built in the Adamesque-style between 1800 and 1804. Across the street, on the northwest corner, stands the Charleston County Courthouse, originally constructed in 1753 as South Carolina's provincial capital. The building was remodeled in 1792 for use as a courthouse. On the southwest corner are the United States Post Office and the Federal Courthouse. The term "Four Corners of the Law" represents the presence of these institutions from federal, state, local, and ecclesiastical law, on each corner of the famed intersection. The joke in Charleston is that a person could get married, divorced, commit a crime, and be sentenced, then write a letter detailing the events and mail it from jail, all in the same day. Oddly enough, apparently one couple accomplished this feat in the long history of these institutions.

Manuel Hernandez was brought in on an early morning flight and would depose first since he had to have the most security and was potentially the most dangerous to be out in public. Two federal marshals, on either side of Hernandez, were constantly by his side to deter an attack team from attempting to free him. The shackles he wore around his wrists and ankles further limited any chance of flight.

The same was true with Pablo Esteban, although the two men who escorted him were sheriff deputies. Though jurisdictional lines overlapped, thus far, all branches were cooperating seamlessly. Esteban held dark secrets, but had not given Dibbs and Mendez much to go on, fearing for his life. Puerto Ricans value freedom the most and having that taken away was extremely difficult for him. He never imagined himself in jail.

The depositions were scheduled as follows: Manuel Hernandez - 9:00 AM, Pablo Esteban - 10:00 AM, and J. Thomas Denby - 11:00 AM. Around noon, the lawyers and staff would meet to collect their thoughts for about thirty minutes. From 12:30 PM until 2:00 PM, they had lunch, which would be spent setting strategy for the afternoon depositions. At 2:30

PM, they were scheduled to depose Paul Walker, and lastly, at 3:30 PM, Eleanor Parks Eastwood.

The cat was out of the bag regarding the Eastwoods' marriage when the Charleston Courier printed a public announcement. Chuck and Eleanor did not have any idea that the news of their marriage on the cruise-liner would hit the local newspaper. It caused quite a stir in Charleston, with rumors throughout town that they had the judge killed. Apparently, an obscure policy of the Caribbean Queen was to release news of all marriages to the hometown newspapers of the newlyweds.

The clipping read: "Jazz trumpet player, Chuck Eastwood, marries Eleanor Parks, the recent widow of the late Honorable Judge Wilmont Parks. The two were on a cruise in the Caribbean and were wed in a private ceremony." A recently issued insurance policy prior to the judge's premature death was motive enough to raise the ire of the Feds, but the wedding hoisted red flags in the minds of the prosecutors, who were sure to examine this suspicious fact.

Manuel Hernandez, escorted by the two marshals, sat in the hallway waiting for his name to be announced. His attorney, Mr. Anderson, was present to defend his client every step of the way. The federal prosecutors called the first witness.

"Mr. Manuel Hernandez, you may come in now," said one of the prosecutorial team.

The prosecutors were in their mid-thirties, but seasoned enough, having served for seven years in the Federal Court System. Hernandez, in his shackles, sat down, wearing a gray jumpsuit issued to him by the US Federal Prison. The questioning began with the usual recitation of normal data, i.e. name, birth date, location of current address, etc. Once the proceedings commenced, the court reporter spoke every word softly, but clearly, into the cupped microphone area of the Dictaphone.

"What, if anything, do you know about the murder of Judge Wilmont Parks?" began Mr. Riley.

Hernandez responded with an answer that surprised the prosecutors. "I have some information that may be of use to you, señor, but I must ask that if I am able to help you identify the murderer of Judge Parks that you will put in writing a deal for me for an early release."

The two prosecutors, Jacobson and Riley, looked at each other briefly, disapproving of his proposal via eye contact and a wag of the heads. Riley eyed Hernandez, "If you refuse to answer the question and hide information, then you are in violation of federal law, and you can be charged with a crime, Mr. Hernandez."

The lawyer for Hernandez spoke up. "I gave those exact words to my client, anticipating your question, and that is our position, Mr. Riley. Is this deposition over now, or are you willing to draw up some papers for us?"

"Let's be reasonable, sir," said Riley to the attorney. "You should know that striking a deal like that is not that easy. We would have to call the Attorney General for guidance."

"Well, then, if you have any other questions for my client, or wish to offer a deal, you can get back in touch with me," spoke the veteran attorney from Miami.

"Wait just a moment, Mr. Anderson." Riley and Jacobson conferred with each other for a few minutes, and then Riley approached Agent Dibbs to confer with him. Turning back to the conference table, he addressed the attorney. "That will be fine. We have no more questions for your client, Mr. Anderson. My office, or Agent Dibbs' office, will be in touch with you regarding any further dealings with your client."

With this brief exchange, the deposition of Manuel Hernandez was completed after only ten minutes. Agents Dibbs and Mendez did not expect Hernandez to offer any future help because the prisoner made gaining any useful information too difficult. Since each suspect was instructed to be present an hour ahead of time, there was no wait between depositions for the next one to begin. Hernandez and his attorney left.

The FBI agents conferred with each other as Pablo Esteban was escorted into the conference room. "Wonder what Hernandez was willing to tell us?" asked Dibbs to Mendez. "Do you think he can really finger who killed the judge?"

"John, he's a very wealthy man, and although his wings have been clipped by the prison system, he still has contacts in many places. He can threaten lives and shell out money through his contacts, same as an incarcerated Mafia boss could do. Remember how we commented on this when we read his dossier last week?"

"So, what are you saying, Mendez? Do you think that Hernandez is responsible for the murders?"

"He could be and is trying to pin his crime on someone else. Then again, he might truly know something and want to work a deal for an early release. It's tough to say at this juncture."

"True enough. Let's just keep going with the depositions and keep an open mind. We can talk to Riley and Jacobson afterwards to find out what they think about cutting a deal. They couldn't negotiate a deal on their own because it would have to be approved by the Attorney General."

"Once again, John, you amaze me with your wisdom, and you're only forty-four? Yeah, let's follow that course of action and see what happens." Mendez said facetiously.

The prosecutors called their next witness.

Esteban waited between the two deputies in the hall for his turn to say his piece. He thought about betraying the trust of the one who hired him, but when he evaluated that the cost of his freedom would likely be a quick death sentence, deciding that jail was not so bad after all. With a good attorney, he would be out in six to ten years, and that surely beat pushing up daisies.

"Deputies, you can bring Pablo Esteban into the conference room now," said a federal marshal, who poked his head out in the hallway.

"Let's go, Esteban," commanded one of the deputies.

Esteban shuffled into the conference room, shackled, wearing an orange jumpsuit. He was unshaven, disheveled, and smelled to high heavens. He had refused to shower or shave when his attorney told him he was required to depose. The Sheriff thought his lack of hygiene was some sort of protest, but actually, Esteban was scared for his life and avoided activities with other inmates.

"Buenos dias, señores," Esteban said respectfully to the FBI agents and the federal attorneys.

"Good morning, Mr. Dreher. Your client can sit here by the second microphone, sir," said Riley.

Esteban's attorney, Bill Dreher, motioned for his client to take a seat in the designated spot. The questioning began, as before, with the usual affirmation of personal information and acknowledgment as to the purpose of the deposition.

"Mr. Esteban, could you tell us why you wanted to harm Miss Paula Cooper by ramming her vehicle on the morning of December 19th as she was crossing SC Highway 517, the Isle of Palms connector bridge?" asked Riley.

"I object to that line of questioning. We are here only to be questioned about the untimely death of Judge Wilmont Parks, are we not?" interrupted Mr. Dreher.

"Yes, of course, we are, Mr. Dreher. We believe the two events are related. We have reason to believe your client was at the party that Judge Parks held the night he was murdered."

Mr. Riley continued his questioning of the witness.

"Now, Mr. Esteban, were you working in the valet staff at Judge Parks' party on December the 14th?"

"Yes, sir, I was working there."

"Did you see, or do you know anything about, who may be involved in the murder of Judge Wilmont Parks?"

"No, I do not."

"Mr. Esteban, do you realize that if you hold back information which would otherwise lead to the arrest and conviction of the murderer of Judge Parks, then you will be charged with aiding and abetting a federal crime? Already you are charged in a separate case, as your attorney so ably pointed out. Do you realize the seriousness of the situation and the importance of being straightforward and honest with us today?"

Dreher had no objection. He waited with a poker face to hear what his client would say.

"I understand this, señor, but do you realize that if I talk to shorten my time in jail, then I will only be signing my death sentence? So, which is better? You tell me."

"What if we are able to provide protective custody for you, Mr. Esteban, so that you are not in danger of being killed by whomever you may be referencing?"

"Señor Riley, how can I be sure that I will be protected?"

"We arrange protection all the time for others in cases like this. There are many people living with assumed names in other parts of the country with new beginnings. We can give you a new identity, a place to live, and a fresh start, including job placement assistance," said Riley.

"I will have to think about this offer. I want to help you so that I can help myself. I miss my family. I have a wife and three small children in Miami, but I also want to live, even if in prison. I am not a bad man. I just got down on my luck and tried to make some quick money so my family would not be thrown out of our apartment."

"I understand," said Riley. "Either you can contact your attorney or call us directly if you have anything to tell us. We are willing to work out a deal, if you can lead us to the person, or persons, who had Judge Parks murdered."

"Gracias, señor, I will tell you this. I am not the one who did that, Señor Riley. I didn't know why we were ramming into the back of the car with the woman in it. The man who I was riding with had been painting some houses with me. We were between jobs when he asked me to come along for the ride. We were to scare this woman, is all he said. The man driving paid me two hundred bucks to ride with him for about an hour. I didn't ask no questions. The job seemed like a quick and easy way to make some cash, which I needed to send my wife, Gloria. I know it was wrong," said Esteban.

"Is there anything else, Mr. Esteban?"

"No señor, not until I know that you can relocate me and my family."

"That will be all for now, Mr. Esteban," said Riley. "We'll get back to you after we talk to the District Attorney about the witness protection program in exchange for your testimony."

Agents Dibbs and Mendez watched carefully as he testified. "He has credibility," Dibbs said to Mendez.

"That, he does," Mendez responded.

27

The deputies escorting Pablo Esteban left the conference room. His chains rattled as he shuffled down the glossy, waxed marble floor of the judicial center and through its wide hallways. They took the prisoner down the steps outside, leading him to the transport vehicle. Lowering his head to avoid injury, the deputies placed him in the back seat of a sheriff's department SUV where a steel cage separated riders from the driver. The doors automatically locked and could be opened only from the outside. This was one of the few times, since being arrested, that Esteban was not handcuffed to a deputy when he was out of his cell. His instinct was to run if he ever got the chance.

The deputies had to complete a comprehensive course in criminal justice and pass with an eighty average to be considered for the sheriff's department. Otherwise, they were not deemed the caliber needed to serve. Instead of the Barney Fife type of deputy of old, these young men and women had high school diplomas and usually some college experience. Most of them were ex-military and acquainted with principles of law enforcement; they were able to handle themselves and their weapons. However, a mundane routine can cause anyone not to perform at his best. The driver of the prisoner shuttle had drifted into a malaise from monotonous, routine transporting of inmates to and from various facilities. He did not take the time to read the file he had on his seat, which gave him information regarding how dangerous this man may be, and how extra care should be given when transporting him.

At the Federal Judicial Center, the next person to be deposed, J. Thomas Denby, pulled up his chair and took the witness oath *to tell the whole truth, and nothing but the truth.* Riley had yielded to his partner, Jake Jacobson, to continue with the next deposition.

"State your name, birth date, and place of birth, please, for the record," said Jacobson.

"J. Thomas Denby, October, 14th, 1956. I was born in Socastee, South Carolina."

"And what is your profession, Mr. Denby?"

"I am an attorney in Georgetown, SC."

"And how long have you practiced law, Mr. Denby?"

"For twenty-nine years, Mr. Jacobson, almost as long as you are old."

He hoped that his arrogant attitude towards the young federal prosecutor would disrupt his rhythm. Denby disdained any attorney who could not set out and succeed on his own. He placed the federal attorneys, who made their living in comfortable jobs with guaranteed pay, shying away from the risk of private practice, in this category.

Jacobson grinned as he took Denby's pot shot without acknowledging his sarcasm. "How did you become involved with the circumstances surrounding the murder of Judge Wilmont Parks? And what can you tell us about it that may be of help in our investigation?"

Open-ended questions were much better than yes or no questions that limited the responses. Denby recognized that Jacobson was good at employing this tactic, yet he could not resist the urge to ramble in his defense.

"I can honestly say that I do not know how or why his murder occurred, Mr. Jacobson, but I will say that I did a thorough investigation of Judge Wilmont Parks. I found that he had an estranged wife who is an alcoholic and given to rage. And, as most everyone knows, the judge was tough on crime, jailing a few notorious drug lords during his ten years on the bench."

"I see, Mr. Denby. And did you have any contact with Judge Parks during the week of his murder or authorize anyone else to have contact with him?"

"If you are referring to Paula Cooper and Dave McCaffery being at his home to do a job I sent them on, I did. In good faith, I told Agent Dibbs about that already to help your investigation, sir."

"Yes, so you did, Mr. Denby, but for the record today, what can you tell us about the details of your plan?"

"I suspected the separated Judge Parks would be vulnerable to an attractive woman, so I sent Paula..., excuse me, Miss Paula Cooper, to hopefully entice him into an embrace. Dave McCaffery, a private investigator, was to capture the embrace on video. We believed his estranged wife, Eleanor Parks, would jump at the chance to have her husband in divorce court, trying to take him for everything she could, if she was privy to his actions. I intended to use the tape to coerce the judge to toss the Colonial Paper Mill case out on a technicality. That was our plan, and the next thing I know, Judge Parks is murdered, and I am being investigated. Like I've said before, I didn't do it, and I don't have any knowledge of it."

"Mr. Denby, why should we believe you didn't have anything to do with the murder since you were bold enough to attempt blackmailing a federal judge?" inquired Jacobson.

"You can choose to believe my innocence, or not. That's up to you, based on everything you discover and how you size me up, but I am not a murderer, Mr. Jacobson."

"Yes, Mr. Denby. That is our job, and that is precisely what we will do."

Jacobson did not believe or disbelieve him. He had learned in law school to suspend judgment until he could gather all the facts and not to believe a liar, not that Denby was lying. Riley took a couple of steps toward Jacobson, passing him a single, yellow, square sticky. Jacobson glanced down at the note and stuffed it in his coat pocket. He kept reading from his prepared list of questions. A few more questions, and then taking a peek at the slip of paper from his coat pocket, he yielded to Riley.

"Mr. Denby, have you ever been investigated for previous involvement in a murder case?" asked Riley.

Denby wondered how in the world the young attorneys had uncovered that bit of information from several years earlier. How he answered this question would change the course of his testimony. If he lied, then the record would show that he violated his sworn oath; if he told the truth, the investigators would know that he was questioned in a murder case years before, and although the charges were dropped, his involvement appeared unfavorable. Denby grimaced as he reluctantly offered an explanation.

"Yes, of course, Mr. Riley, I have nothing to hide. Several years ago, I was questioned as a person of interest, but the investigation was a mistake, and the charges were dropped."

"Would you care to elaborate on the circumstances surrounding these charges, Mr. Denby?"

"Mr. Riley, I'm not going to answer that question because what happened many years ago is totally irrelevant to this case. I'm trying to comply with all your questioning, but this is going beyond the scope of the present investigation. I also move that the previous question and answer be stricken from the record on the grounds that they are both irrelevant."

Riley spoke to the court reporter. "Let the record show that the witness objects to the previous question and answer and is acting as his own attorney."

"Very well, Mr. Denby, we'll move on. Just one more question...have you ever been in contact with a reported Mafia boss in New York City named Frankie Valentino?"

The name was unmistakable, but how did they get his name? *One phone call and they must have recorded it somehow,* Denby thought, as he squirmed. He wanted to dodge the question altogether. This one was touchier than the previous one.

"My memory is not clear on the subject. I talk to as many as twenty or thirty people in a day."

"Think, Mr. Denby. If you are not involved, as you say, then I would think I am making a reasonable request for you to tell us everything you know."

Denby paused for a minute, scratched his head, and calculated whether he should share his recollection or not. "I may have received a phone call on one occasion from a gentleman by that name, but as you know, Mr. Riley, I represent many types of people in trouble with the law. Civil and criminal law have been my practice for more than twenty-five years. Of course, I am selective about what cases I take, and if I remember this gentleman correctly, I turned down his request for representation."

"That will be all, no further questions today, Mr. Denby."

"We'll break for lunch now," said Mr. Jacobson.

The court reporter pulled the blue, cupped mask from her face and tapped the "off" button on the Dictaphone. All parties in the room stood to their feet and exited into the hallway, each going his separate way. Riley and Jacobson lingered behind the others for a few minutes, conferring with Dibbs and Mendez.

The ride back to the county jail began uneventfully as Deputy Ken Abrams drove down Broad Street and took a right on Ashley. There were many tourists and college-aged young people in the streets that day for the beginning of the Spoleto Festival, the largest celebration of art and jazz that came to Charleston each year. The transport vehicle turned slowly down a narrow cobblestone street to avoid the horse and buggy carriages, which were directly in front of the vehicle.

The buggy rides are a highlight of Charleston tourism, as they tour through the Holy City. Usually, college dropouts, in search of themselves, drive the carriages, drawn by a Belgian Draft horse, or two, depending on the size of the buggy. The drivers chant their repetitious versions of Charleston history to their passengers while attempting to be both entertainingly humorous and informative. The most prominent sound, though, is the clippidy-clop of the horses' hooves keeping time, while the tourists gawk at the wonderful architectural schemes of times past.

Olive-complexioned, and muscular with black hair and brown eyes, he could have been mistaken for a tourist, except this man had a different gate to his walk and was taller than most Latinos were. Seemingly, out of nowhere, he trotted up beside the slow-moving transport vehicle, which was delayed by tourists searching for parking. Armed with a deadly, automatic weapon and fully loaded clip, he scooted up to the back of the SUV transporter. With one hand, he grabbed the handle of the back door and hoisted himself to an upright position for a short ride on the bumper. With precision, he drew his nine-millimeter pistol from an underarm holster and pumped five rounds of lead through the back glass, striking Esteban's head and neck.

Four shots were aimed at Esteban, and the final round was fired at the deputy's head but missed. The deputy ducked then whirled around, peeking over the front seat to see what was happening. He prepared to return fire, but before he could, the mysterious shooter jumped off the vehicle and ran down the side street back to the main street, disappearing into the crowd. The deputy, though stunned, was relieved the bullet had missed him. He tried to speed up, but there were so many people walking on the sidewalks and crossing the streets that he could not gain much ground without the danger of hitting a pedestrian.

Frantically, he grabbed his radio from its cradle. "This is Deputy Ken Abrams; we have an emergency, I repeat, a code blue emergency. My passenger has been shot and is seriously wounded. The assailant is male, six feet tall, medium build, wearing dark clothing and sunglasses. He is armed and dangerous, and on foot, over."

"Ten-four, Deputy Abrams, we copy you. Backup is on the way," said the dispatcher. She received his location and other information.

"Copy that, dispatch, I'm taking the wounded passenger to the closest ER. He appears to be bleeding out."

Esteban was losing consciousness and fading into shock from loss of blood. He groaned in Spanish as he choked on his own fluids. "Jesus Cristo, ten misericordia de mí," he said twice, the second time with more difficulty than the first, then passed out in the back seat.

The federal prosecutors had lunch not far from the Courthouse, eating their fried seafood baskets. Jacobson crunched a few fried shrimp and hushpuppies then sipped his iced tea. Riley munched on a cheeseburger and fries then slurped a coke from a straw. Dibbs and Mendez joined the prosecutors to commiserate regarding the morning testimonies and to strategize for the afternoon depositions.

"Man, this case has me smoking again, John," said Mendez, as he took a drag from his cigarette.

"I know what you mean. Give me one of those cancer sticks. I need something to calm my nerves," said Dibbs.

"What bothers me is that the one responsible could be behind bars already, for all we know, or walking around as free as a bird, like us," Mendez quipped.

"You guys are on top of things. Something will break soon," said Riley, attempting to encourage the agents.

"Yeah," said Jacobson, "you men are the best. That's all we ever hear about you two. Don't second guess yourselves."

"Thanks for saying that. We'll try and not disappoint your lofty opinion of us, right, Mendez?"

"That's right, John. We'll do our best. You guys aren't so bad, yourselves," said Mendez.

"You gentlemen ready to get back and finish up with the remaining depositions?" asked Riley.

"Yeah, let's get them behind us," said Dibbs.

The four men returned to the judicial center just before a deputy trotted up the stairs and entered the hallway, handing a note to a federal marshal stationed near the conference room. The marshal glanced at the note intended for the federal attorneys. He approached the prosecutors, passing it to Mr. Jacobson, who read it in disbelief then wagged his head in disgust.

"What have you got there, Jake?" asked Riley.

"Tragic news, I'm afraid."

"I have enough mysteries on my hands. I was hoping to hear good news. What is it?"

Jacobson clinched his jaw as he passed the note to Riley. "Read it for yourself."

"My God, Esteban has been shot and is in critical condition. How the hell did this happen?" Riley asked, in disbelief.

Hearing what just happened; Dibbs and Mendez were suddenly energized, and bolted into action. The frustration level reached a new peak for Agents Dibbs and Mendez.

"I'll call Sheriff Bates and get the details," said Dibbs. "Marshal, do me a favor. Go get the deputy who brought you the note before he leaves the premises. I need to talk with him. It's urgent."

The marshal retrieved the deputy and brought him back inside to the agents.

"Deputy, I'm Agent Dibbs of the FBI. Do you know anything else about the shooting of Pablo

Esteban? To date, he was our most important witness in finding out who murdered Judge Parks and Dave McCaffery."

"Yes, sir, the man who was driving Esteban is a buddy of mine. He told me about the assault. The prisoner was being transported back to the Charleston County Jail down a side street when a lone assailant ran up to the vehicle with a pistol and pumped five rounds into the car. Three hit Esteban in the head and neck. Two bullets exited the front windshield. My buddy says he ducked for his life. He's pretty shaken up."

"Where did this shooter come from?"

"He said the attack happened so fast that he didn't know where the man came from. My buddy had to rush to the ER with the prisoner and never had a chance to pursue the suspect."

"Deputy, thank you for the information," Dibbs said dismissing the deputy to return to duty. *Who, on God's green earth, could be pulling all these strings in a cover-up attempt? Why was Esteban hit?* Dibbs wondered. He hoped the answer to that question would lead to the ruthless assassin.

"We must be on the right track if someone is trying to kill off our witnesses," said Dibbs. "Esteban must have known something worthwhile to be attacked like that."

"We only have half of the depositions completed and already another person has been shot. Geez, how many more such incidents are going to happen before we put the one responsible behind bars?" remarked Agent Mendez.

Riley and Jacobson informed the remaining witnesses that they would be contacted for a new deposition date within seven days and dismissed them. The security was tightened around the Judicial

Center due to the shooting of Esteban. Cancellation of the remaining two depositions seemed to be the only prudent option.

"Let's get out of here, Mendez," said Dibbs. "We've got to get on the trail of this killer."

"Let's roll, John. I want to get a shot at this guy."

Agents Dibbs and Mendez, along with many law enforcement personnel from other branches gathered by their vehicles, as they prepared their weapons and ammunition. They tossed ammunition clips and an assortment of weapons to each other from the trunks and backs of their vehicles as they shared strategy to canvas the area. An all-out search was initiated for the man in a black leather jacket and jeans. Some of them set out on foot, while others drove their squad cars, looking for the armed man. A few city police rode horses.

28

A real-life chess match was in action in which Pablo Esteban was a foot soldier, a mere pawn. He was offered up so that the power pieces, the queen, bishop, rook, and knight, could live to commit more crime another day. The king of law and justice could not capture the king of evil, so readily. Pawns and power pieces were sacrificed along the way before the queen, the second most valued piece, may be surrendered. The king, the author of the murders, could never be sacrificed, or the game would be over, checkmate. Preventing checkmate was the ultimate goal of the murderer of Judge Parks, and he employed the oldest strategy known to man in warfare, "A good offense is one's best defense."

Whenever a criminal was this good at second-guessing law enforcement and keeping one step ahead, he likely had committed similar crimes in the past, but was never caught. He was hidden, known only by very few, as the players performed their parts, one by one, to accomplish the implemented plan. The creator of this heinous deception seemed to have an army of loyal subjects who would kill each other, unwittingly, to protect the king. He was extremely crafty, forcing others to do the dirty work, and he chose the best to execute his ultimate plan. He remained an enigma no one could crack, and now, the best chance to find out the identity of this cold-blooded killer may have been eliminated.

All efforts to stabilize Esteban had been employed. He was in the Intensive Care Unit for thirty minutes, teetering between life and death before he succumbed to his death, and the monitor flatlined. Just an hour earlier, around high noon, Esteban had hopes of cutting a deal and starting a new life, even if he had to spend some time in the penitentiary first. The fact that he was a passenger in the van that rammed Paula Cooper and was unaware of the driver's intentions to harm her was in his favor. Most importantly, law enforcement never found the pistol that the other SC Highway Patrolmen in the shoot out said they saw Esteban shooting. None of these facts would help him now.

The streets of Charleston were buzzing with law enforcement, many of whom were plainclothes Feds, in search of Esteban's killer. Agents Dibbs and Mendez were busy with their fellow FBI agents and other officers in the streets in search of the suspect who had killed Pablo Esteban. The killer's actions were crisp and clean, as were those of Judge Parks and Dave McCaffery's assassin, the night of the Christmas party at Wellington Place. Dibbs and Mendez were in close proximity to each other, scouring a five-block territory from where the hit occurred. Packing their FBI-issued Glocks, both men kept in contact with each other and other law enforcement personnel with radios as they stalked their suspect.

"Let's canvas these two blocks going west, then turn and come back east down the next two. We'll ask merchants and passersby if they have seen anyone who fits the description of the perpetrator," Dibbs said to Mendez.

"I'm with you, John; just lead and I'll follow. We really need to get that guy before he shoots anyone else."

The agents padded down the streets, stopping to ask merchants, tourists, locals, and anyone they could about a man fitting the deputy's descriptions. After two hours of searching and discovering nothing, the agents were exasperated when their break came. To his surprise, Dibbs spotted a man who resembled the shooter, standing on a corner, waiting for a bus.

Dibbs pressed the button on his black Motorola to reach Mendez, who was standing no more than thirty yards away questioning a tourist. "Hey, Mendez, look by the bus stop across the street. Do you see what I do?"

Mendez excused himself and eased closer to the curb to get a better view of the corner. "I sure do. If that's not our man, then he would have to be his double. Let's approach him, John."

"No, wait. You follow me from a distance and let me get close to the bus shelter. I want to close in on him and take him by surprise. If you see me throw one hand up, rush in, and we'll arrest him on the spot. We don't want to flush him out into the streets."

"You're crazy. This man is a trained assassin, and you want to chance sneaking up on him. Let's just walk up nonchalantly and arrest him. If we make a mistake and he turns out to be someone else, he'll get over it. If that's him, he's gonna run or start firing."

"Exactly, Mendez, and just look how many people are in the streets right here. We need to prevent him from drawing his weapon and firing in the middle of this crowd."

"Then how do you want to handle this, then, John?"

"Let's try this. You go stand by the lamppost near the bus stop. I'll follow close behind you and enter the bus stop shelter from the other side. I'll approach the bench in the shelter to sit on the far end. My plan is to surprise him by getting close without him knowing, and then I'll place him under arrest. If he notices me, or begins to move, you will see it and can close in. In any case, get in there as quickly as you can once I make my move. Got it?"

"Yeah, I got it, but I don't like the plan. You're walking in by yourself."

"Two men would only alarm him and take away the element of surprise, Mendez. Trust me on this, or would you rather go in, and let me be your backup?"

"Have it your way. You're the senior agent here."

"Yeah, and don't forget that," Dibbs said, one-upping his fellow agent.

Dibbs unbuttoned his service revolver holster from inside his jacket pocket, as did Mendez. The agents were using an FBI technique to minimize the risk of two agents being injured at the same time, by separating, but staying within the other's line of sight. They wanted to nab the criminal with the least force possible and lessen the chance for injury to everyone in the vicinity. Dibbs and Mendez tried to blend with the crowd, but had just left the courthouse, not expecting to pursue a target, and were dressed in their traditional two-piece suits, white shirts, subdued ties, and dress shoes.

When Dibbs had Mendez's attention, he grabbed his tie, pulling it off in one quick yank, and stuffed it in sidewalk trashcan, to be a little less obvious. His partner followed suit. Dibbs led the way, using the crowd for cover as he ambled down the sidewalk, approaching the bus stop. He advanced within twelve feet of the Plexiglas and metal shelter when a large city bus barreling down the street swerved to the curb, its brakes squealing, as it came to a stop. *I can't let him get out of my sight,* thought Dibbs. From his closer vantage point, Dibbs could see that this man surely fit the description of the suspect.

Passengers waiting at the bus stop paused for a minute to allow offloading before they boarded. The suspect had inched his way through the crowd of waiting passengers, second in line to board. Dibbs got in line near the back, knowing that boarding the bus was his only chance not to lose him. Mendez did not know what to do, but Dibbs gave him a quick glance as he turned backwards, giving a hand signal that indicated that Mendez should not pursue, but rather radio in to headquarters what the situation was.

The suspect took the first available aisle seat near the front. Dibbs climbed the steps of the coach, grabbed an upright silver safety rail, and then turned ninety degrees, walking past the man. He scanned the suspect's face with the blink of an eye and pretended not to notice him. The face was one he had seen in a photo at the office. It was that of the notorious Cuban killer for hire, Juan Delgado.

Dibbs had forgotten about him for a while because he was supposed to be in Italy, according to the last report that he had accessed. He was also known for chasing women when he had breaks between the contracts, especially at the French Riviera when in Europe. At least, that is how Delgado's dossier read. This man was trained in an elite branch of the Cuban army, and in the Dirección General De Inteligencia, Cuba's version of the CIA. He knew how to handle a variety of weapons, and had never been beaten, except by one of his own compatriots in training exercises when he learned his skills. Delgado had defected when he was recruited by one of the Mafia families in New York who needed a man of his skills in their operations in South and Central America. He had eluded law enforcement on several occasions, most recently posing as an Italian woman in Sicily. The DEA was also searching for him in connection with bombings and killings surrounding drug deals.

Dibbs was trained in similar military fashion as a Navy SEAL, served in Desert Storm, and was tops in his class at the FBI Academy. He never feared anyone because his experience and training taught him that fear crippled critical thinking. Juan Delgado was one man who always intrigued him as a possible challenge to his own skills, if their paths were ever to cross. He did not realize that Delgado had seen him. Delgado figured that Dibbs was either highly trained FBI, or a foolish plainclothes cop who would soon become another victim. Delgado spied on Dibbs by glancing in the bus driver's rearview mirror. Both men were observing each other, but each was not sure if the other was privy to it.

Another stop and the bus let off passengers, as more boarded. As the bus rolled down the street again, Delgado rose up out of his seat to walk past Dibbs. *Not a good move for me,* thought Dibbs. *Either I tackle him now, or he will get the upper hand by being behind me.* As Delgado breezed past his seat, Dibbs sprang to his feet and landed on top of the Cuban. Passengers scrambled to get out of the way as the two men fought with a combination of grappling, boxing, and martial arts, each looking for the opportunity to draw his weapons. Dibbs was holding his own, trading blows with the Cuban when he slipped on the bus floor, falling down onto a seat.

Delgado struck Dibbs on the sides of his head with hard elbow blows and dropped on top of the agent, putting him in a chokehold.

Agent Dibbs struggled for air as he looked for an opportunity to whirl his legs around to deliver a kick to the Cuban's face. If Dibbs did not make a move to release quickly, his airway would collapse, and he would succumb to the blackness that flashed before his eyes. He knew the darkness he saw was a precursor to unconsciousness, then death. With all of his strength, Dibbs raised his lower body and spun his legs around with a furious, mule-like kick, delivering a blow to the middle of Delgado's face. The Cuban's nose broke instantly with a crunching sound, and spray of blood, as he released his grip on the agent's throat.

The bus driver, alarmed by the commotion, seeing some of the fight in his rearview mirror, continued along his route without stopping. His training taught him to radio in for help but to keep driving until assistance arrived. Delgado ran to the side exit of the bus, shoving passengers as he went, and then took two steps down to the exit door. Dibbs reached out to grab him by the collar, but Delgado kicked the door open and jumped out of the moving bus, his body hitting the sidewalk, and rolling over twice. Cat-like, he bounded to his feet, ran to the corner, and turned down a small, one-way street out of sight.

Dibbs was amazed at Delgado's quick movement considering the injury he just sustained. He gathered himself and showed his credentials to the driver demanding that he stop the bus immediately. Dibbs kept his eye on the street where Delgado disappeared and hopped off the bus in quick pursuit. Racing to the intersection, he radioed Mendez, and turned, watchfully scanning ahead before entering the one-way street. He knew that Delgado would not care that innocent people may be in danger in a crossfire. The only concern of the elusive assassin was getting away at any price to live freely for another day to make his fast money, as a "gun for hire."

Delgado believed he had to bump off Esteban because he would have revealed secrets that authorities would trace back to him, and then possibly to the mastermind of the judge's murder. Esteban had heard too much from a cell phone conversation Delgado had the day before the car chase with Paula Cooper. Delgado paid the two men to ram her SUV and to cause her serious harm, but they were unable to do because of Paula's daring driving skills. The one who had paid Delgado was still banking that he would never be discovered because he was that good and there were too many suspects involved.

Dibbs walked down a narrow side street made of cobblestone, overlaid with red brick. The street was lined with beautiful old Charleston homes, some dating back to the eighteenth century. Having read Delgado's dossier, he knew that anything was possible because the assassin knew what he was doing and was very resourceful. Many times, a professional would circle back for an attack rather than continue to run from those in pursuit, using the element of surprise, much like a bear in the wild does when being stalked by a hunter. Dibbs was well aware of this tactic and did not want to become a statistic. He was determined, however, to put his own life on the line to subdue this hardened criminal. Dibbs turned the corner at the intersection into a commercial district. He was ready for anything as he stuck close to the shops, hiding behind the crowds on the sidewalk as much as possible.

Suddenly, Delgado appeared, trotting between the tourists and shoppers who strolled down the streets at a leisurely pace. Dibbs kept pace with him, catching a glimpse as the Cuban darted in and out of the crowd. What he did not know was that Delgado was making a move to locate his final target. Turning a corner and jogging down another block, Delgado eluded his pursuer. Dibbs ran on through the intersection, thinking the suspect was straight ahead.

Spring was in the air, and Paula and Jim had come to look at houses in the Charleston area for a possible move in the future. They had talked about the possibility of marriage, but as of yet, Jim had not proposed. There were other things to get past first, and they both knew this. From the beginning of their chance encounter until this messy interruption, there had been some wonderful times. Now, their relationship was tested, although, it had stood up to the trial so far. Paula figured that if they married, her now infamous name and its association with the judge would fade away in time once she took Jim's name. The couple took a break from riding through neighborhoods and went downtown to eat and to browse the shops.

"This is one of my favorite shops, Jim."

"I can see why, dear. The dresses in the window look pretty snazzy."

"Jim, sweetie, look at the champagne colored dress." She pointed to a dress hanging on a mannequin in the corner of the window display. "It's elegant without revealing too much; only the back and arms are exposed."

"Yeah, I like that one a lot, and I like the baby blue dress too...the first one you looked at."

Delgado spotted Paula and Jim in front of a dress shop where everything from wedding gowns, to evening dresses, to sundresses, was for sale. Adrenaline surged through his veins as he thought about which way he would execute the final leg of his assignment. If he could kill Paula and get away, the authorities likely would not be able to pin anything on him, or on the one who hired him. Thinking about the risks of another daylight shooting, he preferred to follow Paula and Jim out of the city first. He figured he could hot-wire a car, but with Dibbs and Mendez on his tail, his preferred plan had to be altered. The stakes were all or nothing now.

Delgado crossed the street as the couple entered the dress shop. Dibbs had circled back to check the intersection again but instructed Mendez to go ahead so that both possible routes would be covered. As Dibbs arrived at the intersection, he looked left, then right. About middle ways down the block, he caught a glimpse of Delgado crossing the street and stopping near a lamppost, where he remained partially hidden. Although the Cuban was his enemy, Dibbs could not help but admire his stealthy movement as he stalked the suspect. He was curious why Delgado did not continue to flee, but rather hung out around a group of shops. Then a realization dawned on him—*another target, but who?* he wondered.

"Let's go inside to take a closer look for a few minutes, if you don't mind?"

"I'm following you, Paula," said Jim, smiling.

She loved that about him, that he was willing to let her be herself and tag along as a friend, not a control freak telling her what she should, or should not do. Jim enjoyed her being happy and doing the things she liked. He knew she worked hard, and with the care of two daughters on her, as well, he realized that she needed times like this to recharge her batteries.

"Well, honey, I'm satisfied with this one," Paula said. She twirled around in a full-length mirror, looking from all angles. "Do you like it?"

"Of course, I do. So long as you are happy, I'm happy," Jim said approvingly.

Mendez circled back to join Dibbs since his route had proven to be a dry hole. Dibbs caught his eye and motioned for him to cross the street and cover the other side of the dress shop. About the same time, he noticed a couple walking to the front of the store. They looked familiar, but he was not sure who it was. The couple took a few more steps to the front of the shop. He recognized Paula carrying a large package, and then he saw Jim walking alongside. The agent's mind went into overdrive. He understood now that the assassin was on his final mission, to kill Paula Cooper.

The Cuban had followed the couple earlier that morning in to Charleston and knew they were heading to this downtown area. He received a tip from the real estate agent who drove them around. The information only cost Delgado a single crisp one-hundred-dollar bill. He convinced the real estate agent that he was a private detective who was tailing Paula because she was cheating on her husband with the man who was with her. The fact that both Esteban and Miss Cooper were available the same day and in the same locale was a stroke of luck for the assassin, and he seized the opportunity.

29

Delgado slipped away from the lamppost to a storefront window next to the dress shop. He looked around and saw Dibbs in the crowd, closing in on him. Their eyes met briefly enough for recognition. Dibbs drew his Glock and held it in a ready position down low by his right leg, but the crowd was too thick for him to take aim.

Jim and Paula exited the door of the shop in time for her to see the steely-eyed Cuban twelve feet away, staring at them. He was partially hidden by a couple of tourists.

"Look, it's the man who was at the party."

"What man?" Jim said.

Quickly, Delgado turned and bolted up to the intersection. Still running, he turned down a street in an adjacent residential section. Wondering why the man ran, they watched him disappear around the corner. Unexpectedly, they saw Agents Dibbs and Mendez in pursuit.

"Did you see what I just saw, Jim?" Paula asked, hardly believing her eyes.

"Yes, I'm afraid I did."

"That guy is the spitting image of the other man from the valet staff at Judge Parks' party. I don't want to interfere, but let's follow them to see what happens."

"I'm sure that federal agents can handle this. Why not let them do their work?"

"Because I'm the reason they are risking their lives. I want to see what happens."

"Paula, no, we need to stay back and give them space to do their jobs."

"I'm sorry, Jim. I can't do that. I'm just going to follow them for a few minutes to see if I can help spot this man that Agent Dibbs is chasing."

"Paula, wait. Come back...not this, again."

She ran off, leaving Jim holding her package from the dress shop. He was perplexed and extremely frustrated that she would become involved in such danger but was powerless to stop her. This stubborn streak in her was what concerned him most, yet also attracted him to her. He marveled that such a beautiful woman had moxy and feared nothing when things were on the line.

Delgado waited, crouched low, using a bush for cover behind an iron fence on the side of a home. He listened for the sounds of Dibbs approaching with his Bulgarian-made Makarov drawn. His plan was to surprise the FBI agent by firing two quick shots and returning to his position to avoid return fire. Then he would pop out again to hit Dibbs when the agent exposed himself on the counterattack. Usually this strategy worked because the return fire was a quick reaction from standard training, executed in a high state of frenzy.

Agent Dibbs had learned to read streets from his training and experience in New York City as a rookie agent. He saw a break between two houses up ahead as a possible place for an ambush and moved to the far side of the street to put some distance between him and the would-be attacker. He also noticed a courtyard that he could duck into, if necessary. He figured that Delgado was hiding and waiting because he did not see him exit the far end of the street. He only saw him disappear quickly, but he could not make out where. For all Dibbs knew, Delgado could have exited the far side of the courtyard, or he may have entered it by climbing a wall and intended to use it to stage a surprise attack.

From the way the agent had fought on the bus, the Cuban knew that Dibbs was among the toughest the FBI had. Dibbs kept a sharpened mental edge, expecting anything. He continued to trek down the old, narrow brick street when he noticed a resident backing out of his driveway just ahead of him. He did not want the resident to be caught in the firefight that was likely to ensue. Remaining steady and sure, he continued pacing down the sidewalk, scanning all areas, left and right.

The resident backed his black Volvo, now beside Dibbs on the sidewalk, and glanced at him. Dibbs motioned with his free hand for the driver to vacate the premises with haste. Seeing Dibbs' service revolver in his other hand, the driver finished backing quickly, and with an instant push of the accelerator pedal, took off, tires screeching. Dibbs recognized his chance to advance with the noise and cover of the car. He bolted up the street to the next property using the vehicle as a shield.

Delgado waited twenty yards up ahead on the same side of the street. As Dibbs loped down the sidewalk, the Cuban assassin rose up from his crouched position, firing the Makarov nine-millimeter three times. Dibbs dove in the air over a four-foot wrought-iron fence, rolling on the grass into a flowerbed with a fountain and statue of St. Francis of Assisi. He took cover behind the statue and returned fire with two quick blasts from his Glock. Delgado did not dip back out of sight because he thought he had Dibbs out in the open where he could pick him off. Now in the same yard, the bullets narrowly missed Delgado, one hitting a magnolia tree and the other ricocheting off the wrought-iron fence where he took refuge. Dibbs lay flat on the ground with his head tucked behind the base of the fountain, which surrounded the statue. He bobbed up and down, looking for an opportunity to fire again.

Both men held their fire and were still for a moment, hoping that the other would give a better target. Delgado spied a white gazebo planted in the spacious yard, which would give him better cover from where the agent was holed up. He calculated making a run for it. Dibbs figured his target would make the first move, so he laid still, waiting and watching. Delgado jumped to his feet, firing twice at the fountain, and ran diagonally, reaching the back of the gazebo. Dibbs fired one shot, which lodged in a wooden rail of the structure, splinters flying.

Mendez was a half block away when he heard the familiar sounds of weapons discharging. He trotted down to the narrow street where the gunfight was in progress and approached from the side of the property. The unmistakable smell of gunpowder became stronger as he approached the residence where Dibbs and Delgado were playing cat and mouse. From the other side of an outer wall of the premises, Mendez could hear the sound of a man breathing heavily and knew it was not coming from his partner. He decided that he would climb the brick wall at the side of the property to get an angle on the assassin. Mendez waited until Dibbs and Delgado exchanged another round of fire and then climbed the five-foot privacy wall, landing on a section of lush green grass, barely making a sound.

Quickly, he ran to the massive trunk of an ancient oak tree and hid behind it. Mendez drew his revolver and had the Cuban in his sights from thirty feet. He stood with his gun pointed at Delgado, "Drop it, or I'll...," but before he could complete his command, the hired gun turned firing one round which hit Mendez in the upper left side of his chest just above his lung. Mendez fell hard to the ground with a groan—his forty-five bouncing out of reach. Dibbs saw what happened but was pinned and could not get to his partner to assist him. He quickly radioed for an ambulance.

"Come out now, or I'll finish off your buddy," shouted Delgado to Dibbs.

Mendez lay helplessly bleeding as he grimaced in pain, his bright red blood making a puddle on the rich green lawn. "Don't surrender, John. I'll be fine, just get that bastard."

Again, the call came as Dibbs hesitated. "Come out now, I said. Throw your gun aside where I can see it and walk out to where your partner is lying on the ground with your hands in the air. This is your final warning."

Dibbs heard the click of the hammer as Delgado cocked his revolver and knew that he would shoot Mendez again if he did not comply. He tossed his weapon on the grass, which bounced and rolled a couple of times before resting in the open where Delgado could see it. Standing to his feet, Dibbs walked out slowly with his hands raised, moving closer to Mendez. The Cuban grinned triumphantly, his gun pointed directly at Dibbs' forehead.

"I don't know who you are, but I do know why you have followed me. You're pretty damn good but no match for me. I guess you know what happens from here."

"Wait, you said to come out and you would spare my partner. I am here. Let him go."

"I admire your chivalry and your love for your fellow man, but that is why you are weaker than me. I don't care about another man's life, if it means mine is safe. I cannot allow him to live. You should know that. He has seen me, the same as you have. I may as well finish him off now," said Delgado, as he glanced at Mendez.

"Freeze or I will shoot!" shouted a female voice from behind Delgado. Paula Cooper pointed a snub-nosed, pearl-handled, thirty-eight caliber Smith & Wesson at the Cuban from fifteen feet away. She had managed to enter the residence yard from the front gate without being spotted. Very few knew, but she had attended the police academy for weapons training when she decided to do private investigative work for her uncle when in college. Very few knew of her concealed weapons permit. She practiced on occasion at an indoor firing range, but did not discuss her skills with handguns. "Now, stretch the gun out to your side and drop it away from you."

Delgado had no idea whether Paula was a good shot, but the closeness of her voice was enough for him to comply. He released his finger from the trigger, stretching the Makarov out to the side, as if to drop it to the ground. He paused a second then spun in an instant, falling on the ground, firing once at Paula. Delgado's move did not surprise her. She leaned to her right and fell sideways on the lawn, and seeing him dip and roll, delivered two shots of her own. One of Paula's bullets found its target, hitting the assassin in the right shoulder, forcing him to loosen his grip on his weapon. He struggled to stand, still gripping the gun.

Dibbs instantly dove to the ground, retrieving his Glock. Delgado regained his balance and steadied his stance to shoot Paula when Dibbs rolled and fired two rounds, striking the target. The Cuban took one of the bullets in his torso and lay writhing on the grass. He squirmed for the gun that had fallen out of his hand, but Dibbs ran up to him, kicking it out of his reach. Quickly, he put the Cuban's arms behind his back, cinching the handcuffs tight.

"Alright, señor, you have me now. Finish me off."

"That's not how we punish criminals here in America, Delgado. If you survive this, you will stand trial like anyone else. We will prove you killed Judge Parks and Pablo Esteban. Now, who hired you?" Dibbs demanded.

"Who do you think had the most to gain from the judge being dead?" asked Delgado, not offering a direct answer.

"I'll deal with you in a minute. Don't move an inch, or you will get your wish." Dibbs took Delgado's gun and ran to Mendez to check his condition, keeping an eye on the injured suspect, as well.

"Albert, are you gonna survive, 'ole buddy?"

"Yeah, John, I will. It's just a flesh wound. He missed my heart...that's the main thing." He winced as Dibbs applied pressure to his chest with a handkerchief he snatched from his hip pocket. "Hurts like hell though."

"And you've got a heart the size of Texas, good buddy. Hang on. Help's coming."

Paula dusted herself off, stood to her feet, and walked over to the agents. She was fortunate not to take a bullet from the trained killer, but she did bruise her shoulder when she fell.

"We've got to stop meeting like this, Agent Dibbs."

"Call me John from now on, Miss Cooper. You've more than earned it."

"Call me Paula," she responded, shaking his outstretched hand. I'm a little past that "Miss Cooper" misnomer, anyway.

"Paula, I can't believe what you just did. A million thanks from me and my partner, here," said Dibbs.

"Yeah Paula, thanks for being the brave one here, and a crackerjack shot," said Mendez, as he sat upright with the help of his partner.

"I do what I can," said Paula. "After all, I'm part of the reason for all this mess anyway. I figured I should pitch in to do my part."

"Well, you've certainly done that. Paula, could you help with my partner for a minute? I hear the ambulance coming around the corner. I need to keep a closer eye on Delgado."

"Sure, I will," Paula said, as she reached down to the handkerchief to apply pressure to Mendez's wound.

Dibbs stood three feet from Delgado with his gun pointed straight at his head. He reached down to the criminal's pants legs, patting them and working his way up. He felt a hard piece of metal bulging from Delgado's left lower leg, then pulled up his pants, removing a six-inch knife which was strapped to his calf. He continued to pat him down. "Any more surprises?" asked Dibbs.

"No, man, that's everything."

Dibbs recited the Miranda rights to his prisoner, placing him under arrest for the murder of Pablo Esteban. Two black Suburbans arrived simultaneously, with two county ambulances. The backup agents evaluated the situation with a brief synopsis from Dibbs and then cordoned off the crime scene for evidence gathering.

Two sets of EMTs hopped out carrying spinal boards and medical paraphernalia to tend to the wounded. Mendez was loaded on a spinal board and rushed off for treatment. EMTs from the second ambulance treated Delgado who was loaded for transport, also. Agent Dibbs and another agent accompanied the assassin for the ride to the ER. There was no way that Dibbs would let his prisoner out of his sight until he was treated and released to other federal agents.

❀

"Miss Cooper is there anything else that you can tell us about what happened?" asked the investigating officer in charge on the scene.

"No, sir, everything I witnessed and did, happened exactly as I heard Agent Dibbs summarize for you before he left."

"Thank you, Miss Cooper. You are free to go, unless you need assistance. I see you are holding your shoulder."

"No, I'll be fine. It's just a bruise from when I fell. I have someone waiting on me."

"You're welcome, ma'am. We'll be in touch for an official statement later on. You take care."

"Thank you, Captain. I will, and you, as well."

Paula backtracked a couple of blocks to the area of the dress shop and found Jim there, seated at a table at a sidewalk café. He was wet with perspiration from fast walking block to block looking for her. He had gotten close to where the action was when police turned him back. Jim stood as he saw her walking up the sidewalk, grass stains on her clothes, as she rubbed her sore shoulder. A huge grin emerged on her face as Paula saw her man. Jim responded with a mischievous grin of his own.

"Have any fun?" Jim asked.

"Just a little, but I'm ready to go home now, if you are?" she said, kissing him on the lips.

"I thought you would never ask."

30

Jostling around in the back of the speeding ambulance, Dibbs peppered his captive with questions, hoping to get a confession. Although he was wounded seriously, the EMTs did an excellent job of stabilizing him. If FBI agents were not riding with Delgado to the ER, then he surely could have overpowered the medical personnel and found a way out of the ambulance. The crafty assassin had been taken into custody on one other occasion, after being caught in a bar room brawl while he was in the armed services in Havana on a weekend pass.

"Do you always run around in the streets of American cities killing innocent people, or is that just a part-time job?" Dibbs probed.

The Cuban did not respond immediately. It was not because he was injured. He was embarrassed that amateurish Americans, in his view, had taken him into custody.

"Delgado, listen to me. You'll be put away for life. If not, you will be executed. Do you read me? Now, tell me who hired you."

The wounded prisoner writhed in pain, rolling his head with his eyes closed for a moment, while he formulated his response.

"I hear you, señor, but I have to weigh my options. I don't know who you are or what authority you have to make deals."

"What options? You don't have any. My name is Special Agent John Dibbs with the FBI, and if you don't want to be executed or put away for life without parole, then you should talk. We can protect your life, but maybe you would rather we release you to Castro, who surely wants you back in Cuba. Didn't you defect while you were serving as a bodyguard for him on a trip? I hear the sentence for that is the firing squad, if they catch up to you. Isn't that right, Señor Delgado?"

"You don't want much, do you?" Delgado said, grimacing in pain as he coughed.

"The best thing you can do for yourself is to start cooperating by telling us who hired you."

Delgado looked surprised that the agent knew not only who he was, but obviously knew many details about his life. He was impressed with Agent Dibbs' knowledge of him and respected him as a professional for being the only one who ever apprehended him, though he did have some help from an unexpected source.

"Yes, you are correct, Señor Dibbs. Castro, the pig, would have me shot before another sun could rise, but I am not afraid of dying. We all have to go sometime."

Although his exterior was tough and portrayed no fear, Delgado did not want to return to Cuba. He had seen the torture and executions in his country's regime and, in fact, had been part of them. He put up a front in an attempt to confuse the agent, which Dibbs saw through, realizing that he might get the Cuban to talk.

Dibbs believed Delgado's fear of being extradited would likely encourage him to rat on his employer. Confessing and gaining protection from the FBI would give him a better chance than returning to certain death in Cuba. Treason in Cuba is not tolerated in any form, and he knew he would be found guilty of high treason. After torture, Castro would have him hung or shot in public so that all who witnessed the grisly event might take heed not to betray the Cuban government.

"What can you tell us about the assassination of Judge Parks? We have reason to believe you are connected with both his murder and the murder of investigator Dave McCaffery."

"Why should I answer anything you ask me?" asked Delgado.

"Like I said, my first phone call when we get you booked is going to be to the Cuban Embassy in Washington, D.C. to determine if they want you extradited, unless you choose to play ball. If you tell me what you know, then I may see fit to ignore what I know about you and not notify them of your whereabouts. We can protect you from whoever hired you."

Dibbs knew they could protect him for a while, and maybe for a long while, but he really could not offer an absolute guarantee; however, the least he could offer was better than shipping him back to Cuba.

Delgado weighed his options for a moment. "If I tell you what I know, then what assurances do I have that you will keep your end of the deal?"

"We'll draw up papers to deny extradition requests from the Cuban government. The District Attorney's office will agree to provide you protection. With the charges you are facing, you will get serious time; however, when you are released you will be given a new identity and a place to live. I handle matters like this all the time in our Witness Protection Program."

"Do it," said Delgado, with a distant stare on his face. "I'll sign the papers, but get it done quickly, or I could change my mind. The person I work for will know about me being arrested within twenty-four hours. Castro will know sooner, trust me."

"Consider it done. Now, who hired you? No more delays," demanded Dibbs, once again.

"Agent Dibbs, you speak to your Attorney General and get the papers in front of me to sign first, and then I'll talk. I'm not as stupid, or desperate, as I may seem."

"I'll personally talk to the Attorney General today. You can expect to see me in the morning with your paperwork."

Several branches of law enforcement met the ambulance and Dibbs at the ER. Federal marshals were dispatched to stand twenty-four-hour guard in the prisoner's hospital room. Dibbs and Mendez knew what a fiasco there would be if their men were to screw up and let this prisoner escape or harm himself.

Word circulated on the streets that the infamous assassin was apprehended for the first time in his long career. Delgado was treated, and then transported to the county jail. Once there, the prisoner was taken out of the vehicle and processed, which included a strip search and showering for head lice. Afterwards, he was locked in a special cell reserved for brutal murderers and high-profile criminals who needed extra attention.

Mendez was treated for a superficial wound, which pierced his flesh just below his collarbone and passed out the other side. Although in pain, and heavily bandaged he decided to celebrate with Dibbs over a couple of beers after calling in to Washington with the news.

"Yeah, Margaret, this is John Dibbs; could you patch me through to the Attorney General's office?"

"Hi, John, I know your voice. I don't need your last name...you know that. How's the weather down there in South Carolina?"

Margaret had worked the switchboard twice as long as Dibbs had been with the FBI and knew most agents' voices and first names. She knew if they were married, their wives' names, and how many kids they had, and she was great at making the agents feel like family, providing a sort of homey atmosphere to the otherwise dry, tough environment of the federal agency.

"It's getting better by the minute, Margaret. We're just wrapping up a case, which has had Mendez and me working around the clock."

"Well, that's good, John, glad to hear it. When are you gentlemen coming back to D.C.?"

"Soon, Margaret, but I can't say exactly when yet."

"Alright, well, you better stop and speak to me when you roll through, or I'll be hurt. Hold on, let me patch you through now while her line is open."

"Okay, Margaret, will do. Take care."

Dibbs waited until the executive secretary to the District Attorney picked up the line.

"This is Carol Browning speaking. May I help you?"

"Hi, Carol, this is Agent John Dibbs. Is the Attorney General available? It's an urgent matter."

"Sure, Agent Dibbs, hold please."

The Attorney General picked up the line. "How can I help you, John? Do we have any good news from Charleston?"

"Yes, we do, Attorney General Leno. We have a notorious assassin in custody, Juan Delgado. We nabbed him after he assassinated Pablo Esteban, our former best witness in the Judge Parks murder case." Dibbs paused for a response.

"Yes, go ahead, Agent Dibbs. You have my ear."

"Ma'am, we have reason to believe that Delgado is the hired gun who killed Judge Wilmont Parks and private investigator Dave McCaffery. He wants protection in exchange for revealing who hired him. Otherwise, he will likely keep quiet until he dies in prison, or is killed by his employer. He fears extradition to Cuba, and is willing to cooperate by pointing to the mastermind of the murders, if we can justify negotiating with him."

"You didn't offer anything foolish, did you, Agent Dibbs? We can provide maximum security at a special location but cannot and will not let him off. He's killed too many people."

"Yes ma'am, I understand. No, I only told him we would recommend that the federal judge be lenient on his sentence, if he cooperates, and that afterwards we could provide protection. Naturally, he doesn't want to be extradited to Cuba, which would mean torture, then death for desertion and treason."

"I will get the papers drawn up tonight and have them faxed to you in the morning. You get all the information and a confession tomorrow, Agent Dibbs."

"Yes, ma'am, Attorney General Leno, I'll look for the papers first thing in the morning. We'll get everything done, and hopefully we can put a lid on this case when we bring in the person, or persons, responsible for bankrolling these murders."

Dibbs was excited that the AG did not have to think about this one. Seeing the FBI in action, busting criminals of such high-profile targets, would give a big boost to the current administration and public confidence.

"That will work, Agent Dibbs. Is there anything else I can do for you to help wrap up this case?"

"No, that's all. I appreciate it very much."

"Thanks for calling me, Agent Dibbs. This news just made my day. The President will be glad to hear about this development. You have a good evening."

Plans were set in motion to obtain the taped confession in the morning. Putting a bow on this case would be a career accomplishment for Dibbs and Mendez, and would likely bring them both promotions. Both men were excited about these prospects but were more gratified that they had put a dangerous man in custody. Word that Delgado had been arrested reached New York in less than twenty-four hours. However, nothing could be done in such a short time by the Mafia to prevent the Cuban from confessing in order to strike a deal. Castro's agents knew about the apprehension in less time.

The next morning at 8:00 AM, Agents Dibbs and Mendez met Delgado at the jail. He was appointed a young public defender who could not have cared less about representing him, but did so out of obligation and for his nominal fees. The tape recorders were switched on to capture the agreement and confession. The public defender spoke first.

"My client is willing to cooperate, if he can remain here in the United States and will not be deported to Cuba. He would also request leniency, by which, we mean a reduced sentence, something less than life in prison. He also tells me he will be in great danger after this confession. Mr. Delgado will need assurance that manpower will be assigned for his protection."

"The Attorney General will agree to all of those terms, sir, but she cannot promise something less than life in prison," responded Dibbs to the public defender. "Here are the papers that your client requested the Attorney General draw up in exchange for his full cooperation. She will speak to the prosecutors about his full cooperation, requesting them to disclose his assistance to the judge when he comes to trial in the sentencing phase."

The public defender examined the documents and passed them to his client to sign. "Things seem to be as good as they can be, Mr. Delgado. The Attorney General has included consideration and future protection."

The infamous Cuban scanned the paperwork, signing it with a pen provided by his attorney then flipped it to the table with a sigh of resignation.

"Mr. Delgado, you may proceed with your statement," said the public defender.

Agent Dibbs turned on the recording device to capture his testimony.

"I will make this quick and to the point," began Delgado in his heavily accented English. "The man who paid me for killing Judge Parks is Vinnie Castano from New York. Paul Walker, the CEO of Colonial Paper, paid him to have the judge killed. Walker got nervous that the blackmail plot that he and Denby were involved in would not work. I was paid one-hundred-and-fifty-thousand to kill Judge Parks, and an additional twenty-five to kill anyone who got in the way, or who might know something to pin the murders on them. I always received half up front and the other half after completion of the job. Those were the terms of the agreement, to be the trigger finger. Esteban talked too much. When he was taken into custody, I knew I had to terminate him. He and another man of mine were trying to run Miss Cooper off the bridge because we thought she knew more than she did."

"Do you mean Vinnie Castano, the Mafia boss from New York City is the one who hired you, Mr. Delgado?" asked Dibbs.

"Yes, Agent Dibbs, he's the one who pulled the strings in hiring me. I had worked for him before, so we knew each other. Walker was scared at first, but when he heard from Vinnie how they would use me, he bought into the plan with large sums of money. I don't know how much. That's not my concern, as long as they pay me, and they do."

"How much money are you referencing? Surely, you must have an idea."

"I have reason to believe that Vinnie got at least four, maybe five-hundred thousand dollars, to hire a professional like me. He always made at least double for these deals."

"Is that all, Mr. Delgado?" asked Dibbs.

"Well, there was that private investigator I killed and dragged off into the bushes. He was just in the wrong place at the wrong time. I couldn't complete my job with him in the way. I used his tripod to steady my rifle."

With many other words, the hired gun laid out the complete story. He was more informed than most hired killers were because of his reputation for getting the job done without being caught. As a result, he asked questions of his payers, which they were obliged to answer to enlist his services. Dibbs and Mendez finished the confession with Delgado and walked outside to the curb.

"Remember, Mendez, what Walker told us about Denby and him being childhood playmates? He said they got good at tricking people by deceiving their friends when they were growing up. Paula told me of stories where Denby bragged to her about the old days when the two sidekicks schemed together. Apparently, Walker decided to have a go on his own this time. He tried to do the ultimate, and his house of cards has collapsed on him."

"Amazing, John, and right here under our noses. That coldhearted bastard! My guess would have been Hernandez, the drug lord, or Eleanor Parks," said Mendez.

"I know what you mean. I thought maybe the widow was involved for a while, but she is just a sick woman who got caught up in a twist of fate that killed her husband."

"Let's get this tape transcribed and faxed to the Attorney General Leno, pronto. She'll be relieved this case is winding down."

"Say hello to the Amazon woman for me," said Mendez, with a maniacal chuckle.

"Careful, now," laughed Dibbs, "I might let her know your pet name for her."

"Yeah, right, John. You do that, and we'll have another murder on our hands," Mendez fired back with a grin.

31

"Hello, this is Paul Walker."

"Yeah, Paul, it's Vinnie. The heat is on. The Feds arrested our man yesterday. We are sure he will spill his guts to get a deal. I thought I would call you in case you want to take a trip out of the country."

"Uh, yeah, thanks, I'll consider that," said Walker. He hung up the phone with the mob boss to call his long-time friend.

"Hello, Tom Denby, here."

"It's Paul. Listen, the whole damned thing is unraveling. Chances are we will be arrested inside of twenty-four hours. I thought I would give you a fair warning."

"Fair warning, hell, you already hung me out to dry while they had me in custody, Paul. I'm trying to save my hide now, and I didn't say you knew anything about the blackmail plot," said Denby.

"No, you just gave the FBI the fax on the bonus. Didn't you say that you would handle all this? I remember you telling me how easy this would be and that our involvement would never become known. Then you got nervous about your plan working. That's when I stepped in."

Walker sounded like a man who had lost his mind as he continued to ramble nonsensically.

"Yeah, I admit I got nervous. So, what are you saying? Did you have the judge killed?" Denby said.

"What did you think I would do?" replied Walker.

"I surely didn't think you would hire a hit man. You didn't even give my plan a chance to work."

"No, I didn't. I was under pressure and used a contact you gave me five years ago. You said something like, 'These guys can have people bumped off, if the need ever arises. Remember? We were drinking heavily at your place that night, as I recall."

"I don't even remember that, Paul. We must have been drunk out of our minds. I don't remember giving you a card," Denby said.

"Why did you turn me in after all we have been through?"

"I didn't spill the beans on you. I didn't even know you had this done. The hit man probably knew more than he should have, and copped a plea to spill his guts."

"You're a sorry bastard! Do you expect me to believe that? You knew I would do anything to save the paper mill and my retirement. I only expected the judge's death, not three murders. I would fly out of here today, but I'm not the running kind," Walker said.

"What you do is up to you. I'm going to stay put, even if I have to serve time in the federal penitentiary. The insides of those places aren't so bad. I can catch up on my reading," said Denby, with a nervous chuckle.

Walker hung up the phone, stunned that what he thought would be the perfect crime had backfired on him. He knew his life was ruined now. Since he could not bear the thought of the shame and disgrace of an arrest and a conviction with life in prison, he went to his bedroom to find the handgun that he kept in his home for protection. Bending on one knee, Walker slid out the lower drawer to his nightstand. He lifted the thin board of a false bottom, which hid the thirty-eight. Lifting the gun out of its place, he laid the nickel-plated revolver across his hand. Opening the cylinder to check for bullets, he found it full like he remembered. Snapping the cylinder back in place, Walker stood upright, and released a heavy sigh of regret.

Robotically, he paced the floor a couple of times then turned on a bedroom television, cranking the volume. He drew the blinds and curtains, wanting to muffle the gun as best he could. He saw a framed picture of his wife, Gladys, standing on his chest of drawers and thought about how it would shake her world. She was away, attending a social function for the Low Country Garden Club, and was wrapped up in being his wife in this small Southern town. Her children were grown and Mr. Walker never had any of his own.

Stepping into his bathroom, he turned the hand-painted ceramic knobs and started the water to the garden tub. His mind was spinning, as he hit the switch to the Jacuzzi to create a little more noise. He slipped his shoes and socks off and stepped into the tub, as it filled. With one hand on the wall to steady his balance and the revolver in the other hand, he slowly sank into the water. He took a deep breath, pondering everything that had transpired, and then put the end of the barrel to the roof of his mouth. Closing his eyes, he pulled the trigger. Blood and brain fragments spattered the ceramic tiled wall, painting an end to Walker's life. His dead body went limp, slipping slowly beneath the water.

Thomas Denby, on the other hand, was much more adept at living the good life. His family was wealthy, and he followed their example. While he did conspire to commit blackmail, he did not involve himself with the murders. Unlike Walker, Denby was a survivor, who knew that he could live through the charges and jail time he would face. With good behavior, he figured he might find a job from within prison to do some type of legal work. He knew from defending a few clients who went to the federal prison system what the inside was like. He remembered the libraries, the computers, and the access to any type of knowledge known to man. When life gave Denby a lemon, he always managed to make lemonade. Committing suicide was not an option for him.

Teams of FBI agents were dispatched to arrest two men, one in Georgetown, SC, and one in New York City. Arriving at the Walker residence and with no one answering the doorbell, Dibbs and Mendez forced entry into the home. They were immediately taken aback by a cascade of water, which flowed from the upstairs master bathroom, to the open hallway, and down the balcony.

"Fan out, men, and search. Be prepared for anything. Come with me, Mendez, we're going upstairs to find out why the running water. If it's from what I think, it's not good."

"I know what you're thinking, John. Let's go."

They climbed the wet carpet runner lining the stairs. At the top of the stairs, a small table with a spray of flowers separated one side of the home from the other. Seeing the dry carpet to one side, they squished their way through the water on the balcony and followed the sounds of a television blaring VH-1 classic rock tunes. They traced the noise to the master bathroom and once inside, they found Paul Walker dead in the garden tub, floating in a pinkish-red pool of water.

A warrant was issued for Vinnie Castano for the murders committed in Charleston, and for other crime-related offenses which he perpetrated as the boss of the family in New York. A team of agents raided Castano's high-rise apartment in New York City. His house cleaner was frightened by the appearance of the heavily armed FBI agents with bulletproof vests, but really could not give them any information on Castano's comings or goings. Vinnie had flown out the night before and had landed in Sicily, where he would be protected and hidden indefinitely. He would be hard to bring to justice and would most likely end up on the America's Most Wanted list. He had no plans to return to America and would likely work through his connections in southern Italy.

One of the two men in the blackmail conspiracy was brought into custody. Delgado, with other charges pending, as well, would soon begin serving time. He later was sentenced to fifty-five years; the best the Feds would give him. Walker was dead from a suicidal bullet. The final culprit had escaped to Italy the night before the authorities could catch up to him.

Later, at Denby's arrest, he was sitting in his den watching college football for entertainment, placing his bets, as usual. He halfway expected the agents to arrive after hearing Walker ramble about how he would implicate him in the judge's death.

A loud knock at the door was followed by a gruff announcement, "FBI," the man shouted. "Open up!"

"Come in. The door's open," responded Denby nonchalantly.

He turned off his television with the remote and walked to the door, offering his wrists for the handcuffs. He knew that this jail stay would be temporary, but knew he would be in court in only a matter of time and convicted for conspiracy to commit blackmail of a federal judge. With the evidence that Paula Cooper had given the FBI, and the vault of secret notes that was discovered, the case against him was secure. He successfully defended himself against the false accusations of conspiracy to commit murder that Paul Walker wrote in a note before he killed himself. Later, Denby was sentenced to ten years in federal prison on the blackmail conspiracy charge. With good behavior, Denby hoped to be released in five to seven years.

John Dibbs and Albert Mendez were invited to Washington, D.C. office for a congratulatory dinner and awards for their heroic efforts in the streets of Charleston against one of the most notorious assassins living. Dibbs was given a promotion to lead the Southeast office in Atlanta. Mendez was given Dibbs' former job as head of the Charlotte office.

The morning after the celebration, the agents chatted at breakfast in their hotel restaurant. They had a vantage point with a window by the street as they waited for their taxi to carry them to Dulles International.

"Congratulations, Mendez, you've got your own office now. Don't screw it up."

"Screw it up? Now, how could I do that?" Mendez said, laughing. "It can only go up from here."

Dibbs finished a piece of toast and jelly, stuffing it in his mouth then chasing it with a gulp of orange juice. Mendez gobbled down his last bit of scrambled eggs and drank the remaining portion of his grapefruit juice.

"Let's hit the road," said Dibbs. "There's the cab to take us to Dulles."

Arriving at the airport, the men paused outside the entranceway to the concourses, each one having a different flight from D.C., now that the Director of the Federal Bureau of Investigation gave the proud agents new assignments, and positions.

"Good luck to you, John, down in Atlanta. When can you move the family?"

"My daughter wants to finish her last year in high school where she is, so probably not until the summer. However, the transition won't be bad because you know how busy I'll be adjusting to a new territory. At least you are where you were, only in a higher position, Mendez. I have to adjust to new people, new roads, and new everything. And I hear the rush hour traffic can be murder down there, no pun intended," said Dibbs.

"Well, whatever the case, I'm sure the adjustment won't be too tough for the new Southeast Director. Tell me, John, are you going to cut me any slack if my Friday report is late?"

"No way, good buddy, yours ought to be early. Everyone else's can be in by eleven AM, but yours is due by ten. Let's get out of here," said Dibbs, winking.

"Yeah, I need to get moving. My plane leaves in thirty minutes. Good luck to you, John. You did a great job down there in Charleston."

"Same to you, Mendez, you weren't so bad yourself. I'll see you down the road."

32

Paula squared her daughters away with her parents for the evening and drove to Jim's condominium at Belle Isle. She had agreed to eat dinner with him as chef some time ago, but their plan was interrupted by her ill-advised and fateful trip to Charleston. Tonight though, she looked forward to a celebration that the case was winding down and the assassin was in jail. Her life was no longer in danger, and she would be in the company of a very special man who had stuck with her through far more than she, or anyone, could have hoped.

Jim had stopped by a local seafood market and picked up two thick salmon steaks, an entree he had worked at grilling to perfection many times before. He was slicing a lemon and an onion to place on the salmon when he heard Paula's vehicle turn into his driveway. Placing the knife down on the counter, he went to the foyer and peeked through the blinds of the narrow window that bordered the front door. He saw his lovely girlfriend getting out of her vehicle, carrying a brown paper bag in her hand. Looking up, she saw Jim standing at the door, waiting with a pleasant smile on his face. His salt and pepper hair, along with his sexy full mustache, always gave her reason to pause a moment to admire his features.

The enormous live oak trees on his property had filled out completely with their thick green leaves, contrasting with the gray drapery of Spanish moss, which hung down from their branches like decorative garland on a Christmas tree. The huge limbs reached out and up, providing shade from the sun just as it had for a hundred years or more. The golden sunlight filtered its beams through the branches and onto the lawn lighting up the thick St. Augustine grass in patches, as Paula did a little dance and twirled on her approach to the steps of the small front porch. Jim's smile broadened then he clapped at her performance. Paula stepped up onto the small porch and Jim met her there with a kiss.

"Are we still on for a home-cooked meal, Mr. Roberts?"

"Does a cat have a climbing gear?" Jim asked playfully. "Are you still up for trusting me with your life, Miss Cooper?"

"Have you ever known me to back out of anything I started?" she said, with a cute smile.

"Well, no, I can't say that I have."

"Besides, after what I've been through these past couple of weeks, I don't think that your cooking poses any threat." He took a brown paper bag from her as she extended her right arm.

"What's this?" he asked.

"Your favorite Chardonnay, hon. I thought it would go well with the salmon."

"Outstanding, thank you, it's cold, too." Jim felt the cold moisture on the bottle as he pulled it from the bag to admire her selection.

"Sure thing, I wouldn't bring it for dinner any other way."

"Let me put this in the fridge. Come on, join me in the kitchen."

They walked to the kitchen area, where Jim left off preparing the garnish just long enough to slip the bottle of wine into the refrigerator. He resumed cutting an onion, keeping focused on his prep work.

"Can I do anything to help you?" she asked.

"Sure, if you want to, you can set the places, Sweetheart. You know where I keep everything."

"I'll see if I remember where everything is; I've only done this once before with you. It was a lunch about two months after we met."

"Yes, I remember it well," he said, with a wink.

The kitchen was of adequate size but not large. Paula brushed against Jim purposefully flirting with him as she collected plates, glasses, and utensils from the cabinets. He pushed gently back against her, reciprocating her advances.

"Are we eating inside, or outside, dear?"

"Outside, I put a tablecloth on that table on the deck. I'm sure it's warm enough outside, if that's good with you?"

"Jim, after what I've put you through and the way you have stuck by me come hell or high water, I'd sit on the floor and be happy to be here with you."

"Okay, well, floor it is, then."

"Hey, that's not to be taken literally," Paula countered, saucily tossing her hair over one shoulder. Jim chuckled as she opened the back door that led to the deck.

He grabbed a box of wild rice from the pantry and a box of frozen broccoli from the freezer. After getting the items started, he opened a package of dinner rolls, buttering four of them. Paula set the table and then took a moment to gaze above the trees that backed up to his property. The trees made up a stand of woods for about thirty yards before they gave way to a marshy area by the Winyah bay.

Paula's mind drifted as birds of various species circled and swooped on the air currents effortlessly.

She believed that the EPA would win its case now, though the litigation was delayed. She hoped for a court order stipulating greater restrictions on the dumping of wastewater from the paper and steel mills nearby. With all the exposure in the news about Colonial Paper, a win for the environment was assured. She lamented, though, because even with clean up and the restrictions that would come, much of the damage that had been done was irreversible.

Jim squeezed lemon on the salmon steaks and let them sit while he went to the deck to fire up the gas grill. "I thought you got lost," he said.

"No, honey, I was just watching the sun go down and daydreaming. It's so gorgeous when it changes to a big, orange ball of fire and slips down below the bay. Since I was a little girl, I've always loved to see the clouds in the sky change to pink, purple, orange, and gray."

"Yeah, I'm glad you told me about these condos. I wouldn't have known where to buy when I moved here."

"I did it for two reasons, Jim. One, this place was a great buy and has an incredible view, and two, you are right across the bay from me," she said, then winked at him.

"I see, so that was your plan." Jim smiled.

"No comment," Paula said then grinned.

He lifted the cover off the grill, turned the knobs, and pushed the auto-lighter button. The burners let out a poofing sound, as the spark ignited the gas and bluish-purple flames vigorously danced, eager to do their job.

"I'm going to let the grill get hot while I cook the wild rice and broccoli. Would you care for a glass of wine?"

"That sounds like an excellent idea, but I'll come get it. You are doing everything, and I'd like to help."

"Well, since you put it that way, sure."

They exchanged a kiss and walked inside, their temperatures rising. Jim continued with the dinner preparations while Paula searched for the corkscrew, continuing to brush against him in the kitchen as she located it. He knew it was intentional and loved her tactile ways. She poured two glasses of wine and made a little throat-clearing noise to get his attention.

"Let's make a toast."

"Okay, I'm game, but you go first." They moved in close, faced each other, and raised their glasses.

"Here's to the most wonderful man I've ever met, one who knows the true meaning of the word loyalty."

"Nice, Paula, and here's to the most fantastic woman I've ever met, who is always striving to be the best she can, someone who brings out the best in me."

They touched their glasses together with a clinking sound, and they sipped the contents. Jim continued to work on the wild rice, giving it a stir then checked the steaming broccoli to ensure it did not overcook. Carefully, he cut thin slices of cheddar cheese to add to the top of the broccoli.

"Okay, time to put the salmon on," said Jim.

"Anything else I can do?"

"I pretty much have everything under control, but I do appreciate your help. Tell ya what, you can stick the rolls in the oven and set the timer for four minutes. I preheated it so it's ready to go."

"I can do that."

Jim returned to the deck and raised the lid to the grill. He adjusted the heat down a little, not to cook the fish too quickly. Expertly, he placed the salmon steaks on the grill, watching them sizzle as they touched the hot grating. Closing the lid, he looked at his watch, timing it so that he would turn the salmon only once. He had discovered, from experience, that turning them once worked best if one wanted to keep the salmon steaks from breaking into pieces.

Paula and Jim loved the way each of them worked together on things, without stress or confusion. They simply meshed well, and there was no denying this. They seemed to always understand when communicating, giving the other the benefit of the doubt. Paula joined him on the deck.

"The rolls are in the oven. How long does the salmon take to cook?"

"Five minutes on each side is what I do. They come out perfect that way, not tough, just right."

"Hmm, sounds scrumptious, I can't wait."

"Let's go back inside and finish prepping the rest of the meal."

"I'm with you," Paula said.

Jim picked up a spoon, gave the wild rice a final stir mixing in butter, then put the cheese on the broccoli to melt.

"Slide over, honey, and let me pull the rolls from the oven."

Jim stepped aside just enough to allow her passage to the oven beneath the stove eyes where he was working. As she pulled a cookie sheet with four sourdough rolls from the oven, the wonderful aroma of freshly baked bread filled the air, mixing with the scent of steamed broccoli and wild rice. Paula placed the rolls in a straw basket lined with a linen cloth, which she folded over the top to keep them warm.

"I'm going to give the salmon a turn, Paula."

"Okay, when you bring the plates in, I'll serve the veggies and rolls," said Paula.

Jim flipped the salmon steaks expertly, with a spatula and timed the second half of the grilling. He closed the lid, took the long grill lighter, and lit the candle on the table. He sat in a wooden rocking chair on the other side of the deck and waited for the salmon to cook. Watching through the kitchen window, Paula waited patiently, warmed by how much effort and care he put into preparing the meal. For a moment, she envisioned Jim thirty years from now, as her husband, sauntering around in the kitchen, and helping her like Mickey Johnson did with his wife.

When the grilled salmon was prepared to perfection, Jim returned to the kitchen with the delectable seafood, causing both of them to salivate like Pavlov's canine. Paula built each plate, leaving just enough room to add a roll. They took their dinner to the deck and took their places at the round slate-top wrought iron table.

"Can we ask a blessing, Jim? I think it would be in order, all things considered."

"Absolutely, honey. Please go ahead."

"Dear Lord, we ask you to bless this meal and bless our children and parents. Keep them safe in all they do. Work everything out in this case, and preserve our wetlands, in your name, we pray. Amen."

"Amen," Jim added. "That was a great prayer. Thank you."

"I don't know about that," Paula said, blushing.

Paula put her utensil in the tender, juicy pink salmon. The layers of the baked fish fell onto her fork, and she took a bite. "Wow. This is as good as anything we could buy in a fine restaurant. It's so tender and tasty."

"It sure is," Jim agreed, eating a little too fast. The food was so delicious that Jim let his appetite overcome him. He was nervously thinking about how the evening might transpire.

"Jim, sweetie, you might want to slow down and savor it more."

He slowed his pace to please her. She was unaware that he had something special on his mind. They continued to enjoy their food while making small talk.

"More wine, sweetie?" Jim asked.

"No, thanks," Paula responded. She wiped her mouth with a cloth napkin. "I will say that the Chardonnay goes well with the dinner, even if I did pick it out myself." Paula looked at Jim, noticing an unusual expression on his face. "What's up with you?"

"Nothing, I just want everything tonight to be special. This evening is something we've long awaited, and it almost didn't happen," Jim said.

"I know what you mean, honey. Our relationship was touch-and-go there for a while. I didn't know if you would stick with me, or not, and I really couldn't have blamed you. I'm glad you did, though."

"I only meant that I came close to losing you."

"That's sweet of you to say, Jim."

"Hey, let's put a cork in the bottle, while there is still enough for a couple of glasses for another time."

"Yeah, one glass is my limit, but I wouldn't mind a cup of coffee, if the kind chef has any?"

"You know a good chef always does. I'll make a couple of cups. I think I could use some, too."

Jim jumped up and went inside to start the coffee. The dinner was unfolding the way he had hoped. Going inside to prepare the coffee gave him the opportunity to get the surprise that he had hidden for her. He measured the grounds, poured the water to start the coffee, and then peeked out the kitchen window to make sure she was not looking in his direction. He slipped over to a small antique secretary against a wall in the den by the kitchen. He pulled out a small drawer then uncovered the little blue velvet box hidden beneath some papers. Dropping it into his pants' pocket, Jim nonchalantly returned to the kitchen to pour the coffee.

Hues of purple clouds faded to a darker shade and then to blackness. Stars appeared and twinkled in the darkening sky. Jim carried both cups of coffee, forcing the back door open with his foot, placing them on the table. Paula picked up her cup, emblazoned with Rainbow Row on the side, the famous row of colorfully painted historic homes on the Charleston Battery. As she took her first sip, she thought, *so this is what being married to Jim will be like,* and smiled. He took a sip as they gazed into each other's eyes in the warmth of the flickering candlelight.

He knew that he was a fortunate man to be in love with such an extraordinary woman. Paula had fallen from grace into Thomas Denby's spider web, but since no longer working for him, and leveling with the FBI, she began to blossom again into the wonderful person and mom she was before. Through their love, which proved to be enduring, she planned to build back what she had lost. In time, with Jim and her family in her life, Paula believed that she would escape the recurring nightmares from the night when Dave McCaffery and Judge Parks were murdered.

"That was great, Jim. The salmon was excellent, along with everything else. I don't know when I've had a better meal."

"Hey, while I'm on a roll, how's the coffee?" he asked jovially.

"It's perfect, too," said Paula, with a cute, whimsical expression.

The candlelight flickered, casting shadows across the table. Cupid's shadow appeared, as he did on the day they met, permeating the air with thoughts of love for each other. A crescent moon emerged with an early, yet bright, evening star, seemingly not far away from its celestial companion. Crickets, katydids, and bullfrogs joined in the chorus of outdoor symphonic sounds.

Jim took a second sip of his coffee then reached into his pants pocket, cupping his hand around the little blue velvet box. He clutched it anxiously; his palm was clammy and moist. His heart thumped so hard he worried that she somehow would hear it. He took a slow, deep breath into his nasal passages to gather his nerves, hoping she would not notice.

"What's the matter, honey?" asked Paula.

"Nothing is the matter, darling. Everything is beautiful with you in my life. I'm glad all the controversy is behind us and that our lives are back on track. We had to put this night off until everything settled down, and a couple of times I even wondered if I had made the correct decision."

Paula sat glued to every word. She knew Jim was better at writing his thoughts than speaking, but tonight it didn't seem to matter. She was curious as he continued, but did not have a clue where it was going. She figured it was an affirmation of his love for her, and she enjoyed the moment nonetheless.

"You know I'm not a man of many words, but I've thought about this possibility since shortly after we met on the beach. Now I know without a doubt that I would be the happiest man alive if you would be my wife." Jim got up out of his chair and knelt down by hers. He opened the little blue box revealing a gorgeous diamond engagement ring and held it up to her. "Paula, will you marry me?"

She welled up with tears, amazed that this rock-solid man had not only stuck with her through the worst of times, but was now proposing. She knew that she did not have to hesitate, and in an instant, she reached out to accept the ring. Her heart beat like a bass drum as she searched for the words to match this special moment.

"Yes, Jim, I'd be honored to be your wife for the rest of my life."

Jim smiled, half in relief, and half in elation.

"The ring is gorgeous, honey. I love it." Paula carefully pulled it from its felt slot and held it closer to the candlelight. The diamond sparkled like the evening star above. Jim sensed she wanted to put it on, but for some reason, she seemed to hesitate.

"I'm glad you do. Try it on if you want. It should fit...size six, right?" said Jim.

She was relieved Jim broke the ice because for a moment she froze in time and did not know how to articulate her thoughts. She slipped the spectacular one-carat diamond ring of fourteen-carat yellow gold on her finger. It settled into position as if it was meant to be there, and had finally found its long overdue resting place.

"Yes, you knew, somehow," Paula, said. She wiped the falling tears from her face. "You really didn't have to do this. It's fabulous. I love the rubies around the diamond, too. You have great taste, dear. Thank you."

"I know I do, honey. I picked you, didn't I?"

She reached down to Jim's head where he knelt, running her fingers through his hair, then pulled him up to her and kissed him on the lips. They embraced as she stood with him. Time had no meaning to them as they held each other, pulling apart only to kiss again and embrace. Jim's former anxiety drifted away, and assurance of their love replaced it. Paula felt secure in his arms and fully loved again. They both knew that their decision was the right one.

33

Charleston has maintained its Southern charm with historic and distinctive styles of architecture of English and French influence. Some of the architecture is endemic to the area itself as the "shot-gun style" homes, which were built long and narrow to take advantage of the sea and land breezes.

Just a couple of blocks away from an old residential area filled with this type architecture, Chuck and Eleanor were at a local coffee and specialty shop with the morning paper and the mail. Eleanor enjoyed reading the daily news. Chuck sipped his black coffee, still trying to awaken completely from the previous night's gig at the Market Place. Eleanor dropped the paper on the table and opened the two pieces of mail she had brought with her, while Chuck glanced at the headlines and settled in reading in the sports section. She opened the first letter from Publisher's Clearing House, which offered her possibilities of great fortune.

"Hmm, I wonder how much money I'd win if I was to subscribe today?" muttered Eleanor.

"There's no telling, dear. Probably the only thing you'll win is a paid subscription, the same as ninety-nine-point nine percent of the people who register," said Chuck, not looking up from his sports articles.

Eleanor scanned the sheets on which to paste stickers for chances to be an "early bird" subscriber for extra money, if she was to win. She never filled them out unless she really wanted to buy a magazine. Tossing the junk mail aside, she picked up the next envelope, which she had purposely saved for last, thinking it would contain news about the payment held in limbo from the largest of her policies. Most of the money she received in the first life insurance policy had already been spent adjusting to her new life, and putting Chuck's CD on the super stations. Her last job had been as a secretary when her husband first started out as a young attorney, so she knew she might have difficulty if she had to find work.

The manila envelope was sent certified mail by from Heartland Insurance Company. She hated receiving letters by certified mail because the last time she had received one, it contained divorce papers from Judge Parks. She had waited out the delays and investigation by Heartland without hiring an attorney to contest their dawdling. She understood that her policy was for a large amount of money and that the circumstances of the judge's death, and their estrangement, warranted scrutiny. This was especially the case since she decided to bounce back on her feet quickly with a marriage to a younger man.

"They don't mind taking your money, but they sure resist like hell when they have to pay it out," Eleanor quipped.

Slipping an ink pen in a small hole that she made in the corner of the envelope, she made an upward motion using it as a letter opener. Eleanor opened the envelope slowly with guarded optimism. Chuck, not aware of what she had in hand, was reading an article on the NBA playoffs. She pulled out two sheets of folded paper. Without looking at the back sheet that was considerably thicker than the first, she read:

Dear Mrs. Eleanor Parks Eastwood,

We have completed our review of your husband's policy. We apologize for the delay in processing the death claim, but we are hopeful that you understand the importance of protecting the integrity of our company. An investigation of the circumstances surrounding the death of the insured is customary for any company when handling policies less than two years old, within the "two-year contestability period."

This process was implemented to maintain your interests as a policyholder, and to ensure Heartland Insurance Company's solvency. Since our findings indicate that Judge Parks died of causes that were unrelated to any actions of impropriety on your behalf, we are pleased to issue the policy benefit check to you, the beneficiary.

Once again, please forgive the delay in processing this check for two-million, seven-thousand, four-hundred, and nineteen dollars. We have included the interest accrued on the benefit amount since the time of your late husband's death.

Thank you for allowing us to serve your needs. We, at the Heartland Insurance Company, wish you the best and offer our condolences in the death of your beloved late husband, Mr. Wilmont C. Parks.

Sincerely yours,

Bob Tisdale
CEO - Heartland Insurance Company

"My God in Heaven, they finally paid off!" She tore the check loose from the second, perforated page and slid the letter back into the envelope. "Two-million, seven-thousand, four-hundred, and nineteen dollars, I won't be worried about making ends meet now. I don't mean that the wrong way, Sweetheart. I know you're a good provider. I'm just so excited."

Chuck dropped his newspaper to the table to share the excitement with her. "That's fantastic, honey! I'm very happy for you."

"I realize that your CD is doing well on the Super Station and that we will be getting money from that for some time, but we can invest some of this money conservatively and live comfortably. I also want to contribute to an orphanage that I've been researching. I may not have had any children in my lifetime, but I can help those in need by investing my time and some of my money."

"That is wonderful, Eleanor. Won't that be great? I'm so glad for you," said Chuck, genuinely happy. He was not the opportunist many thought he was. He had really fallen in love with Eleanor and wanted to make his own way in life, as well. Because Eleanor loved him, she gave him the financing he needed to get started without strings.

He soon would become self-sufficient, earning royalties from orders of his CD. With another one scheduled for production, Chuck planned to get his career off to new horizons. This time, he would pay for the production costs without any help. Financing his project on his own would help his feeling of self-worth, although he knew that Eleanor did not begrudge him. He wanted to be self-respecting and not depend on what his wife had, hoping to never accept help again.

What began as a questionable marriage, to some, was developing into a wonderful union.

In time, the two late bloomers who had found love again late in life, adopted twin toddler girls. Eleanor loved, educated, and dressed them up as a proud mother. Chuck spent more time in the studio and on tour. He loved the little girls as his own and spent time with them when he was at home. Eleanor had become the person she used to be before her bouts with alcoholism. She was warm, caring, and involved in the community. She learned through tragedy, though the circumstances may be strange, things usually would work out if given time. She was at peace with herself for the first time in many years.

34

Two months later

The wedding was set for the newest Charleston couple. The ceremony would be at St. Michael's Episcopal Church across from the Federal Judicial Center where the depositions were conducted. Irony still played its way into the life of Paula Cooper. The County Courthouse where she received her divorce was on the diagonal corner, and the City Hall, where her ex-husband was jailed and arraigned a few times for various charges, was located on the Four Corners of Law, as well.

Immigrants and settlers who were charter members of St. Michael's Church lay in their resting places in the gated cemetery yard behind the picturesque edifice. Over the years, St. Michael's had survived hurricanes, earthquakes, fire, and the Revolutionary and Civil Wars without significant damage. During the Revolutionary War, the British took the church bells as a war prize. A wealthy British merchant discovered the theft, purchased the bells, and eventually they were returned to the church.

Seventy-five years later the bells were transported to Columbia, S.C. for safekeeping during the Civil War, but were burned in a fire while there, causing a crack and other damage. They were shipped back to England where they were melted down and recast in their original moulds, and then brought back to America to St. Michael's, once again.

Several restorations were completed at various times to keep the church in its mid-eighteenth century rendering. The great earthquake of 1886 and Hurricane Hugo in 1989 both threatened to destroy the church but did not. The earthquake caused most of the city to burn and be rebuilt with new building codes, mandating that rods be inserted throughout the structures to better withstand quakes. Likewise, the fabric of Paula and Jim's relationship was rebuilt with new commitment and realizations, which strengthened them for the future. How appropriate that Jim chose this historic edifice, which had withstood many trials, to be the place where he and Paula would wed.

Even though some of their tribulations were spawned by Paula's own misguided actions, she learned from and returned to her roots. Jim remained constant; much like St. Michael's has, faithfully standing with Paula. Although shaken at times, he weathered the storms that tested him.

A small crowd gathered for the afternoon wedding. Paula and Jim kept the invitations to a minimum. Only close friends and relatives were present. Paula's daughters served as bridesmaids, while Jim's sons served as the groomsmen. Longtime friends of both the bride and groom were maid of honor and best man. The priest waited at the front of the church in full Episcopal garb fit for the occasion. Though Paula was Southern Baptist and the couple would attend a Baptist church as a family, Jim was raised Episcopalian and requested that they marry there.

Jim waited in a side room, smartly dressed in a lightweight two-piece charcoal suit, with his best man, a former schoolmate from Pennsylvania. They chatted about days past, before they had ever married and had children, days when they played basketball for their high schools' teams and double-dated, then married for the first time. Both men had children now.

"You're braver than I am, Jim. If I ever broke up with my wife, I don't think I'd have the guts to try it again."

"Alan, when I met her that day on the beach something happened. I didn't know that she would be the one, of course, but I can't put it in words. Our eyes met, and our souls connected somehow."

"Oh, Jim, stop with the crap. She's hot; I can see that."

"Shut up, man, I was speaking from my heart," said Jim, as he slapped his friend on the shoulder.

"I know what you mean, Jim. I'm truly happy for you. It's a rare thing in life to find one's soul-mate and I'm glad you have."

Jim straightened his tie and adjusted his coat. "How do I look, Alan?"

"You'll pass," Alan said. "Just remember, to say "I do" to everything the preacher asks."

"You're not much help."

"I'm here, am I not?"

"You are, and I appreciate it," Jim said.

Paula's mother and her maid of honor were busy putting the final touches on the glorious bride. None lovelier had ever graced the halls of the fine old cathedral. Paula adorned like a princess in an elegant, but modest dress that complimented her lovely figure, anxiously waited for the ceremony to begin. Since this was her second wedding it called for a dressy look, but not the formal attire of a full-blown first wedding. She turned in front of a full-length mirror, checking all details from her hair to her shoes.

"Hold still, Paula, I just want to add a little blush to your cheeks," said Gayle, her maid of honor. "It will give you the *girl-next-door* look. There, you look as if you are getting married for the first time, not the second."

"I know that I am marrying for the right reasons, so in a sense, I do feel that way, Gayle. Life is so strange. Jim is the best thing that ever happened to me. I know it down deep in my heart. My first marriage was for the wrong reasons, and I'm so glad to have a second chance at being happily married."

"You are fortunate to feel that way and to have a man like him, Paula, but he is very fortunate to have a beautiful Southern belle like you, and don't you forget that," said Gayle, with a smile. She lightly touched the blush in a swirling motion to Paula's cheeks then placed it in her makeup bag. Next Gayle applied a curling iron to sections of Paula's hair. "That's it, I can't do anymore. You're perfect."

"Yeah, right, Gayle."

"No, I'm serious. You are absolutely gorgeous."

"Well, thank you, but I'll be glad when the wedding is over, and we get on the plane. I haven't been to the Caribbean in five or six years. I wonder how much it's changed. Jim said the weather is going to be great and he's looking forward to snorkeling by a coral reef. Me, I just want to relax in the sun and read. Of course, I'll do most of the things that he wants to do."

"How's that shoulder feeling anyway? You were wearing a sling for a couple of weeks after catching that killer, weren't you?" Gayle asked.

"Yeah, I was, actually for a month, but the shoulder is well now. It was only bruised from the fall," Paula said. She raised her arm up and down twice demonstrating full movement. Paula had other things on her mind to share with Gayle but could not talk freely to her friend with her mother in the room.

"How long will you be on your honeymoon, dear?" asked her mother, who was checking her camera to make sure it was working properly.

"Four nights, five days, Mom, but we are going to enjoy it immensely before we return to the routine and grind of working and raising kids."

"I know you will. Do you need a chaperone?" her mother asked facetiously.

"Mother, if we did, you would be the last person I would ask. No offense intended."

"None taken, dear. I can't say I blame you."

All three women chuckled.

"Shush, the girls are coming in," Mrs. Cooper said.

Rachel and Christine skipped down the hall from the restroom to the room where their mom prepared.

"How do we look, Mama?" inquired Rachel.

"Adorable, sweetie, both of you look absolutely splendid."

The girls smiled gleefully, as they smoothed their skirts. They looked on with admiration at their mother, whom they noticed looked especially beautiful, as well.

"Time to go," said the wedding coordinator, who poked her head in the door.

"Oh, my God, this is it," Paula said nervously.

"Take a deep breath, honey," said Mrs. Cooper.

Slowly, Paula inhaled and exhaled deeply to regain her composure. The women and girls formed a double line, walking into the foyer with Paula and her bridesmaid close behind. Following a signal from the wedding coordinator, the musician played the majestic pipe organ. The girls led the way down the aisle while the boys and men followed. The familiar bridal processional played as Paula appeared at the entrance to the sanctuary in her glorious moment.

Arrayed exquisitely in her baby blue dress, Paula dazzled the small gathering of friends and relatives. Mr. Cooper swelled with pride, thinking of how his daughter had overcome the many obstacles in her life. He knew the hard times that she went through with her first husband. He believed that his daughter had learned and was more selective in choosing Jim before making this kind of commitment again.

The bride proceeded slowly down the aisle with all eyes on her. She radiated beauty and happiness as she continued steadily to the front where the priest stood with the other parties in the wedding ceremony. The music stopped as everyone looked forward. The priest opened his book and addressed the gathering.

"Dearly beloved, we are gathered here today to join this man and this woman in holy matrimony, and I quote:

"But from the beginning of the creation, God made them male and female. For this cause, shall a man leave his father and mother, and cleave to his wife; and they twain shall be one flesh; so, they are no more twain, but one flesh. What God hath joined together, let not man put asunder" (St. Mark 10: 6-9 KJV).

Paula stepped to the center to join her handsome husband-to-be. Jim, although a few years older than Paula, with his distinctive features and piercing brown eyes, was the object of all the women's fancy who were in attendance.

With many other flowery words, the priest continued the marital ritual. Paula and Jim exchanged rings as the priest prompted, and gently slid the gold bands on each other's fingers while gazing into the other's eyes. Finally, the priest recited the marital vows.

"Do you, Paula, take Jim for your lawfully wedded husband, to have and to hold, to honor and to cherish in sickness and in health, in poverty and in wealth, for as long as you both shall live?"

"I do," she said, with calm assurance.

"And do you, Jim, take Paula for your lawfully wedded wife, to have and to hold, to honor and to cherish in sickness and in health, in poverty and in wealth, for as long as you both shall live?"

"I do," Jim said.

"Then, by the power vested in me by the State of South Carolina and the Holy Episcopal Church, I pronounce you man and wife. You may kiss the bride."

The newly married couple kissed passionately then turned to the intimate gathering of friends and family. The small crowd cheered and clapped. The pipe organ belted the wedding recessional to send the lovebirds on their way. The bride and groom walked briskly down the aisle and out of the old church, as well wishers showered them with birdseed.

Across the street, the newlyweds saw Agents Dibbs and Mendez standing alongside their black Crown Victoria, waving then tossing handfuls of rice at the couple. Jim waved as Paula blew a kiss to the agents and smiled, as if to say, "Thank you for all you have done and for being here for our special moment." Dibbs and Mendez had to return to Charleston to wrap up a few details and figured they would surprise the couple.

Paula and Jim quickly entered their car and left for the airport, tin cans tied to the back-bumper clanging as they bounced on the old brick streets. The lovebirds headed for the honeymoon of their dreams. At the airport, the bride and groom boarded the waiting jet to Miami where they would embark on their cruise aboard the Royal Star Cruise Ship. The jet took off from the Charleston airport rising up over the Atlantic Ocean, banking as it found its flight pattern.

The aircraft dipped its wing as if to wave good-bye to the Holy City. The couple peered out of the window to see the aerial view of Charleston, the adjacent islands, and the coastline of South Carolina. Sunset at Charleston had begun, as the pink, orange, and purple hues spread across a sky of Carolina blue. Small patches of formerly white clouds gave way to purple, as the dark curtain of nightfall fell on the small city's horizon.

"We're leaving one paradise for another, Paula. I'm almost looking forward to returning after seeing a view like this, even though we haven't reached our destination yet," said Jim.

"I know what you mean, honey, but we will have this time all to ourselves, before things return to normal," replied Paula. "Just the sun, the sand, the ocean, and whatever we want to do."

"Things will never be normal for me again, Paula, now that I'm married to the most wonderful girl in the world." Jim squeezed her hand gently and did a little dance with his eyebrows.

"Jim, hush, we can't start anything on the plane," she said, winking at him.

"And why not?" replied Jim, with a wink of his own.

They laughed, holding hands.

Their plane touched down in Miami, and after a short cab ride to the waterfront, the couple boarded the enormous ship to embark upon their honeymoon cruise. Reggae music floated across the deck of the ship as the couple stood arm-in-arm, leaning on the stainless-steel railing. The skyline of Miami in the background lit up like Christmas lights, twinkling for the tourists to enjoy. Pulling out of the harbor, swirling waters gushed beneath the monstrous liner. Chatter from the crowd hummed in harmony with the engines.

They spent together the next few days on the cruise ship and in the Caribbean Islands in perfect bliss without schedules. Strolling down the beach shuffling their feet through the shallow water watching the waves roll in, Paula guided Jim to a quiet spot and unfolded two giant beach towels for them to lie on the beach. They covered each other with oil and soaked up the sun's rays in an effort to bake to a golden brown on their short trip.

On the next day, they rode Mopeds on the winding roads exploring the Bahamas discovering how the native islanders lived. Stopping at roadside outlets, Paula and Jim picked up souvenirs for their families, chatting and laughing with the colorful islanders. They found happiness in the simple life, interacting with all the people with whom they came in contact. On their last day in the Caribbean, the couple returned to the pristine beach to soak up the sun, and enjoy the water. The union that Paula and

Jim had dreamed of with each other culminated in jubilation.

THE END

THE PARALEGAL

97451354R00193

Made in the USA
Columbia, SC
18 June 2018